MOST DEFINITELY DESIRE

He held her close and looked down into her stormy green eyes. "You know, I've always been partial to tall blondes like Elsie," he said casually.

Kirsten stiffened and tried to back out of his embrace. "I've noticed," she said.

Eric smiled wider and allowed his thumbs to move upward along her rib cage. "But lately," he said softly, "I find I'm developing a real fondness for little women with fiery hair and tempers to match."

Kirsten threw her head back to look up at him, but as their eyes met, Eric lowered his mouth and kissed her. His lips were soft and warm. Despite her innocence, Kirsten knew that the feelings radiating from Eric's lips to hers, making her feel shaky and breathless, were caused by desire.

She felt as if she were melting and she knew that if Eric dropped his hands from where they were holding her, she'd crumple to the ground like a rag doll. But he didn't drop her . . . and the kiss went on and on. . . .

CATCH A RISING STAR!

ROBIN ST. THOMAS

Jane Kidder

Mail-Order Temptress

ZEBRA BOOKS
KENSINGTON PUBLISHING CORP.

To my parents,
Fred and Aileen Wigginton,
for the support, the encouragement, the love.

ZEBRA BOOKS

are published by

Kensington Publishing Corp.
475 Park Avenue South
New York, NY 10016

First printing: August, 1992

Printed in the United States of America

Prologue

"What we need is women! Everything would be perfect if we just had some women!"

"No, Olaf, you're wrong. Everything would be perfect if we just had *wives!*"

"Well, that's what I meant!"

A loud guffaw rose from the group of men clustered around the potbellied stove in Lars Bjorklund's general store.

"Ja," agreed Gustav Johnson, his words slow and halting as he struggled to speak English with his thick Scandinavian accent, "it shure vould be nice to taste some good Svedish cooking cooked by a good Svedish gurl."

Ole Lindquist rose from his chair where he had been sitting drinking a beer and smiling broadly. Walking up to the stove, he held his hands up to gain his friends' attention and announced, "Women is exactly why we're here tonight." Reaching into his pocket, he withdrew a page that had been ripped out of a magazine. "I have something here," he began, waving the scrap of paper for emphasis, "that can change all our lives."

The room was suddenly silent as thirteen pairs of eyes looked at him expectantly.

"Vell, vhat?" Gustav finally asked.

"Women!" answered Ole with a grin. "And not just

5

any women, but good Scandinavian girls from the old country who want to get married to good Scandinavian boys just like us!"

For a moment, the men stared at their friend in disbelief. Then, suddenly a whoop went up as his momentous news sank in.

"Really?"

"Where did you hear this?"

"Are you sure?"

If possible, Ole's grin became even wider. "Ja, I'm sure, and I heard about it from this advertisement."

"Read it to us!" a man at the back of the crowd called. "Or, wait . . . let Eric read it. He speaks English better than the rest of us."

In unison, the men turned toward one of their group who was lounging against a post near the store's back counter. "Okay," the man named Eric laughed, walking over and taking the ragged piece of paper from Ole. "I'll read it."

As one, the men waited in expectant silence.

Young, virtuous Scandinavian women are eager to relocate from Vermont to the frontier and become wives of honest, hard-working men. Write for more details and fees.

A man's name and address followed.

"Do you think it's real, Eric?" asked Lars.

"Seems to be," Eric shrugged, handing the paper back to Ole and returning to his place by the post.

"So, what do you say, men?" Ole asked. "Should we write this man and tell him we want wives?"

His suggestion was met by an exuberant affirmative chorus.

"Okay! Everyone who wants a wife, raise your hand, and I'll write your names down."

Every man raised his hand except Eric. Ole laboriously wrote down all the names, checking twice to see that he had included everyone. Then, he looked

6

at Eric curiously.

"Don't you want a wife, Eric?"

"No," Eric smiled. "I'll pass."

"You better think about it," Lars advised. "This may be your only chance. All the women of marrying age in Rose Meadow are already taken except for the Lindbloom girls. . . ."

Eric wrinkled his nose, thinking about the overweight pair of middle-aged siblings. "I'll definitely pass on those two," he laughed.

"Pretty lonely out on that big farm of yours, isn't it? Better get yourself a wife while the gettin's good!"

Eric looked out the window for a moment, realizing there was some truth to that statement. Even now, he could see snow falling outside. In actuality, he dreaded returning to his cold, empty house.

"You know, maybe you're right," he said thoughtfully. He looked out the window again. His cold, empty, *lonely* house . . . "All right. What the hell. Put me down."

A cheer rose, and several men pounded Eric enthusiastically on the back.

"Good!" Ole enthused. "That makes all of us, then." He looked over at Eric who was still wearing an uncertain expression, and laughed. "Don't worry, Eric. You've made the right decision. I promise you, you won't regret this."

Little did he know . . .

Chapter 1

"Next stop is Rose Meadow, ladies. Should arrive in about twenty minutes."

As the conductor bawled this news, fourteen young women, dressed in their very best, shifted nervously in their train seats.

A pretty blonde turned to the girl seated next to her and asked hopefully, "Do I look all right?"

"Yes, just fine. How about me?"

"Your hair's coming loose in the back. Here, let me fix it."

The coach came alive as the girls pulled small mirrors out of reticules and made fussy little adjustments to already perfect coiffures.

"Just think," someone remarked to the group in general, "today, we finally get to meet them!"

"I just hope I'll recognize Ole," sighed Sarah Drake, pulling a tintype out of her bag and studying it closely. Several other girls followed suit, digging into their small purses for frayed letters and well-fingered miniatures.

"Oh, you won't have any trouble recognizing Ole," Elsie Anderson giggled. "With those big ears of his, how could you miss him?"

Several of Elsie's traveling companions joined in her mirth as Sarah pursed her lips in offense. "Ole does *not* have big ears," she defended. "I think it's just the way

9

his hair was combed when the picture was made."

This statement was met by more laughter and good-natured ribbing as the girls continued to compare pictures of their future husbands.

"What about you, Kirsten?" asked Sarah. "Since your man didn't send a picture, how are you going to recognize him?"

All eyes turned toward a petite redhead sitting in the last seat of the coach. Kirsten Lundgren was older than the rest of the girls and her flaming red hair and tawny skin contrasted sharply with her companions' blond-and-pink Scandinavian looks.

Unlike the other girls who all came from the same town in Vermont and had known each other all their lives, Kirsten had met the group a scant five days before, when they'd boarded the train in New York for their mutual destination. Despite her initial shyness, her companions were a bright and lively group and had happily welcomed her into their fold.

"I guess I'll just take whoever is left," she shrugged with a smile. "Anyway, I don't much care what he looks like. All that really matters is that he falls in love with me."

"I bet you'd care a lot if he's ugly as a toad and your firstborn looks just like him!" Elsie hooted.

The mention of "firstborn" had a sobering effect on the girls, and a sudden silence descended.

"Just think," sighed Sophie Olson, "by the end of the month, all of us will be married women, and by this time next year some of us will probably be mothers!"

A nervous titter ran up and down the length of the car and many cheeks pinkened as the girls silently contemplated their upcoming wedding nights.

"I wonder which one of us will have a baby first?" speculated Inga Swenson. "I hope it's me. I want a family right away."

"Well, I'm sure it will be me," Elsie said positively. "My papa always said I could have anything I wanted if I just worked hard enough for it. . . ." Elsie's unwittingly

10

ribald statement set off yet another wave of shrieks and giggles, causing her to blush furiously.

"Oh, quit your bragging," huffed Olga Johannson, a large-boned, big-breasted girl of twenty. "I'll bet you I'm the first. My ma had thirteen children and I'm built just like her." Sitting back in her seat, Olga gave her ample rump a resounding slap.

Elsie looked the large girl up and down disdainfully. "Well, I'll just take you up on that bet, Olga," she challenged. "What should we wager?"

"I know," chirped the effervescent Sophie, "let's *all* bet. We can each wager a little money and whoever gets in the family way first will win the whole amount."

Several girls clapped their hands over their mouths at this scandalous idea, but Elsie quickly picked up the gauntlet. "Fine with me," she said, standing up and facing her companions, "and I'm so sure I'll be first that I'm willing to wager ten dollars!" Dipping into her reticule, she extracted a crisp ten-dollar bill and held it aloft, validating her challenge.

The girls gasped in astonishment at the size of Elsie's wager, but titillated by the thought of possibly winning an astonishing one hundred forty dollars, they eagerly began searching their bags to come up with a matching sum.

All except Kirsten. She didn't need to search her reticule. She knew exactly how much money she had: three dollars and thirty cents. This pitiful amount was all she'd had left after purchasing the exquisite peach velvet traveling suit she was wearing and the other clothes and essentials which lay neatly folded in the large valise at her feet.

There were cries of excitement as more and more of the girls came up with the requisite stake. Finally, all thirteen of them had shown proof of their ability to enter the contest.

"Okay!" Sophie enthused. "We're all in!"

"No, we're not." Elsie shook her head. "Kirsten hasn't proved up yet." Turning to Kirsten," she said,

11

"What's the matter? Don't you want to take a chance?"

"No, thank you," Kirsten said quietly.

A murmur of disappointment rippled down the length of the train car, but Elsie just smiled smugly. "Don't pester her, girls," she said in a sugary voice. "If Kirsten doesn't want to bet, she doesn't have to." Then lowering her voice to a conspiratorial whisper, she added, "Remember how old she is. She probably realizes she can't compete."

Kirsten's cheeks flamed. She was well aware that at twenty-six, she had long since lost the dewy, fresh-faced looks her companions still took for granted, but she was hardly past her childbearing years! She knew Elsie was baiting her, and it rankled. The other girl had, for some reason, taken a dislike to her the moment they met. Kirsten didn't understand the cause of Elsie's animosity, but she was loath to knuckle under to her scornful needling.

"All right," she agreed suddenly, regretting her impulsive words before they were even out of her mouth, "I'll wager, too."

A resounding cheer rose from the other girls, but Elsie threw them a quelling look, saying snidely, "Can you prove your stake, Kirsten?"

"Oh, come on, Elsie!" exclaimed Susan Ingram, a lovely blonde who had befriended Kirsten during the trip. "If Kirsten says she's wagering, then of course she has the money."

"Well, ten dollars is a goodly amount," Elsie snapped. "The rest of us have all shown we have it. Kirsten should, too."

Kirsten blanched. Now what could she do? She was going to be humiliated in front of Elsie and she knew the malicious girl would never let her forget it. With her luck, Elsie would probably tell Eric Wellesley, Kirsten's intended, that his bride didn't even have ten dollars to her name. Wouldn't that be an embarrassing way to start their marriage. Kirsten would rather die than have Mr. Wellesley know the full extent of her penury. As

12

she tried to think of some way to save face, she was unexpectedly saved by the conductor entering the car with a broad smile on his face.

"Five more minutes, ladies, and we'll be there. The engineer told me he received a message at the last station that half the town of Rose Meadow has turned out to greet you, so get ready!"

Squeals of excitement pealed through the coach and the girls promptly forgot the unresolved drama between Elsie and Kirsten.

With a sigh of relief, Kirsten pinned her hat more securely into her thick curls, studiously avoiding Elsie's eyes. For the moment, at least, she was spared. But she knew it was just a matter of time till the subject of the wager came up again and then what would she do? She closed her eyes for a moment, unable to believe, even now, that she had been brought so low. Imagine, not having ten dollars! She, who only a few years before, had never given money a second thought. But that was before her father had died in the fire that had destroyed her family's thriving bakery. *Why, oh why, hadn't Papa carried any insurance?* she wondered for the thousandth time. How could he have been so thoughtless as to leave her, his only child, nearly penniless when he knew she was well past the age of making an advantageous marriage.

The years when Kirsten should have been attending parties and meeting eligible men had instead been spent making exotic pastries and adding up columns of figures on business ledgers. When her father died three years before, she tried to parlay these talents into a living, but no one in New York City seemed to care that her pastries had won numerous prizes or that she could manage a business better than most men. Try as she might, she could not find a job—at least not one that would pay a living wage. And, as time dragged on and no marriage proposals were forthcoming, advantageous or otherwise, she had watched her resources dwindle down to an alarmingly small pittance. Finally, she was forced to seek the recourse of many an aging, penniless spinster: to be a mail-order bride, move to the frontier, and marry a man she'd never met.

Soon after that she saw a small article in a newspaper announcing that a town in Minnesota was seeking brides for eligible men in the area. The only requirement was that the women be young, single, willing to relocate and marry, and of Scandinavian descent.

Kirsten had promptly applied to the agency listed at the end of the article and had been astonished when, soon after, she received a letter from a man in Minnesota which included a train ticket and a marriage proposal.

She had thought about it for five agonizing days and finally decided to accept. Two months later she found herself boarding a train with thirteen other brides-to-be and heading for a town with the unlikely name of Rose Meadow, located in the rich farm country of southern Minnesota.

As outrageous as her decision seemed to those who knew her, Kirsten didn't regret it. As the only child of a widowed father, she had lived a lonely life, raised by governesses and an elderly maiden aunt. She yearned for someone to love her; a romantic man who would sweep her off her feet, wooing her with kisses and whispered promises of lifelong devotion. Becoming a mail-order bride seemed like a sure, although somewhat unorthodox, way of attaining that goal.

In Kirsten's mind, men who wanted wives badly enough to pay to have brides brought to them must surely be the epitome of romance. She just hoped that she and Mr. Wellesley would suit each other. After she had received his initial letter, she had spent the next several weeks in a dreamy haze, envisioning intimate dinners in his quaint wilderness cabin, and long evenings spent cuddled in front of a warm, crackling fire. She put it out of her mind that his letter proposing marriage was short and businesslike. Wellesley had stated that he was looking for a wife to help him run his

14

farm, and warned her that if she accepted his proposal she must be prepared to work hard. He went on to say that he was thirty-two years old, had never been married, and lived alone on his homestead six miles south of town. He finished the terse missive by asking her to let him know what kind of seeds she'd like him to buy to plant a kitchen garden, and had included some money for her to purchase her train ticket.

Even now she smiled at the thought of those seeds. No doubt the two of them would spend many mornings together, watching the dawn break as they lovingly planted the vegetables they would later share while cozily ensconced in the romantic isolation of the long Minnesota winter.

Kirsten had written back, accepting his offer of marriage and assuring him that she would work very hard. She knew she was stretching the truth when she told him she was familiar with the duties of a farm wife, since she didn't have the slightest idea what frontier women did with their time, but she was confident that with her adoring husband's patient tutelage, she could easily learn anything she might not already know. She ended her letter by telling him that she was eager to meet him and asking that he send a picture.

He didn't. In fact, she had not heard from him again, despite the fact that she had written him several more letters.

As the train began slowing, Kirsten pulled herself back to the present. Mr. Wellesley's lack of communication worried her a little. What if he'd changed his mind? No, she told herself firmly, surely he would have let her know if he'd decided against having her come. And, anyway, a man who was buying seeds for a kitchen garden must be serious about a commitment.

The train finally shuddered to a blowing, screeching stop, and the girls looked eagerly through the grimy windows, each trying to pick out her intended. The conductor had been right. There was a sizable crowd gathered at the tiny train station, including an enthusiastic brass band bleating out an off-tune rendition of "Here Comes the Bride," and several older men decked out in faded blue Union Army uniforms and exuberantly waving a slightly tattered American flag.

With a swirl of skirts, the brides rose from their seats, picking up their valises and silently looking at each other with eyes bright with excitement and trepidation. As always, it was the irrepressible Sophie who finally broke the tension. "Well, come on, girls," she cajoled. "Pucker up! The men are waiting!"

Giggling and jostling each other, the girls hurried down the aisle to the back of the car—all except Kirsten, who remained in her seat, suddenly reluctant to leave the security of the train.

Why *hadn't* Mr. Wellesley written to her again, she thought worriedly, and why *hadn't* he sent his picture? Could it be that he was ugly and afraid that if she saw him, she wouldn't come? Kirsten bit her lip. She certainly hoped that he didn't look like a toad as Elsie had predicted. Could she love him if he was homely, or fat, or dirty? A sudden wave of apprehension washed over her and, for the first time, she allowed herself the luxury of doubt.

For several long moments she sat riveted in her seat, pondering this dilemma. She had just about convinced herself that Eric Wellesley must indeed be an ogre and that maybe she should just stay on the train and head back to New York, when Elsie brushed by her. Elsie paused a moment, then leaned close and hissed, "You better hope you win our little contest, Kirsten, because no matter what the others think, I don't believe you have ten dollars! I bet your new husband would be pretty angry if word got around town that his bride was a welsher!"

Furious at Elsie's thinly veiled threat, Kirsten jumped up from her seat, grabbed her valise and made her way to the door.

"Don't you worry about me, Elsie," she declared,

glaring at the younger girl. "Eric Wellesley is going to be so enamored with me that I'll be in the family way before the summer is out!"

At Elsie's snort of disbelief, Kirsten pushed her out of the way, descending the train steps and looking determinedly around for the man who was her destiny.

Chapter 2

Eric Wellesley stood far back from the packed station platform. He knew he should be up with the other men who were crowding close to the coach carrying their brides, but somehow he just couldn't force himself to join the excited melee.

Rubbing his fingers across his forehead as if to ease a persistent ache, he muttered, "This is a mistake. A stupid, stupid mistake. What in hell was I thinking of to get involved in this madness?"

Eric shook his head. Truth be told, he knew exactly why he'd added his name to the list of men requesting mail-order brides. He was lonely. After spending nearly five months isolated on his farm, enduring a bleak and frigid Minnesota winter, he had vowed to find a wife. A strong, hardy Scandinavian girl to help work the farm and keep him company during the dark, endless winters. Someone to clean his house, cook his meals, and warm his bed. So, that night at the general store when Ole had told the men about the mail-order brides, it had seemed perfectly logical to add his name to the roster of interested men.

But that had been in March when winter still held the countryside in its frozen grip and the nights were long, cold, and unbearably lonely. Now it was May and the prairie was alive with the smell of wild flowers and wet earth, newly turned for spring planting. Nights were balmy, dawn came early, and the loneliness that had plagued him was gone. So was much of his desire for a wife.

Eric squinted his eyes against the afternoon sun and watched the first bride descend the train steps. Andrew Patterson, Rose Meadow's mayor, stepped forward and shook the pretty girl's hand.

"Name, please," he asked officiously.

"Sarah Drake," she replied in a voice quaking with fear and excitement.

Andrew turned toward the assembled crowd and boomed, "Miss Sarah Drake!"

"Sarah Drake? She's mine!" came Ole Lindquist's voice from far back in the crowd. People laughed and parted the way as a flushed young man with huge ears and an even huger grin shyly approached the girl, a small bouquet of spring flowers gripped in his hand.

"And where is Miss Drake's host family?" Mayor Patterson demanded.

"Right here!" called a robust woman in her mid-fifties, detaching herself from the crowd and hurrying over to the couple. "I'm Polly Hutton, dear," she said, giving Sarah a bone-crushing hug, "and you'll be staying with me and my family till . . . uh . . . well, till you and this boy here decide to get yourselves hitched!"

Both Sarah and Ole turned crimson, and Eric, backing even farther away from the press of people, moaned in embarrassment. *I can't go through with this,* he thought dismally, *not in front of everybody!*

One by one the giggling, excited girls stepped down on to the platform and endured the town's friendly scrutiny while they were introduced to the men they had traveled so far to meet.

When Olga Johannson made her appearance, Eric took a long look at her big breasts and ample hips and felt his heart take a bound. Now, here was a woman! Big, strong, and glowing with lusty good health. She looked like she'd be as vigorous between the sheets as she would be behind a plow—just the type Eric was hoping for. Casting his eyes heavenward, he offered up a hasty prayer. *Please, please let this one be Kirsten!*

"Olga Johannson," Andrew's voice intoned and Eric's heart plummeted.

Lars Bjorklund, the owner of Rose Meadow's general store, stepped forward and Eric cursed under his breath. "Damn! All that woman wasted on selling ribbons and sugar candy!"

How many was that now? Eric mentally toted up the women who'd already been claimed. By his count, the big girl made eleven. Only three more. *Please, make there be another one just like her still on that train!* he pleaded silently. He was still ogling Olga as another girl appeared and was quickly claimed. That left only two.

Suddenly, amid a flurry of petticoats, two women came down the stairs at once, looking for all the world like they were pushing each other.

Eric eyed them speculatively. One was tall, blond, and very pretty. "Possible," he mused. Sometimes the slender ones were deceptively strong. But it was her companion who really drew his regard. The woman was stunningly beautiful, but it was obvious she wasn't one of the brides. Not only was she small and fragile-looking, but she was considerably older than the rest of the girls. A chaperon, perhaps?

Eric's eyes ran up and down her delicate frame appreciatively. "Just like a little doll," he murmured, "and red hair! What a beauty."

He watched curiously as Andrew approached the redhead, but his smiling countenance suddenly turned to astonished anger when he heard the mayor's next words.

"Kirsten Lundgren."

"No!" Eric blurted, the words coming out in a rush. It couldn't be! This delicate little woman was definitely not what he'd ordered. Oh, she'd be perfect if he lived in Boston like his brother Stuart, or London like his brother Miles, but not here! There must be some mistake. He'd specifically asked for a strong, buxom

21

girl, fit for farm work. Why, this exquisite little creature wouldn't last ten minutes behind a plow—not to mention in his bed! She was so little, he'd probably crush her the first time he touched her . . . especially with his problem.

His thoughts were interrupted by Andrew's voice, again pealing over the crowd. "KIRSTEN LUND-GREN!" When there was still no reply, Andrew turned toward Kirsten, inclining his head to ask her something. She responded and with a nod, Andrew turned back to the crowd and yelled, "Eric Wellesley! Where are you, boy? Your bride's waiting."

Eric quickly shrank back against the wall of the depot as people in the crowd started looking around for him. He was *furious*. This little flower of a woman wasn't what he'd bargained for, and, by God, he wasn't going to accept her! He wasn't even sure he wanted a wife anymore, but he was absolutely sure he didn't want this girl.

He took a hasty step forward, intending to renounce her publicly, but his very proper upbringing and innate good manners would not allow it, no matter how angry he was. No, he thought, stopping. Better to speak to her in private. He knew the woman she was staying with and he'd go round there tomorrow, explain that there must have been a misunderstanding at the agency, and give Kirsten money for her train fare back to New York. Hell, he'd even give her something extra for her trouble. He could afford it and he supposed it was the least he could do.

Nodding decisively, Eric slipped around the back of the train station and climbed into his wagon. With an angry shake of the reins, he clucked to his team and headed for home.

Kirsten stood on the platform, wishing it would open up and swallow her. Mr. Wellesley *had* changed his mind! How could he embarrass her like this and *what*

22

was she supposed to do now?

Andrew Patterson looked at her sympathetically and said, "Now, don't you worry yourself, Miss Lundgren. Eric must have just forgotten that you were arriving today, or maybe some problem came up on his farm and he couldn't get away. It is foaling season, and any number of things could have happened that we don't know about. Anyway, we'll get everything figured out as soon as we're finished here. In the meantime . . ." And, turning away, he bellowed, "Betty! Betty Zimmer! Aren't you Miss Lundgren's hostess?"

A pretty, middle-aged woman with rosy cheeks and rich brown hair hurried forward. "I sure am, Mayor!" she called, smiling warmly at Kirsten. "You just come along with me, honey, and we'll see if we can't find that man of yours."

Kirsten allowed herself to be led away from the crowd, so mortified that she didn't even notice Elsie Anderson's triumphant grin turn into a gasp of shocked dismay as her name was called and a tall, skinny man with a protruding Adam's apple came forward to claim her.

"Do you . . . do you know Eric Wellesley?" Kirsten asked as she trotted along in Betty's wake.

"I sure do!" Betty beamed, "and between you and me, you're one very lucky little lady. Eric is just about the handsomest man around these parts."

Kirsten's heart leaped. So Mr. Wellesley wasn't fat or ugly. Rather, Mrs. Zimmer said he was handsome. The handsomest man around these parts! "But, why do you suppose he didn't show up today?" Kirsten asked, hoping Betty might have a plausible explanation for Eric's nonappearance.

"Well, I don't know," Betty admitted, coming to such an abrupt halt that Kirsten almost ran into her. "I don't think he forgot, though. Eric's much too responsible for that. He's quiet; shy, if you know what I mean. Maybe he just didn't want to meet you for the

23

first time in front of all those people."

At Kirsten's hopeful look, Betty nodded firmly. "Yes, I'm sure that must be it. Why, I bet he's waiting over at my house for you right now!"

"Do you really think so?"

"Only one way to find out. My wagon's right over here. Let's go and see."

Kirsten's hopes soared as they made their way down Main Street. She looked around with interest at the town that would be her home, noting that Rose Meadow seemed surprisingly prosperous. The main street boasted a dry goods store, livery stable, general mercantile, restaurant, hotel, and, of course, a large, noisy saloon.

"What a nice little town," she commented.

"We're pretty proud of it," Betty agreed. "We'll have a new schoolhouse by next fall and there's a Methodist and a Lutheran church over on First Avenue."

Kirsten nodded, pleased that the town was settled enough to support two churches.

As they rode on down the street, Betty took advantage of Kirsten's preoccupation with her new surroundings to take a good look at her. She was very pleased with what she saw. The girl was beautiful and Betty was sure that Eric Wellesley, when he finally saw her, would feel the same.

Kirsten, sensing the older woman's eyes on her, looked over at her curiously. "Is something wrong?"

"Heavens, no!" Betty laughed. "I was just admiring your hair. You have such unusual coloring for a Scandinavian girl."

"Well, my father was Swedish," Kirsten explained, "but my mother was Irish."

"That explains it."

"Yes," Kirsten nodded. "I do favor her. She died when I was only four, but Papa always said I look just like her and her brothers." Kirsten giggled in remembrance. "He also said I have their Irish temper."

Betty smiled widely. "And do you?"

"I'm afraid so," Kirsten admitted. "Like Papa always said, I didn't get this red hair for nothing!"

The two women laughed heartily and Kirsten relaxed for the first time since she'd stepped off the train. "What's Mr. Wellesley like?" she ventured.

"Well, like I said, he's quiet. He doesn't socialize much, but it's always a pleasure to see him when he comes into town. He's friendly in his own way; polite to the ladies, and so handsome! Why, that man's looks just take your breath away . . . even an old widow woman like me!"

Kirsten felt another little shiver of anticipation ripple through her. Surely if Mr. Wellesley was as charming and handsome as Mrs. Zimmer said he was, then he would also be a romantic and ardent lover. Kirsten blushed, embarrassed by her own wayward thoughts.

"But you probably already know all this," Betty continued, "since he must have sent you a picture."

"He didn't," Kirsten responded quietly.

Betty looked startled. "He didn't?"

Kirsten shook her head.

"That's odd," Betty chuckled. "Well, maybe he didn't have one to send. But you can take my word for it. You're in for a very pleasant surprise."

They turned onto Oak Street and Betty pulled the wagon to a stop in front of a large clapboard house with a sign outside that read ZIMMER'S BOARDING-HOUSE. ROOMS TO LET.

"Do you take in boarders?" Kirsten asked.

"Yes," Betty answered, "ever since my husband passed away eight years ago. I have six rooms, and I'm usually full."

"Isn't that an awful lot of work for you?"

Betty shrugged. "I suppose, but we have to keep body and soul together, don't we? Besides, I've never been afraid of a little hard work."

"Oh, neither am I," Kirsten assured her quickly, secretly shuddering at the thought of cooking and washing for seven people.

Betty threw her a distracted smile as she surreptitiously scanned the street for Eric's wagon. Seeing no sign of it, she summoned a wide smile and jumped down from the high wagon seat, motioning for Kirsten to do the same. "Let's go into the house and have a cup of coffee," she suggested. "Best thing I know to clear the head and put things into perspective." Grabbing Kirsten's valise out of the back of the wagon, she headed up the front walk, vowing to give Eric Wellesley a good piece of her mind when she next saw him.

The afternoon dragged on endlessly as Kirsten unpacked her meager belongings and settled into a small but immaculately clean bedroom. Several times she walked over to the window, pulling the lace curtains aside and looking hopefully up and down the street.

At supper she was introduced to Betty's permanent boarders, and she couldn't help but notice their curious looks. They all knew that she was the bride who fiancé hadn't shown up and, although they were too polite to say anything, Kirsten was mortified by their covert glances and sympathetic smiles.

Finally, as she and Betty were washing the mountain of dirty supper dishes, she could stand it no longer. "I don't think Mr. Wellesley's coming," she said dismally. "He must have . . . must have changed his mind."

"Nonsense," Betty insisted stubbornly. "He wouldn't do that—not without telling you. I'm sure he just forgot."

Kirsten laid down her dish towel and stared out into the darkness. "I wish I were as confident as you are," she sighed.

Betty wasn't really confident at all, but she didn't want Kirsten to know it. "Well, I'll tell you what," she said, putting a stack of plates into a cupboard, "tomorrow morning we'll just drive on out to Eric's farm and introduce you."

Kirsten's eyes brightened. "Oh, could we?"

"Sure," Betty grinned. "And, you'll see. This is all just a misunderstanding. The town's planned a big get-together for all the brides and their fiancés tomorrow night, and I just know Eric wouldn't want to miss it. He just needs a little reminding about dates, is all. Probably hasn't turned his calendar over and thinks its still April!"

Kirsten smiled, caught up in Betty's optimism. "Oh, I hope you're right, Mrs. Zimmer," she said, trying hard to believe the older woman's words.

"So do I," Betty muttered to herself. "So do I."

Chapter 3

Kirsten took special care in dressing the next morning and when she walked into the kitchen and greeted Betty, the older woman smiled in approval.

"You look wonderful, dear," she beamed. "Eric won't be able to take his eyes off you."

Kirsten was clad in a rust-colored skirt that fit snugly over her trim hips and accentuated her tiny waist. An ivory silk blouse with a high lacy neck and long, fitted sleeves molded to her generous breasts enhancing her femininity while giving her a look that was properly demure.

Kirsten smiled, grateful for Betty's compliment, and sat down nervously on the edge of a hard kitchen chair, nibbling at a piece of toast Betty handed her. "I hope we're doing the right thing," she murmured, her voice strained. "You don't think Mr. Wellesley will be angry when we just barge in on him, uninvited, do you?"

"Absolutely not," Betty assured her. "That boy is going to be delighted to see you, you mark my words."

Kirsten nodded doubtfully, rising from her chair and pacing the large kitchen in agitation. Betty threw her an indulgent look. "Ready?" she asked.

At Kirsten's nod they walked out to a small shed which served as both barn and chicken coop. Deftly hitching the horses to the wagon, Betty led the team out into the yard and motioned for Kirsten to get in.

Kirsten took a deep breath and climbed onto the high seat, gripping its edges and staring straight ahead.

Betty slapped the reins over the horses' backs. "Giddup, Bess, giddup Sam. We got important business to tend to." Throwing an encouraging grin at Kirsten, she guided the team out of the yard and headed toward Main Street.

The road narrowed as they left town, soon becoming little more than a rutted path. Kirsten looked around with interest, awed by the stark beauty of the tall, waving grasses and the abundance of yellow wildflowers. A large copse of willows and elms off to their left hinted of nearby water. "Is there a creek over there?" she asked, pointing.

"More than a creek," Betty nodded. "That's Big Cedar River. It runs all the way down to Iowa. The water's high right now from the snow melt, but in the summer you can fish and swim, and in the winter it's possible to ice-skate all the way down to Austin. That can be dangerous, though, since there are springs under the water and the river doesn't always freeze solid."

"I don't know how to ice-skate," Kirsten admitted.

"Well, I'm sure you'll learn," Betty chuckled. "Skating and sleigh riding are popular pastimes in the winter, and Eric Wellesley is a demon at both of them. The men have an ice-skating race every December during the town's Christmas celebration and Eric has won it for the past several years."

Kirsten smiled, pleased that Mr. Wellesley was athletic. Certainly a man who enjoyed ice-skating must be fun loving, and probably a good dancer, too.

The open land gave way to newly plowed fields and Kirsten could see a large, square house in the distance, flanked by a massive barn and several outbuildings. "What a big farm!" she exclaimed. "Why, the fields go on for as far as the eye can see."

Betty beamed. "I'm glad you like it, honey, because that's your new home."

Kirsten gasped in astonishment. "That?" she squeaked, her voice quavering slightly. *"That's* Eric Wellesley's homestead?"

"Sure is," Betty confirmed, pulling hard on the reins and guiding the wagon up a long drive. "Pretty place, isn't it?"

Kirsten could only nod, looking around in horrified trepidation.

Bringing the horses to a halt, Betty jumped down and stared quizzically up at Kirsten who remained motionless on the wagon seat. "Well, come on!" Betty laughed. "Let's go find your bridegroom."

Kirsten felt as if she were frozen to the seat. She couldn't manage this! She thought she'd be living on a small plot of land—in a cabin—with a small vegetable garden and maybe a cow and some chickens to care for. But this! This place was huge! She craned her head around, gazing off in every direction, and all she saw was more and more dirt. Plowed up and ready to plant. Or, maybe it already was planted. Kirsten had no idea how to tell.

Suddenly, the half-truths she had written in her letters, assuring Eric that she was experienced in the duties of a farm wife, came back to rest like a lead weight on her shoulders. It would take a lifetime of learning to know how to manage a farm of this size, and there was no way—*no way*—that she was going to be able to do it! Betty might as well turn the wagon around and take her right back to town.

"What are you waiting for?" Betty called, looking over her shoulder at the pale girl. "Come on! Let's go up to the house and see if he's home."

With a weak nod Kirsten climbed down from the wagon and dutifully followed Betty across the lawn. Her mind worked furiously as she tried to figure out a way to extricate herself from this impossible situation. She'd just have to tell Mr. Wellesley, she decided. She'd explain that she hadn't expected a holding of this size, and when he'd written that he wanted a wife to help him with his farm she didn't realize he meant caring for what appeared to be several million acres! Then, she'd just tell him that he would have to find someone else to marry.

Satisfied that this explanation would suffice, Kirsten lifted her chin and hastened to catch up with Betty as the older woman mounted the wide front steps of the big house.

Betty knocked on the door and then waited, glancing at Kirsten who stood nervously chewing a fingernail. When after a few moments there was no answer, she knocked again, louder this time. Again, the two women waited, but still no one answered the summons. With a sigh Betty turned to Kirsten and said, "He must be out back. Probably plowing or cleaning the barn. Come on. We'll go find him."

"Maybe we shouldn't bother him," Kirsten suggested hopefully. "I mean, if he's busy plowing, he probably doesn't want to be disturbed."

"Nonsense!" Betty chuckled, stepping off the porch and striding energetically toward the corner of the house. "We're not disturbing him, for heaven's sake. You're his bride!"

Kirsten winced at this reminder and reluctantly followed along, wishing for all the world that she'd never heard of Minnesota, Rose Meadow, or Eric Wellesley.

Eric had seen the wagon making its way down the road toward his farm. *Who in hell can that be?* he thought irritably, squinting against the sun as he watched the vehicle slowly approaching. "Damn visitors," he muttered, "don't they know it's spring and there's planting to do?" With a grimace of annoyance, he slipped the thick leather reins from his shoulder and wound them around the plow's handle, kicking at a clod of dirt as he started for the house. "Whoever it is is just gonna have to understand that I don't have time to sit around and drink coffee today."

Betty saw him coming before Kirsten did. "There he is," she announced happily, cupping a hand over her eyes to shield them from the sun. "Come on, honey, the bridegroom approaches."

Kirsten turned her gaze in the direction that Betty pointed . . . and nearly fainted. Walking toward her was the most magnificent-looking man she had ever laid eyes on. He was breathtaking; tall and dark with bulging muscles that were easily discernible in his present shirtless state. A pair of suspenders held up closely fitted trousers which hugged his lean legs like a second skin. His hair was as black as a moonless night, without the slightest trace of red or brown to relieve its ebony hue. And as he drew closer Kirsten could see that his eyes were the same color as his hair—pure jet black. His nose was straight and his mouth full and firm, with just a hint of sensuality about it. Prominent cheekbones showed beneath tightly drawn, dark skin, and his jaw was square, jutting, and, at the moment, clenched in what appeared to be anger. Despite his rather forbidding expression, Kirsten couldn't take her eyes off him and all thoughts of wanting to renege on her agreement instantly fled. Instead she felt like she might swoon just thinking of the romantic nights to come, wrapped in this Adonis's muscular embrace as his sensual lips whispered words of love and rained intimate kisses on her.

Eric strode across the field, impatient to reach whoever was waiting for him, find out what they needed, and get back to his plowing. He wanted to finish this section by noon since he knew he had to go into town during the afternoon and talk to Kirsten Lundgren. But as he drew near and caught sight of the flaming red hair of his intended, his steps slowed and he sucked in his breath in annoyance.

33

It was her! A surge of anger coursed through him that she hadn't waited for him to call on her, but rather had decided to just present herself, uninvited. He frowned, suddenly aware of his naked chest and dirty, sweat-begrimed face. Regardless of the fact that he had no intention of ever seeing the girl again after today, he still wished that at least he was fully dressed for their meeting.

"Hello, Eric!" Betty called gaily, raising her arm in an arcing wave. "I brought you a present!"

Kirsten gasped in embarrassment at Betty's outlandish remark and her eyes shifted quickly to the approaching man. What she saw offered no relief to her already pounding heart. Mr. Wellesley did not smile, nor did he look in the least pleased to see her.

"Morning, Mrs. Zimmer," he said quietly when he finally reached them.

With a smiling nod, Betty turned to Kirsten and said, "Eric, may I present Kirsten Lundgren. Kirsten, this is Eric Wellesley."

Had there ever in her life been a more awkward moment, Kirsten wondered as she and Mr. Wellesley stood silently regarding each other. Eric nodded curtly as his gaze roamed over her. Kirsten's cheeks reddened at his perusal, but she politely answered his nod and said, "Mr. Wellesley. How nice to finally meet you."

Eric's eyes narrowed as he weighed the sincerity of her words. Then he looked over at Betty who was staring at the couple with a slight frown clouding her features. "Please excuse the way I look, ladies," he apologized. "I was planning to come by as soon as I got this field plowed. I didn't expect you . . ."

His voice trailed off, embarrassment and a hint of annoyance at their untimely arrival rampant on his handsome face.

"Oh, we understand," Betty offered quickly. "But, since we're here I think it would be a good idea if we visit for a little while now. I'm sorry if it takes you away from your morning plowing, but . . ."

"Fine," Eric interrupted, his impatience obvious. "Why don't you two go on up to the house? I'll be there in a minute." Without so much as a glance in Kirsten's direction, he turned on his heel and headed for the backyard.

Betty's eyebrows rose in surprise at Eric's abrupt departure, but, determined to ignore his obvious displeasure, she said brightly, "Well, Kirsten, why don't we take his advice and go on back to the house?"

Kirsten didn't move a muscle. She was so angry and humiliated by Mr. Wellesley's blatant lack of interest in her that she just stood and stared at his broad, retreating back.

"Kirsten?" Betty prodded, "did you hear me, dear?"

Finally tearing her gaze away from her fiancé, Kirsten turned to Betty and said, "I don't think that's a good idea. We've obviously come at a bad time and I think it would be better if we just went back to your house."

"No!" Betty protested, feeling angry and frustrated as she noted Kirsten's stricken expression. "We've driven all the way out here and we might as well get this settled."

Too upset to argue, Kirsten slowly made her way back to the house. "Something's very wrong here," she remarked. "He didn't forget to meet me yesterday. He's trying to cry off."

"No, he isn't!" Betty's voice was just a shade too loud. "I admit his behavior is a bit odd, but I'm positive there's a logical explanation for it. We just need to wait until he finishes whatever he's doing, and then I'm sure he'll explain everything."

They walked into the big house and Kirsten looked around in stunned surprise. It was beautiful. All the way across the country she had been mentally preparing herself to live in a small, primitive cabin, and the gracious elegance of the large house was the first pleasant surprise she'd had since she'd stepped off the train. Betty led her toward the parlor and Kirsten smiled in delight as her eyes scanned the expensive furnishings. Two beautifully upholstered settees sat facing each other, and in one corner was a rectangular oak table with a splendid cylinder music box on top of it. Next to the largest sofa was an end table with a crystal lamp gracing it that Kirsten was sure was a genuine Comfort Tiffany piece.

Her eyes were drawn to the walls where several expensively framed pictures hung. Intrigued, she walked over to a watercolor landscape to take a closer look, entranced by the subtle shadings and meticulous detail of the work.

"This is magnificent," she murmured, turning to Betty with a look of pleased surprise.

Betty chuckled, vastly relieved that at least *something* was making the girl smile. "I told you he was the best catch in the county!" she whispered conspiratorially. "Not only is he handsome, but he's the wealthiest man in town!"

Kirsten nodded. "I don't doubt that. This artwork alone must have cost a small fortune." Casting another glance around the lavish parlor, she added, more to herself than to Betty, "So, why would a handsome, rich man need to send away for a bride?"

There was no chance for Betty to respond, because at that moment Eric Wellesley made his appearance. He had obviously stopped to wash at the pump before joining them. His face was clean and his hair curled damply around the nape of his neck. He now wore a plaid cotton shirt which had been hastily buttoned halfway up his chest and which he was still tucking into his pants as he entered the room.

Kirsten was again taken aback as she got her second look at him. If possible, he looked even more handsome than he had a few minutes ago. Even in her wildest hopes, she'd never dreamed her unknown

36

fiancé would be so devastatingly attractive. If only he'd smile!

But, Eric didn't feel like smiling. He was annoyed that he was going to be forced to confront Kirsten before he'd had time to fully think through how to let her down, and he was even more annoyed that he'd never get his field plowed today. It was already late May and the corn should have been planted two weeks ago, but heavy rains and lingering cold weather had prevented him from getting the crop in. Earlier in the week the weather had finally cleared and he was now racing against time to get the seeds sown before the spring rains tapered off and the hot weather began.

It seemed to Eric that everything having to do with this girl was conspiring to keep him from his work. Yesterday he'd wasted the whole afternoon making the fruitless journey into town to meet her train, and now, today, his morning was going to be spent trying to explain to her that he'd made a mistake in asking her to come here and marry him.

The room was absolutely silent as the three people nervously studied each other, but finally, with customary aplomb, Betty said, "We missed you at the train yesterday, Eric. I hope nothing was amiss here that prevented you from meeting it."

Her veiled accusation was not lost on Eric and he mumbled contritely, "Ah, no . . . I just couldn't make it."

"Well, no harm done," Betty said smoothly, "we're all here now."

Eric sat down stiffly on a brocade settee opposite the two women. "I wonder, Mrs. Zimmer, if Miss Lundgren and I could have a few minutes alone?"

Betty's eyebrows rose imperceptively at this unexpected request, but feeling that as long as she was in the house, nothing untoward could happen, she nodded. "Yes, I suppose that will be all right. I'll just wait in the kitchen."

When the older woman had departed, Eric leaned forward, turning his attention to Kirsten. His gaze was drawn to her sparkling emerald eyes and again he was taken with her unusual beauty. It really was a shame she wasn't larger, he mused silently. She was so gorgeous that she made his heart pound just looking at her. If only she weren't such a fragile little thing this marriage idea might have worked out and he wouldn't have to say what he was now faced with.

Looking down at his hands, which were clasped between his knees, he said quietly, "I'm sorry you had to come all the way out here, Miss Lundgren."

Mistaking his meaning, Kirsten responded quickly, "Oh, it was no trouble, Mr. Wellesley. It only took us half an hour and I enjoyed seeing the countryside."

"I didn't mean that," he continued, still not looking at her. "I meant that . . . well, I just don't think it is going to work out between us."

He looked up to see how she reacted to this statement, but her face remained impassive. An endless moment passed until she finally said, "Oh? And why is that? Have I done something to displease you?"

"Oh course not," he answered, frowning. "How could you displease me? I don't even know you."

Kirsten felt like someone had just struck her in the stomach, but she carefully composed her features, refusing to let him see how hurt she was. Folding her hands in her lap she asked quietly, "Then, what is the problem?"

For a long moment Eric sat and looked at her flushed face, hating the fact that he was embarrassing this pretty girl. But, realizing there was no help for it, he blurted, "You're too little."

"What?"

"I said, you're too little."

"I'm sorry," Kirsten said, shaking her head. "I don't have the slightest idea what that means."

"It means," he explained, rising to his feet in agitated embarrassment, "that I was led to believe that you were

38

a big, strong, Scandinavian girl."

"And who led you to believe that?" Kirsten asked, her voice becoming frosty.

"Well, you did!"

"Oh? And just exactly when did I tell you that?"

Eric paced the length of the parlor, trying to determine how best to explain his disappointment to her. He knew from her high color and flashing green eyes that she was angry and he really couldn't blame her. "Well, you didn't tell me, exactly," he admitted, "I just assumed too much."

Kirsten was absolutely *livid,* but she fought hard to keep her voice even. "Just what did you assume, Mr. Wellesley?"

"Well, you have a Scandinavian name and I thought . . . well, I thought you'd be . . . big!"

"Big," Kirsten repeated slowly. "You thought I'd be big. Just how big did you want? I mean, were you expecting a Valkyrie warrior woman, complete with a breastplate and a horned helmet?"

Eric turned toward her, a frown settling on his dark features. "I was expecting someone like that girl Lars Bjorklund got," he said frankly.

"Olga," Kirsten murmured.

"I beg your pardon?"

"Olga Johannson," she repeated, looking up at him. "You wanted Olga Johannson."

"I didn't *want* anybody in particular," he protested, raking his hand through his hair. "But, she's the type of woman I was hoping for."

"Yes, I understand now," Kirsten said dryly. *"Big."*

"Please, Miss Lundgren, don't make this any harder than it already is," Eric entreated. "I told you in my letter that I needed a wife to help me work my farm. You wrote back and told me you could do the work. Now that I've seen you, it's obvious you haven't the slightest idea what it takes to be a farm wife."

Kirsten had the good grace to look abashed, knowing she'd been caught in her half-truths.

"Have you ever even been on a farm before, Miss Lundgren?"

"No," she admitted quietly, "but, that doesn't mean . . ."

"I didn't think so," he interrupted. "And, that's my point. You're a small, delicate woman. You couldn't handle the work."

"I beg your pardon!" Kirsten shot back, picking up the gauntlet that Eric didn't even realize he'd thrown. "I can handle anything!" Eric looked at her doubtfully, but that only served to further her resolve. "I *can!*" she repeated stubbornly. "I'm as strong as an ox."

Eric chuckled and again, his gaze swept her petite frame. "A very, very small ox," he murmured.

By this time Kirsten was so angry that she completely forgot that a half hour earlier she had decided to try to extricate herself from the very situation that Eric was now excusing her from.

Several long moments passed as the couple stared at each other, each aware of the powerful attraction which was radiating between them and both resisting it with every fiber of their beings.

Finally, Eric sighed and said, "It wouldn't work, Miss Lundgren. Despite what you think, you're just not what I need."

Enraged tears sprang to Kirsten's eyes at his flat rejection. "Fine," she said in a cold voice. "Well, I'm sorry that I'm such a disappointment." With a dignity Eric couldn't help but admire, she rose and picked up her reticule.

"Wait!" he called, catching her arm as she hurried over to the parlor door. His touch sent a tingle all the way up to her shoulder and she instinctively recoiled from it, wrenching out of his grasp.

"Now what?"

"I want to give you some money."

"Money!" Kirsten gasped in disbelief, losing her

slender hold on her temper. "Sir, this really does pass all bounds of good taste!"

Eric was thunderstruck as he realized what she thought he was offering. "I didn't mean that!" He scowled, his eyes darkening with anger. "I just feel that I owe you something for your time and trouble. I thought maybe if I gave you your train fare back to New York, you wouldn't feel further inconvenienced."

"Mr. Wellesley," Kirsten flared, whirling to face him. "You have inconvenienced me past the point of your ever being able to make up for it. But, I don't want your money. In fact, I'm not even sure I'm going back to New York."

At his look of surprise, she continued impulsively, "I came to Minnesota to get married and just because I do not meet your, ah, *requirements,* I'm sure there are other unattached men in Rose Meadow who are looking for more in a bride than just a good pack mule. Therefore, I would appreciate having your word that I am released from our original bargain and free to pursue another situation."

Eric felt like he'd just been flayed with a piece of velvet. "You can't marry anybody else!" he argued.

"Why not?"

"Because every man around here is going to expect the same as I do and you're just too damn small to be a farm wife! If you're so hot to get married, then go find a preacher somewhere and spend your life pouring tea."

"Thank you for the advice," Kirsten said, "but I assure you that I can choose a husband without any guidance from you."

"Well, fine!" he barked as she stalked down the hallway toward the kitchen. "But, when you drop over dead from exhaustion, don't say I didn't warn you!"

Kirsten slammed through the kitchen door, nearly knocking over Betty whose ear was pressed to it. "I'm ready to go now, Mrs. Zimmer," she said angrily.

Her mouth gaping, Betty could only nod. Retracing

her steps down the hall, Kirsten sailed by the parlor where Eric still stood, his face dark with frustrated anger. "Good day, Mr. Wellesley," she called, never slowing her pace. "When I get back to town, if I see any women who look like they can bring down a bear in hand-to-hand combat, I'll be sure to let them know you're looking for a wife."

Then, without a backward glance, Kirsten swept through the front door and down the steps.

Eric turned to Betty with a look of disbelief.

"Half Irish, you know," Betty chuckled. "Gives her a temper."

"Oh, so that explains it," Eric snorted sarcastically. "I suppose I should have guessed. After all, 'Kirsten Lundgren' is such a good Irish name!"

Chapter 4

"I thought you said he was shy!"

As the wagon jounced along the road back to Rose Meadow Kirsten threw Betty such an accusing glare that the older woman winced.

"Well, normally he is, dear. Whatever did you say to rile him so?"

"Say?" Kirsten said with a huff. "I didn't *say* anything! The man is insufferable. Rude, arrogant, high-handed . . ."

"And so handsome he stops your heart, right?" Betty interrupted with a smile. She was secretly elated by Kirsten's anger, knowing that the girl must have felt a powerful attraction toward Eric to be so upset at his rejection.

"I couldn't care less how handsome he is," Kirsten declared, shifting angrily on the hard wagon seat. "He's an insensitive boor and I'm well rid of him."

Betty said nothing to further anger her already incensed companion, but instead remarked casually, "Well, now that we know that you're not going to be Mrs. Eric Wellesley, we need to make some decisions about your future."

"What future?" Kirsten moaned, her anger dissolving as the seriousness of her predicament settled on her. "I have no future except to find a way to make enough money to buy a return ticket to New York."

"Is that what you really want?" Betty questioned.

"I don't know what I want anymore," Kirsten admitted, "but, I know I can't stay here."

"Why not? Eric Wellesley isn't the only man in town. There are plenty of other eligible young men in Rose Meadow. And you'll have a perfect chance to meet them all at the party tonight."

Kirsten's jaw dropped in astonishment. "You can't think that I'm going to the party! Why, I'd sooner die than bear the humiliation of admitting that I've been jilted."

"You might as well face it, dear. The other brides are bound to find out."

"I know, but it will be easier to bear if I don't have to witness Elsie Anderson's satisfaction when she does."

Betty let the conversation lapse as she eagerly planned her strategy to get Eric and Kirsten together. She had enjoyed a long and loving marriage and had instantly noticed the attraction that had flowed between Eric and Kirsten. Why, the room had fairly crackled with it when they'd all been sitting in his parlor.

Despite what Kirsten might think, Betty knew the couple's relationship was anything but over, and the joy they would share when they finally realized they were meant for each other would more than compensate for their rather shaky start. An incorrigible matchmaker, Betty was eager to leap into the fray if it meant that the two young people would eventually find the happiness she intuitively knew could be theirs.

But the first order of business was to get them together in the same place at the same time, and Betty knew she had her work cut out trying to convince Kirsten to attend this evening's party. "I really think you should reconsider your decision, dear," she remarked blandly. "I can't think of a better way to put that horrid Eric Wellesley in his place than to show up at tonight's party. The last thing you want him to think is that you are devastated by his rejection. Attending

44

the party would be a perfect way to let him know that his decision not to marry you doesn't bother you one bit."

Kirsten remained silent for a long moment, mulling over Betty's logic. "Perhaps you're right," she mused. "The last thing I want Eric Wellesley to think is that I care one whit about him."

"Exactly!" Betty agreed, fighting hard to hold back the triumphant grin which threatened to burst forth. "So, you're going?"

"Yes, I'm going!" Kirsten declared impulsively, "and, what's more, no matter how bad it is, I'm going to have a wonderful time."

"That's my girl!" Betty beamed. Flicking the reins over the horses' backs, she smiled happily. She didn't know of a better way to get a man's attention than to let him think you didn't want it. And if her plans worked out the way she hoped, by the end of the evening, Eric Wellesley would be so besotted with Kirsten Lundgren that he'd be begging her to marry him!

Eric trudged along behind the plow, uncharacteristically ignoring the symmetry of the furrows he was creating. Try as he might, he couldn't get Kirsten Lundgren off his mind. Their meeting that morning had been an unmitigated disaster and he felt a sharp pang of remorse every time he thought about the hurt and bewilderment which had flashed across Kirsten's face when he'd told her he didn't want to marry her.

He never meant to hurt the girl, he thought irritably, but, damn it, it wasn't his fault she was as delicate as a spring flower. He'd made it perfectly clear in his letter that he needed a wife who could help him on his farm and Kirsten had misled him by assuring him she could handle the job. Why, by the looks of her, one morning in the fields would probably send her to her bed for a month!

With an annoyed shake of his head, Eric angrily

45

slapped the reins over the horse's back, urging the meandering animal to lean into the yoke. His annoyance was further compounded when he looked behind him and noticed that he had allowed the plow to wander off course and the entire furrow he'd just dug would have to be rerouted.

Gritting his teeth in frustration, he jerked back on the reins and headed the horse toward the barn. It was useless trying to finish the field today. His mind wasn't on his work and it would take him hours to straighten out the mess he'd just made.

Damn the woman! Everything having to do with her conspired to distract him. Thank God he was done with her and could put the whole fiasco behind him. Tomorrow morning he'd get up, replow the field, and get his life back to normal.

He was just toweling his hair after dunking his head under the pump when he looked up and, for the second time that day, saw Betty Zimmer's wagon pulling up the lane to his house.

Now, what?

"Mrs. Zimmer," he nodded, breathing a sigh of relief that she was alone, "didn't expect to see you so soon."

"I'm sure you didn't," Betty answered wryly, "but I wanted to talk to you."

"I really don't think there's anything . . ."

"Let's go in the house," Betty interrupted, her tone more of a command than a request.

With a sigh of resignation, Eric followed the portly woman up his front steps and into the hall. Belatedly remembering his manners, he said, "Shall we sit in the parlor?"

"I'd rather sit in the kitchen," Betty responded. "I don't think parlors lend themselves to frank talk."

Knowing he was in for a first-class tongue lashing, Eric nodded reluctantly and ushered his unwanted guest into the kitchen.

When they were seated at the small table, Betty drew a deep breath and said, "I don't mean to interfere, Eric, but what you did to Miss Lundgren this morning was unforgivable."

Eric winced, knowing the indomitable old matron was right. "Was she upset?"

"What do you think?"

"What I think," he said "is that it was better to set things straight right away than to let Miss Lundgren continue to think I'm going to marry her."

"You really found her that unattractive?" Betty prodded, concealing a small smile when Eric hurriedly looked away in an attempt to mask his true feelings.

"Attractive has nothing to do with it," he muttered. "She's just wrong for me."

"You couldn't possibly know that from five minutes of conversation."

"I knew it the minute I saw her get off the train yesterday," he blurted, then immediately wished he'd kept his mouth shut.

Betty's eyebrows rose. "So you *were* there, after all! I thought as much."

Eric rose from the table and hurriedly turned his back on the smug old dowager. "Would you like some coffee? I think it's still hot."

"No, thank you," Betty responded, determined not to let him off the hook. "I don't want coffee. What I do want is an explanation of why you made that sweet little girl feel like a freak."

"Freak!" Eric exclaimed, setting the coffeepot down with a resounding bang. "No woman as beautiful as Miss Lundgren could ever feel like a freak, no matter who said what to her!"

"So, you think she's beautiful, do you?" Betty asked slyly.

"Of course I think she's beautiful!" Eric shot back. "What man wouldn't?"

He could have bitten his tongue off when he saw Betty's self-satisfied smile. "But, being pretty isn't important," he quickly added, setting a cup of coffee in front of her. "She's all wrong for the kind of life I could

47

offer her. She belongs in some Eastern drawing room, pouring tea and entertaining the ladies' auxiliary."

"If she'd wanted that life, she could have stayed in New York," Betty pointed out.

"I know," Eric agreed, his brows drawing together, "and I don't understand why she didn't marry some lawyer or banker and do just that. With her looks, she must have had plenty of offers."

Betty shook her head sadly. "Well, after the way you made her feel this morning, I'm sure she doesn't believe there's a man alive who would have her! Her confidence is completely shattered."

"Oh, come on, Mrs. Zimmer! I didn't say anything that would shatter her confidence. I just told her she was wrong for me!"

"And for every other man around these parts," Betty reminded him.

Eric sank back down in the chair across from her and held out his hands in a beseeching manner. "But, it's true! All the men around here farm, and we need wives who can plow and plant and cook and clean."

"What a shame that Mr. Lincoln has already abolished slavery," Betty remarked, spooning sugar into the cup of coffee she'd said she didn't want. "Sounds like that's what you were really looking for when you requested a bride."

"That's not fair," Eric muttered.

"And do you think it was fair to tell Kirsten that you'd prefer a big cow like that Olga to her!"

"But, I would!"

Betty sighed dramatically, pulling on her bonnet and standing up. "All right, Eric. You want to talk fair, let's talk fair. That girl left everything familiar to come here and marry you. The only security she had was your promise to make her your wife, and now you've broken that. So, what are you going to do to make it up to her?"

"What *can* I do?" Eric shrugged. "I already offered to pay for her ticket back to New York and she turned me down flat."

"Then, obviously, you need to think of something else."

"But, what?"

"That's up to you," Betty retorted, heading for the door.

Leaping to his feet, Eric hurried down the hall after her. "Mrs. Zimmer, wait! Do you have any suggestions?"

Betty hesitated a moment before turning back toward the distraught man. The interview had gone even better than she had hoped and she was now ready to play her trump card. "Yes, as a matter of fact, I do. I think you should go to the party tonight and give Kirsten the opportunity to publicly tell you to go to the devil. That way she can save face with her friends and it will also let the other men in town who might be interested in her know she is available."

"Are you suggesting that we have a public falling out?" Eric asked, horrified at the thought of becoming the object of town gossip.

"Of course not!" Betty negated, throwing him a disgusted look. "But, surely you can think of a way to make it look like this breakup was her idea and not yours."

"How?" Eric asked, completely at a loss.

"I don't know," Betty snapped, annoyed by his lack of imagination. "Think of something! But, whatever it is, just make sure that Kirsten comes out the winner. You owe her that much."

Dumbly, Eric nodded, not having the slightest idea how to orchestrate this confrontation which was not supposed to look like a confrontation, and make Kirsten Lundgren publicly reject him when he'd already privately rejected her. Why, the girl was already so angry with him that she probably wouldn't even speak to him! And with the poise and self-control he'd seen her exercise this morning, he couldn't imagine her making a scene in front of half the citizenry of Rose Meadow.

With a sigh, he faced Betty Zimmer's forbidding countenance and said quietly, "All right. I'll try to make amends tonight."

"Good!" Betty nodded, her stern expression softening. "I can assure you you'll feel much better for it." With a quick pat on his arm, she marched off across the yard.

Eric stood on the steps and watched Betty's wagon rumble off toward town. "Yeah, sure I'll feel better," he muttered. "I always feel better when I encourage someone to publicly embarrass me."

Stomping back into the house, he slammed the door behind him, wishing he'd never heard of Kirsten Lundgren.

There must be some other way out of this!

All afternoon that thought kept running through Eric's mind. A solution . . . he had to come up with a solution! A way to prevent Kirsten from having to go back to New York, and yet free him from having to marry her.

Eric sighed as he shrugged into a beautifully tailored broadcloth coat. This whole situation would have been so much easier if only Providence had seen fit to match Kirsten with Lars Bjorklund and Olga Johannson with him.

As he reached for his hairbrush, his hand stilled in midair. Kirsten and Lars . . . Olga and him. That was it! The answer to the problem! And it was so simple and logical that he couldn't believe he hadn't thought of it before.

A swap. He and Lars could swap fiancées! There was nothing in the agreements the men had signed that said they *had* to marry the particular woman whose passage they had paid, and Eric was sure there must have been cases of men finding themselves drawn to brides other than the ones they had originally corresponded with.

So, why not trade? Kirsten could marry Lars and spend the rest of her life safely tucked behind the counter of the general store, and he could have Olga. Big, strong, strapping Olga.

With a whoop of delight, he tossed the hairbrush in the air, catching it with one hand as it came down, and quickly running it through his thick, dark hair.

He'd go talk to Lars right now—on his way into town. That way, if Lars agreed, and considering Kirsten's beauty, Eric couldn't imagine why he wouldn't, the men could approach the women with the idea of the trade at tonight's party.

Eric grinned at his reflection in his shaving mirror. It was an inspired plan!

Picking up his hat, he strode toward the front door. "Stroke of genius, Wellesley," he congratulated himself as he bounded down the steps. "Goddamn stroke of genius!"

Chapter 5

"I don't want to swap."

Eric frowned. His conversation with Lars Bjorklund was not going at all as he'd hoped. "But, Lars, you haven't even *seen* Kirsten Lundgren. She's gorgeous."

"I don't care." Lars shrugged. "Olga and I have already settled things between us. We talked today and we liked each other so much that we think we'll be the first ones married."

At Eric's stricken expression, Lars's eyes narrowed. "Why do you want to trade, Eric? If this Kirsten is so beautiful, why don't you want her?"

"It's not that I don't want her," Eric explained patiently. "It's just that . . . well, the girl is like a little golden wildflower and I need a big, strong mustard weed."

Lars stared at Eric, his expression completely blank. "What does that mean . . . a mustard weed?" Although he had lived in the United States for over ten years, Lars, like so many of his Scandinavian neighbors, had a limited grasp of the English language, preferring to speak his native Swedish whenever possible.

"What I mean," Eric responded, noting his friend's bewildered expression with amusement, "is that Kirsten is small and delicate, sort of like a flower. She belongs behind the counter in a store like yours, selling ribbons and candy to the other ladies in town. Olga is big and strong, like the mustard weeds that grow by the side of the road. She's the type of girl who could handle working in the fields. And, that's the kind of wife I need."

"Oh, no!" Lars protested, holding up his hands as if to ward off evil spirits. "I don't want a wife who's weak and sick."

Eric sighed. "I didn't say Kirsten was weak or sick. I said she's delicate. Fragile. Little and pretty."

A long silence hung between the men as Lars pondered Eric's words. "Well . . ."

"Oh, come on, Lars! What do you have to lose? If you don't like Kirsten, I can't force you to marry her. But, believe me, friend, once you see her . . . Well, you just wait."

"She's really that pretty? Like a flower?"

"Exactly." Eric nodded eagerly. "So, what do you say? Will you spend some time with her tonight at the party?"

Reluctantly, Lars nodded. "Maybe a couple of dances wouldn't hurt. But, don't you count on anything, now."

"Great!" Eric exclaimed, leaping to his feet and clapping Lars on the back. "You won't be sorry."

Lars looked doubtful. "What do I tell Olga?"

"Nothing! Leave her to me. While you're courting Kirsten, I'll take care of Olga. I need to get to know her anyway, since she's going to be my wife."

"Now, Eric," Lars hedged, "I never said I was going to swap with you, so don't you start calling Olga your wife."

"Okay," Eric said quickly, not wanting to anger the other man. "But, after tonight, you'll feel differently."

Lars saw Eric out his front door, then slowly climbed the stairs to his bedroom to finish dressing for the party. He frowned, wishing that he'd never agreed to this crazy scheme. He liked Olga Johannson. She reminded him of the girls he'd grown up with in Sweden and, up until fifteen minutes ago, he'd had every intention of marrying her. So, why had he allowed Eric Wellesley to talk him into courting another woman?

"Damn natives," Lars cursed as he looked out the window, watching Eric mount his horse. "They talk so good, they can make a man agree to anything!"

Kirsten sat on the edge of a small settee in Andrew Patterson's parlor, her back straight, her eyes focused straight ahead. Why, oh why, had she allowed Betty Zimmer to talk her into attending this party? The only reason she'd come was to show Eric Wellesley she didn't care that he'd jilted her, and he wasn't even here! And, despite what Betty had said, there wasn't another man in the room paying any attention to her, except to look at her curiously, wondering why she was at the party alone.

Kirsten's eyes swept the crowd in the mayor's parlor, noting that all the other brides were present, and all of them were accompanied by their fiancés. All except Olga Johannson, who was standing against a wall, looking hopefully out the front door as she waited for Lars Bjorklund. Suddenly, the big woman's face split into a happy grin as Lars walked in. Kirsten smiled as she looked at Olga and Lars. If ever two people were a match, they were. Lars was just as big and beefy as Olga was, and Kirsten could only imagine what giant children the couple would produce. As she sat watching them, she suddenly became aware that Lars was casting furtive glances in her direction.

Kirsten's brow wrinkled as she tried to figure out why Lars was eyeing her so closely. His expression was almost assessing, and she couldn't imagine what was causing his sudden, intense interest. Uncomfortable with Lars's scrutiny, Kirsten shifted her gaze away from him, just in time to see Eric walk through the front door.

She was furious when she felt her pulse quicken. The

man was a cad, a welsher, so why did she feel a thrill race through her, just seeing him enter a room? Irritated with herself, she quickly turned toward Betty who was sitting on the settee next to her.

"Pay no attention to him," Betty whispered. "Just act like you don't care."

"I *don't* care!" Kirsten hissed.

Betty nodded knowingly and patted Kirsten's hand. "Hold that thought, dear, because here he comes."

Kirsten sucked in her breath and quickly shot a glance in the direction of the door. Sure enough, Eric had spotted her and, for some unaccountable reason, was purposely heading her way.

In three long strides, he was in front of her, sweeping off his hat and saying in that warm, rich voice, "Good evening, Miss Lundgren, Mrs. Zimmer. Lovely night for a party, isn't it?"

Although he had addressed both women, his eyes never left Kirsten and, to her horror, she felt a flush brighten her cheeks.

"Lovely indeed, Mr. Wellesley," Betty answered, rising to her feet. "Now, if you two will excuse me, I believe I'll get some punch." Before Kirsten could protest, Betty hurried off toward the refreshment table.

"May I sit down?" Eric inquired softly.

With a thin smile, Kirsten rose. "Certainly," she answered, and, turning on her heel, walked away.

Eric frowned, realizing the girl was even angrier than he'd expected. *Haughty little chit,* he thought irritably. *Why doesn't she understand that I'm doing her a favor by not marrying her?*

With a sigh he turned and followed Kirsten over to the refreshment table, determined not to let her pointed dismissal deter him.

Kirsten was unaware of Eric's approach and nearly jumped out of her skin when she heard his voice near her ear. "After you get your punch, why don't we walk around and meet some of the other couples?"

Furious at the game he was obviously playing,

Kirsten whirled around and said bluntly, "Mr. Welles-ley, I don't want to mingle with you, I don't want to talk to you, I don't even want to see you. I also do not want to embarrass either you or myself by making a scene in public so I would really appreciate it if you would just leave me alone."

Eric winced, realizing it was going to be much more difficult to introduce Kirsten to Lars than he had originally thought. "Oh, come now, Miss Lundgren," he smiled, laying a full measure of his considerable charm on her, "can't we be friends?"

Kirsten looked at him levelly. "No."

Despite his annoyance at Kirsten's obstinacy, Eric felt a grudging respect for her. She obviously had a great deal of pride and he couldn't help but admire her cool self-possession. At the same time, it was annoying him no end that she was being so stubborn when he was just trying to rectify the situation between them. Of course, she didn't know that that was his intention, and he certainly couldn't tell her, but, still, it wouldn't hurt her to at least be civil!

Undaunted, he tried again. "Miss Lundgren, you told me this afternoon that you were interested in staying in Rose Meadow and finding another husband. I am merely trying to help you. I can introduce you to several men here tonight who would be good candidates for marriage."

Kirsten stiffened. "I also told you this afternoon that I don't need your help in finding a husband."

"I know that," he placated, "but I feel an obligation toward you."

"Don't."

Damn her! Eric cursed silently. She was being impossible!

For a long moment, the couple stood glaring at each other, a fact which was not missed by anyone in the room, including Betty Zimmer, who was again seated on the sette, smiling like a cat who'd swallowed a canary.

The frigid tension between Kirsten and Eric was finally broken when Lars and Olga joined them. Eric looked at Lars gratefully and said, "Well, Lars Bjorklund! How are you?"

Lars didn't answer. Rather, after getting his first close-up look at Kirsten, he merely stood, jaw slack and eyes wide, thinking that she was the most ravishing woman he had ever seen.

Olga looked at her fiancé curiously, her mouth tightening as she saw where his gaze was riveted. With an unsubtle nudge to his ribs, she demanded, "Lars, introduce me to your friend!"

Finally remembering himself, Lars made the appropriate introductions, but his stumbling words were soon followed by another awkward silence.

At that moment, however, the same raucous band that had greeted the girls at the train station started energetically warming up and couples drifted toward the center of the room, preparing to dance.

Olga grabbed Lars's arm and unceremoniously hauled him off toward the gathering dancers. Kirsten, who was utterly bewildered by the little drama which had just unfolded in front of her, turned to Eric and said, "What was that all about?"

"Dunno," Eric said quickly. "Let's dance." Before Kirsten could turn him down, he circled her waist with one arm and swept her into the whirling mass of dancers.

They didn't talk, but as the dance progressed, Eric was more and more taken with the graceful beauty of his partner. Kirsten was an exquisite dancer; so light and supple in his arms that it seemed as if she were floating. "You're a good dancer," he complimented when the music finally slowed.

"Thank you," Kirsten acknowledged, smiling despite herself. "You are, too."

The beauty of her smile nearly blinded Eric and before he could catch himself, he found himself smiling back. Their eyes met and clung for a moment, then both of them looked quickly away.

"Let's change partners," Eric suggested.

"What?"

"It's . . . ah . . . tradition," he explained hurriedly. "Come on." And before she could protest, he led her off toward Lars and Olga.

"Let's swap partners," Eric said pointedly to Lars as they neared the other couple.

"Okay," Lars agreed, his eyes again glued to Kirsten. The women suddenly found themselves being nearly hurled into the opposite man's arms and whisked off for another dance.

Kirsten looked over Lars's massive shoulder and found Eric in animated conversation with a seemingly spellbound Olga.

What a peahen I am, she silently chastised herself. *How stupid can I be to think he actually enjoyed dancing with me? Olga's the one he wants.* Furious with herself that she had been flattered by Eric's momentary interest while they had danced, Kirsten turned a brilliant smile on Lars.

If possible, the big man's eyes widened even further at Kirsten's overt flirtation. He desperately wished that he could think of something clever to say, but he was so dumbstruck by this green-eyed goddess's sudden interest in him that he was totally tongue-tied.

The dance continued as Kirsten's mounting anger simmered just behind her radiant smile. When the music finally ended and Lars herded her back toward Eric, she dropped her gay facade and quickly excused herself, heading for the safety of the settee. Olga followed her, as confused by Eric's seeming interest in her as Lars was by Kirsten's in him. The two women sat down on the sofa and stared at the men, trying to figure out exactly what was going on.

Never one to mince words, Olga looked at Kirsten and said, "When are you and Eric getting married?"

"We're not," Kirsten answered with equal candor.

Olga's eyebrows shot into her hair. "You mean Eric

is . . . available?"

Kirsten looked at the big woman and smiled bitterly. "Totally available, and I'm sure he could be yours for the asking."

A loud guffaw exploded from Olga, causing several people to turn and look at her. "Oh no, Kirsten." She shook her head. "Eric's not for me."

"Why do you say that?"

"Because he's not what I want. I want Lars."

Kirsten was thunderstruck. "But, Olga, Eric's the most handsome man in town and," she leaned over and lowered her voice to a whisper, "he's rich, too."

Olga nodded. "I know, but he's not for me. He's for you."

"No," Kirsten protested. "You don't understand. He and I have talked and we . . . we've agreed that we just don't suit."

"Well, Lars and I *do* suit," Olga said firmly, slapping her hands on her knees. "He reminds me of the boys I grew up with and that's what I want. Oh, Eric's handsome, but he's not even Scandinavian and I wouldn't have accepted him even if he'd been the one to pay my passage."

Kirsten looked at Olga in complete shock. What woman in her right mind would turn down a man like Eric Wellesley? "But, why?"

Olga shrugged. "He's too high class for me."

"High class? He's a farmer!"

"He may be a farmer, but he's rich and educated, and I bet his people were nobility in England."

Kirsten's jaw dropped. "Did he tell you that?"

"No," Olga laughed. "He didn't have to. I just know. Just like I know the same thing about you. You two were meant for each other."

Kirsten sighed. "Oh, Olga, you don't know how wrong you are."

"I'm not wrong, Kirsten," Olga said. "I'm going to marry my Lars, and you're going to marry Eric. And we'll all be happy, you wait and see."

Kirsten looked at Olga sadly, but said nothing.

Just then, Lars walked over and asked Olga to dance. Olga looked at Kirsten hopefully, reluctant to leave her friend sitting alone, but dying to dance with "her" Lars again. Kirsten read the beseeching look in Olga's eyes and smiled. "Go ahead, you two. I want to talk to Mrs. Zimmer."

Skirting the area where Eric was standing drinking a glass of punch and talking to Elsie Anderson (who, to Kirsten's annoyance, appeared to be hanging on his every word), Kirsten approached Betty who was with a group of matrons gathered by the door.

"Are you having a good time, dear?" Betty asked cheerily.

"Yes, fine, thank you," Kirsten answered, her voice cool. "May I talk to you a moment, please?"

Excusing herself from her companions, Betty and Kirsten moved into a private corner.

"I want to go home, please," Kirsten said quietly.

Betty quickly covered the look of distress which flickered across her eyes. "Are you feeling sick?"

"No." Kirsten shook her head. "But, I'm not going to meet anyone tonight since Mr. Wellesley is here, and I really don't want to stay any longer."

Betty frowned, trying to think of some means to waylay the determined girl. Thankfully, she was saved by Eric joining them.

"Miss Lundgren, would you like to dance again?"

"No, Mr. Wellesley, I wouldn't," Kirsten answered. "I'm going home."

"Home! You can't go home!" Eric exclaimed, his voice betraying a distinct note of panic. Kirsten threw him a puzzled look and he quickly masked his feelings by adding casually, "After all, the evening's just begun."

"Mr. Wellesley," Kirsten started, "I really don't see . . ."

Suddenly the looming presence of Lars Bjorklund appeared at Kirsten's elbow. "You can't leave yet. You

61

promised me another dance."

Olga's eyes narrowed as she looked at Lars, but Eric enjoined smoothly, "Absolutely. You dance another dance with Lars and I'll dance with Olga."

Again, the couples swooped onto the dance floor. Kirsten was very confused as to why Lars Bjorklund was being so attentive, but his next words made everything painfully clear.

"I hope you'll like working in my store."

"I beg your pardon?"

"I said, I hope you'll like working in my store. Of course, it will probably only be for a short time. I want to start a family right away and since I'm hoping for a baby every year, you won't have much time to spare after we have two or three."

Kirsten stopped dead, causing Lars to nearly trod on her toes. "What in the world are you talking about, Mr. Bjorklund?"

It was Lars's turn to look confused. It had never occurred to him that Eric had not proposed the planned swap to Kirsten before speaking to him. "I'm talking about after we're married."

"Married!" Kirsten gasped. "Why would you think we're getting married?"

"Well," he stammered, "because that's the plan."

Kirsten's voice was deadly quiet. "What plan?"

"Eric's plan! You know, the plan that he'll marry Olga and I'll marry you."

Kirsten was so angry she could barely control herself, but knowing Lars was as innocent in this latest ploy of Eric's as she was, she forced herself to remain calm. "Mr. Bjorklund," she said slowly, "it's obvious that you have been misled. I have no intention of marrying you."

At Lars's hurt and confused expression, she quickly amended, "It's not that I don't like you, but I know that Olga is counting on you. She told me so and I wouldn't think of interfering in the path of true love."

"But," Lars protested, "Eric just told me that Olga

suits him fine, and since he wants her, I get you."

Kirsten bit her lip, trying to hold back tears of rage and humiliation. "I appreciate the offer. I really do. But I'm not going to marry either you *or* Mr. Wellesley and I think we'd better go talk to him and Olga before his, ah, 'plans' go any further."

Lars, suddenly realizing that he was in jeopardy of losing both Olga *and* Kirsten, stiffened. "I think you're right."

The couple marched over to where Olga and Eric were standing, talking to Elsie and her skinny fiancé, Olaf Swenson.

Putting her hand on Olga's arm, Kirsten said, "Are you aware, Olga, that Eric and Lars have decided to trade?"

Olga looked blank. "Trade what?"

"Trade us," Kirsten said, her voice rising angrily. "They have decided to swap fiancées—like swapping horses at an auction."

"Lars!" Olga cried. "Do you want to trade me away?"

"Well," Lars stammered, "it was Eric's idea!"

"I have no doubt of that," Kirsten said icily. "You see, Olga, Mr. Wellesley told me he wanted a big, strong, workhorse of a wife who could toil all day in the fields and still cook the meals, do the wash, clean the house, and raise children. Since he thinks I'm too small to handle all that, he's set his sights on you."

Olga whirled on the crimson Eric. "Is this true?"

"Now, Miss Johannson, please don't get upset. It isn't like that at all."

"Oh yes it is!" Kirsten interrupted. "It's exactly like that!"

"She's right," Lars added, turning accusing eyes on Eric. "Eric told me just this afternoon that he wants a mustard weed."

"A what?" the women chorused.

"A mustard weed," Lars repeated. "You know, those big strong weeds that grow by the side of the road. Eric

63

told me he wants a wife who's a mustard weed like Olga, not a little, golden wildflower like Kirsten."

Kirsten shot Eric a fleeting look when she heard that he'd likened her to a "little, golden wildflower." She was flattered, despite herself.

Olga, however, was far from flattered. Wheeling on Eric, she said, "So you think I'm strong, do you? Well, I'll show you just how strong I really am!" And pulling back her arm, she slugged Eric in the stomach so hard that the air left his lungs in a breathless "whoosh" and he doubled over with a soft groan.

By now the entire congregation in Andrew Patterson's parlor was listening to the little drama being played out in the corner of the room. Several of the girls tittered and Elsie Anderson laughed out loud when Olga's fist slammed into Eric's stomach.

But Olga wasn't finished. Turning on Lars, she said, "I may be a mustard weed, but I'm not *your* mustard weed. Our engagement is off!"

"Ours too!" Kirsten chorused, looking at both men since she was unsure of whom she was engaged to, if anybody. Turning in unison, the two women stomped out of the parlor.

For a moment Eric and Lars just stood looking at each other; then suddenly Lars bellowed, "Eric Wellesley, you've lost me a wife!" and, for the second time in two minutes, Eric received a gut-wrenching punch in the stomach. This time he dropped to his knees, clutching his belly and moaning.

"Enough, now!" thundered Andrew Patterson. "I'll have no fisticuffs in my parlor. Get out, both of you!"

Like two wayward boys, Eric and Lars stumbled out of the house, leaving the other twelve men and their fiancées gaping in disbelief.

Suddenly, Sophie Olson looked over at her fiancé, Gustav Johnson, who was standing with another of the brides whom he had just been dancing with, and yelled, "And, what about you, Gus? Are you planning on swapping me, too?"

Pandemonium broke out as every bride who was not currently standing with her betrothed looked at her man and the women he was near. There were many protestations from the men as they hurried back to their intendeds' sides, but the women turned cold shoulders and leveled accusing stares on their hapless fiancés.

"Well, I'll tell you one thing," Sophie announced to the group. "If Mr. Wellesley isn't going to marry Kirsten, and Mr. Bjorklund isn't going to marry Olga, then Mr. Johnson isn't going to marry me either. We came as a group to get married as a group and, I say, we must stand together as a group!"

"I agree," chorused in Elsie Anderson, delighted to have an excuse to shuck off her unwanted fiancé. All day she had been trying to formulate a plan to get rid of Olaf and get Eric Wellesley for herself. Tonight's little peccadillo was exactly the out she'd been looking for. "All for one and one for all, right girls?" she called.

Several more of the brides voiced their support and, one by one, the girls started out the front door.

"Ladies, wait!" called Andrew Patterson desperately, racing out to his front hall. "You're making a big mistake!"

"No mistake, Mayor Patterson," Sophie called over her shoulder. "Tell the men that until they *all* live up to their promise to marry us, they can keep company with each other. We're not interested in associating with rogues and mashers."

Andrew stopped in his tracks, knowing there was nothing he could say to sway the outraged women. Throwing up his hands in utter frustration, he turned back toward the parlor, having not the slightest idea what he was going to say to the twelve jilted, furious men waiting inside.

Chapter 6

The next week was a nightmare.

It started the morning after the ill-fated party. Eric was still in bed when he heard someone pounding on his front door. He rose slowly, grimacing at the pain that knifed through his bruised stomach.

Trudging slowly down the hall, he peered out of the oval beveled window in his front door, groaning when he saw who stood on the other side.

"Ole Lindquist and Lars Bjorklund," he muttered. "Just what I need to start the day."

He opened the door, forcing a welcoming smile. "Hi, boys. What brings you two visiting so early on a Sunday?"

"I think you know," Lars responded, his expression black.

"Ja, I think so, too," Ole chorused.

"Come to punch me in the stomach again?" Eric asked in a small attempt at humor.

"No," Lars said slowly. "And I'm sorry about that, too. It was wrong. Ole and I are here this morning to find out what you are going to do now to set things right for us men."

Eric stared at Lars blankly. "What do you mean, what am I going to do? What do you want me to do?"

"We want you to make things right with our girls," Ole said.

Eric blew out a long breath and stared vacantly down at his bare feet. Finally, he looked back at the expectant men on his front porch. "Why don't you two come in and we'll talk. I'll make some coffee."

The two men looked at each other, then nodded curtly and stepped into the foyer.

Eric led the way down the hall to the kitchen, trying desperately to think of a way to placate the angry men. With slow deliberation, he filled a pot with water and threw in a handful of beans.

"Be sure you crack an egg in that," Ole advised from the table, "or it won't be worth drinking."

Eric grimaced, but acceded to the old Scandinavian custom and dutifully cracked an egg against the edge of the pot and threw it in with the coffee and water, shell and all. Finally, unable to think of anything else to postpone the confrontation he knew was brewing, he sat down and faced his two neighbors.

"So, what do you want from me?" he asked bluntly.

"Well," Ole said in his slow, halting English, "we think you made the mess last night, so you must clean it up."

"And just exactly how do you propose I 'clean it up,' as you put it?"

"You heard the women," Lars interrupted. "They said unless we all get married, none of us do."

"Yeah, I heard that ridiculous threat," Eric acknowledged with a shake of his head.

"Ridiculous?" Ole bristled. "Why do you say, 'ridiculous'? My Sarah was the one who said that, and I won't have you calling her 'ridiculous.'" Angrily, he started to rise from his chair.

Eric held up his hands in supplication. "I didn't say that *Sarah* is ridiculous, Ole, I said it was a ridiculous threat."

Ole sank back into his chair, but his angry scowl remained.

"Why do you think it's ridiculous?" Lars asked. "The girls were so mad last night that they wouldn't even let us walk them home. And as for Olga, well, you just better stay away from her. She wants your blood after what you said about her being a mustard weed."

Eric clamped his mouth shut, forcing himself to remain silent and not remind Lars that it had been he who had told Olga that little tidbit.

"Ja," Ole enjoined, "and my Sarah, she told me she never wants to see me again—just because I was dancing with that Inga. I don't even like Inga. I was just being polite by asking her to dance, but Sarah thinks I was trying to talk Inga into swapping, too."

"This whole thing is completely out of hand," Eric growled. "The women got hysterical, that's all. One just set off another until they were all acting crazy." He paused for a moment; then a thought occurred to him—one that might end this whole absurd situation. "But, you know what, boys? Now that the women have had time to think on it, I'll bet every one of them is regretting that threat. I bet if you two go to church this morning, you'll find your fiancées more than willing to make up. *More* than willing."

Ole and Lars looked at Eric dubiously. "You really think so?" Ole asked hopefully.

"Absolutely," Eric assured him. "Think about it! These women came all the way out here to get married. They're not going to give up that dream just because they were momentarily piqued."

Ole nudged Lars. "What does 'piqued' mean?"

Lars shrugged.

"It means 'mad,'" Eric volunteered. "And, I'm just sure the ladies regret their rash words. Why, I bet they're all standing in the churchyard right now, just hoping that you men will give them the opportunity to apologize. If I know anything about women, it's that given enough time, they'll eventually come around and be reasonable."

"Well, maybe," Lars conceded. "But, what about you? What are you going to do about Kirsten?"

"Nothing," Eric answered firmly. "That's finished."

"You can't have Olga!" Lars suddenly decreed, rising to his feet with clenched fists. "If she's willing to forget last night and still get married, then she's going to marry me!"

"Fine," Eric soothed. "She's all yours. Last night was all I needed to remind me why I've stayed a bachelor all these years . . . and why I plan to continue to do so."

"Well, all I have to say is, you better be right, Wellesley," Lars grumbled, slamming his hat on his head and heading for the front door. "Come on, Ole, we've got to hurry if we're going to make it to church before services start."

Ole raced down the hall after his companion, then paused to look back at Eric. "You better be right, Wellesley!"

With a smiling nod, Eric ushered the men out the front door and watched them clamber into Ole's old wagon. Turning back toward the kitchen, he paused to look in a mirror which hung in the hall. Smiling wryly at his reflection, he whispered, "You better be right, Wellesley!"

By early afternoon, Eric was positive his plan had worked. Ole and Lars had not reappeared, and that, in itself, was a good sign. Eric did wish, however, that *someone* would stop by and tell him how church had gone. He chuckled to himself as he looked down the empty road. "Must have gone so well that everybody's forgotten to come tell me."

Happily, he sat back to wait, confident that when the day's courting was over, the men would stop by to thank him for his excellent advice. But as the afternoon passed and still no one appeared, he began to feel a little put out. Finally, he could stand it no longer.

Hitching up his wagon, he headed for town. After all, he told himself, if the couples had reconciled, he deserved congratulations for encouraging the men to give the girls another chance.

70

He tethered his horse in front of the Rose Café and sauntered down the boardwalk toward the Sweet Treat Ice Cream Parlor, confident that that's where he would find the men and their fiancées. But, when he pushed open the door to the ice cream shop, he stopped cold. Instead of being met by the welcoming calls of his grateful friends, he was greeted instead by a sudden, icy silence—from seven, unescorted brides.

As fourteen accusing eyes glared at him, Eric swept off his hat. "Good afternoon, ladies," he said, his rich voice flowing over them. His attempt at charm didn't work, however, and, in one accord, the seven heads turned away.

Eric paused, considering the possibility that maybe his plan hadn't gone as well as he'd hoped. He stood just inside the door for a long moment, unsure of what to do next.

Taking a deep breath, he strolled over to the table where the girls were seated. Looking hopefully at Sarah, he said, "I wonder if you know where Ole is, Miss Drake?"

Barely glancing at him, Sarah responded coldly, "I'm sure I don't know, Mr. Wellesley, and I'm equally sure I don't care!"

Eric gulped. Things *definitely* had not gone as planned. "I see," he said slowly. "Well, thank you anyway." Backing toward the door, he added, "Enjoy your phosphates, ladies," and bolted from the shop.

Safely out on the boardwalk, he breathed a sigh of relief. But, his respite was short-lived. As he turned toward his wagon, determined to get out of town before he met anyone else, he ran smack into Kirsten's friend, Susan Ingram. He lifted his hat to greet her, but before he could utter a word, she swept her skirts aside and, with a look of disdain, walked past him.

"Shit!" Eric cursed as he watched Susan continue on down the street. "I haven't done anything to deserve this!"

His plans of escape momentarily forgotten, he

71

stalked off down the boardwalk toward the Cedar Queen Saloon. Pushing through the bat-wing doors, he marched up to the bar and ordered a whiskey.

Dan Morrison, the bartender, poured him a shot, then set the bottle on the bar and grinned. "Heard you caused a whole lot of trouble over at the mayor's house last night, Eric."

Throwing him a jaundiced look, Eric tossed back the drink. "Well, you heard wrong, Dan," he growled, wiping his mouth and slamming the glass down on the bar. "All I did was try to right a wrong. Those ladies at the party just heard half the story and went nuts, that's all."

Dan chuckled. "Women folks will do that now and again."

"Yeah," Eric agreed sullenly, "won't they though?"

"But, still," Dan continued, pouring Eric another drink, "there's a lot of folks who are pretty mad at you today—both women *and* men."

"I know." Eric grimaced. "Everybody I've seen today has made that more than clear."

"So, what are you going to do about it?"

"Do?" Eric repeated. "Everyone keeps asking me what I'm going to do? What *can* I do? What would *you* do?"

"Well, if I was you, I'd hightail it over to Betty Zimmer's place and try to make my peace with that little redheaded gal. She's the only one can lift the hex off you."

"God spare me!" Eric pleaded, casting his eyes heavenward. "She's the last person I want to see. I never had any trouble in my life till that woman arrived, but ever since I laid eyes on her she's caused me nothing but one problem after another."

"They'll do that, for sure," Dan chuckled. "But, the way I see it, you ain't got no choice."

Eric sighed. "You're right. I guess I have to go over to Mrs. Zimmer's and try to talk some sense into Miss Lundgren."

"Be careful," Dan warned with a chuckle. "I never knowed a woman yet who liked having sense talked into her. And just remember, you catch a whole lot more flies with honey than vinegar."

"This is one fly I don't want to catch," Eric grumbled, tossing back one last shot for the road. "I just want her to take off and buzz around somebody else!"

Dan threw back his head and laughed heartily. "Good luck, Eric."

"Thanks," Eric acknowledged. "I'm gonna need it!"

"She's not here."

Eric looked at Betty Zimmer through narrowed eyes, trying to figure out if she was telling him the truth. "You sure of that, Mrs. Zimmer?"

"I said, she's not here," Betty answered firmly. "You want to come in and search the place?"

"I'm sorry, ma'am," Eric apologized. "I'm just having one hell of a day and I've got to get things straightened out."

"I know," Betty relented. "Why don't you come on in? She just went to catch a breath of air and watch the sunset. She'll be back soon."

Nodding, Eric followed Betty into her tiny parlor and perched uncomfortably on the edge of a worn settee.

With a sympathetic smile, Betty sat in a chair across from him. "So, what are you going to do now?" she asked.

Eric thought that if one more person asked him what he was going to do, he just might smack them. Shaking his head, he posed the now familiar question. "What *can* I do?"

"Marry her."

"What?"

"Marry her. That's what she wants, she just won't admit it."

73

"Well, I'm sorry, Mrs. Zimmer, but it's not what I want."

"You must have wanted it once or you wouldn't have sent for her in the first place."

"Yeah, well, once I thought I did, but I don't anymore."

Betty sat back in her chair, gazing speculatively at her guest. "Tell me, Eric, is it marriage you've decided you don't want, or is it just Kirsten?"

Eric sighed, suddenly so tired of the whole subject of Kirsten Lundgren that he could hardly stand talking about it anymore. "I've explained all this to her, ma'am. She and I just don't suit."

"Pshaw!" Betty waved her hand in dismissal. "You suit too well, that's your whole trouble. You're plumb stubborn and so is she. If you two would just quit spitting and clawing at each other, you'd see what a fine match you really are."

"She's too damn small!" Eric nearly shouted. "Excuse my language, Mrs. Zimmer, but, how many times do I have to say it? She'd never stand up to the work!"

"Try her," Betty suggested.

"Pardon?"

"Try her!" she repeated. "Hire her on as your housekeeper. See if she can handle the chores."

"No."

"Why not?"

"Because that wouldn't work."

"What's the matter, boy?" Betty chuckled. "Scared she might prove you wrong?"

Eric looked away, unable to meet the shrewd woman's eyes. "No, it's not that, exactly," he responded uneasily. "There's . . . lots of reasons."

Betty looked at him closely, then suddenly laughed out loud, slapping her knees with the palms of her hands. "Yeah, I've noticed how pretty she is, too."

Eric was mortified by his transparency. He rose abruptly from the settee. "I can't wait around any longer, ma'am. I have milking to do."

"Sure, I understand," Betty chuckled.

They walked to the front door, but as Eric reached for the handle Betty put a staying hand on his arm. "Think about it, Eric. You could make everything right with two little words."

Eric frowned. "It wouldn't work."

"Suit yourself," Betty shrugged, "but keep in mind that until you and Kirsten come to some agreement about this situation, no one in town is going to have anything to do with you. As far as the men are concerned, you've ruined their love lives. As far as the brides are concerned, you've ruined their whole lives. That's a fierce combination."

Eric stared at Betty for a long moment, admitting, despite his frustration, that she was right. Throwing his head back and closing his eyes in defeat, he said, "Would you see that Kirsten is here tomorrow afternoon about three?"

"Certainly," Betty smiled. "Are you coming to call?"

"No," Eric responded quietly, "I'm coming to propose."

Betty beamed. "She'll be here."

Chapter 7

"I won't see him. I don't care what he has to say, I don't want to hear it."

Betty frowned at her obstinate charge. "Don't you think you owe it to him to hear him out?"

"I don't owe him anything," Kirsten sulked. "After the embarrassment Eric Wellesley has caused me, I just want to forget that I ever heard of him."

Betty sighed. "Well, I don't know what to do, dear. It's too late to send him a message. He's going to be here in less than an hour."

"Why didn't you tell me about this last night?" Kirsten cried. "That way there *would* have been time to let him know I don't want to see him."

Betty shrugged and feigned an innocent expression. "It just slipped my mind," she lied, having purposely not told Kirsten of Eric's impending visit, anticipating that the headstrong girl's reaction would be exactly what she was now encountering. She had also intentionally not told Kirsten of Eric's plan to propose, deciding that it was more prudent to keep that bit of information to herself. After all, Betty thought, it was a very personal matter and far be it for her to interfere!

She turned beseeching eyes on Kirsten. "Please, dear, just spare him a few minutes. I'm sure all he wants to do is apologize for everything, and after he does, you never have to see him again. But at least by seeing him

77

today, it will give you the satisfaction of ending this unfortunate situation graciously."

Kirsten closed her eyes and sighed heavily. "Oh, all right," she acquiesced. "I'll give him ten minutes, but that's it! Then he's out the door and out of my life . . . for good!"

Betty beamed. "I'm sure ten minutes will be more than enough time. Now, you better go change. Why don't you wear that lovely yellow dress of yours? It's so pretty with your hair, and I'm sure you'll want to look your best."

"What do I care if I look my best?" Kirsten muttered sourly. But, noting Betty's shaming look, she threw her hands up in defeat and said, "All right, all right! I'll change!"

"I don't believe I'm doing this!" Eric growled to himself as he turned his horse onto Oak Street. "This is crazy! She's crazy and I'm crazy for humoring her."

With an impatient jerk on the reins, he pulled his horse up in front of Zimmer's Boardinghouse and dismounted, flinging the reins over the hitching rail and irritably pulling off his hat. Reaching behind the saddle, he untied a small bouquet of wild summer violets and, raking his fingers through his hair, stomped up to the front door.

He was just raising his hand to knock when the door was abruptly flung open and Kirsten, exquisitely dressed in a yellow sprigged muslin afternoon dress, greeted him. "Mr. Wellesley."

Eric could hardly take his eyes off her. *God, she's beautiful!* Remembering himself, he nodded and held the bouquet out. "Miss Lundgren."

Kirsten reluctantly reached out, accepting the bouquet as she allowed her gaze to covertly sweep over him. *Lord, he's handsome!*

"Won't you come in?" she asked, holding her skirt aside to allow him to enter.

"Thank you." He silently followed her into the parlor and sat on the same hard settee he'd occupied yesterday.

"Would you care for some lemonade?" Kirsten asked stiffly, gesturing toward a pitcher sitting on a nearby table.

"No, thank you."

Glancing down, Kirsten noticed that she was still gripping the bouquet. "Oh!" she said, as if seeing the flowers for the first time. "These are lovely. I better put them in some water."

Eric nodded absently, his eyes riveted on her hair where the sunlight was shining on it. As she disappeared through the parlor door, his eyes followed her, one eyebrow lifting appreciatively at the graceful sway of her full skirt. *She's got the smallest waist I've ever seen. And that red hair! I wonder if it's as soft as it looks?* With a sharp shake of his head, he pulled himself from his reverie, annoyed with himself for allowing his thoughts to stray so provocatively.

Kirsten returned and sat down stiffly on the settee next to him. Eric looked at her hopefully, wishing she'd say something to break the tension, but she didn't. The strained silence lengthened until he finally cleared his throat and said, "I guess I owe you an apology."

"Yes, Mr. Wellesley, I'd say you do."

Eric's lips thinned. *She didn't have to agree so fast!* "Well, you have it."

"Have what?" she asked, forcing him to say the words.

"An apology," he said through gritted teeth, incensed that she was goading him.

"Thank you," Kirsten answered coolly and stood.

Eric looked up at her in bewilderment, then suddenly realized that she expected him to leave. His brows snapped together in consternation. *Now* what was he supposed to say?

"Mr. Wellesley?" Kirsten asked expectantly.

Eric threw her such a troubled look that she sat down

again. "Is there something else?"

"Yes."

She waited . . . and waited . . . and waited. "Well, what?" she finally asked.

Eric's gaze darted over to her, then immediately fled. "I, um, I was wondering . . ."

"Yes?" Kirsten coaxed, completely mystified by his nervous, nearly tongue-tied demeanor.

"Will you marry me, Miss Lundgren?"

His head was down and she didn't hear his muttered words. "I beg your pardon?"

His head snapped up and in a loud voice, he asked, "Are you deaf, Miss Lundgren? I said, will you marry me?"

Kirsten's jaw dropped. She had no idea what she'd expected him to say, but it certainly wasn't this! She answered with the first thing that came to her mind. "No!"

"No?" Eric asked incredulously. *She puts me through all this and then she says "no"?*

Kirsten looked at him closely. *Is that relief in his eyes?* "No, Mr. Wellesley. I won't marry you."

"Why?"

Kirsten sighed and looked down at her hands, which were, to her surprise, trembling. "I don't mean to offend you, but, frankly, I don't like you much."

It was Eric's turn to gape. "You don't mean to *offend* me? Lord, woman, I'm finally giving you what you want and, now, you've decided you don't *like* me? What the hell is wrong with you?"

Kirsten's chin lifted a notch. "I appreciate your sacrifice, sir, but, whether you can believe it or not, marriage to you is *definitely* not what I want. And, as for your other question, there is absolutely *nothing* wrong with me!"

Eric shot to his feet, clapping his hat on his head. "Fine. Great. But just make sure you tell all your girlfriends that you turned me down, okay? I'm tired of being the fall guy in this mess. I've offered, you've refused, so that's the end of it, right?"

Kirsten blinked, so startled by his vehemence that she didn't respond.

"Right?" he repeated, his voice demanding an answer.

"Yes, right," she nodded.

"You're sure about this, now." Eric continued. "I want to be absolutely positive that 'no' is your answer, so I'll ask you one more time. Do you or do you not want to marry me?"

"NO!" Kirsten nearly shouted. "I do NOT want to marry you. Now, please go!"

"Okay." Eric let out a long breath and smiled. "That's settled, then."

Kirsten stared after him as he hurried down the hall. He was smiling! The man was so pleased she'd turned him down that he actually had the audacity to smile—and right in front of her!

Pushing open the front door, Eric looked over his shoulder and said pleasantly, "Good day, Miss Lundgren."

"Get out, Mr. Wellesley!" she yelled in return.

He bolted out the front door, throwing his hat in the air in sheer jubilation. Well, I'll be damned, he thought as he galloped down the road toward home, she turned me down!

He was free. IT WAS OVER!

The word spread like wildfire. Kirsten wasn't sure how everybody found out, but by the next afternoon people she didn't even know were aware that Eric Wellesley had finally proposed and she'd turned him down.

At first she suspected it was Betty who'd told everyone, but as the days passed she changed her mind. Betty seemed genuinely upset that Kirsten had refused Eric's suit and refused to talk about the particulars, even when questioned by her closest friends. Her only comment was that Kirsten's decision was "a mistake—a terrible mistake."

Kirsten didn't feel that way. Although she was embarrassed to be the object of so much gossip and speculation, there was one positive aspect to everyone in town knowing about her breakup with Eric. The rest of the brides had reunited with their fiancés. As soon as the other girls heard that Kirsten had rejected Eric—and not the other way around—they happily began mending fences with their own men. And the men, delighted to suddenly be back in the good graces of their ladies, willingly put the whole fiasco behind them and resumed their courtships.

No one was more pleased to hear of Eric and Kirsten's breakup than Elsie Anderson, but not for the same reasons as the other brides.

Elsie didn't want to resume her relationship with Olaf Swenson. The first moment she'd seen Eric Wellesley she'd decided he was the one she wanted, and now she had been handed the perfect opportunity to make that wish come true.

Eric was available for the taking and Elsie quickly decided that she was going to have him. She spent hours strolling idly down Main Street, hoping to catch sight of him coming into town. She spent precious coins from her fast dwindling cache of money on frivolous items at the general store, just on the off chance that one of the other shoppers might mention him. But her efforts were to no avail. She didn't see him, didn't even hear his name mentioned except by older matrons who pumped *her* for information about his break-up with Kirsten. And, when she finally became so desperate that she asked the other brides if any of them had seen him, they all just shook their heads and returned to their excited chatter about wedding dresses and honeymoons.

Meanwhile, Olaf continued to shyly press his suit, coming to call each night, regardless of the fact that he spent most evenings answering a barrage of Elsie's none too subtle questions about Eric.

Finally Elsie decided to take matters into her own hands. If Eric wouldn't come into town, then she would just ride out to his farm. It took her a whole week to screw up her courage, but, finally, on Sunday afternoon, she dressed in her best dove gray velvet riding habit and walked down to the livery stable to rent a horse.

It was a hot, muggy June day and Elsie knew long before she reached the livery stable that she had made a terrible mistake wearing velvet. But, unwilling to waste the time it would take to return home and change into cooler clothes, she ignored the clinging material and the sweat trickling uncomfortably down between her breasts. Renting a docile, old mare, she headed out of town on the road she knew led to Eric's farm.

Eric was dozing in a hammock when Elsie arrived and he didn't hear her approach until she was standing next to him.

"Mr. Wellesley?"

He jerked awake, pulling the St. Paul newspaper away from where it lay covering his face, and clumsily sat up. The hammock lurched crazily for a moment, then suddenly the rope securing one end to a tree snapped with a loud twang and Eric suddenly found himself sprawled on the ground at Elsie's feet. Elsie took a startled step backward and clapped her hands over her mouth. "I'm sorry," she giggled, "I didn't mean to frighten you. Are you all right?"

Eric threw her a jaundiced look, then scrambled awkwardly to his feet, brushing off the back of his pants as he looked down at the broken hammock in astonished disbelief.

"Yes, I'm fine, Miss, ah, Miss . . ."

"Anderson!" she supplied, trying hard not to let on how annoyed she was that he didn't remember her last name.

"Right . . . Anderson," Eric repeated, looking down in embarrassment as he noticed Elsie's eyes feasting on

83

his naked chest.

"Well, Miss Anderson," he smiled, crossing his muscular arms over his chest in a lame effort to cover it, "what brings you way out here? You're not lost or hurt or anything, are you?"

"Oh, no," Elsie assured him, giving her blond curls a coy shake. "I just decided that it was such a lovely afternoon that I'd take a ride."

"Kind of a hot day for it," Eric noted.

"Oh, not really," she demurred. "But I would appreciate a cup of water if it wouldn't be too much trouble."

"'Course not. Come on," he said, striding off across the yard, "the pump's out back."

Elsie frowned at his retreating back, realizing that he obviously had no intention of inviting her in. "Ah, Mr. Wellesley?" she called, hurrying to catch up to him. "Do you suppose I might sit in your parlor for a few minutes and rest? I'm afraid the heat *has* gotten to me a bit."

Eric wheeled around and looked at her flushed face. "You're not gonna faint, are you?"

"Oh, no! I just need to cool off a little. If I could just sit down inside for a minute with a glass of water . . ." Her voice trailed off.

Eric frowned. "Does Olaf know you're out alone?" he asked pointedly.

"No," Elsie said, trying hard to control the exasperation she knew was creeping into her voice, "but, there's nothing settled between Olaf and me and I don't think it's necessary that he knows where I am and what I'm doing every minute of every day."

Eric Wellesley was a handsome man and he knew it. Women had been throwing themselves at him since he was eighteen years old and now, at thirty-two, he knew a proposition when he heard one.

"You're welcome to sit inside, Miss Anderson," he said, taking care to keep his voice even and polite. "I have some work to do in the barn, but there's a pitcher of water on the sideboard and glasses on the shelf above the sink."

"Oh, I wouldn't feel right being in your house alone, sir," Elsie protested, dropping her eyes.

Eric threw her a hard look. "Well, I'm afraid I wouldn't feel right being in my house alone with you, miss."

Elsie let out a melodic little thrill of laughter. "Are you always so concerned about what's 'right,' Eric?"

Eric didn't miss her sudden use of his first name. He looked directly at her, and in a voice that brooked no argument said, "Always, *Miss Anderson*."

"I see." By now, Elsie was furious. Who did this bumpkin think he was, reminding her of proprieties? In a haughty voice, she added, "Well, since you're obviously so busy, I'll just be on my way."

Eric followed her back to where her horse was tethered. "Don't you want that drink of water before you go?"

"No, thank you," she said, her voice sharp and angry. Mounting, she jerked at the horse's reins.

"Miss Anderson?" Eric asked, stepping forward and putting a hand on her bridle.

"Yes?" she said, trying hard to hold enraged tears at bay.

"I'm flattered you stopped."

"Well, don't be," she snapped, giving the mare a hard kick in an attempt to free the bridle from his grasp. "There was no particular reason I stopped here. I wanted a drink of water and it was purely coincidence that it was your farm I happened to be passing."

Eric smiled. "Still, I'm flattered. Oh, and, Miss Anderson?"

"What!"

"Say hello to Olaf for me when you see him."

With a murderous look, Elsie kicked the poor old horse soundly in the ribs and headed down the drive at a bone-jarring trot.

*   *   *

Elsie was mad. Oh, was she mad! Never in all her nineteen years had any man, handsome or plain, rich or poor, *ever* snubbed her like Eric Wellesley just had. There had to be a reason for his disinterest. After all, he didn't want Kirsten, and now he didn't want her either. And, if he didn't want *her,* Elsie thought vainly, then he must not want anyone!

She pulled back the reins and slowed the wheezing mare to a stiff-jointed walk. Maybe *that* was it. Maybe Eric Wellesley just didn't like girls.

Elsie had heard about men like that. Men who didn't like women. Maybe Eric was one of *them!* It would certainly explain why he had rejected both Kirsten *and* her.

Elsie felt much better. Obviously Eric's rejection had nothing to do with her personally . . . he was just one of *those!*

Suddenly she threw back her head and giggled delightedly. Wasn't this rich? Little Miss Perfect Kirsten Lundgren had traveled all the way across the country to marry a man who would probably rather sleep with his pigs than with her!

Then a new thought occurred to her. "I wonder if Kirsten knows?" she mused aloud. "Well, if she doesn't now, she will soon . . . and very, very publicly!"

Elsie beamed. The afternoon hadn't been a total waste, after all!

Chapter 8

"You're all getting married at once?"

"That's right," Sarah nodded, giggling at Kirsten's incredulous expression. "We decided that rather than have thirteen little weddings, we'd just have one huge one. The biggest celebration Rose Meadow has ever seen!"

"I'm sure it will be that," Kirsten agreed.

"And, what's more," Sarah added, "we want you to make the cake. The biggest wedding cake in history!"

Kirsten stared at her friend in disbelief. "Oh, I don't know, Sarah. I've never tried to make anything that big before. Why, it would have to feed hundreds."

"Only about two hundred."

"*Only* two hundred!" Kirsten laughed. "Think of the cost!"

"Don't worry about that," Sarah responded, reaching out and patting Kirsten's hand. "The cost is all taken care of."

"What do you mean?"

Sarah hesitated, hating the fact that she had to lie to her friend. But she knew if she told Kirsten the truth about where the money was coming from to pay for the cake, she would probably refuse to bake it. "The men have decided to all chip in to buy the ingredients, plus they're going to pay you fifty dollars for baking it."

Kirsten was stunned. "Fifty dollars? Are you sure?"

"Absolutely sure."

Kirsten rose from her chair and paced across Betty's parlor, shaking her head. When Sarah had unexpectedly arrived at the front door, telling Kirsten she had to talk to her about something important, Kirsten had never dreamed her friend's news would have such a shocking impact on her. Fifty dollars! Enough money to pay her train fare back to New York and give her a small nest egg to resume her life there. It was the answer to a prayer . . . but, could she do it?

Turning back toward her smiling friend, Kirsten threw her hands in the air. "Where would I get enough pans? Enough ovens?"

"Don't worry about a thing," Sarah assured her. "All the ladies in town will help."

"When is the wedding?"

"Saturday afternoon."

Kirsten's eyes widened. "This coming Saturday? You must be joking! Why, that's only five days away!"

"I know," Sarah said calmly, "but the men don't want to wait any longer. Now, quit worrying. I've already talked to Helga over at the general store and she's ordering the supplies from St. Paul. She says they'll be here by Wednesday, so you'll have three whole days to bake and decorate and whatever else you'll have to do."

"Oh, Sarah," Kirsten wrung her hands, frowning, "I just don't know if I can handle this. At my father's bakery we made individual tarts and pastries. I've never tried anything like this. And a wedding cake is so important. If it didn't turn out, I'd never forgive myself!"

"Don't be a goose," Sarah said, pulling on her gloves and rising. "It will be wonderful. Just say you'll do it, Kirsten. If you won't, we won't have any cake at all!"

Kirsten stood for a long moment, biting her lip as she thought about the mountain of work ahead of her . . . but, she also thought about the fifty dollars she'd receive.

"All right," she nodded. "I'll do it."

"Wonderful!" Sarah enthused, racing across the room and giving Kirsten a quick hug. "Everyone will be so excited!"

Kirsten grimaced. "Just don't expect too much, okay?"

"Quit worrying!"

The two girls walked toward the front door. "Oh, by the way," Sarah said, "the town hostesses are throwing a party for all the brides on Friday afternoon. Will you come?"

Kirsten felt a little catch in her throat. "All the brides," and she was no longer one of them. Now she was just another attendee at a party where she should have been one of the guests of honor. "I . . . I don't know," she stammered. "I probably won't have time, what with making the cake and all."

"Nonsense. You can spare a couple of hours. Come on, Kirsten, it wouldn't be the same without you."

Kirsten looked at the floor, fighting the tears that threatened. Taking a deep breath, she looked up into Sarah's sympathetic eyes and nodded. "All right, I'll come."

Sarah's concerned expression melted into a wreath of smiles. "Wonderful! It's at two o'clock on Friday at Mayor Patterson's."

"Oh, Lord save me," Kirsten groaned, thinking about the last party she had attended at Andrew Patterson's house.

"Oh, come on," Sarah giggled, "Let bygones be bygones. Besides, it's just us girls. No men allowed!" Placing an airy kiss on Kirsten's cheek, Sarah headed down the front steps. "See you Friday! And, be sure to talk to Helga about those ingredients."

Kirsten nodded and, with a last wave at her radiant friend, closed the door. *Damn you, Eric Wellesley,* she thought angrily. *Damn you, damn you, damn you!*

The next few days flew by in a flurry of sugar, eggs,

flour, and cake pans. Every available oven in town was put to work baking layer after layer of fluffy, golden cake, and the children of Rose Meadow found themselves relegated to playing outside so they wouldn't run across kitchen floors and risk making the precious layers fall.

When Friday finally arrived, Kirsten was so absorbed in mixing up huge quantities of egg white frosting that, had it not been for Betty's reminder, she would have forgotten this afternoon's party.

As it was, she was late. When she finally hurried into Mayor Patterson's cluttered, gaudy parlor, all the other brides were already there with their hostesses, giggling with excited speculation as they pored over the huge stack of gifts which were laid out on a small table.

"Here she is!" exclaimed Sophie as Kirsten walked into the room. "Now we can start!"

Kirsten looked around apologetically. "I'm sorry if I held everyone up. I was so involved with the cake that I nearly forgot."

"That's perfectly all right," soothed Mrs. Patterson, noting Kirsten's embarrassment. "The important thing is that all of you brides are here now and the festivities can begin."

"Kirsten's hardly one of us brides anymore," whispered Elsie, leaning over to Olga and smirking with satisfaction. She'd been just dying for this afternoon to arrive so she could tell Kirsten what she suspected about Eric. She just hoped that someone else brought up his name so she could drop her little bomb without seeming too obvious.

The afternoon progressed happily with much teasing and giggling about the big events of the next day . . . and night. Several of the town hostesses pursed their lips in disapproval as the girls tittered behind their hands about their impending wedding nights, but, for the most part, the matrons simply smiled and nodded knowingly.

Kirsten couldn't help but feel out of place, knowing that she really didn't belong to either group. It made her feel lonely and bereft to listen to her friends' excited chatter, and, yet, she didn't want to sit with the married ladies, since she wasn't one of them either.

For the most part she just stayed on the edge of the crowd, trying to assume an interested expression and smiling blandly as the other girls exclaimed over the gifts their hostesses had made for them.

For the first time the finality of her broken betrothal hit her. Next week when these same girls gathered at church with their new husbands and stood in small groups after the service to whisper about the secrets of the marriage bed, she would be on a train back to New York. Alone.

Unbidden, her thoughts drifted to Eric and a wave of regret washed over her as she thought of what might have been. The man was everything she'd hoped for. Hard working, prosperous, handsome. The attraction she felt toward him had been so profound that it astonished her, and she wondered if she would ever feel that same giddy breathlessness again. Somehow she doubted it. After all, she'd never felt it before and she'd met countless men during the years she'd worked in her father's bakery, many of them young, handsome, and available. Some of them had even flirted with her over the high glass display cases, but none of them had ever made her feel the way Eric Wellesley had.

Kirsten sighed, chastising herself for mooning over a man who had made it very clear from the outset that the attraction was not mutual. And even though he'd made the halfhearted eleventh hour proposal, she knew he hadn't wanted her and was only doing the honorable thing. Still, she mused, what if she had said yes?

Put him out of your mind, she told herself sternly. You'll probably never even see him again. But, still, her feelings of longing remained and it took every bit of willpower she could muster to pull herself out of her doldrums and concentrate on the festivities around her.

When the mountain of gifts had finally been opened and the last shrieks of delight had faded, the party moved toward the dining room where a veritable feast had been laid out. As the women clustered about the table, Elsie saw her chance and sidled into line beside Kirsten.

"So, I hear you're leaving soon," she said loudly enough that everyone in the room could hear.

Kirsten threw her a sidelong glance. "Yes, on Monday," she confirmed.

"Well, you really shouldn't feel too bad," Elsie advised, leaning across the table to spear a large dill pickle from an etched glass dish. "I found out something about Eric Wellesley that is so awful you should be grateful you escaped him."

Conversation around the buffet table instantly died as twenty-seven heads swiveled in Elsie's direction. Feigning surprise at the attention she had gained, she smiled innocently and said, "I'm sorry. Maybe I shouldn't have said anything."

Betty slammed her half-filled plate down on the table and planted her hands on her hips. "All right, Elsie, since it's obvious you want us all to hear your so-called 'awful news' about Mr. Wellesley, let's have it."

Elsie blinked with feigned chagrin and made a great show of fluttering her hand against her chest. "Really, Mrs. Zimmer, I meant for only Kirsten to hear me. I was just trying to make the poor thing feel better by telling her that even being an old maid is better than being married to *that* kind of man."

Kirsten clenched her icy hands and kept her eyes riveted on the lacy tablecloth, unable to look up and meet the pitying glances of her friends.

"Just exactly what do you mean by '*that* kind of man'?" Betty demanded.

92

"Well . . . of course, I don't know anything for sure," Elsie hedged, feeling for the first time like she might be in over her head.

"Maybe you better just tell us what you think you know," suggested Polly Hutton, her lips thin with anger.

Elsie was cornered and she knew it. Wishing desperately that she'd never started this, she nevertheless raised her chin, and looking Mrs. Hutton straight in the eye stated, "From what I've seen, it's clear to me that Eric Wellesley is one of those men who doesn't like women."

There was a collective gasp around the table and several more plates clattered to its surface.

Polly stared at Elsie, stunned. "Are you saying that you think Eric prefers the company of, ah, men?"

"Well, it certainly would explain why he rejected Kirsten, wouldn't it?" Elsie responded, her voice defensive.

"You're wrong, Elsie!" Kirsten suddenly exploded. "In fact, that's the most ridiculous thing I've ever heard. Why, Mr. Wellesley is the most charming, most masculine, most attractive . . ." Her voice trailed off in embarrassment as she noticed everyone staring at her.

"Enough of this nonsense!" Betty exclaimed, saving Kirsten further humiliation. "I don't want to hear another word about it. Now, let's eat."

"Well, I never," Elsie muttered self-righteously. "I was only trying to make Kirsten feel better."

Everyone strove to recapture the gaiety they'd been enjoying before Elsie's outrageous announcement, but for most of the celebrants the afternoon had taken on a pall, and Kirsten's mortification was so great that it was all she could do to maintain any sort of composure at all.

Shortly after lunch the girls started gathering up their booty and making hurried preparations to depart. Kirsten smiled as each of her friends pressed a cheek against hers and stammered an excuse for leaving so abruptly, but deep down she knew that what they really wanted was to get away from the unbearable tension that had been building all afternoon between Elsie and herself.

She tried to comfort herself with the thought that at least the party was finally over and she, like everyone else, could flee Elsie's odious presence. But she was wrong. The worst was yet to come.

Infuriated that her plan to embarrass Kirsten with the shocking news about Eric had backfired, Elsie decided to throw one last barb. Hurrying toward the door, she paused with her back against it, subtly blocking everyone else's exit.

"You know, Kirsten dear," she said to the group in general, "even though you're leaving next week, I want you to know that we'll always think of you as one of our little group."

"Why, thank you, Elsie," Kirsten responded, completely taken aback by this unexpected compliment. "I really appreciate that."

"Yes, of course," Elsie continued, "and since you do still want to be one of us, then we need to settle up on our little bet."

"The bet?" Kirsten's face was ashen.

"What bet?" Betty asked. "What are you two talking about?"

Several of the brides cast uneasy glances at their perplexed hostesses, hoping they would not be asked to explain what the bet entailed.

"The bet, Kirsten," Elsie repeated. "After all, you did agree to participate. Since this is probably the last time that all of us will be together, don't you think it would be a good time to pay your share? If I remember correctly, you never did put up your stake when we were on the train."

Several of the other girls gasped as the memory of the confrontation between Elsie and Kirsten the day they'd arrived came rushing back.

94

"Oh, Elsie, how could you?" Susan Ingram demanded.

Elsie's eyes were flinty as she looked over at Susan. "Well, if she still wants to be treated like one of us, then she has to pay. It's only fair."

"It's not fair at all," Olga interrupted loudly, throwing Elsie a malevolent look. "Kirsten's not getting married and she shouldn't have to pay."

Kirsten could take no more. She bit the inside of her lip and blinked hard, but the tears couldn't be dammed and rushed unchecked down her cheeks. Placing her hands over her mouth, she fled down the hall toward the sanctuary of the Pattersons' deserted kitchen.

Suddenly the entire group erupted with anger. En masse the brides turned on Elsie, flinging a stream of very unladylike epithets at her and demanding to know why she was being so intentionally cruel.

Elsie thrust her hands out, palms up, and said, "What did I do wrong this time?" Then, assuming a hurt, bewildered expression, she added, "Maybe I should just leave. I can't seem to say anything right this afternoon." And with a swirl of petticoats she flung open the door and swept down the front steps of the mayor's gingerbread latticed home.

Betty Zimmer was so incensed she nearly went after her. "What in heavens is this all about?" she demanded, rounding on Sophie who had the bad luck to be standing next to her. "What bet? Why is Kirsten crying?"

"Well," Sophie choked, looking desperately at her compatriots for support, "we all made a wager on the train about who would be the first of us to have a baby."

A gasp of shocked outrage rose from the hostesses who together turned shaming glares on their charges.

"Yes?" Betty prodded. "So, why is Kirsten crying? Because she lost her money?"

"No," Sophie admitted. "You see, we all bet quite a bit . . ."

"How much?"

"Ten dollars."

"TEN DOLLARS!" chorused the older ladies.

By this time, Betty had the hapless Sophie backed up against Mayor Patterson's mahogany spooled bannister. "I repeat," she thundered, "why would this make Kirsten cry?"

"Well," Sophie gulped, "Kirsten never proved that she had ten dollars to bet and I guess Elsie thought she didn't really have it and wanted to prove that today by demanding that she pay it now."

Betty's face was nearly purple with rage as, wheeling around, she pointed an accusing finger at Elsie's hostess. "Rebecca Jamison, I don't know how you have sheltered that hateful wench under your roof all this time!"

"Well, it's not like I had any choice," Rebecca countered, offended that her friend of thirty years was making it sound as if she were responsible for Elsie's rudeness.

Miriam Patterson, who had been standing at the back of the crowd assembled in her vestibule, now pushed her way through the throng with surprising speed. "All right, all right, ladies. Let's all calm down. Elsie's behavior is no one's fault but her own and I think the best thing we can do for Kirsten right now is just leave quietly and pretend this unfortunate incident never occurred."

Nodding in agreement, the women moved toward the front door, anxious to be away from the vexing scene.

Susan stayed behind for a moment and walked up to Betty who was standing by the front door. "Please tell Kirsten to just forget this whole thing. In another week Elsie Anderson will be nothing more than a bad memory. And let her know that none of the rest of us

96

expect her to pay that ten dollars. That was just Elsie talking."

Betty smiled. "I know, dear, and thank you. I'll tell her."

After Susan left, Betty walked slowly down the hall toward the kitchen, sighing heavily as she wondered what she could possibly say that would right the myriad of wrongs which had been perpetrated against sweet little Kirsten Lundgren.

Chapter 9

Eric Wellesley was a creature of habit and every Saturday morning he drove into Rose Meadow to pick up the week's supplies. Today was no different, except that when he arrived in town the sight that met him made him look around in surprise. There wasn't a soul anywhere and the normally bustling Main Street was completely deserted of horses and wagons.

Pulling his wagon to a creaking stop in front of the general store, he jumped down and walked through the door, pausing briefly to greet Joe Dawson, Ezra Quackenbush, and the Locke Brothers, Harold and Hershel. The four old men amicably returned his greeting, then went back to their whittling and chewing, a pastime which occupied the greater portion of their days.

Hearing voices, Lars Bjorklund looked up and smiled a welcome to Eric from behind the counter.

"Where is everybody this morning?" Eric asked. "Do we have an outbreak of plague in town?"

"No," Lars chuckled, "we have an outbreak of weddings."

"Ah, yes, today's the day, isn't it? So, what are you doing here, Lars? Shouldn't you be home slicking back your hair and dousing yourself in that flowery cologne you're always trying to sell me?"

Lars blushed, embarrassed because that was exactly

what he planned to do as soon as his brother arrived to relieve him. "Oh, it won't take me long to get ready," he mumbled, ducking his head and hoping that Eric wouldn't notice the red stain creeping up his cheeks. "You know I don't go in for any of that fancy dude stuff."

"Yeah, sure," Eric chuckled. "No different from getting ready for church on Sunday, right?"

"Well . . ." Lars conceded, unable to contain his excitement any longer. "You coming to the wedding?"

"Me?" Eric asked, clapping a hand to his chest. "Hell, no! I'm afraid the good ladies of Rose Meadow would run me out on a rail if I showed my face in that church."

Lars nodded in wry agreement, picking up the list Eric had dropped on the counter and turning toward the shelves behind him. "You might be right about that. Especially after what happened yesterday."

Eric had stepped away from the counter and was looking through a pile of flannel shirts which had just arrived from St. Paul. "Oh?" he asked, glancing absently over his shoulder. "And what was that?"

"Haven't you heard?"

"Heard what?"

"Well, it seems the ladies in town gave a party for the brides yesterday afternoon and there was some kind of argument between somebody and that little girl you were supposed to marry, and she ended up crying."

Eric was astounded at the jolt of anger which coursed through him at the thought of some little witch making Kirsten cry. Wheeling back toward the counter, he demanded, "What was she crying about and who made her cry?"

Lars held up his hands as if to ward off Eric's sudden anger. "I don't know much about it. Olga didn't give me many details. She just said that somebody said something about you and . . ."

"About me?" Eric blurted. "What the hell were they talking about me for?"

"Calm down, Eric!" Lars exclaimed, taking a step backward. "I'm telling you everything I know. Olga said that one of the girls said something bad about you and Kirsten got mad and started defending you and . . ."

"She defended me?" Eric interrupted again.

"That's what Olga said," Lars nodded patiently. "Anyway, whoever it was that said something about you, she and Kirsten had words right there at the party and Kirsten got so upset she began crying and ran out of the room."

Eric was dumbfounded. Why in hell would Kirsten Lundgren defend him? He would have been less surprised to learn that she was the one maligning him.

"And you don't know what this other girl said about me, or who said it?"

"I keep telling you," Lars sighed, "I don't know. But Olga said that Kirsten was so mad that she was ready to bust with it."

"Well, I'll be damned," Eric muttered, staring thoughtfully out the store's front window.

"So, anyway," Lars continued, going back to Eric's list and pulling three cans of beans off the shelf, "I guess the argument ruined the tea party, and now everyone is mad at everyone. If you're smart, you'll get out of town quick before one of those ladies sees you and decides to take it out of your hide that you spoiled their fun."

Eric didn't respond to this piece of advice but continued staring off into space.

Noting his friend's pensive expression, Lars's eyebrows rose slightly. "Why *do* you suppose that little girl defended you, Eric?"

"Hell if I know," Eric responded, walking back to the counter.

"I bet I know," Lars continued casually, measuring out a pound of coffee.

"Yeah? And what's your theory?"

"I think Kirsten Lundgren cares about you . . . a lot. I think she might even be a little bit in love with you."

101

Eric snorted. "You're wrong."

"And what's more," Lars added cautiously, "I think you care about her, too. You just won't admit it."

Eric remained silent.

Encouraged, Lars took a deep breath and plunged on. "So, why don't you just marry her like you promised?"

Eric's lips thinned. "Because," he gritted, leaning over the counter, "I don't want to and neither does she."

Lars backed up a step. "For a man who doesn't care, you're awful mad. You want to know what I think?"

"Not really, but I'm sure I'm going to anyway."

Lars grinned. "I think you're scared."

"Don't be ridiculous."

Lars continued as if he hadn't heard. "But, so are all the rest of us. We're all scared to death. Who wouldn't be?"

"If you're so scared, then why in hell are you doing it?" Eric asked.

"Because," Lars smiled, "there are some things about marriage that make it all worthwhile."

"Yeah? And what things are those?"

Lars wriggled his eyebrows meaningfully. "Well, one of them is obvious. But, there are other things, too. Things like having someone to sit by the fire with on a cold night. Someone to eat with. Someone to talk to. And kids. That's the best thing of all. Don't you want some kids, Eric?"

This last point hit home. Eric badly wanted a family. Every day as he worked his land he wondered who would continue on with it after he was gone. The farm was his legacy and he secretly yearned for a son to leave it to.

"Sure," he admitted. "I'd like to have kids sometime."

"Sometime!" Lars chuckled, dropping a half-dozen potatoes into a sack. "You're not getting any younger, friend. If I were you, I'd quit thinking about 'sometime' and start thinking about 'now'!"

102

"That's easy for you to say. You've found your perfect woman and she's right down the street waiting for you."

"Your perfect woman is right down the street waiting for you, too, if you'd just admit it," Lars muttered.

Eric shook his head. "No thanks. All I'm buying today is what's on that list."

Lars sighed. "Have it your way." Turning over the list, he began totaling the supplies. "That'll be two sixty unless you want that shirt, then it's four even."

Eric looked down in surprise at the flannel shirt he hadn't even realized he was holding. "Oh. Yeah, what the hell, I'll take it. Cold weather will be here before we know it and I might as well get ready while you still have these in stock."

"Four dollars it is, then," Lars proclaimed, slapping his stubby pencil down on the counter.

Eric fished in his pocket and withdrew the required amount, then picked up his purchases and started out of the store. "See ya, Lars," he called over his shoulder.

"Not for a few days," Lars called back. "I'm taking Olga up to St. Paul to see the sights. Won't be back till Wednesday."

Eric turned back, flashing a knowing grin at his friend. "Why waste the money going all the way to St. Paul?" he teased. "After all, ceilings look the same all over and I'll bet that's the only sight you two will see."

Lars threw back his head and laughed. "Get out of here, Eric," he chortled.

"Okay, okay, I'm going. Give Olga my best and, ah . . . have a good trip." Rolling his eyes meaningfully, Eric disappeared out the door.

All the way home, Eric thought about what Lars had said. Why *had* Kirsten defended him? And, who had said something about him, and what could it have been that would be so disparaging that Kirsten would start to cry?

He felt a sharp stab of guilt as he thought of everything that had passed between him and Kirsten. But, damn it, he had tried to right things, hadn't he? He had offered to marry her and she had turned *him* down. If she really did care about him like Lars said she did, then why hadn't she said yes to his proposal?

You know why, Wellesley, his conscience answered. *She knew you were just being honorable, that you didn't really want her and that you hoped she'd say no. It was probably written all over your face!*

Eric pulled his wagon to a stop and gazed off toward the river as he let his thoughts drift further. Maybe Kirsten had found out that he was the one who was paying the fifty dollars for the wedding cake. Maybe Sarah Drake had told her after all and Kirsten had been so humiliated by the thought that he was trying to buy her off that she had started to cry.

Eric shook his head, discounting that theory. It just didn't make sense. Sarah had promised she wouldn't tell Kirsten who was really behind the outrageous payment for the cake and, besides, she and Kirsten were friends. Why would Sarah betray his confidence when she knew it would only hurt Kirsten?

But, what could have been said that would make the woman he had jilted jump to his defense? Had someone questioned his integrity? His honesty? It had to be something that would be a direct reflection on Kirsten, or she probably wouldn't care what was said about him. After all, she hated him, didn't she?

Or did she? Could it be that she regretted not accepting his proposal? And what if she did? What could he do about it now? More importantly, did he *want* to do anything about it?

Let her go, he told himself sternly, slapping the reins over the horses' backs and moving slowly down the road toward home. *So what if she's the prettiest woman you've ever seen? So what if just looking at her makes you feel like you can't take a deep breath? So what? It would never have worked. She's too little, too delicate, too genteel. She's much better off back in New York where she belongs. Just let her go.*

Kirsten slipped into a pew at the back of the Rose Meadow Lutheran Church and heaved a huge sigh of relief. She had done it! The cake was finished—baked, decorated, and delivered. And she had to admit it looked beautiful. She was sure that even her father, with his discerning eye and formal Paris training, couldn't have found fault with her creation.

She should feel an enormous sense of accomplishment. So, why did she only feel sad? *Because it should have been your wedding cake you were baking,* a tiny voice deep inside her answered.

Kirsten pressed her hands together and looked down at her lap, determined not to cry. *Not now,* she told herself. *You can cry later and everyone will just think it's out of happiness for your friends. But, not now!* She concentrated hard on that thought, finally leaning back in the pew and letting out a long-held shaky breath as she felt the threatening tears recede.

The whole town was seated and waiting in a high state of anticipation when a small door near the altar opened and all thirteen grooms marched, single file, into the nave. Kirsten smiled at the line of faces staring solemnly out into the congregation. Could these thirteen somber men with their oiled hair and starched collars be the same merrymakers who had done an impromptu jig at Mayor Patterson's home the previous Saturday night? She looked around, noticing similar smiles playing around the corners of other people's mouths and guessed they were thinking the same thing.

Then suddenly everyone's attention was drawn to the back of the church as the double doors were opened with a flourish and the brides started down the aisle. Many a handkerchief was raised to discreetly wipe a teary eye as the young women, dressed in their best gowns and adorned with flowers woven into their loose, flowing hair paraded slowly down the aisle. They all looked beautiful and happy. Even Elsie, who had finally accepted Olaf Swenson's proposal, was smiling. The dam of emotions that Kirsten had been so bravely holding back suddenly broke and her vision blurred as tears coursed unchecked down her cheeks. As the last bride reached the crowded altar and took her place beside her prospective husband, the congregation sat down.

It was then that it happened.

Kirsten never saw him coming, never heard him behind her, but, suddenly, she felt a firm grasp on her arm as someone pulled her up out of her seat. She turned startled eyes to see Eric Wellesley, dressed like the other grooms, leaning over the side of the pew.

"Come on," he whispered. "They're going to start without us."

There was no chance of that, however, since the Reverend Mr. Dahlquist had seen Eric bound down the aisle and haul the unsuspecting girl in the back pew out of her seat. He now stood, his prayer book open in his hands, gaping at the little scene unfolding at the back of his church.

One by one, the couples at the altar, as well as the parishioners seated in front of Kirsten, began turning around. There were muffled gasps from the brides and several of the town's matrons began wildly fanning themselves in nervous reaction to this unprecedented interruption of the ceremony.

But Kirsten was oblivious to all that was going on around her. She just stood and stared at Eric who, as calmly as if they were at an ice cream social, continued to hold onto her elbow.

Finally she found her voice. "What are you doing here?" she hissed, looking around in embarrassment at the hundreds of pairs of eyes trained on them.

"Marrying you," he whispered back, " and the guests are starting to get restless, so come on."

She looked at him searchingly, a million thoughts

106

crowding her befuddled brain. And then he smiled—a smile so dazzling that she knew she couldn't deny him.

"All right," she whispered, and taking his arm, began walking slowly down the aisle to join her friends.

With a little squeal of delight Sarah Drake and Olga Johannson each took a step to the side, making a space for Kirsten and Eric.

The whispering among the members of the congregation had now increased to the level of an active beehive. Reverend Dahlquist noisily cleared his throat and threw a shaming look at his flock, bringing about instant silence. Then, scanning the long line of people standing in front of him, he asked, "Are we *all* here now?"

Several of the girls tittered and looked meaningfully over at Kirsten and Eric.

"Yes, Reverend," Eric answered, his voice firm. "All here and ready."

The minister nodded with satisfaction and looked down at his book. "Dearly beloved . . ."

Kirsten felt like she was in the middle of a bizarre dream. She cast a covert glance up and down the line, noticing that most of the brides were beaming at her instead of listening to Reverend Dahlquist. All except Elsie, who was standing like she had a stick up her back, her eyes straight ahead, her small bouquet crushed in a punishing grip.

As the minister moved down the line, asking each couple to vow to love, honor, and cherish each other, Kirsten became more and more apprehensive. What if Eric again changed his mind? It was possible, even at this late juncture.

But she needn't have worried. When the minister got to Eric and asked if he would take Kirsten for his lawfully wedded wife, he responded "I do" without a moment's hesitation.

Kirsten looked over at him, surprised that he had answered so readily. Then it was her turn. As she softly repeated the minister's words, she was so nervous that her voice didn't even sound like her own. It wasn't until the reverend moved on to the next couple that she realized she had actually just agreed to marry the handsome man next to her. Regardless of all that had passed between them, she had promised to spend the rest of her life with him. And suddenly she was ecstatic. Her heart pounding, she glanced at Eric and found him looking back at her. Quickly, she looked away, afraid her expression might give her away and reluctant to let him see how excited she really was.

The long ceremony finally concluded with Reverend Dahlquist closing his prayer book and saying, "You may now all kiss your brides."

As the congregation burst into spontaneous applause, Eric turned Kirsten gently by the shoulders and said quietly, "Is it all right?"

Kirsten stared at him, her eyes wide, her breath coming fast. "Yes," she murmured.

Pulling her toward him, Eric bent and placed his lips firmly on hers, tightening his grip on her shoulders as his gentle caress deepened.

Kirsten had spent many nights lying in her bed in Betty Zimmer's house and fantasizing what Eric Wellesley's kiss might feel like. She wasn't disappointed. His lips were warm and soft, and as he moved them over hers something deep inside her seemed to turn to liquid, and she felt a rush of weakness sweep over her. Unconsciously leaning toward him, she parted her lips slightly, then opened her eyes in surprise when she heard his sharp intake of breath. Immediately, he lifted his mouth from hers and took a startled step backward.

Averting his eyes, he folded her arm through his and turned her toward the congregation. Kirsten noticed that several of the couples had already begun walking down the aisle toward the double doors and her cheeks turned crimson as she realized that she and Eric had shared the longest kiss at the altar. She was further embarrassed to see Betty Zimmer standing in the third pew, grinning broadly. Ducking her head, Kirsten stepped down from the altar and followed the other couples down the aisle.

Everyone poured out the doors, gathering around the couples and offering felicitations as they showered them with rice. Several of the girls broke away from their new husbands and pulled Kirsten to one side, pelting her with questions.

"Were you surprised?"

"Did you know he was going to do this?"

"What do you think made him change his mind?"

"Weren't you embarrassed when everyone turned and stared at you?"

"Lord, that was some kiss!"

This last comment came from Olga who gave Kirsten a good-natured shove on the shoulder. "Maybe you better get back into the bet, after all!"

Shrieks of laughter erupted from the excited girls as their bridegrooms looked at them in confusion.

"And," Olga lowered her voice conspiratorially, "tonight's the night the wager really goes into effect!"

This was met with more giggles and much eye rolling from the brides until Sophie ventured, "Not for me, it's not."

"Why?" asked Sarah.

"Oh, you know," Sophie whispered.

"Oh!" Sarah breathed as Sophie's meaning suddenly dawned on her. "You poor thing! How embarrassing!"

"I know," Sophie agreed. "I just don't know how I'm going to tell Gustav."

"Don't be embarrassed," Olga advised. "He'll understand. It's something we'll all have to face."

"I know, but not on the first night!"

The other brides nodded solemnly, sympathizing with Sophie's plight and breathing collective sighs of relief that the same tragedy hadn't befallen them.

Buggies were brought around and the couples again paired off, making their way to Mayor Patterson's where the reception was to be held.

The brides had thought that yesterday's party was lovely, but today they were rendered nearly speechless as they entered the mayor's home. Flowers adorned every available surface, including a long garland artfully woven around the staircase bannister. White streamers had been hung from the dining room ceiling and attached to the chandelier, creating a bowerlike effect over the table.

Kirsten's cake served as the centerpiece and she felt a rush of pride as the guests oohed and aahed over her masterpiece. Eric stayed by her side, as attentive as any of the other grooms as he nodded at people offering congratulations and smiled at Kirsten's obvious happiness over her culinary triumph.

Kirsten had never been so happy. Even when she saw Elsie standing on the edge of the crowd glaring at her, she simply smiled and turned away.

When the cake had been cut and everyone was enjoying the huge feast the town's ladies had provided, Susan approached Kirsten whom she found standing alone near a window.

"Here," she said, holding out a small leather bag.

"What's this?" Kirsten asked.

"Your money for the cake."

Kirsten looked at her in surprise. "I can't take this now," she protested. "After what happened today, I won't be leaving and I wouldn't feel right taking the money. Why don't you just give it back to the men?"

Susan's eyes widened in dismay. *Now,* what was she supposed to do? She was saved from having to think of a reply, however, by Eric, who had heard the exchange as he returned from the refreshment table, laden with two glasses of punch.

"I'll take it," he offered, holding out his hand.

"Oh, thank you!" Susan said with a relieved little sigh, thrusting the bag at him. Then with a quirky little smile, she added, "And you'll make sure it's returned to its rightful owner? Ah, owners?"

Eric grinned. "Absolutely. Don't give it another

thought. I'll take care of it."

Susan nodded happily and with a quick smile at Kirsten, hurried off to rejoin her husband.

The afternoon waned and, one by one, the couples began gathering up their belongings and preparing to take their leave. The girls hugged as if they might never see each other again while the eager grooms stood, shuffling their feet and quietly encouraging their brides to hurry.

After the last couple had said their thank you's, the town hostesses stood in the front yard, congratulating themselves on the success of their venture.

"We did it!" Miriam Patterson rhapsodized. "We actually got the girls here, got them paired up, and got all fourteen of them married!"

"I just hope they'll all be happy," Polly Hutton sighed. Then, turning to Betty, she asked, "Are you worried about Kirsten?"

Betty grinned. "Not a bit. If any of those marriages is going to work, it's that one."

Polly looked at her in surprise. "After the rocky start they've have? What would make you think that?"

"Look at them," Betty pointed at the couples heading toward their respective wagons. "Kirsten and Eric are already more intimate than the rest."

"What are you talking about?"

Betty laughed, amazed that none of the other women had noticed what she had. "Why, it's as plain as the nose on your face. Every one of those men has his bride by the elbow, except Eric. He's holding Kirsten's hand and, what's more, he's got his fingers laced with hers. Doesn't that tell you something?"

The other women stared at the retreating couple, slowly nodding their heads in dawning understanding. "You're right," laughed Miriam. "He *is* holding her hand . . . and in public, too! Ah, what a night that lucky girl has in store for her!"

Suddenly, the staid, proper matrons of Rose Meadow, Minnesota broke into peals of gusty laughter, clapping their hands over their mouths and staring at each other with eyes bright as schoolgirls'.

As they turned back toward the house, Polly said, "There's just nothing like a wedding to make a woman think about those things, is there? By the way, has anyone seen Ben? I'm ready to go home!"

Chapter 10

The ride home was quiet. Now that Kirsten and Eric were alone, the giddy excitement of the wedding and reception began to fade and the reality of Eric's impetuous act settled upon both of them.

Why did he marry me? Kirsten thought, nervously playing with her gleaming, gold wedding band. What had made him change his mind? She shot a quick glance at her new husband, wondering if she could find the courage to ask him. But she didn't, because somewhere in the deepest recesses of her mind a little warning bell went off. *Don't ask! You've gotten what you wanted—a good, decent, unbelievably handsome man to build a future with. Don't press your luck by asking "why"!* The important thing was that he *had* married her. He was hers—to love and honor and cherish—just like she'd promised in church this afternoon. That was all that really mattered. Any problems they might encounter could be worked out together. Kirsten sighed, happy that she could at last feel a sense of security about the future.

Eric's thoughts, however, were running in a much different vein. Far from feeling optimistic about the future, he was suffering agonies of doubt. What *had* he been thinking this morning when he'd suddenly decided to keep his promise and marry this stranger seated next to him? Deep down he knew the answer.

113

Guilt—pure and simple. After Lars had told him about what had happened at the girls' party the previous day, a mantle of guilt had dropped over him until he thought he would suffocate.

He'd made his decision to go through with the wedding on the way home, but by the time he actually reached his farm he'd barely had time to bathe, shower, and dress before turning around and racing back into town. It wasn't until he was again on the outskirts of Rose Meadow that he'd slowed his wagon and allowed himself a moment to ponder the momentous step he was taking. To his surprise he'd found that he felt good about his impulsive decision. So good, in fact, that by the time he reached the church, he was almost excited at the prospect of having this pretty girl as his wife.

Even now a peculiar little chill ran through him as he thought of the night to come. Kirsten *was* beautiful and, in the sight of both God and man, she was his. Out of the corner of his eye, he stole a quick look at her. She was sitting stiffly on the seat next to him, staring straight ahead and toying with her new wedding ring. Totally misreading the expression on her face, Eric interpreted her faraway look as regret and, immediately, a like feeling settled over him.

She's having second thoughts! he thought suddenly. *She doesn't want this any more than I do.* Well, that wasn't exactly true, he admitted silently. He did *want* her, but surely a good marriage should be built on more than just easing one's conscience and satisfying one's lust. Scowling with irritation, he slapped the reins over the horses' backs, causing the daydreaming Kirsten to nearly somersault over the back of the wagon seat.

Yanking back hard on the team, he barked, "Whoa there!" then turned to Kirsten and said contritely, "Sorry. Didn't mean to startle you."

"It's all right," she assured him, gripping the side of her seat.

The silence that again descended was so deafening

that Eric thought he would burst from the tension. "Kirsten . . ."

"Yes?"

He suddenly had her full attention and realized that he had no idea what he was going to say. "Never mind."

Kirsten looked at him anxiously. "What were you going to say, Eric?"

The sound of her voice saying his name made the hair stand up on the back of his neck. Desperately, he cast about for something to respond. "We're almost home," he said lamely.

Kirsten looked at him in surprise. "I know," she responded, pointing. "I can see your farm down the road."

For the first time since they'd left town, they looked at each other and Eric was nearly undone by her shy, hopeful smile. "I just wanted to warn you that my house is kind of a mess," he stammered. "I've been busy and I'm not much of a housekeeper."

Kirsten smiled, relieved that this was all that was bothering him. "Don't worry. That's my job now. But I guess I should warn *you*, I don't know much about housekeeping either. We had a staff at home to take care of those things."

Eric felt his heart sink. A staff, for God's sake! What had he done marrying this high-tone little woman? He should have followed his first instinct and let her go back where she belonged. There was no way she was going to be happy scratching out a life in this harsh, unforgiving land. Just wait until she was met with her first, full-blown Minnesota blizzard!

She'll be out of here on the first train East next spring, he thought miserably, *if she even makes it that long!*

They turned into Eric's long driveway and pulled to a stop in front of the house. "You can go on inside," he invited. "I'll put the team away and then bring in your stuff."

Kirsten's "stuff" consisted of only her one small

valise. Unlike the other brides who had been lavished with small, useful gifts by the townspeople, she had nothing to bring to her new home. "All right," she nodded, painfully aware of her total lack of a dowry, "I'll wait for you inside."

Wait for me? Eric thought as he led the team toward the barn. *Wait for me to do what? Make her dinner? Draw her a bath? Take her to bed?* His eyes closed involuntarily as he allowed his mind to play with that thought. Take her to bed, he mused. Just the thought made his loins tighten.

He turned, looking out the barn doors at where Kirsten still stood in the yard, gazing out over his fields and absently petting his dog's head. She had been delighted when the big brown mutt had loped out to meet them, confiding that she loved dogs but had never owned one of her own. Eric had told her the dog's name was Durango and that he was a companion, but he also helped herd cows and served as a watchdog against intruders—animal or human. Kirsten had squatted down to get a closer look at the dog and had been rewarded with a wet cheek as the huge beast greeted her with a long slurp of his pink tongue.

Now, as Eric stood gazing at her through the barn door, he thought again about how pretty she was—how delicate and tiny she seemed as she stood framed against the backdrop of the vast Minnesota prairie.

"And that's exactly why this is never going to work!" he growled out loud, berating himself for his wayward thoughts. *Delicate and tiny is not what you need, Wellesley! Why, you'll kill her in bed, if the work doesn't get her first.*

In a fit of frustrated anger, he threw the harness he was carrying into a corner of the barn. Who was he kidding? This girl wasn't going to stay with him. Why, she'd admitted that she didn't even know how to dust the house, much less plow fields or put up vegetables. As soon as she saw what this life was all about, she would be gone. He was positive of it.

The best thing he could do for both of them would be to show her exactly what farm life was like. And the worst thing he could do was to take her to bed! That was an entanglement neither of them needed.

Just forget it, he told himself firmly. *She's not for you. One night in the sheets with her and you'll only want her more than you do now.*

Leading the horses into their stalls, Eric resolved that the only way to extricate both of them from the situation he'd gotten them into was to do everything in his power to hasten Kirsten's departure. Becoming intimate with her was definitely not the way to do that!

He walked out of the barn, closing the door hard behind him and exhaling a long sigh. It was going to be one hell of a summer!

They ate a light supper of cold meat, bread, and cheese. Eric had brought a bottle of wine up from the cellar that morning, intending to share it with his new bride, but in light of the decisions he'd made in the barn he made no move to open it. Kirsten said nothing, but several times while they sat quietly eating the simple repast, Eric noticed her eyes straying to the unopened bottle on the sideboard.

She had changed out of the dress she'd been married in and now wore a gauzy, violet-colored day dress. Although it was hardly appropriate attire for a farm wife, it was the plainest dress he'd ever seen her wear and he felt a moment of sorrow as he realized how hard she was trying to fit in to her new surroundings.

When they'd both finished eating, Eric rose from the table and headed down the hall to the parlor to smoke a pipe, turning in surprise when he saw that Kirsten was following him. With a glance back at the uncleared table, he asked, "Do you need some help with the dishes?"

"The dishes?"

"Yeah. Do you want me to help you clean up the dishes?"

"Oh! No, I can do it." With flaming cheeks Kirsten turned on her heel and returned to the dining room.

"Damn!" Eric thought as he tamped tobacco into his pipe. "Did she think some maid was going to appear from somewhere and clean up the kitchen?" Flopping down in an overstuffed chair, he put his head back and closed his eyes.

Kirsten was mortified as she picked up dirty dishes from the table. She hadn't meant for Eric to think she wasn't going to fulfill her wifely chores and clean up the kitchen, she'd merely wanted to sit with him while he had his pipe. Now, she thought dismally, he probably thought she was lazy as well as inept. She spent the next hour scouring and cleaning, determined that when he next entered the kitchen he'd see that she was well able to take care of this feminine domain.

When the room was finally spotless, she wearily laid down her dish towel, glancing at a clock which hung in the dining room. Nine-thirty. Time to go to bed. A knot of excitement and trepidation formed in her stomach. How should she handle this delicate subject? She didn't even know where the master bedroom was since she'd never been upstairs.

Where was her valise? she wondered, looking around for it. Had Eric taken it up to his bedroom when he'd brought it into the house? Kirsten hoped so. That way she could just nonchalantly go upstairs and wherever she found it she'd know that was their bedroom.

Entering the parlor, she looked over to where he was still slumped in the chair. "I . . . I'll be getting ready for bed now," she said, her voice hardly more than a whisper.

"All right," he nodded, opening his eyes and looking at her. "I put your things upstairs. First door on the right."

"Thank you," she murmured, ducking her head with embarrassment. Turning quickly away, she flew up the

118

stairs, not wanting him to see her flaming face.

She walked into the bedroom he'd indicated, pausing to light a small kerosene lamp which sat on a table near the door. As the flame caught, she looked around with interest, then surprise. This surely wasn't the master bedroom. It was small, with a single bed along one wall and a washstand and tiny closet along another. There wasn't even a rug on the floor and the room's barren, dusty appearance attested to its disuse. Kirsten thought that maybe she'd misheard Eric until she noticed her valise sitting at the end of the small bed.

She stood and stared at the suitcase for a long moment, trying to determine his intentions. Was she supposed to sleep in here ... alone? No, surely not! They were married and married people slept together ... didn't they?

Maybe Eric had just given her the use of this room so that she could wash and change into her nightclothes in private. Yes, that must be it. Kirsten smiled at her husband's thoughtfulness. Hurry! She must hurry! She could hear Eric moving around downstairs, letting Durango outside and closing windows.

Feverishly, she unbuttoned her dress, scattering hairpins all over the wooden floor as she yanked it over her head. Grabbing her brush out of the valise, she pulled it through her hair then threw it back on the bed. She rummaged through the bag, finally lifting a gossamer sheet nightgown from the bottom. She gave it a shake, then threw it on the bed while she divested herself of the rest of her clothes. Picking up the petal pink gown, she lovingly smoothed the wrinkles from it and slowly pulled it over her head, closing her eyes as the sensuous material settled over her hips. She walked over to a small mirror which hung over the washstand, reveling in the sensation of the silk rustling against her bare legs. Leaning down, she gave her head a shake and fluffed her hair, then pinched her cheeks and bit her lips to give them color. Satisfied with her appearance, she hurried out into the hall, relieved that there was still no sign of her groom.

Tiptoeing down the hall, she peeked into three more bedrooms before she came to the one she sought. It was at the end of the hall and as she peeked around the doorjamb, a shudder ran through her. This was undoubtedly *their* bedroom.

The chamber was large and sumptuous, and as she stepped through the door, her feet sank into a carpet so thick and luxuriant that they seemed to disappear into it. She looked around, noticing that the rug covered the entire surface of the floor.

In the middle of the room was a huge bed—longer and wider than any she'd ever seen before. She drew in her breath in awe, wondering where Eric could have found such a piece. It was covered with a feather tick that was so puffy that Kirsten feared that once she lay down on it, she'd never be able to get up.

With a little giggle she hurried over to the bed and pulled down the coverlet. Slipping inside, she plumped a pillow up behind her and turned the covers back invitingly on the opposite side.

Taking a deep breath, she settled herself back carefully against the pillow, raking her fingers through her hair until it billowed out from her shoulders and the ends curled provocatively around her breasts.

This was how Eric found her when he entered the room a few minutes later. For a moment he just stood and stared, mouth open, eyes wide. Finally, he collected himself, and directing a black frown at his wife, said, "What are you doing here? I told you the first room on the right is yours."

Kirsten gaped at him, unable to believe what he was saying. He didn't want her here! He hadn't meant for her to sleep in this big, beautiful bed with him. He'd meant for her to sleep alone—in that little bare room at the other end of the hall!

"I'm sorry!" she blurted, throwing back the covers and struggling mightily to extricate herself from the enveloping mattress. "I'll go right now!"

"Damn!" Eric cursed, turning his head away from the vision of flying hair and bare limbs she presented as she fought to keep the mattress from swallowing her. "Just stay where you_are. It's okay."

"No!" Kirsten protested, her voice muffled as she clawed her way toward the edge of the bed, trying to get a grip on the sideboard. "I'm sorry. I misunderstood. I'll be gone in just a . . . minute!" With a mighty heave, she threw herself over the side of the bed.

Landing clumsily on her feet, she straightened, allowing Eric a full view of her voluptuous little body, barely concealed by the clinging, shimmering night-gown. Instantly he felt his loins tighten with the beginnings of an erection.

"Kirsten, I . . ."

"No!" she protested as she rushed past him, heading for the door. "Please, don't say anything. I . . . I'm sorry. I just presumed . . ."

Completely moritified by what he must be thinking of her wanton behavior, she whirled away from his outstretched hand, sprinting through the door and down the hall toward the room she'd been assigned.

"Goddamn it!" Eric gritted through clenched teeth and spun on his heel to follow her. "Kirsten, wait a minute! Let me explain!"

"There's nothing to explain!" Kirsten assured him as she disappeared around the corner in a flash of pink silk.

She slammed the door behind her just as he reached it, but he didn't pause a moment before flinging it open and charging into the little bedroom after her.

Kirsten leaped backward in startled surprise as the door bounced off the wall, then she made a frantic lunge toward the small bed, grabbing her discarded dress and holding it up in front of her in a lame attempt to cover herself.

"Look, let me explain!" Eric shouted, looking at the door in astonishment as it bounced off the wall and vibrated noisily.

"No!" Kirsten shook her head wildly. "Please, just leave! I didn't understand, but I do now, so please go!"

Eric took a deep, calming breath. "I want to talk to you first," he said, forcing his voice down to a normal level.

Kirsten stared at him, wild-eyed for a moment. Then with a shuddering sigh she sank down on the edge of the bed. "All right, I'm listening."

Now that he had her attention, Eric had not the slightest idea of what he should say. He couldn't tell her that he didn't dare sleep with her because if he did he might never be able to let her go.

For an endless moment he just gazed at her, trying to think of something—ANYTHING—to explain his outrageous behavior. "Look," he said slowly, playing for time, "tomorrow is gonna be a busy day. We've got to . . ." *Got to what?* he thought desperately. "um, slaughter a hog!" he finished triumphantly.

Kirsten blanched. "Sl . . . slaughter a . . . a hog?" she gulped.

"Yup," Eric confirmed, breathing a huge sigh of relief that she was obviously no longer thinking about their wedding night. "And it's a hot, dirty job, so we better call it a night."

"I'm sure it is," Kirsten murmured, feeling her stomach roll just at the thought of it.

"So," he continued brusquely, "get some sleep because we need to get up by four."

"By four . . ." Kirsten repeated dumbly.

"Yeah, by four." With a decisive nod, he backed toward the door. "Well, good night."

Kirsten watched him hastily close the door, but long after his footsteps had receded down the hallway she still sat and stared at the portal. Slaughter a hog. SLAUGHTER A HOG! She'd envisioned them spending a least a couple of days getting to know each other. Sharing intimate meals, taking walks, holding hands, talking, making love. But, no. They were going to spend the first day of their marriage *slaughtering a hog!*

In a daze Kirsten lay back on the hard little pillow on the hard little bed and stared at the ceiling. Were they really going to kill a pig tomorrow? Of course she understood that every time she ate pork chops someone had killed a pig, but . . . not her! A butcher killed them, or someone like that. Someone in a bloody apron with huge, brawny arms and a name like Spinozza or Kascmarski!

The closest she ever got to food preparation was mixing up fluffy batters for pastries and tarts. She didn't kill animals and then sit down and eat them for dinner!

But, she was going to tomorrow . . . at four in the morning!

Eric lay back in his huge bed, clasped his hands behind his head, and stared at the ceiling. *SLAUGHTER A HOG!* What the hell had he been thinking? No one slaughtered a hog in June! Hogs got slaughtered in the late fall when the weather was cold enough that the meat could be salted down or smoked for the winter or packed fresh into barrels and frozen in a snow drift. Only a madman would slaughter a hog in June, guaranteeing that ninety percent of the meat would be lost. So *why* had he told Kirsten that they were going to do just that tomorrow morning . . . at a god-awful hour like four o'clock in the morning?

Because it's the ugliest, grossest job on the farm and the one sure to make her run screaming out the door and back to New York! And the sooner she gets out of your house and out of your life, the better.

Eric sighed, realizing that his impulsive plan really wasn't such a bad idea after all. If he wanted Kirsten Lundgren out of his life, this was certainly the way to do it. By tomorrow night she'd undoubtedly be back at Betty Zimmer's. Hell, she could probably still make the

Monday train she held the ticket for.

Good idea, Wellesley, he complimented himself. *End it quick and get things back to normal. No more walking into your bedroom and finding gorgeous women in transparent nightgowns nestled down in your bed waiting for you.*

With a groan, Eric shifted to another position, gritting his teeth against the erection that again threatened. "I just hope to hell this damn hog thing works!"

Chapter 11

"Wake up, Kirsten. It's nearly four-thirty."

Kirsten shrugged the offending hand off her shoulder and pulled the blanket over her head. From far away she heard a man chuckle.

"Oh, no you don't. Now, come on, get up."

Feeling her blanket being pulled off, Kirsten groaned and turned over, opening one eye and trying to focus on the intruder looming over her. "Go away. It's the middle of the night."

"No, it's not. It's time to get up. We've got to butcher the hog today."

At the mention of the word *hog*, Kirsten's eyes snapped open and in the soft glow of the kerosene lamp she stared up at Eric. Her mouth parted slightly as she drank in his masculine perfection. His black hair was haloed by the light dancing behind him, and his dark eyes were luminous in its reflection. He was dressed in snug-fitting pants which molded to his muscular thighs and left little to the imagination regarding his masculine attributes. His shirt was old and soft, with the look of cotton that had been washed many, many times. The sleeves were rolled up above his elbows, exposing sun-bronzed forearms ribbed with tightly corded muscles.

Kirsten's blatant perusal of her husband did not go unnoticed and Eric seized the moment to return her admiring gaze, sure that he had never seen a more arousing sight than his new wife with her hair spread across the pillow like a flame and her emerald eyes soft and limpid with sleep.

Swallowing hard, Eric forced himself to look away before his flaring desire completely overcame his reason and he consummated his marriage right there. "Come on, Kirsten," he said tightly, "we're wasting time. Now, get up."

With a resigned nod, Kirsten pushed back the covers and sat up, pushing her tousled hair back from her face.

The simple act of lifting her arm caused her nightgown to stretch taut against her thrusting breasts and Eric felt his mouth go dry. Taking a deep, shuddering breath, he headed for the door. "Wear your oldest dress because after today, it will probably be ruined."

"The oldest thing I have is what I was wearing last night," Kirsten called after him.

Eric stopped in his headlong flight out the door and looked at her in astonishment. "That pretty little thing you had on is your *oldest* dress?"

"As a matter of fact, yes!" Kirsten nodded.

Eric snorted and clapped his hands on his trim hips. "Well, you can't wear that! We'll go into town sometime this week and get you some decent clothes."

"Decent?" Kirsten bristled. "Are you saying you think my clothes aren't decent?"

Eric frowned. "That's not what I meant. I guess 'appropriate' would be a better word. But, for now, I'll see if I can find something of mine you can wear."

"Yours?" she exclaimed, tossing her mane of hair over her shoulder. "I can't wear something of yours. You're huge!"

Eric's breath caught in his throat as he was treated to another of Kirsten's unconsciously provocative movements. *Yeah, little girl, and if I don't get away from you right now, you're going to find out just how "huge" I really am!*

"I'll figure something out," he rasped, and fled out the door.

Racing down the hallway, he tore into his bedroom, slamming the door behind him and leaning against it, breathing heavily. "Dumb! Dumb thing to do!" he chided himself. "First lesson. Never, *ever* go in her room when she's in bed!"

Walking over to his closet, he opened the door and flipped through the clothes inside, wondering what he could give her to wear that he wouldn't want to immediately rip off her.

This situation was going to be a lot tougher than he'd anticipated. Although he was not totally inexperienced with women, he had never been as intrigued with the pleasures of the bedroom as, say, several of his brothers who reveled in their reputations as renowned cocksmen. Miles, his oldest brother, had bedded his way halfway across America and then taken ship for England. Although everyone knew that Miles had actually gone to Britain to finish his education, Eric and his other brothers had always joked that Miles had left because there weren't any women left in America whom he hadn't already sampled.

And Adam, Eric's youngest brother, seemed to be trying his damnedest to follow in Miles's footsteps. Although Adam was still just a kid of eighteen, he was gaining such a reputation in their hometown of Durango, Colorado that their baby sister, Paula, who was a year younger than Adam, had confided to Eric that she was embarrassed to accompany Adam out in public, the women made such fools of themselves over him.

But Eric was different. Although he'd done his fair share of wenching with his brothers during his youth, as he'd matured, his priorities had changed. Women had not held much importance in his life over the past few years. In fact, he'd not been involved in any romantic entanglements since moving to Minnesota six years before, but had concentrated all his efforts into making his farm a success. Even his decision to send for a bride had been based more on the need for a helpmate than a desire for a wife and lover. Granted, the long winter nights got lonely and a warm body next to him in his big bed held a lot of appeal, but it wasn't really *important*. Besides, there was that other thing about him that was so embarrassing that it, in itself, had served as a strong deterrent to any sort of physical intimacy for most of his life.

Therefore, his immediate passionate reaction to Kirsten this morning had stunned him. What was it about her that made him react so strongly? Still staring blindly into his closet, Eric shook his head and blew out a long, irritated breath. He sure as hell didn't know, but whatever it was he didn't like it and he wanted her gone as soon as possible. Hell, he'd already wasted half an hour, and with a farm the size of his he couldn't afford that kind of lost time. He knew from experience that men who were so infatuated with their wives that they spent their time rolling around in bed instead of plowing their fields and tending their stock usually ended up bankrupt. Although Eric knew there was no possible way his farm could bankrupt him even if it did fail, he wasn't about to throw six years of hard work away to spend his days making love instead of tending to business.

He smiled as he grabbed a pair of shortened pants and the flannel shirt he'd bought at Lars's store the day before. This morning's activities should do it. There was no more odious job than slaughtering animals, and although he knew he was being grossly unfair in forcing Kirsten to do so her first day on a farm, it was a sure way to get this mistake behind him.

Satisfied with his plan, he walked back down the hall, opening Kirsten's door a crack and tossing the clothes into her room. "Put these on and then meet me outside," he directed, quickly closing the door. "And hurry! Time's a'wastin'."

"All right," came the small reply.

Choking back his laugher, Eric bounded down the staircase, grabbed his butchering knife from the kitchen, and headed out toward the pigpen.

He had no intention of wasting a good hog on this little exercise, but there was one runted little shoat who was never going to amount to anything and could be sacrificed. The pig had developed enough to provide a few good chops and some spareribs that could be eaten in the next few days. Past that, he'd just have to bury it. His smokehouse wasn't even outfitted for the fall's curing yet and one runty pig wasn't worth all the work of setting it up.

Entering the pigpen, he separated his victim, looping a rope around the shoat's neck and yanking the stubborn animal away from the feeding trough.

He was driving the pig toward the butchering block when he glanced up to see Kirsten cross the yard, carrying two coffee cups. Eric stopped so suddenly that he was nearly pulled off his feet as the pig continued lumbering on toward his doom.

His mouth dropped open as he watched his wife bounce, and that was the only word for it, *bounce* across the yard toward him. He didn't know what she had on under his shirt, but it sure as hell wasn't much!

Lesson number two, he thought wryly, never, *ever* lend her your clothes!

Kirsten had donned the outfit he had provided, but it had never occurred to Eric how it would look on her. The shortened pants were secured about her waist by a tightly cinched leather belt. They hit her just above the knees, exposing her shapely little calves and trim ankles. It didn't help his rapidly increasing pulse that she had failed to put on stockings.

The flannel shirt was tucked into the waistband of the pants and with the tight belt clung to her ample breasts like a second skin.

Jesus Christ! he thought desperately, *kill the hog—quick!*

Kirsten, who seemed to be totally unaware of the enticing picture she presented, smiled as she approached. "Thought you might like this," she offered, holding out a cup of coffee.

"Thanks," Eric answered dumbly, his gaze riveted to her deep cleavage showing above the shirt's gaping neckline. He took a sip of the coffee, then suddenly choked and spat the black liquid out on the grass. "God, Kirsten, how much coffee did you put in the pot?"

Kirsten's eyes widened. "Is it too strong?"

"Strong? Have you tasted it?"

"No."

"How much coffee did you use?"

"Just one cup, Eric."

"And how much water?"

"Two cups."

"What?" he gasped. "You used one cup of coffee for two cups of water? No wonder it's like mud!"

Kirsten bristled at his insult and took a cautious sip. It *was* terrible! Looking up from the cup, she said, "I guess it *is* a little strong."

"Yeah," Eric snorted. "Just a little. Haven't you ever made coffee before?"

Kirsten shook her head.

"Unbelievable," he muttered. "A woman not knowing how to make a pot of coffee."

Despite the fact that he was muttering to himself, Kirsten heard his words and looked away quickly so he would not see how hurt she was. "I'm sorry, Eric," she said softly. "I just thought some coffee might taste good since it's so early . . ."

"Yeah, well, next time you want coffee tell me and I'll make it, okay? The rate you use it, you'll bankrupt me buying beans."

"Fine," she mumbled, still looking away. "Give me your cup and I'll take it back into the house."

Eric tipped the cup to the side, spilling the remaining contents on to the ground, then handed the empty vessel to her. "Here. Take it back if you want, but hurry. It's nearly five and we've got to get started here or we'll be at it all day."

With a quick nod Kirsten whirled around and headed back toward the house.

Eric had seen the sheen of tears in her eyes and felt a sharp stab of remorse. After all, she was just trying to please him. But at least their little altercation had taken his mind off her cleavage! Turning back to the pig, Eric poked it sharply with the stick he still carried, causing the shoat to snort belligerently.

Kirsten was walking back toward where Eric stood leaning over a wooden block when she heard the pig scream. "Oh, my God!" she shrieked, clapping her hands over her mouth. Running toward her husband, she grabbed him by the arm and yelled, "Don't! You're hurting the poor thing!"

Eric turned toward her, the bloody knife still in his hand. "What the hell are you talking about? I'm not hurting it. It's already dead. Look for yourself."

"No! I don't want to look!"

"Well, you better get used to looking, city girl, because this is what farm life is all about!"

"That's not true!" Kirsten cried. "There's more to running a farm than killing living things. Torturing them!"

Eric's eyes blazed with anger. "I didn't torture it, for God's sake. I know what I'm doing and it didn't feel a thing!"

"Then why did it scream?" Kirsten accused.

"How the hell do I know? But I didn't torture it!"

"Oh, I hate this!" Kirsten blurted.

Eric turned his back on her, surprised how upset he was by her words. "Like I told you before," he said, throwing down the knife, "you'd better get used to it because it's the only way we get meat on the table around here. There isn't a nice, clean butcher shop to send your maid to and have it brought back all cut up and wrapped in white paper. We have to do the dirty

131

work here and if you 'hate' it, then you better get out right now."

Kirsten looked at him for a long moment, aware of the challenge in his voice. "I'm not leaving," she said quietly. "What do you want me to do?"

"Help me drag the carcass over to the pot."

"What pot?"

"That pot." Eric pointed.

Over by the barn sat a large cauldron with a fire blazing under it. From the amount of steam rising from the surface, Kirsten knew it must be filled with boiling water.

"Are you going to boil the poor thing now?" she gasped. "Are you *sure* it's dead?"

Eric rolled his eyes. "Yes, I'm sure the 'poor thing' is dead and, yes, I'm going to scald it so I can scrape the hide after I skin it."

Kirsten swallowed hard but doggedly stepped forward to help Eric drag the small pig over to the pot. Once there, Eric dunked the pig up and down in the boiling water, causing a smell to arise with the steam that very nearly sent Kirsten to her knees.

Turning away, she walked swiftly toward the house, drawing in great gulps of air as she told herself she wouldn't be sick. She stayed as far away from the pot as possible until Eric called her.

"Okay, I need your help again."

Turning, she walked slowly toward him, keeping her eyes averted. "What now?"

"We're going to hang the carcass so I can gut and bleed it."

Kirsten closed her eyes in horror. This was *much* worse than she could have imagined. Maybe if she told Eric she didn't really like pork and didn't care if they ever ate it, they could stop this gruesome procedure. "You know," she said, trying hard to summon a smile, "I'm really not much of a pork lover."

"Yeah?" he said, throwing her an exasperated look, "well, I love it."

132

That ended that conversation.

"Do me a favor?" Eric asked suddenly. "There's a big rope just inside the barn door. Get it, will you?"

Relieved that she had an excuse to leave the scene of carnage, Kirsten hurried off toward the barn. Finding the rope, she returned at a much slower pace, saying, "Where do you want this?"

"Over there by that tree. Next thing we do is string him up."

"String him up?" she croaked.

"Yeah. I just told you, I have to gut him."

By the time the hog was hanging head down from the tree, Kirsten's head was swimming from fatigue and revulsion. "Eric," she said quietly, "can I take a little break now?"

"Sure," he nodded, not looking at her. "I won't need you for a few minutes."

Before she could turn away, he slit the carcass end to end, leaping out of the way to avoid being spattered with blood.

This last step was more than Kirsten could take. She took three quick running steps, then stopped, bent over, and vomited.

Hearing the retching sound from behind him, Eric whirled around just in time to see her crumple to the ground.

"Jesus Christ! Kirsten!" He raced over to where she lay in a heap and dropped to his knees, cradling her head in one arm while he lightly slapped her cheeks. "Kirsten! Kirsten, are you okay?"

No response.

Eric felt like a vise was tightening around his chest. Why didn't she come to? He slapped her cheeks a little harder. "Kirsten! Kirsten, wake up!"

No response.

Eric was terrified. He'd never witnessed a woman faint but he'd always heard that the way to bring them around was by slapping their cheeks or waving ammonia salts under their noses. Well, he didn't have any smelling salts on him and slapping her wasn't working at all. So, now what?

Picking up her limp body, he headed over to the water trough. He knelt in front of it and grabbed Kirsten around the chest, unceremoniously tipping her over and drunking her head under the water.

Kirsten came to with a shriek which instantly filled her mouth and nose with water. Fighting against the hand which seemed to be holding her under, she threw her head back and reared up like a cornered horse.

The first thing she saw was Eric, kneeling next to her with his hand on the back of her head. What in the world was going on? Was he trying to *kill* her?

Coughing and sputtering, she wrenched out of grasp and fell back on the ground. Looking up with eyes filled with confusion she gasped, "What are you doing? You almost drowned me!"

Eric's relieved expression instantly darkened. "What are you talking about? You fainted dead away over there and I couldn't bring you to, so I thought I'd try this."

"Well," Kirsten sputtered, still choking on the large amount of water she'd inhaled, "it worked. But, please, next time I faint, just leave me where I drop. It's safer than having you try to help."

"Next time!" Eric exploded. "Do you do this a lot? And why the hell did you do it now? Are you sick?"

"Yes, I'm sick! You and your pig made me sick!"

Eric rose to his feet, dusting off his pants and wiping his face free of the water he'd been sprayed with when Kirsten had reared out of the trough.

"You're useless, you know that?" he accused, furious that she should take him to task for merely trying to help. She'd scared the life out of him and she didn't even care! In fact, she was acting like *he'd* done something wrong!

"Useless!" she yelled, struggling to her feet and pushing her sopping hair back from her face. "Why? Because I don't know how to gut a hog?"

"Gut a hog!" he yelled back. "No, I could understand that. But, you can't even make a cup of coffee fit for a man to drink!" He could have bitten off his tongue when he saw her stricken expression.

"Well, I'm sorry that I'm such a disappointment," she responded, her voice quiet. Turning on her heel, she walked off toward the house without looking back.

Eric watched her go, raking his hand through his hair in utter frustration. What a damn mess this was! Why had he been stupid enough to get himself into it? And why had he thought that he could extricate himself from it with no one getting hurt? The girl had been in his house less than twenty-four hours and already he had screamed at her, insulted her, half drowned her, and lusted after her. His behavior was reprehensible and he knew it. What he didn't know was how to make amends for it. He didn't want to hurt her—he just wanted her to leave!

With a tired sigh he turned back to the pig, wishing, for all the world, that he could just bury the damn thing. Hell, he really didn't like pork that much either!

Chapter 12

Kirsten slammed into the house in a high rage. Unless! Eric had said she was useless! Well, by God, she'd show him! If that pompous, arrogant farmer thought she was going to stand for him telling her she was useless, well, he had another thing coming!

"And all because I don't know how to gut a hog!" she muttered furiously. "Well, he'll be singing another song after he sees how well I do the things I understand!"

Stopping short in her tirade, she glanced at herself in the hall mirror. *And just what do you know how to do, miss?* The unbidden thought shook her. Eric was right. She *didn't* know how to do much of anything, but, blast it, she could learn! And she would, too. She just needed someone to explain what was expected of her and show her how to do it. But, who?

Betty. That was it. Tomorrow, she'd go see Betty and ask her what to do.

But, until then, there must be something she could do around the house to prove to her husband that she wasn't worthless. Wandering into the parlor, Kirsten looked around the room, noticing, as she had the first time she'd been there, the magnificent works of art which hung on the walls. Walking up to the largest of the pictures, a mountain scene, she peered at it closely, awed by the detail and the depth and shading of colors the artist had used. Kirsten had never seen mountains of the stature of those in the painting, but she was sure that whoever had painted it had. The greens, blues, and mauves which blended together as the peak rose to its magnificent summit could only have been painted by someone who had witnessed the subtle color changes firsthand.

Intrigued, Kirsten moved on to another picture which hung over the room's huge fireplace. This one was a portrait of a young girl sitting in a meadow of wild flowers. The child was enchanting: angelically blond and blue-eyed, but with a whimsical smile that betrayed a sense of mischief lurking behind the innocent beauty of her exquisite face.

As she had that first day, Kirsten again wondered who had painted these beautiful works. Her gaze wandered from one picture to the next and she suddenly realized that the mountain she had seen in the first painting was present in all of them. Obviously, the pictures had all been painted in the same place. It must be somewhere that means a great deal to Eric, she mused, resolving to ask him about it.

How little she really knew about her new husband, she thought as she meandered through the room, straightening small knickknacks on tables and running a finger lightly over the highly polished surface of a large plant stand. She lifted her finger, noticing for the first time how dusty the furniture was. Her discovery brought a smile. Here was something she could rectify. She knew how to dust or, rather, she'd at least seen other people do it. It had never looked like a very difficult task. You took a rag and you wiped off the surface of whatever was dusty. That was all there was to it.

With the newfound resolve of a budding housewife, Kirsten marched into the kitchen, determined to find where Eric kept the cleaning supplies. After fifteen minutes of fruitless searching, she sighed in frustration. There was nothing in the kitchen or pantry or back porch that even resembled a dust rag. What now?

Improvise! You're a creative girl. Think of something! Glancing down at Eric's flannel shirt, she smiled. Flannel. The maids at home had always used rags made of flannel when they'd cleaned. Fingering the soft material, Kirsten felt a moment of doubt. The shirt didn't seem old or worn. Its red-and-blue plaid colors were vibrant and there was no sign of fraying on either the cuffs or collar. "Oh well," she shrugged, reasoning aloud, "Eric wouldn't have given it to me to wear to kill a hog if he'd cared about it."

Hurriedly, she unbuttoned the shirt, dashing up the stairs as she peeled it off. Entering her small, sparsely furnished room, she donned one of her own blouses, then walked over to the dresser and extracted a pair of nail scissors from her manicure kit. With quick, precise snips, she severed the buttons from the flannel shirt. Finally, she cut a small wedge into the shirt's hem and neatly tore it in half.

There, she thought with satisfaction, two good flannel cleaning rags. Tripping back down the stairs, she hurried into the parlor and began energetically polishing the furniture.

Two full hours passed before she stood back and surveyed her work. What she saw pleased her immensely. The beautiful mahogany furniture gleamed, reflected by the sun pouring through the freshly washed windows. She wished the windows weren't quite so streaked, but she was still proud of her accomplishment. The room definitely looked better. Not perfect, maybe, but much better. The only thing left was the floor.

Frowning, Kirsten stared down at the polished planks which were heavily marred by black boot marks. Squatting down, she rubbed at a mark with the flannel she held. Nothing. With a determined scowl, she attacked the mark again, rubbing the flannel hard against it with the heel of her hand. Nothing. Standing up, she planted her hands on her hips and glared down at the offending stain. What would take that off?

Water? She didn't know, but it was certainly worth a try.

She walked back through the kitchen and out to the porch where she had seen a bucket. Filling it with water from the cistern, she lugged it back toward the kitchen door, then set it down. She opened the door and turned to again pick up her bucket. It was then that she noticed a large mound of what appeared to be clothing lying in a heap in the corner. Curious, she walked over to take a closer look. She was still ten paces away when the smell of sweaty clothing assailed her.

Phew, she thought, wrinkling her nose with distaste, when was the last time the man had done laundry?

Suddenly, though, her frown disappeared and a small smile lit her face. Here was something else she could do to impress her husband. It was only one o'clock—there was still plenty of time left in the day to get some of these filthy clothes washed and dried.

Lugging her bucket back to the cistern, she poured out half the water and reached for a jug of liquid chlorine bleach which stood against the wall. Upending it, she filled the bucket to the top with bleach, then carried it into the house and hefted it onto the stove. Lighting a flame under the burner, she took a long wooden spoon and mixed the bleach and water together, then left it to heat.

She returned to the porch and, holding her nose, sorted out all the white socks and underwear from the odorous pile, carrying the dirty clothes at arm's length into the kitchen and throwing them into the now boiling pot of bleach and water. There, she thought happily, that should whiten them and take the smell out. She threw open the kitchen windows, dispelling the noxious smell of the boiling bleach, then filled another bucket with water and returned to the parlor to scrub the floor.

An hour passed before she went back to the kitchen. Her arms and back ached, but the black marks on the parlor floor were gone. So was much of the wax, but she told herself that nothing could be done about that. At least the floor was clean.

Looking into the pot of bleach water, Kirsten noticed that the level of liquid had dropped sharply, but the clothes floating in what was left look white and clean. She was looking for a pair of tongs to lift the clothes out of the water when Eric came in the back door.

He was shirtless and dripping wet, having stopped at the pump in the backyard and washed. As he stepped into the kitchen, still toweling his hair, he took a deep breath and coughed. "What in hell smells so bad in here?"

"Your clothes," Kirsten laughed. "But, they don't smell anymore. I boiled them and they're fresh and clean now."

Eric lowered the towel from his face and gaped at her. "You *boiled* my clothes?"

"Yes," Kirsten nodded happily. "It was the only way to get them white again." At that moment, she found the tongs she was looking for and brandishing them over her head, added, "Come here, I'll show you."

Leaning over the pot, she dug into the clothing with the tongs and grabbed a pair of underwear. "Now just look how white this is," she said, and glanced over her shoulder at Eric to see his reaction.

But instead of the approval she expected to see, Eric's face registered first shock, then disbelief, and finally horror. Kirsten whirled back toward the stove, wondering what could possibly be making him react so strangely, then gasped in dismay. What she was holding in the tongs had once been a pair of light, linen underwear. It was now a button attached to a scrap of waistband from which dangled several shreds of material which had once been legs.

Kirsten again looked over her shoulder at her husband who had not moved or altered his horrified expression. She quickly dropped the underwear back into the pot, praying that perhaps it was just an old pair

141

that had fallen apart due to too many washings. She fished around for a sock, finally finding one and lifting it gingerly. Again she gasped. There was nothing left but the toe.

"Oh dear," she groaned, "I think maybe I boiled them too long." She turned to find Eric standing right behind her, peering over her shoulder into the pot of mutilated garments.

"Kirsten," he said very quietly, "did you boil all of my clothes?"

"Well, of course not!" she responded, "just your socks and underwear. You don't put colored clothes into bleach, for heaven's sake."

Eric took a deep breath, willing himself to hold on to his temper. "Are you telling me that all of my socks and underwear are in that pot?"

"Well," Kirsten stammered, "yes. All of the white ones, anyway."

"Kirsten, I don't have any colored underwear. All of it is white."

Kirsten swallowed hard. "Then, I guess it's all in here."

Eric nodded slowly. "Tell me, what made you decide to boil my clothes?"

"They smelled!" she responded defensively. "I figured boiling them in bleach would take the smell out and get them white."

"Hasn't anyone ever told you that soap and water does that, too—without turning the clothes into oatmeal?"

Kirsten looked at the floor. "I'm sorry, Eric. I was just trying to help."

He nodded again and sighed. "It's okay. I have some more underwear upstairs. Just promise me you won't boil any of my clothes again—ever!"

"I promise."

"Good." Then, in a voice that clearly said he was afraid to ask, he added, "What else did you do today?"

Kirsten brightened. "I cleaned the parlor."

"What do you mean, *cleaned* it?" he asked warily.

"You know, I dusted, I washed the windows, and I scrubbed the floor."

Despite himself a small smile quirked the corners of Eric's mouth. "This was really nice of you, but you didn't have to do it. I have a woman who comes in once every couple of weeks and cleans."

Kirsten bristled. "Well, you have a wife now so you can just tell that woman, whoever she is, that her services aren't needed any longer."

Eric threw her a doubting look.

"You don't believe me!" Kirsten accused, obviously offended. Well, you just come here and take a look! Impulsively, she took Eric's hand and led him toward the parlor. "I'll show you!"

Later she realized that if she had not insisted on showing off her accomplishments, the fireworks that ensued might never have happened. It all started so innocently. At first Eric even seemed genuinely pleased with the job she had done.

"It looks great," he acknowledged, wishing for all the world that she didn't look so damn fetching in her bare feet and his short trousers. Quickly he looked away, steeling himself against her happy smile. "What's that?" he asked, pointing at a red heap in the corner.

"Oh, that's my rag," she explained, hurrying over and picking it up. "I forgot to put it out on the porch when I finished."

Eric felt a sudden surge of apprehension as he stared at the piece of red flannel she held, noticing, for the first time since coming into the house, that she was no longer wearing his new shirt. "Kirsten," he asked slowly, "where did you get that rag?"

"Oh, that!" she giggled nervously, wishing she didn't have to confess that she'd used his old shirt. "I couldn't find anything to clean with so I cut up that old shirt you gave me to wear this morning. I hope you don't mind."

The next moment it became painfully obvious that

143

he minded very much. *"What?* You cut up my shirt?"

"Well, yes," she admitted, taking a startled step backward, "I had to use something!"

"Jesus Christ," Eric thundered, his face dark with anger, "that was a brand new shirt! I hadn't even worn it yet and you cut it up for a rag!"

Tears sprang to Kirsten's eyes, but she held her ground. "Well, how was I supposed to know that? I never dreamed you'd give me a new shirt to wear while we killed a hog!"

Although Eric knew her argument was reasonable, he was too frustrated with everything that had happened in the last thirty-six hours to care. "I can't believe you're so dumb that you can't tell the difference between a new shirt and an old one! Good God, girl, first you boil away my underwear, then you cut up my new shirt. If you're trying to make a statement about my clothes, a simple 'I don't like what you wear, Eric,' would do just fine!"

Kirsten remained silent, realizing that all the work she'd done today to try to impress her new husband had been for naught. He thought she was stupid and useless. What's more, he wasn't even attracted enough to her to want her to sleep in his bed with him.

Blinking hard to fight the tears that threatened, she raised her eyes to his and said, "I'm very sorry, Eric. I'll pay you back for whatever I've ruined."

Then, with a dignity that Eric couldn't help but admire, she walked out of the room and up the stairs, closing her bedroom door softly behind her.

Eric stood for a long time staring at what was left of his shirt, then slowly walked out to the kitchen and threw it into the pot with the rest of his ruined clothes. Grabbing the pot by the handles, he marched out into the backyard and threw the soggy, bleachy mess into the ash can.

The sun slowly disappeared, casting a blue-green shadow over Eric's newly tilled fields. Still he stood there, the empty pot dangling from his fingers. *What in*

144

the hell have I gotten myself into? he thought disconsolately.

But he knew the answer to that question. It wasn't the shirt or the socks or the underwear that was bothering him. He could afford a thousand shirts if he wanted them.

It was Kirsten. In one day she had proven herself to be everything he'd feared. Beautiful, alluring, well-intentioned, and totally unfit for the life she had married into. It had been all he could do not to grab her and kiss away her tears when she'd apologized to him in the parlor. His only defense had been to hide his frustrated longing behind the guise of anger. If he hadn't, he knew he would have burst out laughing, swung her up in his arms and taken her straight to his bed, confessing that he couldn't care less about his stupid shirt and that he loved the fact that she was trying so hard to please him.

But what would that have proven? "Nothing!" he growled to himself. "Absolutely nothing except to make this mess worse!"

It was dark when Eric finally went back into the house, dousing lights as he went. Slipping his heavy work boots off, he silently climbed the stairs, vaguely aware that he hadn't really eaten all day, but too tired and confused to care.

He hesitated for a moment in front of Kirsten's door, wondering if she was still awake and if she, too, was hungry. *Maybe I should ask her if she wants a sandwich,* he thought, knowing full well that he was just looking for an excuse to go into her room.

Pushing the door open a crack, he peered into the dimly lit room. Kirsten was sound asleep on the narrow little bed, still dressed in his short trousers and the blouse to her traveling suit.

Tomorrow we're going into town and get her some proper clothes, he thought as he crept quietly toward the bed.

He looked down at his sleeping wife, feeling a

moment of guilt. There were dark shadows under her eyes and a splotchy redness to her cheeks that betrayed the fact that she had cried herself to sleep.

Picking up a comforter which lay across the bottom of the bed, Eric gently spread it over her. Carefully, so as not to wake her, he leaned across the bed and extinguished the kerosene lamp on the night table, then turned and started toward the door. He had almost reached it when he turned back and took another look.

Slowly, he retraced his steps until he again stood by the side of the bed. He reached out and lightly brushed a knuckle against her dirty face, wishing he dared wash the grime away, but knowing it would wake her.

Shaking his head as if to persuade himself not to linger, he started back toward the door. But something stopped him and he knew he would never make it out of the room until he fulfilled the desire which was now driving him, despite his attempts to quell it.

Once more he leaned over his sleeping bride, but this time he allowed his head to dip until his lips softly caressed hers. He kissed her for a long moment, indulging his senses as he drank in the taste and texture of her. Finally lifting his head, he whispered, "Good night, sweetheart. Sleep well in your little bed and tomorrow I promise I'll show you a better day."

Turning away, he walked to the door and silently let himself out, never noticing that Kirsten's eyes had opened and her soft, longing gaze had followed him as he left her room.

Chapter 13

Betty Zimmer opened her front door, then blinked with surprise to see Kirsten standing on her stoop. "Hello, dear," she smiled. "I certainly didn't expect to see you today. What brings you to town?"

Kirsten smiled back at the kindly older woman, knowing that she'd made the right decision in seeking her counsel. "Eric had some errands in town and I thought I'd stop to visit while he's at the store."

It was a perfectly plausible explanation, but there was something in Kirsten's voice which belied her nonchalance. Opening the door wider, Betty stepped aside and ushered Kirsten into her little foyer, watching the young woman closely as she took off her bonnet.

There was definitely something wrong, Betty surmised as she herded her guest toward the big, welcoming kitchen, and she aimed to find out what it was. "So tell me," she asked pleasantly, "how is married life?"

"Oh, it's fine, just fine," Kirsten answered quickly, refusing to meet Betty's eyes.

Betty's eyebrows rose. Kirsten's abrupt answer and overly bright smile was proof positive that things were not "fine." Waving Kirsten into a chair, she turned toward the stove, filling two cups with tea and wondering how to subtly get the girl to confide what was bothering her.

"I'm surprised to see you in town so soon. We

147

haven't seen hide nor hair of any of your friends."

"Well, like I said, Eric had supplies to pick up, so I decided to ride along."

"Ah, the fate of a farmer's wife," Betty sighed. "Not much time for a leisurely honeymoon, is there?"

"No," Kirsten replied, sipping her tea and wishing now that she hadn't come. "There certainly isn't." Quickly changing the subject, she asked, "How have you been? Has Mr. Potts moved out or is he still with you?"

Betty set her cup down on her saucer with a decisive clink. "All right, my dear, enough of this. You don't care about cranky old Mr. Potts and neither do I. Now, what's wrong?"

For a long moment, Kirsten was silent, staring into her teacup. Despite her resolve, tears welled in her eyes and when she looked up at Betty, they overflowed down her cheeks. "Everything's wrong!"

Betty was shocked by the girl's obvious misery. "What is it, honey? Is Eric being mean to you?"

"No, it's not that," Kirsten assured her hurriedly, "he's not mean, exactly. But he told me I was useless and when I tried to prove I wasn't, I ruined everything!"

Betty leaned back in her chair, unable to believe that she could have so grossly misread the couple's attraction for each other. "Okay, start from the beginning and tell me what has happened."

Kirsten launched into an account of the past forty-eight hours, confiding everything except the fact that she was still a virgin bride. As the story unraveled, Betty sighed in relief, realizing that the only problem in the Wellesley house was an inexperienced bride trying much too hard to please. By the time Kirsten got to the part about boiling Eric's underwear, it was all she could do to keep a straight face.

"So you see," Kirsten concluded, wiping her eyes and sniffing, "I can't seem to do anything right."

Betty smiled a knowing little smile. "Honey, at this

point in your marriage, there's only one thing you should be worrying about doing right . . ."

It took a moment for Kirsten to grasp the older woman's meaning, but when she did, she quickly averted her eyes, saying nothing.

Betty's eyebrows rose again as she speculated on Kirsten's silence. But she could think of no way to tactfully pursue that particular subject and so let it drop.

Kirsten kneaded her handkerchief and looked at Betty with beseeching eyes. "Is there anything you can think of that might help me? I want to do things right around the house. I just don't know how."

"Yes, I can think of something." Betty smiled and rose from the table. She walked over to a cupboard and extracted a book from the bottom shelf, holding it out to Kirsten. "I bought this for you, thinking I'd give it to you at the party. It's a bride's handbook and it's full of wonderful recipes and household hints for a new wife. I think it will be a lot of help to you."

Kirsten took the book from Betty and looked at it curiously. Carefully opening it, she stared down at the dedication page.

To Those
Plucky Housewives
Who Master Their Work Instead of Allowing It
to Master Them
This Book is Dedicated

Paging farther into the text, she came across a chapter entitled, "Pickles—Every Man's Favorite Snack." She looked up at Betty in wonder. "Is that true? Do men really like pickles?"

Betty shrugged. "I guess so. My husband, Hank, always ate them."

Kirsten bolted out of her chair, circling the table and throwing her arms around Betty's neck. "Oh, thank you!" she enthused. "This will be a great help. With all these recipes, I'm sure to make things that Eric will like!"

Betty grinned and gave Kirsten a little squeeze. "There's more than just recipes, honey. Look in the back."

Kirsten again picked the book up, flipping to the back until she came across a chapter headed "Housekeeping." Eagerly, she read the first paragraph aloud:

> Housekeeping, whatever may be the opinion of the butterflies of the period, is an accomplishment in comparison to which, in its bearing on woman's relation to real life and to the family, all others are trivial.
>
> Your husband may admire your grace and ease in society, your wit and your school day accomplishments, but all in perfection will not atone for an ill-ordered kitchen, sour bread, muddy coffee, tough meats, unpalatable vegetables, indigestible pastry, and the whole train of horrors that result from bad housekeeping. On the other hand, success wins gratitude and attachment in the home circle, and adds luster to a woman's life.

Kirsten closed the book reverently. "You may just have saved my marriage," she sighed. "Thank you so much. I'm going to read every single word in here and do everything it suggests!"

Betty laughed and rose from her chair. "I hope it helps, dear. But, just remember, regardless of what any book says, the best wives are those who make their husbands feel like men . . . especially during their most private moments."

Kirsten looked at her blankly. "I don't understand. The book says that the best way to keep a husband happy is good cooking, a clean house, and well-laundered sheets."

"Well, yes, that's true . . . to a point. But, keep in mind that no matter how clean the sheets are, a warm

150

and willing wife between them is what men really care about."

Kirsten blushed furiously. How could she tell Betty that, obviously, Eric was different. He didn't care about her being warm and willing in his bed. He didn't want her in his bed at all, willing or otherwise! She remained silent, gripping the book tightly as she and Betty walked toward the front door. When they reached it, Kirsten turned and gave Betty a light kiss. "Thank you for everything. I don't know what I'd do without you."

"You're welcome, honey. You just take care of that man of yours and keep him happy."

"I will," Kirsten promised, clasping the book to her breast. "I have all the help I need right here."

"Not all," Betty warned. "Like I said before, there are some very important aspects of marriage that aren't covered in that book. Just keep them in mind and you'll be fine."

Kirsten nodded and headed off down the sidewalk. *Aspects of marriage that aren't covered in the book* . . . Would she ever have a chance to find out about those? She sighed and shook her head. Eric's seeming disinterest bothered her more than she cared to admit. Why didn't he want her to sleep with him? Could it be that Elsie's accusations at the party were right? Didn't he "like girls"? And, if he didn't, why not? Had he once been hurt by a woman . . . had a bad experience with one? Or was it what Elsie had intimated . . . that he didn't like girls because there was something peculiar about him?

Growing up in New York, Kirsten had heard whispers about men who preferred the company of other men to that of women. But surely Eric wasn't one of those. He was just too . . . too comfortable with women. And besides, the way he had kissed her last night when he'd thought she was asleep certainly destroyed that theory. That kiss . . . Kirsten closed her eyes, trying to recapture the hot tingly sensations which

Eric's lips had evoked. Why had he done it? She had spent half the night lying in her hard little bed trying to figure it out. But, still, she had no answer. Why would a man sneak into his wife's room and kiss her but not want to take her to his bed? It was all very confusing!

Maybe it was something physical. Kirsten slowed her step as she pondered this possibility. There certainly didn't seem to be anything physically wrong with Eric. He was tall, broad-shouldered, muscular, and strong. But, did strength have anything to do with the ability to perform the marital act? Kirsten wasn't sure since no one had ever really explained exactly what the participants in the marital act had to do, but she did know enough to think that there didn't seem to be anything about Eric that would prevent him from doing it. After all, his back looked strong and straight, and there didn't seem to be anything wrong with his knees.

Kirsten shook her head. She really didn't think there was anything physically preventing Eric from taking her to his bed. Rather, she was afraid his disinterest was caused by something lacking in her. And, despite the problems they'd had during their courtship and the first few days of their marriage, Kirsten was determined that, eventually, she would be Eric's wife in every way. Her first step was to learn the skills which she knew would make him proud of her. Hopefully, if she accomplished that, everything else would just fall into place.

Armed with her new resolve, she hurried down the sidewalk toward Main Street, silently making a vow that Eric would never again have a reason to call her "useless." Never!

A few minutes later Kirsten entered Bjorklund's General Store to find the object of her musings standing at the counter talking to Sven Bjorklund, Lars's younger brother.

As she walked toward them, Sven looked up and with a broad smile said, "Here's your bride now, Eric."

Eric turned around, his breath catching in his throat at the winsome picture Kirsten presented. Her eyes were bright and her cheeks tinged a deep rose from her walk from Betty's house. Hastening to meet her, he said, "You didn't have to walk all the way down here. I would have come to fetch you."

"That's all right," she smiled. "I enjoyed it. Have you gotten your supplies?"

"He sure has," Sven laughed. "'Bout cleaned me out of dry goods."

Eric threw Sven a quelling look and said, "Is there anything you need before we go?"

Remembering her book, Kirsten nodded and answered, "As a matter of fact, I'd like a peck of cucumbers if you have them, Mr. Bjorklund."

"A peck of cucumbers!" Eric exclaimed, "what for?"

"To make pickles."

"Pickles!" Sven guffawed, slapping Eric on the back. "Already? I thought it'd take at least a couple of months before any of the brides would be wanting pickles!"

Eric's eyes widened at this suggestion and he whirled on Kirsten. "Why do you want pickles?"

"I . . . I just thought I'd make some pickles!" she stammered, completely nonplussed by Eric's sudden, intense scrutiny.

With a nod, Eric turned back to Sven. "You heard her. She just wants to make pickles. Now, do you have a peck of cucumbers or don't you?"

"Don't know," Sven admitted. "There's a few back there, but it's pretty early yet. I don't know if Lars has that many."

"Well, we'll take whatever you have."

With a nod Sven pushed through a curtain and disappeared into a back room, leaving Eric and Kirsten standing alone at the front of the store.

"Do you like pickles?" Kirsten asked casually.

"Nope. Can't stand them. I don't like anything that has to do with cucumbers."

Kirsten's face fell. "Oh."

Eric was surprised at her sudden, woebegone expression and quickly amended, "But, that doesn't matter. If you like them, make as many as you want."

Unwilling to tell him that she didn't like pickles either and was only making them because her book said all men loved them, Kirsten nodded wanly.

Sven reappeared with the cucumbers and pushed them into a bag. "There's not a peck here, but there's enough for a pretty good batch," he said with a grin.

Eric picked up the bag and took Kirsten by the elbow, herding her toward the front door.

"Don't forget your clothes," Sven called, coming around the counter and handing Eric another sack.

"Oh, yeah, thanks," Eric mumbled, again taking Kirsten's elbow.

Kirsten closed her eyes, mortified as she suddenly realized why Eric had been so insistent on coming to town today. He had to replenish his underwear and sock supply. Well, she thought, clutching her book, at least nothing like that will ever happen again. From now on I'll know exactly how to wash his clothes so they come out clean and still in one piece!

Her good humor restored, Kirsten flashed a brilliant smile at her husband and clambered into their wagon, determined to use her newfound wealth of recipes to make him the best supper he'd ever tasted.

It wasn't the best supper either of them had ever tasted, but it was reasonably successful. They had pork chops, and although Kirsten had been unable to find a recipe in her new book specifically for them, she found a paragraph which instructed her to cook them like beefsteak. The one thing the book didn't mention, however, was that pork took much longer to cook than beef, so when she put the chops on the table, they were still rare in the middle.

Eric cut into his, made a face and rose from the table, stabbing his chop and then hers from off of their plates and returning them to the skillet. "Eating rare pork can make you sick, Kirsten," he said. "You have to cook it till it's done all the way through. It's different from beef."

Different from beef, Kirsten thought angrily. Then why hadn't her book *said* that? Mentally, she catalogued this bit of information, determined that the next time she made pork, she'd double the cooking time.

The rare pork had been her only major mistake, however, Her biscuits were light and fluffy and the snap beans edible, if a little overcooked.

Kirsten scoured the kitchen until it shone, hoping Eric would notice. But he remained out on the front porch where he'd gone directly after the meal, smoking a cigarette and staring out at his newly seeded crops.

When Kirsten was finally satisfied that even the author of her book would be pleased with her cleaning efforts, she joined him, sitting on the top step and covertly watching him as he smoked.

Eric glanced over at her, admiring her delicate profile silhouetted against the waning sun. "Good dinner, Kirsten. Those biscuits were the best I've ever had. Even better than my ma's."

She turned toward him, pleasure lighting her eyes. "Why, thank you. Tomorrow I'll make doughnuts, if you like. I was famous in New York for my doughnuts!"

Eric smiled. "I love doughnuts."

"Good! First thing in the morning, I'll make some so they're ready in time for you to take a sack to the field with you."

"Sounds great." And it did, Eric thought suddenly. In fact, the whole day had been great. He could get real used to having this gorgeous woman around, cooking his meals, making him doughnuts, going into town with him. *Real* used to it . . .

155

"I'm also going to wash all the curtains," Kirsten continued. "They're so dusty."

Eric turned and looked at her in horror. "No bleach!"

"I know," Kirsten giggled. "No bleach!"

Their eyes caught and Eric suddenly found that his throat felt dry and his chest tight. *Don't do this!* his mind warned. *Don't start liking this.*

Steeling himself against Kirsten's soft, melodic laughter, he snapped, "There's a lot of chores outside you could help with, too. There are cows to be milked, chickens to be fed, and the garden could use a good weeding. All of that needs doing more than the damn curtains need washing."

Kirsten's smile disappeared and her eyes widened in stunned surprise. What in the world had caused this sudden change of mood? "All right," she murmured. "Just tell me what needs doing most and that's where I'll start."

Eric lurched out of his chair, furious with himself for acting like such a boor, but having no idea how to make amends. "Time for bed, Kirsten," he barked. "Milking time comes early."

Kirsten's heart leaped. *Time for bed!* Did he mean he wanted her to come to bed with him? He must! Why else would he care when she retired? Blushing profusely, she stood up on shaky legs and entered the house in front of him. Standing at the bottom of the massive oak staircase, she shyly waited for him as he moved about the house, dousing the lights.

When he returned to the front hall, he looked at her curiously, wondering why she was still downstairs. "You need something?"

"No," she answered softly, completely misunderstanding him. "I was just waiting for . . ." But she never finished her sentence because the look of panic which suddenly crossed Eric's face told her everything she needed to know. He didn't want her to go to bed with him. He'd never intended her to think that when he'd

156

mentioned it on the porch. He merely wanted her to go to bed, period!

"Good night!" she blurted and raced up the staircase, praying that he hadn't noticed her flaming face.

Eric's troubled gaze followed her flight up the stairs. "Goddamn it," he cursed softly, "GodDAMN it! This is never going to work! She's got to get the hell out of here or I'm gonna do something I'm gonna regret. I just know it! A couple more nights of eating supper together and sitting on the porch together and putting out the lights together and I'm gonna *carry* her up those stairs and show her there's more to being a wife than washing curtains and making pickles!"

Exhaling a frustrated sigh, Eric jammed his hands into his pockets. What in hell was he going to do?

Kirsten rushed into her little room, slamming the door behind her and leaning on it heavily. She'd never been so embarrassed in her life! What must Eric think of her? That she was some kind of brazen hussy who spent her time lurking around the bottom of staircases waiting for men to give her a sign?

"Oh, God," she moaned, dropping her head into her hands, "he probably thinks I'm a cheap trollop! And, what's worse, he still isn't interested!"

Sinking down on the edge of her narrow little bed, Kirsten stared blindly at the wall. She was falling in love with him. She couldn't deny it. But, what did a woman do when she was in love with a man and he wasn't in love with her—especially when they were married? Was this a common thing? Were there other marriages like hers?

Somehow, she doubted it. She'd always heard that one of the things men liked best about marriage was making love. She'd even heard that men who weren't married sometimes bought women's favors just so they could make love—that's how much they liked it. But something was definitely wrong with her man. He didn't want to make love at all—unless of course . . . Kirsten drew in her breath as she allowed her mind to reel out the rest of the appalling thought—unless he was making love to someone else and that's why he didn't want her!

This thought was so distresing that she could hardly stand to ponder it. Eric in love with someone else? No! It was absurd. If he loved another woman, why would he have married her? It certainly wasn't for the pleasure she could give him in bed. He'd proven he didn't care about that. And he had told her she wasn't suited for farm life and that he wanted a wife who was. So, why *had* he married her?

Kirsten's thoughts whirled in an endless circle, but she could come to no conclusion as to her husband's motives. Finally, exhausted, she lay back on the bed. It was then that she saw the package. It was a small sack, similar to the one which Eric had carried out of Lars Bjorklund's store earlier that day.

Curious, she sat up and opened the bag, shaking out its contents. A pile of material plopped onto the bed. She looked down at it, realizing that it wasn't just material, it was dresses. Made up, ready to wear dresses. Three of them!

Jumping off the bed, Kirsten shook out the first dress and held it up in front of her. It was a brown-and-rust calico print, with tatted lace around the yoke and a high, stand-up tatted lace collar. The other two were similar in design, but with different patterns and colors.

Excitedly, Kirsten stripped off her skirt and blouse and pulled on the first dress. It was a bit difficult to catch all the buttons running down the back, but, finally, after much stretching, she triumphed. Racing over to the small mirror above her bureau, she gazed at her reflection. The dress fit amazingly well. The waist was a little large and the bodice a little snug, but the length was right and, all in all, it was very wearable.

"He bought me a dress!" she rhapsodized. "No, he

bought me three dresses!"

In a frenzy of delight, she danced around the room, holding the dress's full skirt out until it whirled around her like a bell. Eric did care about her! He must!

She turned back to the mirror, her eyes shining and her cheeks pink with pleasure. Her quiet, enigmatic husband had bought her three dresses! THREE DRESSES!

For a moment she plucked worriedly at the too-tight bodice where it stretched across her generous breasts, wondering how she could alter it to make it more demure. Oh, but, she was too happy to worry about it now. She'd figure out something tomorrow. Or maybe she'd just leave it the way it was, she thought wickedly, then clapped her hands over her mouth and giggled.

In a gesture of sheer happiness, she blew a kiss in the direction of Eric's room. "You just wait, you big, handsome, wonderful man. You just wait until you taste the doughnuts I'm going to make you tomorrow!"

Chapter 14

No sloven can make good butter. The *one thing* to be kept in mind, morning, noon, and night, is neatness, neatness, neatness.

Kirsten smiled down at her book, closed it and walked out to the porch. Sitting down on a small stool, she wrapped her hands around the butter churn's broomsticklike handle and happily began driving it up and down into the cream. She enjoyed making butter. The first few times had been hard since her arms were not used to the repetitive motion required, but now she found it to be the most pleasurable of all her chores.

She had been married for almost two months now, although she and Eric had actually lived together less than half that time.

Three weeks after their wedding, Eric had received the horrifying news that his younger brother Seth's wife and young son had been brutally murdered. He had immediately left for Colorado to be with his grief stricken brother. Although he had wanted Kirsten to stay in town with Betty during his absence, she had insisted on remaining at the farm, using the time to practice her cooking and generally improve her housewifely skills.

Her hard work had paid off. Since Eric had returned the previous week, he'd mentioned several times that her cooking was delicious and his house had never been so clean.

His extended absence had not been without its negative aspects, however. The camaraderie that Kirsten had felt budding during those first few weeks of their marriage had disappeared while he was gone, and the man who had returned to her had once again seemed like a stranger.

Looking up, Kirsten saw the object of her musings striding toward her, carrying what looked like a shirt. Kirsten smiled as Eric approached, hoping that he might stop to talk a minute. But the annoyed expression on his face as he mounted the steps did not portend a friendly chat. Instead, he waved the cloth he was holding at her and demanded, "Kirsten, why the hell was my shirt buried in the garden?"

Kirsten's eyes widened. "How did you find that?" she asked with a nervous giggle.

"I stopped to pull a weed out of your beans and noticed somebody had been digging next to the garden. I was afraid we might be getting gophers, so I went over to take a look. I couldn't believe it when I found this." He stared down at the dirty shirt. "What is it doing there?"

Kirsten was embarrassed. The shirt in question was an old one which Eric wore while plowing and, somehow, no matter how hard she scrubbed it or how long she soaked it, it never smelled fresh, even when it had just been washed. In desperation, she had consulted her book and found a passage that directed:

Articles of clothing, or of any other character, which have become impregnated with bad-smelling substances, will be freed from them by burying them for a day or two in the ground.

Early that morning before Eric had arisen, she had stolen out to her garden where the ground was soft and buried the offensive item. She thought he wouldn't miss it since he wouldn't be expecting her to wash until Monday, but it was just her bad luck that she'd gotten caught. Who'd have thought he'd be out weeding? He never went near the kitchen garden. It was her domain and he left it to her.

Now, how was she going to explain her actions without offending him? Such a long time passed while she ruminated on this that Eric finally repeated, "Kirsten? Why was my shirt buried in the garden?"

"Well," she gulped, "actually, I put it out there."

"I pretty much figured that," he retorted, "but, why?"

Kirsten swallowed, unable to think of a tactful way to explain her actions. "Because it smelled," she murmured.

Eric's eyebrows rose. "You buried my shirt because it smelled? Why didn't you just wash it?"

"I have! But, the smell never seems to come completely out and my book said . . ."

"What is this book you're always talking about?" he asked.

"It's a book of household hints that Betty gave me. It's been a great help."

"Is that where you got the idea to boil my under-wear?"

"No. That was my idea. But, really, Eric, this book is wonderful. All the good things we've been eating lately came from recipes from it."

"Well, the recipes have been great," Eric admitted, "but the household hints, as you call them, are a little weird, if you ask me."

Kirsten's expression was mutinous. "I was just trying to get that awful shirt clean. I'd tried everything else I could think of and I figured this was worth a try."

"Look," Eric smiled, "if the shirt's that bad, throw it out. Better yet, rip it up and use it for a rag if you want to. Maybe that way, my new shirts will be safe."

Kirsten threw him a furious look. "You don't need to be sarcastic. I've apologized for that over and over. I

163

wish you'd just let it drop."

Eric's teasing expression changed abruptly. "I'm sorry. I wasn't trying to hurt your feelings. I didn't know you were so sensitive about it."

"Well, now you do," Kirsten muttered, pointedly turning away as she returned to her churning.

Eric stood on the step for a moment, wishing that he could call back his hasty, hurtful words. "Tell you what," he said, his voice placating, "how about you and I go into town tomorrow and buy me some new shirts. That way you can throw away any of them that smell or that you don't like, and I'll still have enough to get by."

Kirsten's heart leapt. It was the first time Eric had ever asked her to go anywhere with him, and she was thrilled. But she still wasn't ready to forgive him for his teasing and so said, "I have a lot to do tomorrow. I don't know if I'll have time."

"Oh, come on," he cajoled. "We'll have lunch at the new hotel. I hear their new dining room is terrific, and we haven't tried it yet. Come on, Kirsten, the house looks great, I've got plenty of clean clothes and we have enough bread to feed an army. You deserve a day off, and so do I. Say you'll go."

Kirsten's heart was slamming so hard against her ribs that she was sure he could probably hear it. "Well," she murmured, trying hard to hide her smile, "all right. I'll go. But only if you promise not to tease me anymore about that shirt!"

Eric grinned. Bounding up the steps and leaning over, he ran a calloused hand over her cheek. "Okay, I promise." Then, drawing his hand away, he disappeared into the house.

Kirsten swiveled around on her stool and watched him disappear down the hall toward the kitchen. Absently, she lifted her hand to her cheek, touching it where he had caressed it. With an ecstatic little smile she closed her eyes, allowing herself the luxury of reliving the brief intimate moment. It was so seldom that he ever showed her any physical affection that she felt as if she'd been transported to heaven and back by the small gesture.

With a happy little sigh she turned back to her churn. Long after the butter was creamy and smooth, she still sat there, smiling out at the fields and dreaming about an intimate lunch at the plush new hotel with her handsome husband. She allowed her imagination free rein as she mentally pictured them ensconced at a small private table in a shadowy corner, sharing a glass of wine and offering each other delectable tidbits from their respective plates.

And afterward, when they were both sated with food, wine and each other's company, they'd return home to their beautiful house and make love.

Kirsten shivered as goose bumps rose on her arms. Just the thought of making love with Eric caused tremors to course through her. How she wished her romantic dreams of languishing in his passionate embrace would become reality! But, as always, a little knot formed in the pit of her stomach as she thought of Elsie's words. Was there really something strange about Eric that caused him not to want to make love to her? The thought of her husband's inability to consummate their marriage haunted Kirsten day and night. She had spent enough time with the other brides since their marriages to know that for the rest of the girls, making love occupied a great deal of their time. Olga constantly laughed about how she was afraid for the future of Lars's store because he never wanted to leave their bed long enough to go into town and tend his business. The other brides always smiled knowingly at Olga's lusty recountings, nodding at each other wisely, as if they also were experiencing the same problem with their grooms.

Kirsten always made a point of smiling and nodding also so no one would know that she had no fears about Eric's farm going to rack and ruin because he would rather spend his time in bed with her. She had not told anyone that her marriage was, as yet, unconsummated and had no intention of doing so. It was just too embarrassing, too humiliating to admit that her husband had no romantic interest in her. But she dearly wished she could talk to someone, if only to find out if she was doing something wrong. What had the other girls done those first few days of marriage that had made their husbands desire them?

Kirsten shook her head, firmly putting the distressing thoughts out of her mind. Tomorrow might be just the chance she was hoping for. She would have Eric all to herself for a few hours and she vowed to do everything she could to subtly let her reluctant husband know that she would welcome his attentions.

She had long since formulated a plan about how she would go about seducing her husband, given the opportunity, and now she closed her eyes, uttering a small prayer that her carefully planned seduction would be successful. Opening her eyes again, she smiled to herself. With any luck, the next time the brides got together to whisper and giggle about marital intimacies, she would be able to join the conversation. In fact, she thought excitedly, she might even be able to introduce the subject!

Eric stood in front of his shaving stand and peered anxiously in the mirror, carefully forming a perfect knot in his tie. Today was the day!

Ever since he'd returned from Colorado he had fought the overwhelming attraction he felt for Kirsten, and today he was determined to lose his battle.

Lord knew he had done everything in his power to show Kirsten the least appealing aspects of being his wife. He had forced her to accept more responsibility than any woman should have to, and had worked her unmercifully, expecting, every day, that she would finally get fed up and tell him to go to hell. But she hadn't. He knew by the tired droop of her shoulders that many nights she was so exhausted she could hardly stay awake at the supper table. But she had never complained, had never said she regretted their marriage and wished to return to her comfortable life in New York. Rather, she had accepted every new task he assigned her with unfailing good humor.

Eric smiled at his reflection. Despite his misgivings, despite his fears that his high-class, pampered little Eastern bride would abandon him, she had stayed. And, try as he might to deny it, as the weeks passed, he realized he was falling in love with her. He had tried so hard not to, but her beauty, charm, and wit, coupled with her tenacity and stubborn determination to succeed as a farm wife had finally won him over. His fears that she would be miserable and ultimately leave him had slowly disappeared, and with their abatement had come the startling realization that he wanted Kirsten to be his wife . . . to stay his wife . . . to live with him, have children with him, grow old with him.

So today he was going to try to show her how good life with him could be. For days he had been looking for a way to set the stage for a romantic encounter. But it had taken Kirsten's ridiculous act of burying his shirt in the garden to finally give him the opportunity he'd been looking for. He'd take her to town to shop, maybe find her a little gift she'd like, ply her with wine and food at the hotel, and, if his seduction was successful, bring her home and make her his wife in the truest sense of the word.

Eric looked down, smiling wryly at the bulge which was beginning to stretch the front of his trousers. Closing his eyes, he willed himself to get control. There would be time enough later tonight to give his passion free rein, and he didn't want to shock his innocent little wife with his blatant, masculine interest until he was sure she'd be receptive to it.

Casting a longing glance at the big soft bed sitting in the middle of his beautiful bedroom, Eric sighed and pulled on his jacket. Taking a last look at himself, he took a deep breath and muttered, "Later, man. Later."

Closing the bedroom door firmly behind him, he started down the stairs, eagerly anticipating the day . . . and the night to come.

Olga Bjorklund smiled broadly at Eric Wellesley. She had long since forgiven both him and Lars for the "swap" they had tried to perpetrate when the brides had first arrived, and now she enjoyed seeing him whenever he came to shop at the general store. Not only was he incredibly handsome, but he always spent a tremendous amount of money. Just today he had bought four shirts, a new pair of overalls, two pairs of jeans, and a set of navy suspenders.

Olga had questioned Lars at length about the seemingly endless amount of money that Eric had, but Lars just shrugged, saying that he'd once heard that Eric came from a wealthy family in Colorado and farmed just to have something to do. Although, to most Scandinavian men, this sort of "gentlemanly pastime" was hardly a worthy pursuit, Eric worked as industriously on his farm as any of his neighbors, and everyone in Rose Meadow liked and respected him.

Olga didn't particularly care whether Eric was respected for his farming abilities or not. She just liked the fact that he spent lots of money at her husband's store and often bought extravagant little items which were usually hard to sell to the thrifty, conservative Norwegians.

Although it was not unusual for Eric and Kirsten to be in town, today was unique in that they were shopping together. Not only that, but they were both dressed in their Sunday finery, a fact that Olga immediately noted and was dying to ask Kirsten about. She was heading over to the ribbon counter to do just that when Eric waylaid her.

"Olga," he hissed, his voice lowered to a conspiratorial whisper, "I want to buy something as a surprise for Kirsten and I don't know what she'd like. Can you think of anything you have in stock that she's admired?"

Olga smiled at him, touched by his obvious devotion to his wife. "I have just the thing," she whispered back, crooking her finger and motioning Eric over to a small, glass display case. "These earbobs just came in from Chicago. I showed them to Kirsten last week when she was in, and she was very taken with them."

Eric bent over the case and covertly inspected the garnet earrings. "I'll take them," he nodded. "Wrap them up, but don't let Kirsten see."

Olga nodded and turned away with an envious little sigh. Maybe she shouldn't have been so hasty in rejecting Eric Wellesley's suit. But before she'd even completed the disloyal little thought, she felt guilty. Kirsten was her friend and she was glad that after all their early problems, she and Eric had obviously found happiness together. Besides, Lars was the best of husbands, and no one could have made Olga happier. Even if Kirsten had gotten the richest, most handsome man in Rose Meadow, Olga truly loved her big, strapping husband. And, oh, the pleasure he gave her in their big Scandinavian sleigh bed!

Kirsten returned from the ribbon counter and joined Eric. "Do you have everything you need?" she asked.

"Yeah, think so. Anything else you want?"

"Just lunch," she said softly, giving him a shy little smile.

Eric grinned. "Think I can arrange that, ma'am. But, before we leave, will you go over and look in the button bins and see if you can match the ones off my brown shirt? I lost one yesterday and I can't find it."

Kirsten looked a little disappointed, but nodded and headed off toward the counter which held the sewing supplies.

Eric immediately turned back to Olga and with a sly wink, whispered, "Got those earrings wrapped yet?"

Delighted to be a part of such romantic goings-on, Olga giggled and handed Eric a small package which he immediately plunged into his jacket pocket. When Kirsten returned, carrying two brown buttons, he said, "You know, Kirsten, I guess we won't need those after all. I just found the button in my pocket."

"What?" she asked, completely confused. "How did the button from your brown shirt get into your jacket pocket?"

"Don't know," he shrugged, "but it doesn't matter. Let's go."

With a bewildered little shrug Kirsten handed the buttons to the smiling Olga and allowed herself to be herded out the front door by her grinning husband.

As they swept through the front doors of the new Minnesota Hotel, Kirsten felt her excitement rise. By New York standards Rose Meadow's finest was hardly impressive, but it did have its own rustic charm. The lobby was bright and clean, and carpeted with a lovely rose patterned rug. The front desk was made of the finest black oak, polished to a high sheen, and manned by an immaculately clad attendant. Off to the left stood several large, potted ferns, flanking a wide arch which led to the dining room.

Eric steered her in the direction of the arch, but before they reached it, Kirsten put a staying hand on his arm, whispering, "Before we have lunch, I'd like to freshen up a bit. I'll meet you inside in just a minute."

With a nod Eric gave her arm a little pat and discreetly pointed in the direction of the door leading to the facilities. With a smile of eager anticipation he watched Kirsten disappear down the narrow little hall, then continued on into the dining room.

The dining room was nearly empty, and Eric glanced at his watch in surprise, noting that it was already two o'clock. No wonder he was so hungry! Actually, the late hour could work in his favor. He and Kirsten could share a leisurely, late lunch and then return home just as dusk was falling. A perfect setting for romance . . .

For several long minutes Eric stared off into space, lost in lusty rumination. He finally pulled himself back to reality when a waiter, who had been hovering solicitously at his elbow, cleared his throat and said loudly, "May I help you, sir?"

Eric quickly stated his preferences, and the man led him toward a remote table for two, set back in a secluded corner. "Will this do?" he asked solicitously.

"Perfectly," Eric smiled. "Do you have wine?"

"Yes," the man nodded. "Just got some in from New York yesterday. Would you like a bottle?"

"Please. Chilled. And right away."

With a nod the waiter hurried off and Eric sat down. He was deeply absorbed in the menu when suddenly he felt someone's presence and looked up to find Elsie Anderson Swenson standing next to him.

"Why, Eric Wellesley," she cooed, looking him up and down like a hungry cat, "whatever are you doing here all alone?"

Eric rose to his feet and forced a smile. "I'm not alone. Kirsten is with me. We just came in for a late lunch."

"Oh?" Elsie said, glancing behind her to see if she could spot Kirsten. "Well, isn't that a coincidence. I did, too. Olaf had some errands to run in town today and I told him I just *had* to see the new hotel."

Eric looked relieved. "So, you're waiting for Olaf to join you?"

"Oh, heavens, no!" Elsie trilled. "Olaf wouldn't come here. Why, I can hardly get him to dress up for church on Sunday, much less ask him to put on a suit in the middle of the week. No, I'm here alone . . . eating alone . . . spending the afternoon alone." She let her voice trail off meaningfully.

Eric looked away for a moment, closing his eyes as his innate good manners warred with his desire for privacy. What could he do? It would be inexcusably rude not to invite Elsie to join them for lunch when she was so obviously hinting toward that end. He looked back at her expectant face and smiled weakly. "I'm sure Kirsten would be delighted to have a chance for a visit," he said slowly, not wanting her to think that *he* was interested in her company. "Why don't you join us for lunch?"

"Why, thank you!" Elsie's face lit up with a brilliant smile. Then, coyly demurring, she lowered her eyes and said, "Oh, but I probably shouldn't. I mean, I wouldn't want to intrude, and you have already taken a table for two. You've probably even ordered."

For a brief second Eric actually thought he might be able to extricate himself from this infuriating situation. But the ever helpful waiter had overheard their conversation and suddenly appeared behind Elsie's shoulder. "Is there a problem, sir? Do you need a bigger table?"

Misinterpreting Eric's annoyed look, the waiter continued eagerly, "It's no problem at all, sir. I have plenty. Let's just move you and the lady over here." With a sweeping motion, he retrieved the bottle of wine he'd set in a stand by the table and strode off toward a table for four in the middle of the dining room. Looking back over his shoulder at Eric, who was still sitting at the small table, he added, "Really, sir, it's no trouble. I'm sure you'll find this table very comfortable for three."

With a resigned nod, Eric rose from his seat and escorted the ecstatic Elsie over to the larger table, holding out a chair for her and then seating himself.

Flipping her napkin open, Elsie spread it across her lap and said, "This is so nice of you, Eric. I certainly hope I'm not interrupting something private."

"I'm sure Kirsten will be delighted that we ran into each other," Eric answered politely, silently cursing his rotten luck.

Just then, Kirsten appeared in the dining room doorway. She hesitated a moment as she scanned the large room for her husband, then her eyebrows rose and her lips thinned as she spotted him sitting with Elsie.

172

Walking quickly over to the table, she stopped and stood stiffly next to it, her gaze darting between her embarrassed husband and the gleeful Elsie.

"Hello, Elsie," she said quietly, looking closely at Eric. "What are you doing in town?"

"I came in to see the hotel and try the new restaurant," Elsie explained, smiling at Eric as she talked, "and your charming husband invited me to join you for lunch."

"Wonderful," Kirsten muttered, seating herself before Eric could assist her.

"So, Eric, what have you been doing with yourself since the wedding?" Elsie asked, turning her attention back to Eric and pointedly ignoring Kirsten.

"Farming."

Elsie laughed. "Well, I sort of expected that, but surely you must do more than that with your time."

"He's been helping me learn to be a wife," Kirsten said a shade too loudly. Then, seeing Eric's astonished expression, she added, "You know, Elsie, how ill-prepared I was for farm life."

"Yes," Elsie answered sweetly, "I know how worried you were that your lack of experience would be, ah, a disappointment to Eric."

Eric shot a quick glance at Kirsten and, realizing that Elsie's double entendre had not gone unnoticed, growled, "Let's order."

"Yes, let's," Kirsten agreed, opening her menu with a snap.

The meal lasted forever. Elsie chattered incessantly, directing all her conversation to Eric and acting like Kirsten wasn't even present. Finally, the food came, which at least gave Kirsten something to do with her hands other than clench them under the table.

"My fish is delicious!" Elsie announced, spearing a piece and waving the fork over the middle of the table. "Would anyone like a taste? Eric?"

"No thanks," he said, shaking his head.

"Oh," Elsie pouted. "You have no idea what a treat you're missing."

Kirsten knew exactly what "treat" Elsie was offering Eric, and it was all she could do not to reach over and slap the hateful woman. But years of training asserted themselves and she maintained her composure, sitting calmly in her chair, delicately chewing her food, and watching her nemesis fawn all over her husband. Her father would have been proud of her. Her aunt would have said that she was showing good manners and decorum. But even though she knew she was conducting herself like a well-bred lady, all she really wanted to do was slap Elsie Anderson. She wanted to stand up and shriek and rail and threaten the woman with bodily harm if she didn't get her nasty little fish fork away from her husband's mouth. But she didn't do any of those things. Instead, she remained poised and calm. Miserable, but poised and calm.

Finally, the dishes were cleared and coffee was served. Elsie sat back in her chair and groaned contentedly. "I must say, even though this is backward old Minnesota, that was wonderful. You really should have tried my fish, Eric."

Eric smiled and sipped his coffee.

Kirsten frowned and clenched her hands under the table.

Realizing that flirtation was getting her nowhere, Elsie decided to drop the bomb that she was sure would end Kirsten's ladylike struggle. "By the way, Eric," she purred, "did you ever get that hammock of yours fixed?"

Eric nearly choked on his coffee. "What?"

"Oh, you know. Don't you remember? That day right before we all got married when I was at your house and the hammock broke?"

"Yeah, I remember," Eric muttered.

"Well," Elsie pursued, "were you able to fix it?"

"Yes, I fixed it!"

"I'm so glad. It's such a wonderful hammock. I'd hate to think that I was the cause of its loss."

"You had nothing to do with it," Eric answered, throwing Elsie a hard look. Then, turning to the furious Kirsten, he said, "We better go. It's getting late, and the cows need milking."

"Oh, Kirsten, I'm so sorry,' Elsie laughed, "I didn't mean to dominate the conversation. You've hardly said a word!"

Kirsten still didn't say a word. She didn't even look at Elsie. She just stared at Eric, trying to judge the truth of Elsie's hammock story.

Had Elsie and Eric had a secret tryst before the wedding? And, if so, what had happened the day the hammock broke? Had he and Elsie had some sort of argument that had made him suddenly decide to marry her? Kirsten knew that Elsie had put off accepting Olaf's proposal until the day before the wedding. Was Eric the reason why?

By the time the three of them left the hotel, Kirsten's mind was reeling with wild speculation. From far off she heard Eric offer Elsie a ride home and heard Elsie respond that she was meeting Olaf at four o'clock and that he would take her home. As they parted on the street, Elsie made a great show of kissing Kirsten on the cheek and giving Eric a quick hug. By this time Kirsten's imagination had conjured up so many devastating possibilities about a love affair between her husband and her nemesis that she didn't even notice how Eric stiffened at Elsie's embrace.

Kirsten silently followed Eric over to their wagon and accepted his lift up without making eye contact. As they drove out of town she stared straight ahead, refusing to give him the satisfaction of seeing her distress.

Eric was furious. Why the hell did this have to happen today? he thought angrily. He had planned everything so carefully, setting the scene for his wife's seduction with the precision of a military campaign. Now, God knew what was going on in Kirsten's head. He glanced over at her. What was she thinking? Was she upset by Elsie'd broad hints and innuendos, or didn't she care? He could tell nothing by looking at her.

"Kirsten," he said quietly, "nothing happened that day when Elsie came to the house. She was out riding and she just stopped for some water."

"You don't need to explain," Kirsten said coldly, her lips compressed and her eyes riveted on the horizon. "What you and Elsie might have done before we were married is none of my business."

"We didn't *do* anything!"

"It doesn't matter."

Eric jerked back on the reins. "Like hell it doesn't matter. If it didn't matter, you wouldn't be so mad."

"I'm not mad," Kirsten answered, looking over at him and forcing a smile. "It's none of my concern."

Eric stared at her for a long moment, trying to gauge her real feelings. He could tell by the stony look on her face that she was struggling to keep her emotions in check, but he didn't know why. He would have much preferred that she scream at him, demand an explanation, threaten him with wifely retaliation if he ever cheated on her. At least, then, he'd know she cared something for him.

"You don't have to pretend to be so understanding," he said, hoping to get a rise out of her. "I know you're upset, and after what Elsie said, I suppose you have a right to be. But I want you to know that there's never been anything between Elsie and me, not before you and I got married and not since."

Kirsten's head snapped around, her emerald green eyes blazing. "There better not have been anything since we got married!"

"There hasn't," Eric hastily assured her. He quickly looked away before she noticed the pleased smile he couldn't restrain. She *did* care! That furious look had told him everything he'd wanted to know. Maybe the day wasn't going to be a total loss, after all, he thought happily, clucking to the horses and steering the wagon onto the road again. Kirsten was jealous! And, with any luck at all, maybe he could turn that jealousy into passion. One thing was for sure. As soon as they got home and he got the damn chores done, he was certainly going to try!

Chapter 15

They pulled into the yard, and before Eric even brought the horses to a full stop, Kirsten was gathering her skirts to make the long leap to the ground.

"Sit down!" he ordered. "Just wait a minute, and I'll come over and help you."

Kirsten sat down with a thump, then, throwing an angry look over her shoulder, announced, "I can get down myself," and again stood up, preparing to jump.

"Kirsten, for God's sake! You're going to break your neck. Just sit down and wait till I get over there!"

Again Kirsten sat down, this time staring straight ahead. Eric looked at her quizzically, then, shaking his head, jumped down and came around to her side, holding his arms up expectantly.

She didn't move.

He continued to stand there, his arms outstretched. When she still didn't move, he reached forward and tugged on the hem of her skirt. "Hey, lady, want some help?"

Kirsten smiled, despite herself. "I suppose," she admitted, and standing, leaned toward Eric until she felt his hands clasp her around the waist.

It seemed like a long, long trip to the ground. Eric lifted her slowly, causing her body to slide down the length of his. When her feet finally touched the ground, he didn't remove his hands, but, instead, held her close against him and looked down into her stormy green eyes.

"You know, I've always been partial to tall blondes like Elsie," he said casually.

Kirsten stiffened and tried to back out of his embrace, but Eric tightened his hold slightly and continued smiling down at her. Finally, realizing she wasn't going to get away from him until he was ready to release her, she answered coolly, "I noticed."

Eric smiled wider and allowed his thumbs to move upward along Kirsten's rib cage until they rested just below the curve of her breasts. Leaning forward until his lips were touching her hair, he whispered, "But, lately I find I'm developing a real fondness for little women with fiery hair and tempers to match."

Kirsten threw her head back to look at him, but as their eyes met, Eric lowered his mouth and kissed her. Kirsten didn't even have time to take a breath before she was caught up in the whirling, giddy sensation of her husband's caress. His lips were soft and warm, just like they'd been the day of their wedding. But today there was something else in his kiss. An urgency, a need she'd not felt before. Despite her innocence, Kirsten knew that the feelings which were radiating from Eric's lips to hers, making her feel shaky and breathless, were caused by desire. Gentle and restrained, but most definitely desire.

She felt like she was melting and she knew that if Eric dropped his hands from where they were holding her around the waist and shoulders, she'd crumple to the ground like a limp marionette.

But he didn't drop her, and the kiss went on and on and on. Kirsten shivered as his tongue, warm, wet, and probing, sought entry into the secret recesses of her mouth. Although she felt a moment of shock at his erotic play, her lips softened and opened.

She thought she heard a small groan escape him—or

maybe it had come from her own throat—she wasn't sure. All she knew was that the sensation of Eric's tongue in her mouth, delving into the dark caverns of her cheeks and skimming over the sensitive skin inside her lips, made her feel like she couldn't catch her breath.

Eric moved his hand up the side of her face, sliding his palm along her cheek and weaving his fingers into her hair near her temple. He pulled her more tightly against him and deepened the kiss. Just when Kirsten was sure she was going to swoon, he lifted his lips, feathering light kisses along the side of her nose and across her eyelids.

She drew a deep, shuddering breath and her head dropped back, allowing him free access to her face and neck. Again she felt his tongue run along the edge of her eyelashes and she squirmed against him.

Smiling at her reaction, Eric dipped his head, running his parted lips down the sensitive cords of her neck, then nibbling and kissing his way back up her chin until his lips again settled on hers.

Kirsten tightened her grip on his shoulders, pulling him closer and holding on to him as though she were drowning. Eric answered by pressing against her, letting her feel his rapidly rising desire. The provocative movement caused a hot rush of sensation to suddenly spin downward from Kirsten's stomach and unfurl through her abdomen until it settled with a throb between her thighs. This graphic proof of her stirring passions made her draw in her breath and take a startled step backward.

Eric's eyes snapped open, his breath coming harsh and fast as he looked at her in bewilderment.

"I . . . we better get to the chores, don't you think?" She backed up another step and nervously ran her hand across her hair where it had come loose from its pins.

"Chores?" he repeated, staring at her in dumbfounded astonishment.

"Well, yes," she nodded, fighting to control her quivering voice. "You told Elsie back at the restaurant that we had to get back to do chores."

Eric closed his eyes and clenched his jaw in frustration. *Elsie.* Now that Kirsten had said her name, she stood between them like a wall. The moment was over, and he knew it. Blowing out an angry, exasperated breath, he turned toward the house. "Yeah, sure. We better change and do the chores since we told Elsie that's what we were going to do. Wouldn't want Elsie to find out we lied to her, would we?"

Kirsten stared after him as he stomped off to the house to change his clothes, bewildered by his sudden anger. After all, she was the one who should be mad. She was the one who had been forced to sit through a two-hour lunch, watching that hateful shrew fawn all over her husband! What did Eric have to be mad about?

A little voice far back in a corner of her mind pricked her. *You know why he's mad. He's mad because you stopped him.*

Kirsten thought about that for a moment, trying to sort out her feelings. Why *had* she pulled away?

Because he scares you, the voice promptly supplied. *You've never been with a man who makes you feel hot and cold and shaky the way he does. You lose control every time he comes near you and it scares you to death!*

But, why was she scared? He was her husband. Wasn't his affection, his kisses, his passion what she wanted? What she hoped for?

Yes, but not if Elsie Anderson had it first.

"We have to talk about this," Kirsten said aloud. "Tonight at supper I'll just tell him that once and for all, we have to get this Elsie thing behind us. Then he'll tell me there's nothing to it, that it's just my imagination and then . . ."

Her mind drifted to "and then . . ." and a little shiver ran down her spine as she thought of the ecstasy Eric's

182

kiss had brought her. What other secrets could the man unlock within her? Just the thought made her smile and look impatiently at the slowly setting sun.

Eric didn't come in from the barn until very late, and as the evening waned so did Kirsten's hopes. Still, when he finally walked in the back door, she looked up hopefully from where she sat at the kitchen table and said, "Would you like something to eat? A sandwich maybe?"

"No, don't bother," he answered with a shake of his head.

Kirsten's face fell, her disappointment so obvious that Eric's heart took a bound. "Well, maybe just a sandwich," he amended.

"There's some roast beef left from last night. It'll only take me a minute."

"Sounds good," Eric nodded. "Why don't you make us each a sandwich and we'll go out and eat on the front porch. There's a nice breeze tonight."

Kirsten rose from the table and hurried over to the counter, praying he wouldn't see the smile she couldn't conceal. After all, she thought primly, even if tonight was going to be *the* night, it wouldn't do for her to seem *too* enthusiastic. Her father's maiden sister who had helped raise her after her mother's death had always preached that men might like a bold, brazen woman for a moment's pleasure, but they expected their wives to conduct themselves like ladies at all times.

Eric's thoughts as he climbed the stairs to his bedroom were much the same. Although he knew that, based on Kirsten's reaction to his kiss, she could probably be easily seduced into his bed, he didn't want to rush her. Her obvious innocence and startled reaction had touched a deep, protective chord in him he hadn't even known existed. Now that he finally realized that he wanted to make Kirsten his wife in the most real sense, he didn't want to scare her. He just hoped he could recreate the passion he'd stirred in her that afternoon. He was sure he could—if only they could keep that damn trollop Elsie out of the conversation.

After washing and donning fresh clothes, he returned to the kitchen to find Kirsten putting two plates and two large glasses of milk on a tray.

"Ready?" he smiled.

She nodded and turned toward him, almost dropping the tray. Never, in all the time they'd been together, had she ever seen her husband look as magnificent as he did at that moment. His hair was damp, and loose sable curls clung to the back of his neck. He was wearing one of the new pairs of jeans he'd bought earlier that day and a loose cambric shirt. The stark whiteness of the linen against his sun-bronzed skin and ebony eyes was such a stunning contrast that Kirsten's eyes widened in awe. She had thought him the handsomest man alive at their wedding, but even that day, decked out in his finest clothes, the sight of him hadn't made her heart pound the way it was pounding right now.

Kirsten chided herself for not having spent more time preparing herself for the evening. She would have liked Eric to have the same reaction to her that she was having to him. But after arriving home from town, she had spent the rest of the afternoon putting away the supplies they'd bought and washing the breakfast dishes which she'd left behind that morning. Plus, she thought defensively, the way he had hightailed it out to the barn after he'd kissed her, she never dreamed he'd pick tonight to have a cozy dinner on the front porch.

Oh, well, she sighed, picking up the tray and passing through the door he was holding open. No help for it now. He'll just have to take me as I am. But she vowed that tomorrow night she'd be ready for him—freshly bathed, coiffed, and dressed.

They walked out onto the porch, and Eric took the tray from her, setting it on a small table and gesturing

Kirsten into a wicker chair. He then sat down on the table's opposite side and handed her a plate.

"So, what'd you do this afternoon?" he asked, taking a bite of his sandwich.

"Not much," she replied. "Just some household chores."

"I'm gonna spend the day checking the fields tomorrow. The corn's starting to tassel and I want to make sure it's okay. You want to go along?"

Kirsten looked at him in surprise. "Go along?"

"Sure," he nodded. "It's your farm, too, and I thought you might be interested in seeing the whole thing."

"Well, yes," Kirsten stammered, dumbfounded by his admission that the farm was partly hers. "I'd like to go. Very much."

"Good." Eric sat back in his chair and took a long drink of milk. "We'll start early. Takes a while to look at all of it."

"How big is the farm?"

"Six hundred forty acres. A whole section."

"Are all farms that big?"

"No. Most of the men around here have a quarter section—one hundred sixty acres. But, I wanted enough space to expand so I bought a whole section. I'm only planting part of it this year though."

"How come" Kirsten asked, thrilled that Eric was carrying on a real conversation with her. Usually he didn't say ten words in a day, and he'd never spent any time telling her about the farm. Of course, she'd never asked him either . . .

"I didn't want to hire any help this year and I knew I couldn't handle more than a quarter section by myself."

"Why didn't you want to hire help?" The words were out before Kirsten could stop them, and she could have kicked herself for prying.

Eric set down his empty milk glass and cocked his head as if he was pondering exactly what to say. "Well,

185

actually," he started, then paused and cleared his throat, looking suddenly shy and uncomfortable.

Kirsten knew she should tell him that he didn't have to confide in her, but she was dying to know what had caused such a look of discomfiture. "Yes?" she prompted.

"Actually, after I decided to get married, I figured it would be better to have our first year together with just the two of us. You know—so we'd have the privacy we needed to really get to know each other. So, I decided to work just part of the farm and not hire anyone on."

Kirsten felt herself blush. "I see," she murmured and jumped to her feet, grabbing his milk glass. "I'll go refill this for you and I'll bring a plate of cookies. I made some oatmeal ones yesterday."

She whirled toward the front door, but like a striking snake, Eric's hand whipped out and clasped her by the wrist, gently halting her flight. "Did I embarrass you? I didn't mean to."

"No," she whispered, mesmerized by his soft, dark eyes. "I'm not embarrassed, it's just that . . ."

"That we've never taken the time to get to know each other, even though we've been married for months? I know."

Kirsten looked up from under her lashes to see him smiling at her. Her heart took another bound at the hopeful, boyish expression on his face.

"Sit down, Kirsty," he murmured. "I don't want cookies and I don't want any more milk. I want to talk to you."

No one had ever called Kirsten by a nickname. Her father hated pet names and had insisted that everyone call her Kirsten. Somehow, though, despite the strangeness of it, she liked having Eric call her "Kirsty." It was special . . . intimate.

She set the glass down with shaking hands and perched on the edge of the wicker chair. Eric looked at her and smiled.

"Let's sit on the swing."

186

Getting up, he held out a hand to her, then led her over to the opposite side of the porch where a wooden swing sat suspended from chains attached to the porch's roof. Kirsten sat down at one end, and Eric dropped down next to her—not as close as he wanted to be, but near enough that their thighs nearly touched.

With a push of his foot he set the swing into a gentle rocking motion. "Do you miss New York?" he asked softly.

"Yes," Kirsten admitted. "I miss the shops and the people and the activity. It's so quiet here."

"Boring, too, huh?"

"No," she answered honestly, looking at him and shaking her head. "I'm never bored. I have too much work to do to be bored."

Eric's heart dropped like a stone. Her response was exactly what he'd feared. She was miserable.

"Guess it's not what you were hoping for, is it?"

"No, it's not that, exactly, but, you were right. Being a farm wife is a lot more work than I ever expected. There's one good thing about it, though. I'm so busy that I don't have time to be lonely for what I left behind. Honestly, I've hardly given New York a thought. It's just that I sometimes miss the noise and the excitement.

Eric looked away so she wouldn't see his dejection. "I've never been to New York, but I imagine Minnesota must seem pretty dull by comparison."

"You've never been to New York?"

"No. I haven't traveled too much. I've got a brother in Boston and I've been there, but never to New York. I spent most of my life in a little town way up in the Colorado mountains and then I came here."

"Why?" Kirsten asked.

Eric sighed, his spirits sinking lower every moment. Obviously Kirsten was trying to tell him that she couldn't imagine why *anyone* would want to live in Minnesota, and he didn't know if he'd be able to explain how he felt. "I wanted to farm," he said simply.

"My folks owned a ranch in Durango and I liked the life there, but I wanted to grow crops, not just raise animals, and the Colorado Rockies isn't the place to do it."

"Durango," Kirsten mused. "Is your dog named for the town where you grew up?"

"Yeah," Eric smiled. "Dumb, huh?"

"I don't think it's dumb," Kirsten said. "I think it just shows that you love your hometown . . ."

Eric's eyes grew wistful. "I do," he admitted. "It's a spectacular spot. But, I wanted to be a farmer, so I had to move."

"But why Minnesota?" Kirsten asked. "Why not Kansas or Nebraska? It would have been closer to your home."

"Yeah, it would have. But I had a friend who told me about the soil here. He said it was so black it would grow anything—wheat, corn, soybeans, alfalfa. Anything. And Minnesota doesn't have the wind that Kansas does so there isn't as much problem with erosion. Besides," his face took on a faraway look, "I love the trees and the water. Kansas is too dry. I came here to take a look and once I saw this soil I knew my friend was right. I filed a homestead and never left."

Kirsten stared at him for a moment, then burst into a peal of tinkling laughter. "You moved here because of the color of the dirt?"

Eric gave the swing another push, trying hard to cover his embarrassment. Love of the earth must seem simple and crude to a woman who had just admitted that she longed for the shops in New York. "Yeah, I guess you could say that."

"And, are you glad?"

"Yes," he admitted, "I love it here." Turning to face her, he added meaningfully, "But I understand that it's not for everybody. The winters are hell. It snows in November and it's still snowing in April. The temperature reaches thirty below in January and everything freezes solid. If this year is anything like the last few, we'll get snowbound and won't be able to get out for days, maybe even weeks—even to go to town. December, January, and February are killers."

"Are you trying to scare me?" Kirsten asked.

"No, I'm just telling you how it is. We're gonna be here cooped up together for a lot of months. I just want you to be sure that you're gonna be able to handle being alone with me that much."

Kirsten couldn't think of anything she'd like more than to be "cooped up" with her handsome husband. Nights spent lying by the fire . . . long, quiet days spent sharing confidences. It sounded like heaven. But not knowing how Eric felt about her, she couldn't bring herself to say so. "I'm sure I'll be fine, Eric. I can handle a lot more than you think."

"Think about it, Kirsten," he warned. "It's cold and dark and boring as hell. If you think it's dull around here now, just wait till you can't even leave the house!"

Kirsten looked at him closely. What was he really trying to say? That he didn't want her to stay? That he wanted her to go back to New York? Well, she wasn't going to! He was her husband, this was her home, and she was staying. With a bright, determined smile, she said, "I know I'm probably not going to enjoy the winter but, between the two of us, I'm sure we can think of some way to amuse ourselves."

Eric's eyes widened at her provocative comment and he threw her a quick, startled glance, but her expression was so guileless that he was sure she hadn't a clue how it had sounded.

He was wrong though. Despite her innocence Kirsten was trying her best to let her husband know she wanted him. *Why doesn't he kiss me again like he did this afternoon?* she thought. *What more can I say to let him know that I want him to?* She shifted ever so slightly toward him, wishing he'd move closer to her.

But he didn't. Instead, he stared out into the darkness, an enigmatic expression on his face. Kirsten had no way of knowing that he was fighting a battle that had been plaguing him for months. *You can have her. You can take her right now, and she'll be yours forever. Just lean over and kiss her. Then, you can pick her up, carry her up those stairs and this torture will be over.*

Just the thought of carrying Kirsten up the stairs and laying her down on his big, soft bed made Eric's loins tighten uncomfortably and, impulsively, he started to reach for her. But the word "forever" drummed through his brain like a litany, staying his impetuous move.

Think about what she just said! She misses New York. She's dreading the winter. If you make love to her tonight, you'll forge a bond that neither of you will be able to break. You can't do it to her. YOU CAN'T!

A long, stiff silence ensued. Kirsten sat, desperately wishing that the easy comaraderie they had shared just a short time ago would return, and Eric sat, desperately wishing that he had never brought up the subject of New York. Neither of them knew how to recapture what they had lost. Finally, with a small, troubled sigh, Eric said, "Guess we better go to bed."

Kirsten's head snapped around, hoping to see in his expression that he meant "together." But he was already getting up and moving toward the table to collect the empty dishes. Slowly, she rose from the swing and followed him.

They walked silently back into the kitchen. Eric deposited the dirty dishes in the sink and turning, said simply, "I'll see you in the morning." Without giving her a chance to reply, he pushed through the kitchen door and disappeared down the hall.

Kirsten heard his slow, heavy tread as he climbed the stairs, but it was a long time before she followed. The thought of facing her empty bed made tears spring to her eyes, and for the thousandth time she wondered what she could do to make Eric Wellesley love her.

Chapter 16

"What do you mean, you're not really married? Of course you are! I was at your wedding—along with half of the rest of the town. What nonsense, Kirsten. Not married, indeed!"

Kirsten looked imploringly into Betty's eyes, hoping that the wise older woman would realize what she was really trying to tell her without her having to explain it in plain language. "That's not what I mean, Betty," she said softly, placing her coffee cup on its saucer with shaking hands.

Betty sat back in one of the worn, overstuffed chairs in her parlor and frowned. "Kirsten, I'm completely confused. What are you talking about?"

"What I'm trying to say," Kirsten gulped, "is that Eric and I have never . . . never done what people do when they're *really* married."

Betty's eyes widened as the realization of what Kirsten was saying finally hit home. "What?" she gasped. "Are you telling me that you and Eric have been married for two months now and you still haven't . . . haven't . . ."

"That's right," Kirsten interrupted before the other woman could say the words "we haven't."

"Well, why not?"

Kirsten hung her head. "I don't know. I think there might be something wrong with Eric."

191

The last response Kirsten expected to her startling statement was the great gust of laughter that escaped Betty. She looked up in astonishment as her friend laughed until she doubled over, tears running down her face.

"I'm sorry, dear," Betty wheezed, wiping her eyes and trying to compose herself, "I know you're upset and I shouldn't laugh, but *where* in the world did you ever get the idea there's something 'wrong' with Eric Wellesley? Why, I never saw a more virile specimen of manhood in my entire life!"

Kirsten's lips thinned. This was not a funny situation, and she resented the fact that Betty was taking it so lightly. It had taken her nearly two weeks to gather up the courage to come and talk to her mentor about her problem, and she didn't expect to be laughed at! "I think there may be something wrong with him because he has never so much as tried to . . . you know."

Betty sobered instantly. "Wait a minute, Kirsten," she said, leaning forward and putting her hand on Kirsten's arm, "don't you two sleep together?"

"No," Kirsten answered softly, averting her eyes, "I have my own room."

"But, why?" Betty was genuinely puzzled.

Kirsten's lower lip trembled as she tried vainly to hold back the tears. "I don't know!" she blurted. "When he took me home after our wedding, he showed me this little bedroom at the opposite end of the hall from his and said it was mine. I've been sleeping there ever since."

"Well," Betty mused, "I have heard of couples who don't sleep in the same bed. Rich folks, mainly. But still, hasn't he ever . . . come to you?"

"Never," Kirsten pronounced solemnly.

Betty again sat back in her chair, crossing her arms across her large bosom and staring out the front window. "Well, I never." Flicking her eyes back to Kirsten, she said, "Okay, young lady, let's talk frank

ENJOY ALL THE PASSION AND ROMANCE OF...

Heartfire

ROMANCES from ZEBRA

After you have read HEART-FIRE ROMANCES, we're sure you'll agree that HEARTFIRE sets new standards of excellence for historical romantic fiction. Each Zebra HEARTFIRE novel is the ultimate blend of intimate romance and grand adventure and each takes place in the kinds of historical settings you want most...the American Revolution, the Old West, Civil War and more.

SUBSCRIBERS $AVE, $AVE, $AVE!!!

As a HEARTFIRE Home Subscriber, you'll save with your HEARTFIRE Subscription. You'll receive 4 brand new Heartfire Romances to preview Free for 10 days each month. If you decide to keep them you'll pay only $3.50 each; a total of $14.00 and you'll save $3.00 each month off the cover price.

Plus, we'll send you these novels as soon as they are published each month. There is never any shipping, handling or other hidden charges; home delivery is always FREE! And there is no obligation to buy even a single book. You may return any of the books within 10 days for full credit and you can cancel your subscription at any time. No questions asked.

Zebra's HEARTFIRE ROMANCES Are The Ultimate
In Historical Romantic Fiction.
Start Enjoying Romance As You Have Never Enjoyed It Before...
With 4 FREE Books From HEARTFIRE

TO GET YOUR
4 FREE BOOKS
MAIL THE COUPON BELOW.

FREE BOOK CERTIFICATE

GET 4 FREE BOOKS

Yes! I want to subscribe to Zebra's HEARTFIRE HOME SUBSCRIPTION SERVICE. Please send me my 4 FREE books. Then each month I'll receive the four newest Heartfire Romances as soon as they are published to preview Free for ten days. If I decide to keep them I'll pay the special discounted price of just $3.50 each; a total of $14.00. This is a savings of $3.00 off the regular publishers price. There are no shipping, handling or other hidden charges. There is no minimum number of books to buy and I may cancel this subscription at any time. In any case the 4 FREE Books are mine to keep regardless.

NAME _____

ADDRESS _____

CITY _____ STATE _____ ZIP _____

TELEPHONE _____

SIGNATURE _____

(If under 18 parent or guardian must sign)
Terms and prices subject to change.
Orders subject to acceptance.

HF 104

Heartfire Romance

GET 4 FREE BOOKS

HEARTFIRE HOME SUBSCRIPTION
SERVICE
P.O. BOX 5214
120 BRIGHTON ROAD
CLIFTON, NEW JERSEY 07015

about this. I don't believe for one minute there's anything physically wrong with your husband. If there was, it would show up in other ways. Does he seem strong and healthy to you?"

Kirsten nodded. "He works all day in the fields, does barn chores, all the normal things, and he never seems tired or anything. We sit up at night and talk or play cards or go visiting. I don't think he's sick."

"Well, what do you think is causing his . . . disinterest?"

Kirsten shook her head. "I really think it might be what Elsie said that day at the party."

"Piffle!" Betty retorted. "That little theory of Elsie's is absolute nonsense and I'm ashamed of you for giving it any credence at all. Now, tell me, has Eric ever done *anything* to show any interest in you?"

Kirsten nodded. "Oh, yes. He kisses me all the time."

"What kind of kisses?"

Kirsten's blush told Betty everything she was hoping to hear. "Oh, you know. Like you would expect a man to kiss his wife."

"Good," Betty nodded. "That proves right there that he's not disinterested. Now, I want you to forget everything Elsie Anderson has ever told you. It's my personal opinion that she's sweet on Eric—always has been—and is just trying to brew up some mischief to make you miserable. Sounds like she's doing a pretty good job of it, too."

Kirsten nodded. "I've thought that, too, only I was afraid it was just my imagination. But, frankly, I can tell you that I've always thought Elsie was jealous that Eric married me and not her. There have been several times since we've been married that she's been somewhere that we are and she always makes a point to be close to him."

"What do you mean, 'close'?"

"You know," Kirsten said, wishing that she didn't have to explain all of the embarrassing incidents. "When we've been at parties and things, she always seems to sit by Eric or be near him when it's time to dance. Things like that."

"And how does Eric react to all this?"

"He doesn't seem to mind, exactly, but he's never given her any encouragement that I can see."

"Well, there. You see?" Betty smiled. "It's just as I suspected. Elsie is jealous of you and trying to make you miserable by making you think that your husband is dallying with her. That, and the fact that for some reason you and Eric aren't intimate, is enough to make any wife feel unloved and unwanted. But, don't worry, dear. You and I are going to figure out what's wrong and fix it!"

Tears welled in Kirsten's eyes. "Oh, thank you, Betty. I knew you would help me!"

"Don't give me too much credit, Kirsten," Betty warned. "The only person who can really help this situation is you. All I can do is give you a couple of suggestions."

"I'll do anything you tell me to," Kirsten promised.

"The first thing you need to do is quit blushing and talk to me like I was your mother. Now, I'm going to ask you some personal questions and I want straight answers from you. Agreed?"

Kirsten swallowed hard. She'd never had a mother to confide in and it didn't come easily to her to share the intimate details of her personal life. But Eric was worth whatever embarrassment she had to endure. "All right," she smiled nervously, "I'll try."

Betty chuckled. "Relax, honey. You're not on trial here. I'm only trying to help you get to the bottom of your problem. Now, tell me, have you ever just gone and gotten into bed with Eric?"

"You mean go into his room, uninvited, and get into his bed—when he's in it?" Kirsten gasped. "Of course not!"

"*Why* not?" Betty asked, her voice brooking no nonsense.

"Why, because, because it wouldn't be proper!"

Kirsten blustered.

"Who's to say what's proper between a man and his wife?"

Kirsten looked down at her lap, mortified. "I just couldn't do that."

Betty sighed. "Okay, but tell me this. Would you like to?"

Kirsten didn't look up, but Betty detected just the slightest nod.

"Then why don't you?"

"I just told you. It would just be too forward of me. Besides," she continued, lifting her head and looking at Betty squarely in the eye, "I think it's Eric's place to come to me, not the other way around."

Betty smiled. "I think you're right. But, something is keeping him from it and I think it's you."

"Me?" Kirsten blurted, her anger obvious, "I haven't done anything at all."

"Exactly," Betty smiled. "And that's your problem."

Kirsten's expression was mutinous as she stared silently at the older woman.

"Honey, what I'm trying to say is that Eric Wellesley is shy. I told you that the first day you arrived. Maybe he's as uncomfortable making the first move as you are. I think what might have happened here is that when you two were first married, he felt that after all the problems you'd had, you wouldn't *want* an intimate relationship with him right away. So he decided to wait until both of you had a chance to get to know each other and, hopefully, fall in love a little bit. Now it looks like he's waited so long that you two have gotten into a routine with your marriage and he doesn't know how to change it . . . probably doesn't even know if you want him to try. If you're not giving him any signs that you'd welcome more intimate attention from him, then he probably figures you're happy with things the way they are and he's scared to press you."

"I don't believe Eric Wellesley has ever been scared of anything in his life," Kirsten said defensively.

"Okay, then, why don't you climb into bed with him tonight and find out?" Betty challenged.

Kirsten closed her eyes, shaking her head. "Because I just can't," she moaned. "What if he threw me out?"

"He's *not* going to throw you out," Betty assured her, praying she was right, "but if you don't feel you can be that forward, then try something else."

Kirsten looked at her hopefully. "Like what?"

"Think of something! You're a bright girl and you've been living with the man for two months! What were you doing when he's kissed you in the past?"

"Nothing, usually," Kirsten shrugged. "Sometimes it's when we're sitting on the porch at night. But, sometimes, it's at really strange times. Like the other day, we drove all over the farm so Eric could check the corn. We stopped at one field, and he was explaining something called 'tasseling' to me, and while we were standing there looking at the plants, he just grabbed me around the waist and kissed me! Pulled me right down on the ground and began kissing and tickling me like we were a couple of children!"

Betty closed her eyes, thinking how lucky Kirsten was. "And what did you do?"

"I . . . I pushed him off and got up," Kirsten answered, her voice uncertain.

"Oh, Kirsten!" Betty moaned.

"Betty!" she defended. "It was broad daylight and we were in a field right by the road! Anybody could have driven by. I mean, can you imagine?"

Betty closed her eyes, her mind awash with memories of her own happy marriage. "Yes, I can imagine," she murmured. "And, believe me, honey, there's nothing wrong with that man that a little encouragement on your part won't fix."

"Do you really think so?"

"Absolutely," Betty smiled. "Now, here's what I want you to do. And I don't want you to tell me you can't, because you have to, whether it embarrasses you or not."

196

Kirsten took a deep breath. "Okay. Tell me."

"I want you to go home, take a bath, and put on a pretty dress." She paused a moment, then snapped her fingers. "Better yet, a dressing gown if you have one. Then fix Eric his favorite dinner."

"I *can't* serve dinner in a dressing gown!" Kirsten protested, blushing just at the thought of it. "What will Eric think?"

"He'll think it's his lucky day," Betty chuckled. "Quit arguing with me and do it. If he asks why you're in your nightclothes, tell him you were warm and wanted to take off your corset. Something like that."

Kirsten moaned. "Tell Eric I wanted to take off my corset? Oh Lord, I'll never make it through this without swooning from embarrassment."

"You'll be fine," Betty said matter-of-factly. "Now, pay attention because I'm not finished."

Kirsten looked at her warily.

"Have dinner by candlelight and afterward, don't, I repeat, *don't* clear up the dishes. Don't even make a *move* toward that kitchen. If Eric gets up from the table and goes outside to have a smoke, you go with him. Do you understand?"

"Yes," Kirsten nodded.

"If he sits down on the porch swing, you sit down next to him . . . and I mean close. Better yet, sit on his lap. That always works."

Kirsten gasped, truly scandalized. "I don't think I can do that, Betty. I'm not trying to be difficult, but unless Eric invited me to, I don't think I could just sit down on his lap!"

"Okay, okay," Betty relented with a wave of her hand. "Forget that. You can save that for later. Just sit down next to him. And make sure that after your bath you put some perfume in your hair and behind your ears so he can smell it."

Kirsten nodded and waited expectantly. "What else?" she prompted when Betty remained silent.

"Believe me, that should be enough," Betty answered

wryly. "You do everything I say and I guarantee you, you won't be a maiden tomorrow morning."

Kirsten colored to the roots of her hair, but her eyes were sparkling with excitement. "Do you really think it will work?"

"If it doesn't, then I'll believe Elsie's right," Betty laughed.

A look of dismay crossed Kirsten's face. "Oh, what if she is?"

"She's not!" Betty retorted firmly. "Believe me, that man is going to be all over you, so you just be ready and don't push him away! If he starts kissing you, you kiss him back! If he starts rubbing his hands all over you, you do the same to him!"

"All right," Kirsten smiled, thinking about how wonderful it would be to run her fingers over the smooth planes of Eric's muscular chest. She'd seen him shirtless many times, and maybe tonight, finally, her dreams of caressing that taut, bronze skin would become reality.

Betty watched the faraway, dreamy expression crossing Kirsten's face and smiled. Everything was going to be just fine. "Okay, my dear," she said, hefting her large bulk out of her chair, "it's time for you to go home and put our plan into action."

Kirsten nodded and rose too. "Betty," she asked shyly, "how do you know all these things?"

Betty laughed. "Honey, I was married for almost thirty-five years. Every woman, no matter how innocent she is in the beginning, learns a few tricks in that length of time. And how did you think I got those four fine sons of mine?"

Kirsten giggled at her suggestive comment. "Thank you," she whispered, giving her a quick kiss. "You're just like the mother I never had."

Betty's eyes pooled and she bit her lip. "Get on with you now," she smiled, giving Kirsten a little push. "Go home and be a wife!"

With a last gay wave, Kirsten disappeared down the

front steps. Betty closed the door behind her and leaned against it for a long moment. Ah, what an experience that little girl had in store! And what a lucky woman she was that her life was going to be spent with a man as sensitive as Eric Wellesley.

With a sigh Betty walked into her kitchen to start dinner for her boarders. Casting her eyes heavenward, she whispered, "If you were listening, Frank, I hope you'll forgive me giving away some of our little secrets. I just want that little girl to be as happy a wife as I always was."

With a pleased little chuckle, she upended a big bowl sitting on the counter and energetically began kneading bread dough, wishing she could turn back the hands of time.

Chapter 17

Kirsten fairly flew home, so anxious was she to put Betty's plan into action. As her horse trotted along the road leading to the farm, she excitedly mulled over how best to make the coming evening a success. Should she use the precious beeswax candles she had found in the sideboard drawer? She wasn't sure if Eric was saving them for something special, but wasn't tonight going to be the most special night of their lives? She nodded decisively as she turned into the yard and pulled the horse to a halt. The candles would certainly lend an air of romance to dinner and she was sure Eric wouldn't be angry once he realized what her intentions were.

It wasn't until she dismounted that Kirsten noticed a strange horse tethered to the hitching post in front of the house. She frowned at the unfamiliar animal. Who was here? Blast it, she thought irritably, if someone was visiting, it was going to slow her down and she needed every available minute if she was to have time to prepare the dinner she had in mind.

With a sigh she started up the back steps, hoping the unwanted visitor was someone to see Eric about buying part of his corn crop. That way she wouldn't feel obliged to serve as hostess and she could get started on a pie. She had counted on Eric being out in the fields, not in the house, but she'd just have to work around his presence.

Kirsten briefly considered whether she should try one of the new recipes Betty had given her, but decided against it. She still wasn't completely confident of her cooking skills and thought that tonight she better stick to recipes she was familiar with. The last thing she wanted to do was start the evening badly by presenting Eric with a culinary disaster.

She entered the house through the kitchen, pulling off the beautiful leather riding gloves Eric had bought for her and tossing them onto the small table. Tiptoeing across the room, she gave the kitchen door a little push, hoping to discreetly discover who was visiting. She peered through the crack and a little gasp of outrage escaped her.

Elsie!

What was *she* doing here—alone in *her* house being entertained by *her* husband?

Kirsten ground her fingernails into her palms as she fought back an immediate surge of anger. Well, by God, there was one way to find out! Pushing through the swinging door, she swept into the parlor.

Eric and Elsie were sitting on a settee facing away from the door, but Kirsten caught Elsie's quick sidelong glance and knew the other girl had heard her enter the room.

"Good afternoon," Kirsten said pleasantly, rounding the back of the sofa and facing the couple.

"Why, Kirsten!" Elsie cried, jumping to her feet in a pretense of surprise. "We didn't hear you come in!"

Kirsten's blazing green eyes flicked from Elsie to Eric as he also jumped up, smiling at her warily. Was that guilt in his eyes? Kirsten's heart sank.

"Elsie stopped just a minute ago to invite us to a party tomorrow night," Eric blurted, a little too quickly for Kirsten's peace of mind.

"That's true," Elsie giggled, placing a possessive hand on Eric's arm, "but, I'm afraid it was far longer than a minute ago." Making a great show of checking her lapel watch, she gasped and added, "In fact, I've been here absolutely forever!"

Eric's head snapped around as he gaped at Elsie, his look of surprise quickly turning to one of anger. He opened his mouth as if to say something, but then seemed to think better of it and closed it again.

His startled reaction was lost on both Kirsten and Elsie, however, as their eyes met; Elsie's, smugly satisfied, and Kirsten's, tormented and outraged.

"It's terrible how time can get away from you, isn't it, Kirsten?" Elsie goaded mercilessly. "Eric was showing me his artwork, and I fear I was so entranced that I just completely lost track of the hour. I must run!"

Kirsten's narrowed eyes widened in sudden astonishment. "Artwork? What artwork?"

"Oh, come now, Kirsten!" Elsie chided, making a sweeping gesture toward the parlor walls. "Surely you aren't as modest about your husband's talent as he is. Why, if I had an artist of Eric's caliber for my husband, I'd be doing everything I could to encourage and help him. I'm really surprised you aren't."

Kirsten glanced briefly toward the south wall as the import of Elsie's words sank in. How many times had she stared at the beautiful paintings which graced this room? She had even asked Eric about the art collection, but never once had he admitted that he was responsible for the magnificent works. She looked over at him now, her expression quizzical and hurt.

"Elsie studied art in New York," he explained. "She thought these were Atwaters and I figured I better set her straight."

"Well, they're every bit as good as Atwater's work," Elsie proclaimed, leaning over to pluck her reticule off the table, where it sat next to a nearly empty coffee cup. "You should be very proud of Eric, Kirsten."

Kirsten bristled at the accusing tone in Elsie's voice. Willing herself to not lose her temper, she said, "So, when is your party, Elsie?"

"Tomorrow night. Seven o'clock sharp. I'm inviting everyone, but I would most especially like you and Eric

203

to be there."

Kirsten blinked, trying to glean the real motivation behind Elsie's words. Why did Elsie want them to be there? Had she thought of some new way to make her look like a fool in front of their friends?

"Well, I don't know," Kirsten hedged. "My snap beans are ready to be canned and I'd planned to do that tomorrow."

"Oh, pooh!" Elsie laughed. "Nobody cans beans on Saturday night. At least, I hope that's not how you spend your evenings, Kirsten."

Kirsten glared at the laughing woman, knowing by her syrupy tone, that's exactly what she suspected. "We'll be there," she said quietly. "That is, unless you have other plans, Eric." She looked hopefully at her husband.

"No," he shrugged, seeming to be unaware of the battle of wills being played out between his wife and her nemesis. "If you want to go, Kirsten, then we will."

"Oh, good!" Elsie crowed, flashing a brilliant smile in Eric's direction. "I was counting on you being there!" The way she stressed 'you' while looking coyly into Eric's eyes made Kirsten think that Elsie actually couldn't care less whether she attended, as long as her husband did.

"Now I really must go," Elsie announced, heading out of the parlor and toward the front door. She put her hand on the doorknob, then turned back to Eric. "Thank you so much for the wonderful afternoon, Eric. I can't remember when I've had such a *stimulating* time."

Kirsten glanced at Eric out of the corner of her eye, trying to interpret the intense look he was giving Elsie. *What was going on between these two?*

"Give my best to Lars, Elsie."

"Yes, I'll do that," Elsie promised. "See you tomorrow. Now don't you dare be late!" With a cursory nod in Kirsten's general direction, Elsie threw Eric one last blinding smile, then sailed down the steps and headed across the yard toward her horse.

Eric closed the door and turned to Kirsten. "Sounds like fun, doesn't it? We haven't all gotten together in a long time."

"Oh, yes," Kirsten replied, unable to keep the sarcasm out of her voice, "it sounds like to truly *stimulating* time."

Eric's brow knitted with confusion. "Look, if you don't want to go, we don't have to."

"No!" Kirsten protested. "I want to go. Maybe not as much as you do, but I want to go."

Eric frowned. "What's that supposed to mean?"

Kirsten looked at him for a long moment, then sighed. "Why didn't you tell me you painted the pictures in the parlor?"

"I don't know. You never asked."

"Oh, and Elsie did?"

"Well, yeah, as a matter of fact, she did."

"I see."

Eric was completely nonplussed by Kirsten's hostility, but decided the best thing to do was ignore it. "So, how was your visit with Betty?" he ventured.

"Fine," Kirsten snapped, and turning away, strode off down the hall to the kitchen. "Just wonderful. *Stimulating,* in fact."

Eric stared after her, watching the kitchen door swing back and forth in her wake. Then, with a little smile, he, too, headed down the hall, pushing open the kitchen door to find her standing by the sink, staring out the window.

"You know, Kirsten, if I didn't know better, I'd say you're sounding a lot like a jealous wife."

Kirsten whirled around to face him. "Jealous! Me? Of what?"

"I don't know," Eric shrugged. "I'm wondering that, too."

"Well, you can just quit wondering. I'm not jealous of anybody or anything, thank you very much!" With a haughty lift of her chin, she again presented her husband with her back.

"Okay," Eric chuckled, delighted by her fit of temper. "I'm going out to the east field. I'll be back in a couple of hours." He waited for a moment, expecting a response, but she didn't turn around. "Did you hear me, Kirsten?"

Kirsten's only response was an infinitesimal nod of her head.

Eric looked at her a moment longer, then walked up behind her. Gently laying his hands on her shoulders, he eased her around to face him. "What's wrong?" he asked.

"Nothing," she answered, twisting out of his grasp and turning back toward the window.

"Don't tell me that," he ordered, turning her around again. "You're mad as hell about something, and I want to know what."

"It's nothing, I told you."

"Yes, it *is* something and we're going to stand here until you tell me what it is I've done."

Eric's obvious concern for her feelings took much of the wind out of Kirsten's sails. "It's just that you told Elsie about your pictures and you never told me. It was embarrassing, that's all."

Eric sighed and took a step back. "Look, Kirsty, I never told you about my painting because you never asked me. It's as simple as that."

"That's not true!" Kirsten protested. "I asked you about the paintings the first week we were married."

Eric shrugged. "You didn't really *ask*. You just said you thought they were pretty. What did you expect me to say? *Well, I'm glad you think so because I've spent the last six winters creating them?*"

"Well, yes," Kirsten blurted, "I guess I would have expected you to say something like that."

A wry little smile tipped a corner of Eric's mouth. "Actually, I was hoping you might guess."

Kirsten planted her hands on her hips. "Now, why would I have done that?"

"Well, they're all of Colorado and you know I grew up there."

"That's true," she conceded, throwing him an apologetic little smile, "I did know that and I suppose I should have guessed. So, who's the beautiful little girl in the picture of the meadow?"

"My baby sister, Paula."

"Sister? I didn't know you have a sister."

"Well, I do," Eric affirmed. "I've also got six brothers."

Kirsten nodded. "You did tell me that. So, why haven't you ever painted any of them?"

"I don't know," Eric shrugged. "Probably because they're all big hulks like me and I never thought they were worth painting."

Kirsten giggled despite herself. "Do you ever see them?"

"Not much. We're all spread out and we don't seem to ever get together in the same place at the same time. Last time I saw everybody was at my father's funeral a couple of years ago."

"I'm sorry," Kirsten murmured, "I didn't know your father had passed away."

"Scarlet fever," Eric said quietly. "He went real quick." A look of intense sadness crossed his face and Kirsten cast about desperately for a new topic that would lighten his mood. "Your sister is a beautiful little girl," she said brightly.

"Well, she *was,*" Eric nodded, the light returning to his eyes. "She's not little anymore. She must be about, let me see, if I'm thirty-two, then she must be . . . my God, she's sixteen already! Poor Ma!"

"Why 'poor Ma'?"

Eric laughed "'Poor Ma' because Paula was always wild—even when she was a little kid. I can't imagine what a handful she must be by now. God help us if Paula's discovered men! I can't imagine Ma having to put up with all that nonsense at her age."

"How old is your mother?" Kirsten questioned. She

was delighted by the course their conversation had suddenly taken. Eric had never talked much about his family and she had always been curious, but today was the first time she had felt comfortable enough with him to ask.

"Well, she's no kid. I think she was thirty-nine when Paula was born so she's got to be on the far side of fifty. Too old to be worrying about a sixteen-year-old little hellcat rolling around in the hay with one of the ranch hands, that's for sure!"

Kirsten blushed as the thought ran through her head that she wished Paula's older brother would show a little interest in 'rolling around in the hay'—unless, of course, he already *was*— with someone other than herself.

This devastating thought instantly wiped the happy smile off Kirsten's face and a sudden, weighty silence descended. Finally, Eric cleared his throat and said, "Well, like I said, I better get back to work." He waited for a long moment, hoping Kirsten would ask another question, but when it became obvious their cozy little conversation was over, he picked up his hat and walked out the back door.

After he left, Kirsten poured herself a cup of coffee and dropped wearily into a chair at the kitchen table.

Was there something going on between Elsie and Eric? And, if so, why had Elsie told Kirsten that Eric was incapable of having a normal romantic relationship with a woman? Unless . . . unless . . . the thought was so painful that Kirsten could hardly bring herself to think it . . . unless Elsie had simply lied to her so Kirsten wouldn't even try to win Eric's love. That way Elsie could continue to have him all to herself.

But if that was the case, why hadn't Eric just married Elsie? As far as Kirsten knew, he had never even tried to win Elsie away from Lars. Why? Because Lars was his best friend? That could be it. Eric was far too honorable to try to steal away his best friend's fiancée. But not too honorable to cuckold him?

Kirsten clapped her hands to her flaming cheeks. "What are you thinking?" she chastised herself. "You're assuming they're lovers and you have no basis for it at all!"

But, if they weren't, then why did Elsie always seem to be around? And why had Eric been sitting so close to her on the settee? And why had he invited Elsie to have lunch with them that day at the restaurant? Why?

Kirsten's tortured thoughts tumbled over one another till she was sure she would go crazy. Jumping up from her chair, she paced the kitchen like a caged animal.

"All right!" she cried out to the empty room, "I give up! If they want each other that badly, they're welcome. I'll not interfere.

Mentally conceding defeat, Kirsten slumped back down on the chair and buried her head in her hands. How could she not interfere? Eric was *her* husband! And, whether he cared for her or not, she loved him. *So,* whispered the familiar little voice, *isn't he worth fighting for?*

"You're damn right he is!" Kirsten proclaimed. Jumping up with new resolve, she hastened toward the stairs, intending to begin her preparations for tonight according to Betty's plan. But by the time she was halfway up the staircase, she had changed her mind. If she attempted to inflame Eric's passion tonight, might he not think it was merely jealousy prodding her?

Kirsten paused, her hand clutching the bannister. Maybe she should wait a day or two. Eric already thought she was jealous. The last thing she wanted to do was reinforce that. No. Better to wait until this afternoon's episode had faded from his mind.

What are you afraid of? That he'll turn you away?

"I'm not afraid!" Kirsten declared. "But what difference does a couple of days make? Besides, this way I'll be able to see how he acts toward Elsie tomorrow night." Nodding, she continued on down the hall, satisfied with her decision.

"The day after tomorrow," she murmured. "All the questions will be answered. By Monday at this time, I'll know whether Eric *can* make love to me, but, more importantly, I'll know whether he *wants* to."

It was a terrifying thought.

Chapter 18

"Your tarts are delicious, Kirsten. It was so thoughtful of you to bring them."

Kirsten looked up from Elsie Swenson's heavily laden dining room table to find her friend, Susan, standing at her elbow. "Thank you," she smiled. "Now that the apples are ripe, I finally have something to make the filling out of. Eric brought home a whole bushel the other day so I thought I'd make a batch."

"Well, they're absolutely wonderful. I think we should all get together at your house sometime so you can teach us how to bake like this."

Kirsten laughed. The thought of anyone wanting her to teach them to cook was almost comical. She'd have to remember to tell Eric. After some of the disastrous meals she'd put in front of him during the first days of their marriage, he was sure to get a kick out of it.

She glanced over to where her husband stood talking with several men, a beer glass dangling casually from his fingers. *Tomorrow night,* she thought, a little shiver of excitement and apprehension coursing through her. *Tomorrow night, I'll know.*

Suddenly a sharp clapping sound jolted Kirsten out of her reverie. "Attention, everyone. I have an important announcement to make."

Every head turned toward Elsie who was standing in the parlor doorway, looking extraordinarily pleased with herself. Susan sidled closer to Kirsten and whispered, "Oh, Lord, what do you suppose she's done now that we're all going to feel obliged to compliment her for?"

Kirsten giggled and looked over at Susan with a knowing nod.

Elsie again clapped her hands to ensure she had the full attention of everyone in the room, then said, "I'm sure you are all wondering about the reason for my party tonight."

"Notice how now that it's a success, it's *her* party," Susan muttered under her breath. "If it was a disaster, I'm sure she'd announce that it had been all Lars's idea and she'd been against it from the first."

Kirsten bit the inside of her lip to keep from laughing out loud at Susan's wry comment. "Shh!" she hissed, throwing her friend a shaming glance, "someone is going to hear you."

"I don't care," Susan whispered back, "I just wish she'd get her stupid announcement over with— whatever is it—so I can get back to that plate of tarts!"

Kirsten clapped her hand over her mouth and turned away, trying hard to get control of herself while Susan rolled her eyes and turned back toward Elsie, clasping her hands in front of her in a great show of interest.

Elsie had noticed the mirthful exchange between Kirsten and Susan and had paused in her dramatic little speech, obviously hoping to embarrass the girls into silence. She waited in frowning impatience until she was satisfied that both women were again looking at her raptly. With a condescending smile, she continued. "I'm sure that some of you think you know what I'm going to say—and you're right."

She paused and looked around at the little clusters of women gathered about the room, noting with pleasure their various expressions: shock, anger, embarrassment, and disappointment. It was a grand moment!

She drew out her moment of triumph as long as possible, then, with an expression of delighted superiority, declared, "That's right, ladies. It's time to pull out your pocketbooks because *I* am expecting a baby in the spring!"

The effect of Elsie's bold statement was a chorus of gasps from the ladies and looks of complete bafflement from their husbands.

No one was more astounded by Elsie's scandalous announcement than her husband Olaf. As the room erupted in conversation, he suddenly found himself surrounded by the other men, clapping him on the back and offering congratulations.

"Good job, old boy!"

"Didn't know you had it in you, Swenson!"

"Thought for sure I'd be the first. Sure have been trying!"

"Me, too, but looks like we've been beaten fair and square."

Olaf accepted the men's good-natured felicitations with a stunned smile, all the time wondering how this could have happened. Only he knew how seldom Elsie allowed him into her bed. How many times had it been? Three? Four? Certainly not enough to put her in the family way. But, looking over quizzically at his smiling wife, he realized it must be true. Surely Elsie wouldn't lie about such a thing! He just wished she'd thought to mention it to him first—and in private. Her announcement had been as much a shock to him as to everyone else—and he didn't like being caught so off guard regarding such an intimate event.

But as more and more men gathered around, hoisting their beer steins and congratulating him on his prowess, he relaxed and threw Elsie a broad grin. If his wife was proud enough to tell the whole world of her condition, then he guessed he should be, too! But, damn! It would have been nice to have a little warning!

Gradually, the men drifted away, returning to their wives' sides as they bent their heads toward their spouses and asked what Elsie meant by the "get out your pocketbooks" comment.

Eric was no different. Walking up behind Kirsten, he put a hand on her shoulder and whispered, "What do you have in your pocketbook that Elsie wants?"

Mortified, Kirsten stammered, "She wants ten dollars."

Before Eric had a chance to question Kirsten's shocking response, Elsie's voice again rose above the din. "Since I'm sure all of you men are asking your wives the same question, why don't I explain?"

Again, twenty-seven heads swiveled toward her, and this time she had everyone's full attention.

"A long time ago, we brides each wagered ten dollars that we'd be the first among the group to get, ah, in the family way. Since, obviously, I've won the bet, I'll be collecting tonight."

As one, the men turned disbelieving eyes toward their wives. "Ten dollars? You wagered ten dollars?" Gustav Johnson's voice was loud with outrage as he looked accusingly at his wife, Sophie. "Do you have any idea how many seeds I could buy vith ten dollars?"

Never at a loss for words, Sophie planted her hands on her hips and declared, "Don't you look at me like that, Gus Johnson. It was my money and I'll spend it any way I want to!"

"Trow it away, yu mean," Gustav muttered angrily.

A general hubbub broke out as all over the room, voices were suddenly raised—some accusing, some defensive. But a deathly stillness suddenly dropped over the group as Olga Johannson stood up from where she was sitting on a ladder-back chair and said, "How are you so sure you're the winner, Elsie? Maybe there are others of us in the room who are in the same condition but are too modest to say so in front of half the town."

Elsie's face paled. "Well," she blustered, "if there is anyone else, say so now."

No one moved.

"Well?" Elsie demanded, her bravado quickly returning in the face of the heavy silence. "Anyone?"

Several husbands turned hopeful eyes toward their wives, but were met with quick, negative head shakes as many faces flamed with embarrassment.

"Well, then," Elsie smiled, relieved that her thunder was not about to be stolen, "Then I guess that's that. Now I understand that not all of you have the money with you tonight, and that's perfectly all right. I'll just come around in the next couple of days and collect it."

"Elsie!" Olaf pleaded quietly, mortified by his wife's brazen handling of this whole unseemly affair. "I think you've said enough!"

Elsie shot him a scathing look, then turned back to the crowd with a syrupy sweet smile. "Just pay me when it's convenient, ladies. I know none of you would have entered into the wager if you weren't good for the money."

Her gaze circled the room, coming to rest on Kirsten with such meaningful intensity that the rest of the girls gasped in astonished outrage.

Ironically, the one person in the room who missed Elsie's pointed glance was Kirsten. During the entire course of the shocking dissertation, she had not taken her eyes off the floor. What she had most feared had happened. Where was she going to get the money to pay off her wager? She couldn't ask Eric—especially considering how things stood between them with regards to marital intimacy! Never in her life had she been so embarrassed.

But Kirsten underestimated her husband. Not only was he aware of her embarrassment, but he was also furious that Elsie would put everyone in the room in such an uncomfortable position. Giving Kirsten's shoulder a little squeeze, he leaned close and said, "Did you bet?"

Kirsten nodded without raising her eyes, looking up only when she heard him stride purposely across the parlor. When he reached the doorway where Elsie and Olaf stood, he reached into his coat pocket and withdrew a flat wallet from which he withdrew a ten-dollar bill. "Congratulations to you both," he said loudly, smiling and holding forth the bill. "I hope it's a boy."

Then, returning his wallet to his pocket, he walked back to Kirsten and casually draped an arm around her shoulder. "Do you want to go home now?" he whispered, his lips close to her hair.

"Please," she nodded, looking up at him gratefully.

"Come on then, let's get your wrap." With a hand under her elbow, he guided her toward the front door.

Out of the corner of her eye, Elsie saw Eric rummaging through the pile of shawls by the front door and hastened over. "You can't leave already!" she protested, as Eric plucked a soft magenta shawl from the pile and laid it across Kirsten's shoulders. "Why, we haven't even started the dancing yet!"

"Kirsten's tired," Eric responded shortly, "she's been canning beans all day."

"Oh, that's right," Elsie clucked, her face a study in condescension, "she did mention that yesterday when I was over."

The reminder of Elsie's solitary visit to Eric made Kirsten's lips thin with suppressed anger. "Thank you very much for the lovely evening," she said quietly, holding her hand out. "And, again, congratulations on your wonderful news."

"Oh, but you just can't go!" Elsie repeated. "Why, the evening's hardly begun. Listen, Kirsten, if you're tired, why don't you just go upstairs and rest. Surely you don't want to ruin Eric's good time just because you're too tired to join in."

"Thanks for the offer," Eric said quickly, "but I've got corn to harvest and it's getting late."

Elsie frowned, her displeasure obvious. "Will we see you at church tomorrow?"

Eric shook his head. "Don't think so. I think we'll just spend a quiet day at home."

"Harvesting corn and canning beans?" Elsie said snidely, distraught that she couldn't convince Eric to

216

stay long enough that she could dance with him.

"Yeah," Eric smiled. "Something like that. Thanks again for a great party. Good night."

Before Elsie could form another protest, he put his hand on the small of Kirsten's back and ushered her out the front door.

The ride home was quiet with only the chorus of late summer crickets breaking the peaceful silence. The early September night was balmy, and a full moon lit the sky until it was almost like daylight. Kirsten waited in the yard while Eric bedded down the horses, enjoying the beautiful evening as she drank in the sweet scent of newly mown hay. As they walked into the house together, Eric finally broke the long silence.

"Want to sit on the porch for a while before we call it a day?" he suggested.

Kirsten turned to him with a look of pleased surprise. "That would be wonderful. I'll make some tea."

"I've got a better idea," Eric smiled, and walked over to the sideboard in the dining room, pulling open one of the intricately carved doors and reaching inside for a beautiful cut-glass decanter. "I have some excellent cognac that my brother Miles sent me for Christmas last year. Let's have a snifter."

Kirsten had never tasted cognac in her life and had no idea what a "snifter" was, but not wanting to ruin her husband's mellow mood, she nodded. "If you like."

Looking at her over his shoulder, Eric allowed his gaze to ripple over her. "I like a lot."

Kirsten blushed and turned away, bedazzled by the warm intensity in her husband's eyes. Walking out onto the porch, she perched on the edge of one of the chairs for a moment, then crossed over to the swing. She had just settled herself on one end when Eric came out the front door, holding two bowl-shaped glasses filled with an amber liquid.

"Ever had cognac?" he asked, extending a glass toward her.

"No," she replied, shaking her head.

Slowly, Eric eased himself down on the swing, just close enough that their thighs touched. "Sip it slowly, and I think you'll enjoy it."

Kirsten took a small sip and gasped in surprise as the liquor blazed a fiery trail down her throat. Closing her eyes to blink back the tears which had suddenly formed, she wheezed, "I'm sorry, Eric, but I don't think so."

Eric chuckled and took a sip from his own glass. "I told you to drink it slowly," he admonished gently. "Try it again, it gets better."

The last thing Kirsten wanted was another sip of the liquid fire, but in an effort to please her husband she tried it again. Eric was right—it *was* better. This time it didn't burn as it slid down her throat, but, rather, she experienced a warm, glowing sensation which seemed to spread out from her stomach all the way to her fingertips.

Eric smiled contentedly as he saw her reaction. "Like it?"

"Yes," Kirsten answered, surprised to find that she did. "As a matter of fact, I think I do."

Eric smiled and leaned back in the swing, giving it a lazy push with his toe.

Kirsten couldn't remember when she'd felt so relaxed. Taking another sip of her drink, she sighed and looked up at the huge moon. "It's a beautiful night."

Eric looked up also. "Some moon, isn't it? Not quite a harvest moon, but getting close."

"Ummm," Kirsten agreed, "the sky is so big here. In New York it never looked so big, or so black."

"I think it's because there are more lights there. They reflect off the ground somehow, and the night sky doesn't look the same."

Kirsten shrugged, too relaxed to ponder the point

any further. For a long time they sat in silence, looking up at the moon and enjoying each other's company.

"Kirsty, why did you get in on that bet?"

Instantly, the tranquillity Kirsten was feeling disappeared, and she looked at Eric, her expression wary. "I'm really sorry about that," she gulped. "I'll find a way to pay you back, somehow."

"I don't care about the money. I just wondered why you bet."

Without her even realizing it, the cognac had worked its insidious magic on Kirsten, loosening both her tongue and her inhibitions. "I figured I'd have a chance to win."

Eric looked at her for a long moment, his heart in his throat. "Pretty hard to win a game you're not even playing," he murmured.

Kirsten shook her head. "It was a long time ago. We made that bet on the train before we ever arrived in Rose Meadow, long before I found out you can't . . ." Even in her slightly inebriated state, Kirsten realized what she'd almost said and her voice trailed off.

Eric suddenly leaned forward, causing the swing to sway crazily. "Can't what?"

"Never mind. It was a dumb thing to do and I'm sorry. I promise I'll pay you back." Lifting her nearly empty glass to her lips, she drained it of the last of its contents. "This is really good. Could I have a little more?"

"No," Eric responded sharply. Reaching out, he cupped Kirsten's chin in his big, work-hardened hand and said, "Now, tell me. What is it that you think I *can't* do?"

The warm glow from the cognac was rapidly disappearing in the wake of Eric's rising anger, and Kirsten shifted uncomfortably on the hard swing. "I don't want to talk about it."

"Well, you better talk about it! Now, I'm asking you one more time. What is it that you think I can't do?"

Kirsten looked at him for a long moment, cursing the

cognac. "Make love," she murmured.

"What?"

"Make love!"

Eric gaped at her in disbelief. "You think I can't make love? Why?"

"Someone told me you couldn't," Kirsten whispered, staring down at her clenched hands.

"What? Look at me so I can hear you!"

With a deep sigh Kirsten looked up, meeting Eric's angry, bewildered eyes. "Someone told me that you have a . . . problem and you can't have a normal relationship with a woman."

"WHAT?" Eric jumped to his feet, his hands clenched at his sides and his eyes blazing. "WHO TOLD YOU THAT?"

"It's not important," Kirsten said.

"What do you mean, it's not important! Someone tells my wife that I'm incapable of making love to her, and she says it's not important? What made you believe such nonsense, Kirsten?"

Kirsten again dropped her gaze.

"Answer me!"

Despite her efforts to quell them, tears rose in Kirsten's eyes. "Well, you've never tried to make love to me, and so, naturally, I assumed . . ."

"I've never tried because you've always acted like you didn't want me to."

Kirsten looked up at the outraged man and the last vestiges of the cognac fled as her own anger flashed. "Well, what did you expect me to believe? The day we were married, you brought me home and told me that little room was mine and you've never come to me or given me any sign that you wanted me!"

"Do you think I wanted you to sleep in that damn room? I was just trying to be considerate since we'd gotten off to such a bad start. I didn't think you'd stay with me once you found out what farm life was like and I didn't want to complicate the issue."

"That's rubbish, Eric," Kirsten flared. "You didn't

220

want to sleep with me because you didn't want to feel obligated. You were hoping I'd leave!"

"Now, wait just one damn minute," Eric raged, looming over her, "you're changing your story here. You just told me you thought I didn't sleep with you because I'm incapable of fulfilling my husbandly duties!"

"Well, that, too," Kirsten admitted.

"I don't believe this!" Eric growled, pacing the length of the porch as he thought about the nights he'd lain in his empty bed and ached for the woman sleeping so peacefully down the hall. The nights he'd crept into her room and stood at the end of her narrow little bed, wanting her so badly he could hardly breathe . . .

Marching back across the porch, he railed, "Whoever told you I'm incapable of making love to you was lying, lady, and if you want me to, I'll prove it right now!"

Kirsten looked up into his red, angry face and shook her head, not fully understanding what he was saying. "What do you mean?"

"I mean that all you have to do is say the word and I'll carry you up those stairs and show you just how 'capable' I am!"

Kirsten was speechless in the face of his blatant suggestion and merely stared up at him, dumbfounded.

"Answer me, Kirsten," he pursued, leaning over her in the darkness. "Do you want to make love?"

"Now?"

"Yes. Right now."

"No," she lied.

Her rejection hit Eric like a cannonball in the chest, but he gritted his teeth, determined that she wouldn't see his pain. "That's what I thought."

He turned away, intending to return to the house, but her next words stopped him dead in his tracks. "Do you want to make love, Eric?"

For the briefest moment, Eric closed his eyes, his head reeling at Kirsten's impulsive question. *Did he want to make love?* Oh, God, if she only knew! He wanted to scream, "Yes, Yes, Yes!" but common sense finally won out. *Not now, Wellesley. Not like this when you're both angry.*

Turning back to face her, he asked impersonally, "Now?"

Kirsten nodded.

Gazing at her upturned face, he took a deep breath and responded in an almost inaudible voice.

"No."

A surge of disappointment coursed through Kirsten and she released a long breath she hadn't even realized she was holding. "That's what I thought," she said quietly, dropping her gaze.

"But, let's get one thing clear," Eric interjected hotly. "It's not because I can't. It's because I don't want to."

"I understand," Kirsten nodded, rising from the swing and picking up her empty brandy snifter. "If you'll excuse me, I think I'll retire."

"Fine. Sleep well, *Mrs. Wellesley.*"

Chapter 19

Not because I can't, because I don't want to!

Long after Kirsten heard Eric stomp up the stairs and slam his bedroom door, she lay in her small bed thinking about his hurtful words. He really *didn't* want her. He had told her plainly enough. Only a fool would attempt to prolong this sham of a marriage. It was time she faced facts.

He doesn't love you. He doesn't even desire you.

But even as she admitted this hard truth, other thoughts crept into her mind, giving the lie to this conclusion.

Betty's words: *"He's quiet—kind of shy."*

And Sarah's: *"He must really care for you to grab you out of a church pew and make you marry him even after you told him you didn't want to!"*

And Eric's own: *"I never tried to make love to you because you always acted like you didn't want me to."*

Kirsten turned over restlessly, tormented by her thoughts. Was she to blame for the shambles of her marriage? *Had* she been cold and aloof, leading her husband to believe she would reject his attentions?

With a dejected sigh, she flopped over on her back, nodding to the ceiling. The answer was yes. At least partially. True, Eric *could* have been more aggressive toward her, could have insisted that she fulfill her conjugal duties. But would she have wanted him to

223

force her?

No, of course not.

Then what *did* she want?

To be wooed, seduced, romanced! she thought stubbornly. But, what had she done to encourage that seduction?

Nothing!

Without even consciously realizing her intent, Kirsten threw back the covers and sat up, reaching for a light robe which lay on the end of the bed.

She cinched the satin sash around her waist and shoved her feet into her slippers. She would talk to Eric. Tonight. Right now. She needed to tell him that she wanted their marriage to work, and tomorrow morning was too late. By then he would probably have decided to send her back to New York—regardless of what she said.

It wasn't until she was stepping into the hall that she realized what a chance she was taking. It was possible that Eric would refuse to listen—would resent her intrusion into his private chamber. She knew he wasn't asleep yet because she could hear him moving about in his room, but what if he wouldn't open the door to her? Kirsten paused. Did she actually dare go to him?

For a long moment she stood motionless, paralyzed with indecision. What choice did she have? She had to know how he felt, and the only way to find out was to ask him.

Taking a deep breath, she girded up her courage and started down the hall.

She hadn't gone more than three steps when she heard Eric's door open and saw his shadowy figure emerge into the hall. For a moment, both of them stopped, looking at each other from opposite ends of the long corridor. Then, in the same split second, they both started forward, quickly swallowing up the chasm between them.

When Eric was less than a yard away, Kirsten let out her breath in a rush and said, "Eric, I want . . ."

She never finished her sentence because suddenly she found herself caught up in a crushing embrace. Eric buried his hands in her fiery hair, his lips a mere inch above hers. "I know, sweetheart, I want it too."

"But, Eric, I have to tell you . . ."

Again, he silenced her. "Don't talk, Kirsty. Just kiss me."

And she did. For what seemed like an eternity, they stood in the darkness of the hall and kissed—a gentle touching of lips which soon blossomed into an eager seeking of tongues and culminated in a fusing of their mouths that sucked the very breath from them.

When Eric finally lifted his lips, Kirsten was shaking and dizzy, and his breath was coming in short, harsh rasps. Without a word, he bent and scooped her into his arms, pivoting on his heel and heading back for his bedroom as she wrapped her arms around his neck and laid her head against his bare, bronze chest.

A single candle burning on the night stand cast the dark planes of Eric's chiseled face into sharp relief, and as Kirsten gazed up into his ebony eyes she realized that she had never wanted anything as much as she wanted this handsome, enigmatic man to make her his.

In three long strides, Eric reached the huge, canopied bed and gently lowered Kirsten to its softness. Settling a hip on the edge of the mattress, he placed his hands on either side of her face and again claimed her lips in a searing kiss.

Kirsten felt like she was drowning. The times that Eric had kissed her in the past had always stirred her, but never had she dreamed that a kiss could evoke the feelings she was experiencing now. Her body felt heavy and languid, as if she were drifting in a pool of thick, warm liquid, and yet every nerve was alive and seemed to be centered in her lips, breasts, and deep within the core of her.

She could feel a hot, pulsing need between her thighs, frightening in its intensity. Unconsciously, she shifted her hips toward Eric's thigh, somehow needing to rub that part of herself against him.

Eric felt her sudden shift toward him at the same moment that the pressure of his erection straining against the front of his jeans became almost unbearable. Needing desperately to release himself from the painful constraint, he rose, pulling his mouth away from Kirsten's and panting, "I have to stop a minute . . ."

Eric's breathless words immediately pulled Kirsten back from the sea of passion on which she floated, and alarmed but groggy, she raised herself on an elbow. "Is . . . something wrong?" she stammered, hardly able to form a lucid thought.

"No," he rasped, turning away and quickly unbuttoning the tight jeans, "I just need to get out of these." Shimmying the pants down over his slim hips, he threw back his head and let out a groan of relief as his huge, impassioned manhood was suddenly freed from its torturous confines.

With his back turned to her, Kirsten was not sure what was going on, but she was terrified that she had somehow caused the agony he now seemed to be enduring. What was wrong? Why was she enjoying this so much when it was obviously hurting him? She had always heard that it was the man who enjoyed lovemaking, not the woman. So, what was she doing wrong that her husband was in pain?

"Are you all right?" she asked again, her voice quaking. "Am I doing something that's hurting you?"

With a soft, wry chuckle, Eric answered, "Yeah, you are . . . and I hope you'll keep doing it for about the next fifty years."

Kirsten looked at him in complete bafflement, but as he turned back toward her he smiled and, satisfied that he was all right, her eyes drooped closed in anticipation of returning to the sexual trance she had been enjoying.

Eric had prudently left on his light, linen undergarment, not wanting to scare his innocent wife. He was an extraordinarily well-endowed man, and it caused him real concern as he gazed at the tiny woman awaiting him. Although all his brothers were generously endowed with masculine attributes, even they teased him about his size, calling him "Hose Boy" and "The Stud." Eric had always felt that it was somehow unfair that he, the least flamboyant member of his family, had been granted such a "gift," and deep down he knew that embarrassment over his size had played a large part in his reluctance to get involved in a serious relationship with a woman.

Now, gazing over at the beautiful girl who awaited him in his big bed, the old fears of his youth arose. *God, please don't let her be put off!* His silent plea was so heartfelt that Kirsten, opening her eyes a crack to see what was delaying him, read it on his face.

"Eric," she murmured, "are you *sure* you're okay?"

"Yes," he smiled, pushing his fears to the back of his mind as he slipped into bed next to her. "I'm better than okay—better than I've been in years."

Kirsten smiled in pleased delight and reached out her hand, running her fingertips gently across his massive chest as she'd longed to do for so many months.

Eric closed his eyes, succumbing to the rapture of her touch. Then with a soft smile he sat up, pulling her up with him and kissing her as he dropped his hands to her waist, untying the sash to her robe.

When the sash came loose, Kirsten shrugged the robe off her shoulders, lifting her hips so that he could remove it from beneath her. For a long moment they stared at each other, then, as if in unspoken agreement, Kirsten raised her arms, and Eric ran his hands up her sides, sweeping her nightgown over her head and baring her body to his hungry gaze.

For a long moment he feasted on her delicate beauty. Then, almost shyly, he reached out and feathered his fingers across her breasts, causing her to gasp in response. He paused a moment, afraid that she would pull away. But she remained as she was, and, relieved, he smiled and leaned forward, kissing her breasts and

227

rubbing his face against their exquisite softness.

With a groan of bliss Kirsten lay back in the pillows. She knew she had never felt anything as sensuous as Eric's lips against her breasts and was sure that this must be the zenith of sexual rapture. But in the next moment Eric showed her how wrong she was. As he leaned toward her, she was vaguely aware of his warm breath against her erect nipple, and then all thought fled as his mouth closed over her. Kirsten nearly crawled up the bed's carved mahogany headboard as Eric's warm, wet tongue swirled in small circles around the hard little bud.

He chuckled softly at her reaction and dipped his head lower still, nibbling and kissing her stomach until she squirmed away and gasped, "What are you doing?"

"Making love to you, sweethheart," he whispered, his mouth continuing its splendorous torturing of the sensitive skin on her abdomen. "How do you like it so far?"

Running her hands over the ebony silk of his hair, Kirsten pressed against him and sighed, "I like it very much, but I don't know if I can stand much more."

Eric glanced up at her, his eyes full of laughter. "Baby, we've hardly even begun."

Kirsten's eyes widened as again her stomach muscles contracted in reaction to her husband's passionate assault. "Oh, Eric," she moaned.

Immediately he lifted his head, moving up the bed until he lay next to her. "Kirsty," he murmured, his voice serious, "do you want me to stop?"

Kirsten's eyes flew open. "No! It's just that when you do that, it makes me feel so funny! Like I want . . . something . . ."

Eric smiled, knowing his innocent little wife had no idea what she was asking for.

"I know," he whispered.

"You do?"

He nodded.

"How can you know what I want? I don't even know myself."

"I do," he assured her. "Just lie still a moment and I'll show you."

Kirsten felt him move down her body again, but, still, she was unprepared for the ripple of delight which coursed through her as his long fingers tangled themselves in the fleecy down at the juncture of her thighs. Her entire body broke out in gooseflesh, and instinctively she tightened her thighs.

Eric frowned as she drew away. Removing his hand from where it rested so intimately against her, he murmured, "Kirsten, look at me."

Slowly, Kirsten opened her eyes, her expression a mixture of fear and anticipation. "Sweetheart, if you don't want to do this, we won't, but you have to tell me now."

Kirsten didn't immediately answer, and for a terrible moment Eric thought she was going to tell him to stop. But he didn't realize the level of passion his little bride harbored for him and was astonished and delighted when she smiled, shook her head, and put his hand back where it had been, drawing her knees up and relaxing her thighs.

At her overt invitation Eric's passion flared anew, and he stretched out full length against her, reaching down to where she now lay open to him. Pulling her tightly against him, he gave her a blazing kiss while his fingers invaded her intimately.

Kirsten was wet and ready for him, and at his touch she groaned with the first blush of ecstacy. Her low moan, coupled with the beauty of her glistening body in the candlelight, was almost more than Eric could bear. He felt his erection swell and strengthen, pressing with heated demand against the front of his underwear. Swallowing hard, he knew the time had come. Slowly, he rose to his knees and whispered, "Kirsty, baby, open your eyes."

Very slowly, Kirsten's passion glazed eyes opened.

"Why did you stop?" she whispered. "Is it over?"

Despite his trepidation Eric couldn't help but laugh. "No, sweetheart, we haven't even started, but, before we do, I want you to look at me."

"I am," Kirsten said vacantly, reaching out and running a nail across the tightly corded muscles covering his ribs.

"No," he groaned, gently removing her hand before he completely lost control and buried himself in her that very second. "I mean, really look at me. All of me, Kirsten."

Perplexed, Kirsten sat up.

Satisfied that he had her attention, Eric stood up, turned away for a moment and released the button on his underwear, causing them to drop to the floor. Frowning at the intimidating size of his erection, he took a deep breath and turned back toward the bed.

Kirsten's eyes immediately dropped to the center of his body and, for a moment, she stared in rapt fascination at the bold, jutting proof of his desire for her. It was the most magnificent sight she'd ever seen. Looking up into his tense face, she whispered, "You're beautiful, Eric. More beautiful than I ever imagined."

For a moment Eric just stood and stared at her, feeling like this might be the happiest moment of his life. In the past every woman who had ever seen him naked had either gasped in astonishment or made a lewd comment about his uncanny size. Never, ever, had any woman told him he was beautiful. He'd heard "incredible," "unbelievable," "amazing," but never, ever "beautiful."

With a sigh of relief and joy, Eric bent a knee on the bed and gathered Kirsten into his embrace. Like someone had pulled the plug on a dam, his words tumbled out in a torrent. " . . . the most fabulous woman in the world . . . try not to hurt you . . . God, you're beautiful . . ."

Kirsten couldn't imagine what had unleashed such a torrent of verbosity in her usually uncommunicative

230

husband, but at this moment the last thing she wanted to do was talk. Pushing him away, she looked down at his throbbing arousal and whispered, "May I . . . may I touch you?"

Eric's stream of conversation came to an abrupt halt. Closing his eyes in sheer rapture, he lay back. As Kirsten looked at him with hopeful eyes, he smiled and nodded.

Slowly, tentatively, she touched him, reveling in the satiny smooth softness of his skin as she stroked him. Gently, she ran her fingers up his length, pausing as she reached the tip. Looking at Eric's dark, lusting eyes, she said softly, "Make love to me."

It was all Eric needed. Pulling Kirsten down on top of him, he gently rolled her over, murmuring encouragement and praise as he softly directed her in the ways of love.

Kirsten was an apt pupil. Wildly in love with her husband she wanted very badly to please him, to chase away the ghosts of the other women she was afraid he'd known—and show him that she was all he'd ever need.

With a quick prayer that he wouldn't hurt her, Eric slowly, carefully entered her, then was immediately seized by a pang of guilt as Kirsten gasped in pain. He withdrew quickly, mortified that he'd already hurt her when he hadn't even fully entered her. "I'm sorry, baby," he whispered, his mouth close to her ear, "I know it hurts. You're small, I'm big, and the first time is the hardest."

Kirsten nodded, trying to blink back the tears that the searing pain had brought to her eyes. With a determined little smile that said more than words ever could, she gently guided him back to her. Taking a deep breath, she hooked her heels behind his thighs and propelled herself forward, driving her husband's full length into her. Eric felt the delicate tissue rip and knew she must be in agony, but Kirsten didn't make a sound, except to let out a sharp breath and whisper, "There, it's done."

That single moment was one of the most profound in Eric Wellesley's life. Overcome with emotion, he lay quietly atop his wife, waiting for her to adjust to his huge presence within her and cursing himself for the tears that he saw pooling at the corners of her eyes.

But Kirsten wouldn't allow him to feel guilty and looked up at him with a tremulous smile. "Is there more, or is it over already?"

"Oh, God, Kirsty . . ."

Not fully understanding the depth of her husband's emotions, Kirsten wiggled her hips slightly and said, "If there's more, Eric, then I want it."

And with an exultant grin Eric granted her wish. Setting an easy, rocking rhythm, he showed his wife the full glory of love, clamping down hard on his raging lust until he was sure she was ready for him. Then, with a long, shuddering groan, he poured himself into her, gifting her with his life's essence.

Afterward they lay together quietly, languishing in sublime contentment. So much time passed that Eric thought Kirsten was asleep, and was surprised when he heard her giggle.

"What's so funny?"

"Oh, nothing," she sighed, "I was just thinking that now I now know exactly what 'capable' means!"

Eric laughed and hugged her close. "I didn't hurt you too badly, did I?"

"It hurt a little," she admitted.

"I'm sorry, sweetheart. It'll get easier, I promise."

Kirsten closed her eyes, trying hard to stay awake. "Eric?"

"Umm?"

"I just have one question about it."

"What?"

"When can we do it again?"

A soft chuckle rumbled in Eric's chest, and he brushed a light kiss against her temple. "A little later, baby, after you've rested a bit."

Kirsten smiled and nodded sleepily.

Raising himself on an elbow, Eric blew out the candle, then settled back into the pillows, pulling Kirsten against him until their bodies were nestled intimately and her head rested on his shoulder.

"Kirsty?"

"Hmm?"

"You're wonderful."

Chapter 20

Someone was kissing her, and it felt wonderful. His lips were smooth, soft, and warm. They gently caressed her, feathering lightly over her mouth, teasing the corners until she smiled.

Determinedly, she kept her eyes shut, knowing that if she opened them, the magical kisses would disappear and she would find herself in her small bed in her lonely room.

Her dream lover abandoned her lips and moved down her throat, breathing warm, sweet air against her neck before lowering his mouth to softly caress her breast. He had never done this before . . . never left her mouth . . . never touched her breasts. The sensations his warm mouth was invoking were almost more than she could bear, and despite her resolve her eyes opened.

With a great rush of delight, Kirsten realized she wasn't in her empty room . . . and she most certainly wasn't alone. Looking down, she met Eric's soft, dark eyes smiling up at her.

"Good morning," he whispered, placing a soft kiss on her cheek near her nose.

Kirsten was so bedazzled that her long-held dream of waking up in Eric's arms had actually come true that she found herself unable to answer. Instead, she reached up and gently stroked his tousled hair, pushing back a lock which had fallen over his forehead while he slept.

"Did you sleep well?" she murmured.

"Better than I can ever remember," he nodded, running his thumb provocatively down the side of her breast.

Kirsten held her breath, her eyes closing in anticipatory rapture as she waited for him to touch her erect nipple. But Eric just grinned wickedly and traced a wide circle around her breast, skirting the hard, straining nub and watching with delight as Kirsten waited and waited . . . and waited.

Gooseflesh rose all over her body, and a flush of color suffused her neck and traveled down toward the trembling breast with which he toyed. She bit her lip anxiously and squeezed her eyes tighter, but still Eric offered no relief.

Finally, unable to stand the sublime torture any longer, Kirsten's eyes snapped open and she looked down at the handsome monster who was so tormenting her.

"What's the matter?" he asked innocently, trying hard to keep from laughing.

"You know . . ." she panted.

"Do you want something from me?" Again, his index finger swirled around her straining breast.

"You know . . ." she repeated.

"Don't you like this?" he teased, tightening the circle he was making until his finger traced the farthest edges of her nipple.

"Yes, but . . ."

"But, you'd rather have this?" And dipping his head, he ran his warm, wet tongue sensuously across her nipple.

His touch was so erotic that Kirsten let out a little scream of delight, causing Eric to redouble his ministrations until she was squirming beneath him.

Somewhere in the back of her mind Kirsten was aware of his hand trailing down her stomach, and instinctively she parted her thighs and thrust her hips upward, offering herself to him. As his fingers delved into her creamy depths, she shifted her position, feeling for the first time his rigid shaft pressing insistently against her thigh.

His arousal was scorching hot, and as the tip moved up toward her most intimate spot, he left a warm wet trail on her leg, exciting her as nothing ever had before.

Gasping, she captured his head between her hands, drawing him up so she could kiss him, and shifting herself under him so that his pulsing manhood was nestled between her thighs, at the very threshold of her body. Wrapping an arm around his neck and burying her hand in his thick hair, she slipped her other hand between them and gently caressed him.

Eric groaned as her soft, cool fingers encircled him, enticing him to enter her. His moan was so primal, so utterly male, that Kirsten shuddered and wrapped her slim, silken legs around his hips, extending the ultimate invitation.

And Eric responded, just as she hoped he would. Rising above her, his face dark with desire and need, he entered her, slowly, gently, sensitive to the fact that she must still be tender from last night's initiation.

For a moment Kirsten tensed, waiting for the surge of pain to engulf her. But when none came, she relaxed, opening shining eyes and smiling at her husband. "Oh, Eric," she sighed, "it's so much better this time."

Eric smiled. "You don't even know how much better it's going to be, sweetheart."

Kirsten closed her eyes as she entangled herself in the erotic web her husband was so skillfully weaving. Sinking into a sweet, hot sea of sensation, she relaxed, allowing Eric to bury himself deep within her.

The pleasure was indescribable as, very slowly, Eric rocked back and forth, giving Kirsten time to accept all of his awesome power.

Stroking his back, she kissed him, silently encouraging him to increase his thrusts and allow himself the joy which she knew she had given him the previous night.

But this morning the joy was also to be hers. As

Eric's movements increased in fervor, Kirsten experienced an exquisite pressure building within her—a blinding need for some sort of release that she didn't even yet know existed.

Eric could feel it also, and forcing himself to restrain his own need he waited for Kirsten to find her heaven.

When the moment came, a sharp, gasping scream tore from Kirsten's throat and her eyes opened wide in wonder as wave after wave of ecstasy washed over her.

It was not until Eric felt her spasms start to ebb that he allowed himself to join her in paradise. With one final great lunge, he exploded within her, filling her with his passion.

For a long time neither of them moved, so overwhelmed by what they'd just shared that both were loath to break the magical spell. Finally, when their breathing had slowed and their hearts were again beating normally, Eric gently withdrew and lay beside his exhausted wife, holding her close and stroking her hair.

Kirsten had never felt so relaxed and content, and it was several long moments before she could find the energy to speak. Slowly turning her head, she gazed at her husband in wonder and murmured, "I never dreamed anything could be so wonderful . . ."

Eric smiled and kissed her. "I know. Neither did I."

"Is it like that for everybody?"

Eric looked at her, his expression puzzled. "I don't know, sweetheart. I think there has to be something very special between a man and a woman for it to be like this."

"But you knew it was coming, so you must have found it before," Kirsten insisted.

Eric frowned, wondering what she was really asking. Shaking his head, he said earnestly, "It's never been like this for me before."

Despite his words, Kirsten was still haunted by what Eric might have experienced with other women. How many had there been before her that he knew so well how to bring her to ecstacy? "Have you . . . have you known many other women?" she ventured.

Not liking the direction their conversation was taking, Eric sat up and reached for his robe. "No, Kirsten, I haven't. Now, I've got to get up and milk the cows. I'm sure they're all bawling their heads off in the barn, I'm so late."

Kirsten reached out her hand, touching his arm in an effort to keep him with her. "Eric, I didn't mean to make you mad. You just seem to know so much about this that I thought . . ."

With a sigh Eric lay back down and pulled Kirsten over on top of him so that the entire length of their bodies touched. "Kirsty, there's never been anyone like you, and I've never experienced anything like the last few hours. Please believe that."

From her position above him Kirsten could see the truth in his eyes, and with a smile of relief she whispered, "I do."

Eric grinned and gave her a quick, hard kiss, then playfully tossed her onto the bed next to him and bounded to his feet. "I better get out of here, you vixen, or my cows are never going to get milked!"

At Kirsten's quizzical expression, he looked down ruefully at himself.

Kirsten's eyes followed the path his had taken and she giggled with feminine satisfaction as she saw that his manhood was again swelling.

"Do you really have to go?" she asked throatily. "It seems like such a shame to waste such an impressive effort . . ."

Aghast at his prim little wife's bawdy comment, Eric threw back his head and laughed. "Dear God, I've unleashed a monster!" he quipped, covering his arousal with his hands in a mock display of terror. "Now that you've had a taste of it, I'll have no rest, day or night!"

"You're right," Kirsten cooed, stretching across the bed and reaching out to stroke his rapidly increasing length. "I think I'll just keep you in bed all the time."

Eric pushed her questing hand away and sighed dramatically. "A tempting idea, wench, but for now you're just going to have to control your lust. I have cows to milk and stock to feed. And if you expect me to spend the rest of the day playing with you, then I need some food to keep up my strength, so I want you to get your pretty little bottom out of that bed and fix me some breakfast!"

Kirsten, entranced with their provocative interchange, answered tartly, "Well, all right. But, as soon as you've eaten . . ."

"I know, I know," Eric grinned, holding up his hands as if to ward her off. "A few quick bites and then back to bed, right? I'll be lucky if I live through the day!"

With a shriek of laughter, Kirsten picked up the pillow and threw it at her husband as he raced toward the door.

Whipping it open, he dashed through it, peeking around its protective barrier. "I'll be back in about an hour. Fix me a big breakfast and I promise I'll make it worth your while!"

Before Kirsten could pick up another pillow to hurl at him, he slammed the door and disappeared. She heard him laughing all the way down the stairs.

Kirsten was just taking a pan of bacon off the stove when she looked out the window and saw Elsie coming up the drive.

Oh no, not today! Please! Not today!

Frantically, she looked around, wondering where she could hide so Elsie would think she and Eric weren't home.

You're being ridiculous. Of couse she's going to know you're home. The wagon's in the yard, the horses are in the paddock, Eric's right outside. You're going to have to see her.

With a sigh of resignation Kirsten set down the skillet she still held and wiped her hands on a dish towel, preparing to meet her unwanted guest at the front door. But when she turned back toward the window, she found that Elsie had not headed up to the porch, but, rather, was standing in the yard, talking to Eric.

Kirsten felt an immediate surge of anger as she saw Elsie lean toward Eric, placing a possessive hand on his arm. And Eric was smiling. Smiling!

Why doesn't he shake her arm off? Kirsten thought irritably. *She has no right to touch him. He's mine!*

Slapping the dish towel down on the sink, she whirled around, intending to march straight outside and let Elsie have a piece of her mind. But as she sailed through the dining room, she again glanced out a window and what she saw brought her to a dead halt.

Eric was kissing Elsie!

Paralyzed, Kirsten stared out the window, reeling with horror as she watched the couple embrace. Her shock was so intense that she didn't even notice that the kiss had been only the merest peck on the cheek until Elsie had seen her standing in the window and had thrown her arms around Eric's neck, nearly knocking him off his feet as he struggled to disengage himself from her unexpected stranglehold.

All Kirsten's old insecurities, which she thought had been put to rest last night, came rushing back with the force of a tidal wave. Her head swam, and for a terrible moment she thought she might faint.

Grabbing the edge of the dining room table, she closed her eyes and lowered her head until the dizziness passed. Finally, when she felt sure that she wasn't going to pass out, she raised her head and again looked out the window.

The couple was no longer standing where she had seen them. Rather, Eric was entering the barn and Elsie was heading toward the house, a huge smile on her face.

Determined that she wouldn't give Elsie the satisfaction of knowing that she'd witnessed the intimate little

241

scene, Kirsten raised her chin a notch and strode down the hall toward the foyer. Elsie was just raising her hand to knock when Kirsten jerked the door open.

"Oh!" Elsie exclaimed, lowering her hand and clapping it against her chest. "Kirsten! What a turn you gave me!"

"What can I do for you, Elsie?" Kirsten asked.

With a quick, furtive look over her shoulder, Elsie glanced toward the barn. Satisfied that Eric was nowhere in sight, she said coolly, "I need to talk to you. May I come in?"

Kirsten's stomach lurched, but she refused to let her face betray her turmoil. "Yes, of course," she answered in a polite, impersonal tone and opened the door wider, moving aside so Elsie could enter.

Elsie walked into the house and paused, as if waiting for Kirsten to show her into the parlor. But, Kirsten was not about to let the woman any further into her home than the front hall and remained where she was, her eyebrows raised expectantly. "What is it that you want, Elsie?"

Elsie blinked as if surprised by Kirsten's rudeness, but Kirsten could see a smug look lurking in the back of her eyes.

"I won't keep you, Kirsten," she said sweetly, digging in her reticule, "I just came by to give you this." With a flourish, she withdrew a ten-dollar bill and held it out.

"What's that for?"

"It's the ten dollars you gave me last night."

"I guessed that, but why are you giving it back to me?"

"Well," Elsie prevaricated, lowering her eyes in what she hoped was a properly chagrined attitude, "frankly, I just don't feel right taking it from you."

"Why not?"

"I just don't." Elsie continued to stand with the bill outstretched in her hand and her eyes glued to the floor.

A sudden, terrible rush of understanding caused

Kirsten to flush with anger. "Just what are you inti-mating?" she demanded.

Elsie's eyes flicked upward, then quickly dropped again. "I think you know."

"I don't know anything!" Kirsten insisted, her voice rising, despite her resolve to remain calm. "Quit beating around the bush, Elsie, and say what you're here to say."

"You're not stupid, Kirsten," Elsie said, savoring the anguished disbelief on Kirsten's face. "You know very well what I'm trying to tell you. Do you really want me to say it out loud?"

Kirsten remained silent, refusing to admit, even to herself, what she knew Elsie was going to tell her.

Elsie shook her head, sighing dramatically. "All right. I can see you're going to make me admit to my transgressions. I don't know why you would want to hear this, but since you insist, I'll tell you straight out. It's true that I'm going to have a baby, but . . . Olaf isn't the father."

"So, how does that concern me?" Kirsten asked, making one last desperate attempt to deflect the blow she knew was coming. "I don't care who the father of your baby is."

"Not even if the father is your husband?" Elsie asked, smiling with satisfaction as she watched Kirsten grab for the newel post.

"You're lying!"

Trying to keep from laughing out loud at the other woman's gullibility, Elsie shook her head and sighed, "I'm afraid not."

"You're lying!" Kirsten repeated. "And I'm so sure of it that I think we should just go outside and ask Eric!"

"Fine with me," Elsie shrugged. "He'll deny it, of course, but if you want to put yourself and him through the humiliation of a confrontation in front of me, that's up to you. He and I have already discussed the matter and he feels that, at this point, the best way to keep gossip at a minimum is for him to simply keep his, ah, involvement secret."

"I don't believe you!" Kirsten shrieked, the last thread of her control snapping. "When have you and he ever even been alone together?"

"Oh, come on, Kirsten!" Elsie sneered. "How can you be so naive? Don't you remember the day you came home and found us in the parlor together? Do you know how close you came to catching us? Why, my heart still pounds when I think about it!"

Seeing Kirsten's eyes close in misery, Elsie continued, "And all those Saturdays when Eric would drop you off at the general store. Didn't you ever wonder where he went while you shopped? Well, I'll tell you where, Kirsten. He'd meet me at the hotel. Every Saturday morning at ten o'clock."

"You're lying!" Kirsten repeated. "Eric runs errands while I shop. He goes to the feed store. I know he does! I've seen the feed sacks in the back of the wagon when he comes back to pick me up!"

Elsie nodded agreeably. "You're right. Sometimes he would go to the feed store. I'd hate it when he had to do that since it took away from the time we'd have together. But," she added slyly, "with the passion Eric feels for me, all we'd ever need is about fifteen minutes. A whole hour together was just pure luxury."

As Kirsten shook her head in agonized denial, Elsie feigned a look of sympathy. "I know how hard this must be for you," she said, her tone patronizing, "but you might as well know the whole truth. Eric and I have been lovers since shortly after we were all married."

"That isn't true!"

"Isn't it, Kirsten? Think about it."

Desperate not to believe Elsie's words, Kirsten blurted, "Everything you've said could just be coincidence. Eric told me that you'd only been here a few minutes that day I came home, and when we had lunch at the hotel, we just happened to run into you. He'd spent the whole morning shopping with me."

"I know," Elsie sighed. "We'd planned to meet that

244

morning, as usual, and when Eric didn't appear, I finally gave up waiting in our room and came down to the dining room. When you found us there together, he was explaining why he hadn't been able to see me—that he'd had to go shopping with you for some reason. I don't even remember why."

Kirsten's mind drifted back to that day—to the happiness she'd felt as she'd helped Eric pick out new clothes at Bjorklund's store.

She couldn't believe this. Elsie had to be lying! With a determined shake of her head, she looked Elsie straight in the eye and said, "You've always hated me, Elsie, and I'm sure it would give you great pleasure to break up my marriage. But I can refute everything you're saying. So, tell me, why should I believe you?"

Smugly, Elsie stretched the skirt of her morning dress against the swell of her slightly rounded stomach. "This is why you should believe me."

"No!" Kirsten shouted. "You're going to have to do better than that. You're going to have to prove to me that you know Eric intimately! Tell me something about him that no one but his lover would know. Then, maybe, I'll believe you."

For a moment, Elsie was caught off guard. But then she remembered the time that all the brides and grooms had gone on a picnic together down by the river. The men had gone swimming, and when they had come out of the water she had been awestruck by the huge masculine bulge that Eric's wet swimming clothes had betrayed.

Now, clasping her hands in front of her, she tried hard to conceal her glee. "I know that Eric's very . . . large. Much larger than most men."

Kirsten felt as if the world were crumbling around her, and she slowly sank down on to the second step of the staircase.

It was true. Eric himself had told her he was bigger than most men, had even worried that his size might hurt her. Only a woman who had been intimate with him would know that. Elsie *wasn't* lying, and in a flash of devastating reality Kirsten realized that her marriage, which had only really begun last night, was over.

"Go," she whispered, her voice choked with the tears she was trying so hard to fight. "Get out of my house and never come back."

Elsie looked at Kirsten's bowed head and smiled. Never would she have believed that her lies could hit such fertile ground. There must be serious problems in the Wellesleys' marriage for Kirsten to believe such outrageous lies.

Taking a step forward, Elsie placed the ten-dollar bill on the step next to Kirsten.

"I won't be a hypocrite and tell you I'm sorry about this, Kirsten. Eric and I are in love, and somehow we will find a way to be together. It was inevitable that you would eventually have to be told, but I think you would be doing yourself and Eric a big favor if you didn't let him know that I told you today. He and I need time to work out how best to break the news to Olaf and make the necessary legal arrangements to end our current marriages. I know Eric has been good to you all these months, and the best way for you to repay his kindness is to release him from your marriage." She paused, waiting for Kirsten to respond, but Kirsten sat as if made of stone.

Walking quietly over to the door, Elsie turned back one last time. "Remember, Kirsten, you could save everyone the embarrassment of a scandal if you'd just quietly return to New York. Eric need never know we had this talk. And you will never have to endure the humiliation of him admitting to you that he's in love with another woman."

Slowly, Kirsten raised stricken eyes and stared at the beautiful blonde standing so regally by her front door and dictating the rest of her life.

"Get out, Elsie."

"All right," Elsie sighed. "I'll go. But, please, think about what I've said. You'll see that I'm right."

And slipping out the front door, Elsie Swenson skipped down Kirsten Wellesley's front steps, feeling happier than she had since the day she had arrived in this two-bit, godforsaken town. For the first time she felt she actually might have a chance of achieving her fondest dream—being Mrs. Eric Wellesley.

Chapter 21

Elsie smiled all the way home. She hated Kirsten Wellesley—had hated her from the first time she had seen her at the New York train station. Kirsten was the first girl Elsie had ever met who posed a threat to her. Elsie had always relished her position as the prettiest, most popular girl in her small home town in Vermont. But the moment she met Kirsten she realized that this small woman with her piquant face, soft voice, and beautiful figure could easily usurp her anticipated premier standing in Rose Meadow.

Elsie had immediately set about to turn the other girls against Kirsten. But somehow as hard as Elsie tried, the other brides all liked Kirsten, and no matter what deprecations Elsie bandied about, Kirsten's new friends remained steadfast.

It was incredibly frustrating. And when they finally reached Rose Meadow and Elsie got a look at Olaf and then saw Eric, it was almost more than she could bear. Her hatred toward her rival doubled and redoubled as her jealousy and resentment grew.

But as much as Elsie detested Kirsten, the one thing she had never thought about her was that she was a fool. Until today . . .

When Olaf had demanded that she give the ten dollars back to each and every girl who had participated in the wager, Elsie was furious. But as much as she had pleaded and cajoled, as vehemently as she had threatened, Olaf remained implacable in his decision.

It had been a mortifying experience to return the money, trying to act like it didn't matter and convince the other brides that she was only doing it because she "didn't feel right" about keeping it.

Elsie had saved Kirsten till last, knowing that she would be the hardest to face. But never had she dreamed, as she reluctantly climbed out of her wagon in the Wellesleys' front yard, what a stunning turn her visit would take.

First, there had been the unprecedented moment when Eric had come out of the barn to greet her and had kissed her cheek, warmly congratulating her on her expected baby. And then, the unbelievable stroke of luck when Kirsten just happened to pass the window at that very moment, allowing Elsie to make it look like she and Eric were wrapped in an intimate embrace. The look on Kirsten's face was so gratifying that Elsie hadn't even been offended when Eric had pulled away, startled and annoyed when she had wrapped her arms around his neck. Elsie knew that from where Kirsten was standing, she couldn't see Eric's expression; that from her position at the window, it looked as though Eric were enthusiastically returning Elsie's affectionate caress.

Best of all, Kirsten had jumped to exactly the conclusion that Elsie had hoped for, her expressive face betraying a mixture of shock, disbelief, and, finally, devastation. The rest was easy, with Kirsten accepting Elsie's outrageous story about her baby's paternity as if it were gospel.

Thank God she had spent so much time watching Eric and Kirsten. Her story about her supposed Saturday morning trysts with him was brilliant, and if she hadn't spent so many Saturdays sitting in the Rose Café, hoping for a glimpse of Eric when he and Kirsten came into town to get supplies, she would never have known they didn't shop together.

Of course at some point the truth was going to come out, and Elsie wasn't sure how she would handle the situation when it did. But, for now, her victory was sweet, and she was going to savor the moment. She'd figure out how to cover her lies later. At least for the moment she had the satisfaction of knowing that she had turned little Mrs. Wellesley's world upside down. Elsie smiled again, relishing the thought of how miserable Kirsten had looked.

As her wagon creaked down the dusty little road which led to Olaf's farm, Elsie broke into a happy little song. The day had turned out so well that maybe she'd even allow her clumsy, awkward husband to share her bed that night. No, on second thought, no day could be good enough to warrant that!

Eric pushed happily through the kitchen door, anxious to sit down to the huge, mouth-watering breakfast Kirsten had promised him. But walking into the big room, he was surprised to find it was empty. As he looked around, his eyes widened with alarm at the sight of his morning bacon sitting in the cold frying pan, congealing in its own grease.

With a strange, uneasy feeling that he couldn't quite name, Eric retraced his steps back down the hall till he reached the bottom of the staircase. "Kirsty, are you up there?"

No answer.

"Kirsten, where are you?"

No answer.

He was just about to check the backyard when he heard someone walking around upstairs. With a grin he took the steps two at a time, eager to see his wife.

But as he rounded the corner into her small bedroom, he stopped short, the grin on his face fading to a look of astonishment. Kirsten was there all right— feverishly stuffing clothes into her valise.

Eric's gaze flicked from the open bag on the bed to

Kirsten's angry, tear-stained face. "What's going on here?" he asked.

Kirsten didn't answer, but continued to yank clothes out of drawers and toss them in the general direction of the unmade bed.

Eric's uneasiness increased tenfold and he hurried across the bedroom, taking his wife by her upper arm and turning her toward him. "I asked you what you're doing."

"Packing," she replied, wrenching her arm out of his grasp and turning back toward the bureau.

"I can see that. Why?"

"Because I'm leaving."

"What?"

With an angry snort, Kirsten turned back toward him and said loudly, "Because I'm leaving!"

Eric was flabbergasted. "Leaving for where?"

"Anywhere!"

Dumbfounded, Eric took a step backward and for a long moment just stared at her. "Kirsty," he said softly, "what's wrong?"

"Don't call me that!"

"Call you what?"

"'Kirsty.' I hate it when you call me that. I hate nicknames! My name is Kirsten."

Shaking his head in utter confusion, Eric threw up his hands and said, "Fine! What's wrong, *Kirsten?*"

"You know very well what's wrong," she hissed, elbowing him out of the way as she raced back to the bed, her arms laden with clothes.

Eric looked around the messy room in disbelief. An hour earlier he'd left an enchanting little temptress who had said she wanted to spend the rest of the day in bed with him, and now he was confronted with an outraged virago who was packing her bags to leave him! WHAT IN HELL HAD HAPPENED WHILE HE WAS OUTSIDE?

His mind working feverishly, Eric suddenly lit upon a possible answer. "Kirsten, did Elsie say something that upset you?"

His question hit its mark and Kirsten dropped the pile of clothes she held, gripping the edge of the bureau. "Yes, as a matter of fact, she did, but she wouldn't have had to."

Clenching his jaw as he silently vowed to speak to Olaf Swenson about his bitchy little wife, Eric took a step forward and lifted Kirsten's chin until she was forced to look at him. "Tell me what's wrong," he entreated, dropping his hands to her shoulders. "What could Elsie have possibly said that could have upset you so much?"

"Get your hands off me!" Kirsten raged, her control snapping as she fought to break his hold.

Eric immediately lifted his hands from her, throwing them up in front of him as though she were holding him at gunpoint. "All right!" he barked, his own anger flaring. "They're off! Now, start talking."

"There's nothing to talk about."

"Hell if there isn't. I leave you laughing and happy and come back to find you packing to leave me, and you say there's nothing to talk about? What the hell did Elsie say to you?"

"She told me everything," Kirsten choked.

"Everything about what?"

"Oh, Eric, don't play dumb with me! I saw you two out the window and then Elsie told me about the baby. Do you honestly think I would stay with you now?"

Unlike his volatile brothers Eric had a long fuse. But, still, he was a Wellesley, and right now it took every bit of willpower he possessed to hold his soaring temper in check. Taking a deep, calming breath, he said quietly, "Kirsten, you're making no sense."

Unbidden, tears rose in Kirsten's eyes. Hating herself for her weakness, she again turned away, not wanting Eric to see how he had hurt her. "What doesn't make sense," she said, her voice tight, "is that you made love to me last night as if . . . as if you cared for me, when all the while, you're in love with Elsie."

Eric's jaw dropped. "In love with Elsie? Are you crazy?"

"No," Kirsten answered with a sad little chuckle, "I'm not crazy." Slowly turning back toward him, she continued, "I saw you two kissing."

Eric's brows snapped together. *Kissing? She was accusing him of kissing Elsie Swenson? When? Where?*

"Sweetheart," he said quietly, "when did you see me kissing Elsie?"

"Don't you *dare* call me 'sweetheart'!"

"Goddamn it, Kirsten, *when?*"

"This morning. Outside. I was looking out the window when Elsie arrived and I saw you two kissing.

Eric blew out a long, relieved breath. All of this was because of the congratulatory peck on the cheek he'd given Elsie this morning? A small smile twitched the corners of his mouth. This was not the first time he'd seen evidence of Kirsten's jealous streak. His smile spread as he realized how much her fiery possessiveness pleased him.

It was all Eric could do not to take Kirsten in his arms, lay her back on the rumpled sheets and show her how unfounded her jealousy was. But somehow he knew that trying to make love to her now would not help this situation. He must first convince her that there was nothing between him and Elsie, and prudently he kept his hands to himself.

"Kirsten," he said softly, his voice low and earnest, "I kissed Elsie this morning simply as a way of congratulating her on her baby."

"Oh, so now it's *her* baby!"

"Okay," Eric soothed, "hers and Olaf's baby."

The blow that followed was totally unexpected. Before he ever saw it coming, Kirsten's hand cracked against his cheek like a whip, causing his head to snap around.

"How can you *say* this to me?" she blazed. "How can you stand here, look me in the eye, and calmly call your baby Olaf's. Despite what I've found out about you

254

today, Eric, I never thought you'd deny your responsibility."

Eric's ears were ringing from the stunning blow Kirsten had just landed, and all he clearly heard were the words "your baby." But it was enough. His eyes widened in complete incredulity and his closely held temper broke. "My baby!" he exploded. *My baby! Lady, you are crazy!"

For a moment Kirsten almost believed him. His astonishment and outrage were so genuine that it was nearly impossible to believe he was lying. But then she thought of Elsie's explanations . . . of the times she and Eric had been alone, of her lack of fear when Kirsten threatened to confront Eric in front of her, and, most of all, of her intimate knowledge of Eric's body that only a lover would have.

"It's no good, Eric," Kirsten sighed. "Please don't destroy every positive thought I've ever had about you by continuing to lie to me. Let's try to salvage some dignity from this misbegotten marriage of ours. I just wish you'd been honest enough to tell me the truth about you and Elsie before you . . . before last night."

"Jesus Christ, Kirsten!" Eric shouted, his voice betraying the panic he was beginning to feel. "You've got to listen to me! Elsie's lying. Please, we've got to talk about this!"

To his complete astonishment Kirsten started to laugh. "You know, Eric, for months I've lived in this house with you and every day I've hoped that you might want to talk. But you never did. Most days you didn't say ten words to me."

"What the hell have my conversational abilities got to do with anything?" he interrupted, frustrated beyond all reason.

Kirsten sobered. "I just think it's ironic that now that you want to talk, I don't want to listen. I just want to leave."

Eric couldn't believe this was happening. His anger was so acute that he wanted to lash out, to put his fist through a wall, to wring Elsie Swenson's neck, to somehow hurt someone the way he was being hurt. Wheeling on his mistrusting, unbelieving wife, his face darkened ominously and his voice became icy.

"Okay, if you want to leave, then leave. But tell me one thing. Just where the hell do you think you're going to go?"

Kirsten snapped her valise shut and looked into Eric's angry face, her heart breaking. "I . . . I guess I'll go back to New York."

"I see. And then what?"

"I'll seek an annulment."

Eric chuckled mirthlessly. "'Fraid that's not an option, lady. You yourself just said you wished this had all happened before last night. But it didn't, did it?"

"No, but what difference does that make?"

"Our marriage is consummated, Kirsten. An annulment is out. You'll have to get a divorce."

The shock of Eric's words made Kirsten's head reel, but she was determined not to let him see it. "All right, then, I'll get a divorce."

His eyes black as ebony, he asked quietly, "And just how do you think you're going to afford a lawyer? In fact, how do you think you're going to afford a train ticket back to New York? You don't have any money." He paused, letting the full implication of his words sink in, then added smugly, "Looks to me like you're stuck, *Mrs. Wellesley.*"

"I'm not stuck!" she shrieked, even as she admitted to herself that he was right. "I'll think of some way to earn my passage."

"Oh?" he pursued relentlessly. "And just how do you plan to do that?"

"I'll . . . I'll bake!" she cried triumphantly. "I'll set up a little bake shop in town and sell pies and cakes until I have enough money to buy my ticket."

"That's a hell of a lot of pies and cakes," Eric remarked wryly.

"I know, but somehow I'll do it. I'd be willing to do

just about anything to get away from you!"

Her desperate words almost sent Eric to his knees. Obviously she meant everything she was saying, and knowing her stubborn Irish determination, he had no doubt that she'd do just exactly as she promised. Somehow he had to stop her. A million thoughts raced through his head as he frantically tried to think of some way to keep her from leaving. Suddenly he seized upon an idea. His father had often told him that the best way to stop someone from doing something was to make them think you had no intention of stopping them. Hopefully the tactic would work now.

"Okay," he said shrugging. "If this is what you really want, I won't try to stop you."

Far from having the effect he was hoping for, Eric's words merely cemented Kirsten's resolve. An excruciating pain shot through her as she realized that Eric really didn't care if she stayed or left. His shrugging agreement had said it all. Kirsten felt like a vise was tightening around her chest, and for a moment the pain was so intense she couldn't speak. But somehow her pride asserted itself, and in a calm, dignified voice, she asked, "Will you allow me to take one of the horses? I have to get to town."

"Sure," Eric answered, desperately hoping that she'd call his bluff. "In fact, you can take the small wagon if you want. You'll need it if you're going to take all your stuff with you."

Miserably, Kirsten nodded. Hefting her heavy satchel off the bed, she staggered toward the bedroom door.

"Need some help?" Eric called, making one last bid to rekindle her anger. At least if she turned back to scream at him, it would stop her headlong flight out of his life.

But again the tactic didn't work, and without pausing Kirsten shook her head and disappeared out the door.

For a long moment Eric stood where he was,

realizing his strategy had failed. The woman he loved was walking out on him, and he was encouraging her! Was he crazy? But what could he do to stop her? At this point she was so angry and disillusioned that she probably wouldn't believe anything he said. Maybe it was better just to let her go. At least then he would have time to think—to figure out a way to mend this terrible rift and get her back.

Following Kirsten out into the hall, Eric watched her struggle down the stairs. Quickly he descended the steps, passing her in order to hold the front door open.

As Kirsten stepped out onto the porch, he reached down and took the heavy valise from her hand, then silently headed off toward the barn.

Kirsten watched him go, feeling as though she were in the middle of a nightmare. But the reality of the sun beaming down on her hair, the birds singing in the oak trees, and the crickets chirping in the fields forced her to face the fact that she was very much awake.

With slow, heavy steps she started toward the barn just as Eric appeared in the doorway leading his chestnut gelding, who he'd hitched to a small buckboard.

Without a word Kirsten walked past him and climbed up onto the wagon's seat, unwrapping the reins from the brake pedal.

For what seemed like an eternity they stared at each other, both of them wanting to speak and neither of them knowing what to say. Finally, Eric took a lurching step forward. "Kirsty, I . . ."

His unthinking endearment was almost Kirsten's undoing. But as much as she wanted to, there was no way she could stay with him when she thought he loved another woman. Before he could say more, she stopped him with a quick, negative shake of her head. "Please, Eric, don't say any more. Please."

And clucking to the horse Kirsten moved off down the driveway, leaving her husband standing alone and desolate in front of his beautiful, empty house.

Chapter 22

Kirsten brushed an arm across her perspiring forehead and lifted a tray of blueberry pies out of Betty's oven. Pies, pies, pies! In her whole life, she hadn't baked as many pies as she had in the two weeks since she'd left Eric. Dozens and dozens of them. She hated pies. Hated the crusts, hated the fillings, hated the smell of them baking. But, most of all, she hated Eric Wellesley for forcing her into this humiliating position.

On top of all the rest of her problems, she knew she was *the* topic of gossip in Rose Meadow. Lord, how she hated that! It seemed like every man and woman in town had come in to buy a pie from her in the last week, and she knew it was not because her culinary expertise was that exceptional. All the women in town knew how to cook and were perfectly capable of baking their own pies, but somehow none of them had found the time in the last week and so just *had* to buy one from her.

Kirsten knew she should be grateful that her business was booming, but, deep down, she also knew that it was merely curiosity that was driving the good wives of Rose Meadow to patronize her makeshift little shop. She had quickly learned to dodge their questions, but, more and more, she resented their nosiness and unflagging curiosity.

Thank God for Betty. The kindly older woman had

asked no questions when Kirsten had arrived on her doorstep. Rather, she had simply nodded in silent understanding and helped Kirsten settle back into her old room. And when Kirsten had broached the idea of using Betty's storage room as a bake shop, Betty had merely smiled and said that she thought it was a wonderful idea and just what Rose Meadow needed.

Kirsten knew that Betty was probably dying to know what had precipitated her abrupt flight from Eric, but, to Betty's credit, she had never asked. Until this morning . . .

The late summer dawn had not even purpled the eastern sky when Betty walked into the big kitchen and found Kirsten staring into a cup of coffee. Silently she poured herself some of the strong brew and sat down at the table, gazing at her young guest speculatively.

"It's time you told someone," she said simply.

Kirsten looked up as if startled to see her there, then her gaze immediately returned to her cup. "There's really nothing to tell," she shrugged.

"Balderdash! A woman doesn't leave her man for no reason . . . unless she's a fool or a Mama's girl . . . and you're neither. Something happened between you two and it's time you confided in someone. Why not me?"

Kirsten looked up at her friend with tear-glazed eyes, and suddenly the whole story tumbled out in a torrent, which once started she was powerless to stop.

Betty listened without interruption, merely rising once to fetch a handkerchief. When at last Kirsten's voice trailed off, Betty simply shook her head and said, "She's lying, you know."

"No, she's not," Kirsten protested. "She . . . knew things."

"What sort of things?"

Kirsten hung her head, loath to admit to Betty the intimate details about Eric's anatomy that Elsie had divulged. "Things that only lovers know about each other," she mumbled.

Betty frowned. "I don't believe for a minute that Eric

is a two-timer, and I don't care what Elsie says she knows about him, she's lying."

"But, why?" Kirsten asked, throwing Betty a beseeching look.

"Why? Because she's a troublemaker. Because she's jealous that you have a handsome, charming husband and she doesn't. Because she doesn't want to see you happy when she's not. There's any number of reasons."

Kirsten shook her head stubbornly. "She wasn't lying about them being alone. She *was* at my house with Eric that day when I got home and they were in the hotel restaurant together."

Betty looked at Kirsten quizzically. "You almost sound like you *want* to believe her."

"That's not true! But if you'd been there you'd understand. Everything Elsie said made sense."

"I'm sure it did," Betty nodded, getting up to refill their coffee cups. "Women like Elsie always make sense. They plan their attacks very carefully so gullible girls like you believe every lie they tell."

Kirsten sat for a long time looking out the kitchen window. "I want to believe you, Betty, really I do, but . . ."

"It's not me you should want to believe," Betty interrupted in an reproving tone, "it's your husband."

"My husband!" Kirsten snorted. "And where is he? He hasn't once come to see me since I left. Don't you think if he really cared for me he'd have come around by now? He's just about the only person in Rose Meadow who hasn't."

"Oh, Kirsten, be sensible!" Betty snapped, completely exasperated. "Why would Eric come around when you left him? I'm sure he's sitting at home wondering why *you* haven't come around. To my way of thinking, he's the wronged party in all this and you're the one who should be trying to make up!"

"No!" Kirsten said stubbornly. "You're wrong. Eric never wanted me in the first place. You know that. I'm sure he's delighted to be rid of me. And," she continued vehemently, tears surfacing despite her efforts to hold them back, "I'm glad to be rid of him, too. Our marriage was a mistake from the beginning and something like this was bound to happen, sooner or later. At least now we both know it's over and we can move on. The way my pies are selling, I'll be able to leave here before the winter sets in, and as soon as I get back to New York I can get a divorce and put this whole nightmare behind me."

"You're kidding yourself, girl. You're not over that man and my guess is you never will be. There's ties between you now that are pretty hard to break."

"Ties? What ties?"

"Well, what's to say you're not carrying his baby?"

"Oh!" Kirsten gasped. "That's not possible!"

"What do you mean, it's not possible? You're quick enough to believe that a couple of encounters with Elsie was enough to get her into the family way. What makes you think his time with you wouldn't bear equal fruit?"

Kirsten paled. "It just couldn't be. It was . . . it was only twice."

Betty chuckled. "Twice is exactly once more than it takes, my dear. I know for a fact that I got with my oldest son Christopher on my wedding night. What makes you think it can't happen to you? Some men just seem to hit the bull's-eye every time they shoot the arrow, and it's my guess that Eric Wellesley is probably one of them."

"Oh, God!" Kirsten moaned, dropping her head into her hands in abject misery. "I didn't know it was possible to . . . to get that way so quickly."

"Well, it is," Betty assured her, leaning over and patting the unhappy girl on the shoulder, "but there's no sense fretting about it. Time will tell."

Rising, Betty carried the empty cups to the sink. "Now, I've got to start breakfast and you better start rolling out your pie crusts. It's Saturday and you know how busy you were last week."

Kirsten nodded and slowly got up from the table.

"I'll just get my apron."

Betty listened to Kirsten trudge up the stairs. Shaking her head, she looked out the window to where the sun was just breaking the horizon and muttered, "Please, Lord, if it was ever in your plan to give that girl a baby, make it have already happened." Then with a sigh she picked up a basket and headed out toward the henhouse.

Although he didn't want to, Eric came to town that Saturday morning. He had purposely avoided making his usual trip the previous week, too unsure of what he'd say if he ran into Kirsten. But now he was out of coffee and sugar and baling wire and he knew he had to lay in some supplies. He could no longer put off the inevitable.

Kirsten had been gone two weeks and as each long, lonely day passed, Eric's hopes that she would come to her senses and return home dwindled.

All the way into town he fought with himself as to whether he should try to see her. It annoyed him that he was concerned over her welfare. Was she all right? Where was she staying? What was she doing for money? All of these thoughts had tormented him for two weeks now, and even though he told himself over and over that he didn't care he knew he was kidding himself. His boiling fury had long since cooled to simmering indignation, and as he neared town he finally admitted to himself that there wasn't a chance in hell that he could return to the farm without first seeing his obstinate wife.

To his surprise and dismay, many of the questions which had been nagging him were answered as he entered Bjorklund's General Store. As usual, Lars's four regulars were sitting near the potbellied stove. Eric nodded to the old men as he passed, but instead of responding with their usual disinterested grunts, they looked up in surprise, their small knives growing still in

263

their gnarled hands.

"Quite a little setup your wife has over at Betty's," Ezra Quackenbush cracked, eyeing Eric with a knowing grin.

"Yeah," Joe Dawson interjected, "that must have been some tiff you two younguns had for her to pack up and move to town! What'd you do, Eric? Make her slaughter another hog?"

The four ancients broke into wheezing laughter at Joe's cleverness, the story of Kirsten and the hog having already become a town legend.

Eric frowned, disturbed that his domestic problems had obviously become a target for town gossip. "What setup?"

Ezra leaned back in his chair. "Oh, so you *don't* know, huh?"

Eric threw the old man a dark look and continued walking toward the back counter where Lars stood listening with rapt attention.

"She's started a bakery over at Betty Zimmer's storeroom," Joe called after him. "Doin' pretty well, too, by the looks of the number of men goin' in and out the door."

Eric's jaw clenched, but he wasn't about to give the old men the satisfaction of seeing his anger. Instead he slapped his supply list down on the counter, pushed it toward Lars, and barked, "I've got to run a couple other errands. Get this stuff together for me and I'll be back in a while."

Before Lars had time to do any more than nod, Eric wheeled around and headed back out the store's front door, his anger escalating as he heard the old men's chuckles floating out the door behind him.

He marched down Main Street with huge, furious strides, his hands balled into tight fists at his sides.

The damnable Wellesley temper, erupted with a vengeance, and Eric's usually friendly expression was dark with fury. *Enough is enough. If she thinks she's going to make me the laughingstock of this town, she's got another thing coming. She's coming home today!*

He rounded the corner to Oak Street, not even pausing at the walkway to Betty's house, but proceeding straight for the side door which he knew led to her storeroom.

A small hand-lettered sign tacked to the door proclaimed KIRSTEN'S BAKE SHOP. Eric paused briefly to stare at it before ripping the cardboard off the door and hurling it to the ground.

Grabbing the door's handle, he opened it with an aggressive push and stepped inside the small room.

Kirsten was standing behind a small table which sported an array of pies, cookies, and the tarts she had become famous for. Eric gave the display no more than a cursory glance before his dark eyes rose to look at his wife.

As Kirsten met her husband's stormy gaze, her pleasant smile faded to be replaced by a look of icy indifference. Pointedly she looked away, making a great show of rearranging her wares on the table.

A young man who was loitering nearby noticed the abrupt change in Kirsten's expression and turned toward the door. Seeing Eric's dark visage glaring at him with open hostility, he took an involuntary step backward, nodding hastily as he hurriedly sidled toward the door. Several other customers quickly made their purchases and followed suit.

When the shop was empty of all but the two of them, Eric reached behind him and snapped the door lock into place.

Kirsten's eyes widened in response to his proprietary gesture, and despite herself a prickle of apprehension crawled up her spine. Willing herself to be calm, she asked, "May I help you with something, Mr. Wellesley?"

The sound of her soft, melodic voice did much to cool Eric's flaming temper and with a small sigh he answered, "Yeah, you can help me make supper, Mrs. Wellesley."

Intentionally misunderstanding his meaning, Kirsten

forced a bright smile. "Well, I'd be delighted to take care of the dessert portion of your meal. I have several lovely blueberry pies here and almond cookies and . . ."

"Kirsten!" Eric's anger again surfaced as he interrupted her rambling recitation. "Quit it! I didn't come here to play word games with you!"

Kirsten swallowed hard. "I'm sure I don't know what you mean. Maybe you better tell me what you *did* come here for."

Taking an aggressive step forward, Eric braced his fists on the table, his face inches from hers. "I came here to put an end to this nonsense.

Kirsten's eyes sparked with anger. "I beg your pardon," she hissed, "but what I am doing is not nonsense! What I am doing, *sir,* is what I have been forced to do by a husband who has cheated on me, rejected me, and left me penniless!"

"When did I ever reject you?" Eric shouted, livid at her accusation.

"Every time you climbed into bed with Elsie Swenson!" Kirsten rejoined, her voice shaking with fury.

Eric leaned even further over the table, causing Kirsten to step backward until she was pressed against the wall.

"I never, I repeat, NEVER, climbed into bed with Elsie Swenson!" he snarled. "By God, I wish I had! At least then maybe I'd have had the pleasure I'm being accused of having!"

Kirsten gasped at his outrageous statement. "Pleasure! PLEASURE! Do you seriously think you'd have found pleasure with that conniving little bitch?"

"No!" Eric thundered back, not even realizing that Kirsten had just unwittingly admitted that she didn't really believe he had bedded Elsie. "The most pleasure I ever had in my life was with you . . . and look what that got me!"

"Look what it got you!" Kirsten shrieked. "Look what it probably got me! It probably got me with child, and God knows that's the last thing I want!"

Eric's mouth snapped shut and he took a staggering step backward. His voice was suddenly low and intense. "Are you telling me we're going to have a baby?"

By now Kirsten was in such a fine rage that she didn't even notice that he had spoken about having a baby as "we're," and not "you're." Perhaps if she had noticed his phrasing it would have prevented her from hurling her next stinging barb:

"God, I hope not!"

As soon as the words were out, Kirsten wished them back. A stricken look crossed her face, and she quickly reached across the table, wanting to take Eric's hand and tell him she didn't mean her cruel words.

But black anger, coupled with a look of devastating pain suffused Eric's face, and abruptly Kirsten halted her impulsive gesture. For an endless moment he simply stared at her. Then, in a voice devoid of all emotion, he said, "I see. Then, for both our sakes, I hope not also."

And turning on his heel, he marched out of the small building, so utterly destroyed by Kirsten's comment that he wasn't even aware of the small crowd that had gathered outside the door, peering through the glass while wildly speculating about what might be going on inside.

Elbowing his way through the throng, Eric walked back down the street, mounted the seat of his wagon, and gave his surprised horse a sharp crack on the back with the reins, startling the poor mare so that she fairly flew down the street toward home. It was not until after he reached his farm that he realized that, in his anger he'd forgotten to stop back at the store to get his supplies.

After Eric's furious departure Kirsten stood behind her little display table, so upset that her teeth were chattering. She hardly noticed when the customers gathered outside started to make their way into her shop until several of them were standing right in front of her. Then she looked up at them with surprise and said flatly, "I'm closed for the rest of the day. Please leave."

Ushering her astonished and offended patrons toward the door, she jerked it open, herding the small band back out onto the street. Slamming the door soundly, she snapped the lock into place, pulled the shade, and leaned against the wall, allowing her tears free rein.

She was still crying an hour later when Betty came out to check on the day's sales.

Chapter 23

Eric sat on the front porch moodily smoking a cigarette and staring out into the blackness of the late summer night. It was well past midnight and the wick on the kerosene lamp next to him had long since burned out, but still he sat, knowing there was no sense in going to bed. He'd never sleep.

A breeze sprang up and the air became heavy with the promise of rain. Eric didn't notice. He didn't know how long he'd sat on the porch swing aimlessly rocking and brooding. The only thing he did know was that he was no closer to finding an answer to his marital problems than he'd been that afternoon when he'd stormed out of Kirsten's small bake shop.

I shouldn't have yelled at her, he thought, leaning forward to drop his cigarette butt on the porch floor and grind it under the heel of his boot. But, damn, she'd hurt him! Especially when she said she wouldn't want a baby of his. But even as she'd said it he could tell by her face that she hadn't really meant it. She was just trying to hurt him like he'd hurt her. And if his temper and his pride hadn't gotten the best of him, he would have stayed and tried to talk things out with her instead of telling her he didn't care and walking out.

Leaning back tiredly in the swing, he pushed his toe against the floor, setting the swing into motion. The rhythmic creaking of the suspension chains droned through his beleaguered mind like a litany: Shouldn't have yelled, shouldn't have walked out.

Abruptly he brought the swing to a halt, then dropped his head into his hands. "Christ," he muttered, "you're as bad as Seth!" Despite his despair Eric's lips twitched as he thought of his volatile younger brother whose answer to every childhood problem had always been to simply yell his adversary down.

Eric shook his head in remembrance, and a disparaging chuckle rumbled deep in his chest. "And the tactic didn't work for you any more than it ever did for him!"

With a long sigh he gazed out over his fields of corn, their tall tassels waving eerily against the cloudy night sky. What was he going to do? He couldn't seem to reason with Kirsten, and yelling didn't work. What would?

Eric knew that what he needed was advice. He had so little experience with women that he had no idea how to approach his recalcitrant wife. If only he had someone he could talk to. One of his more worldly brothers perhaps. "Stuart," he mumbled to himself, "where are you when I need you?"

His older brother Stuart, whom Eric considered to be the most accomplished rake he'd ever known, always knew what to do in situations like this. So handsome that women stopped on the street just to look at him, and blessed with the wit and charm to melt the iciest dowager's heart or turn the head of the most aloof debutante, Stuart always knew what to do.

But Stuart was far away in Boston managing his vast shipping empire, happily married to the beautiful and sophisticated Claire Boudreau, and undoubtedly raising his four children to be as sophisticated and worldly as he was.

"No help there," Eric muttered. "But, there's got to be somebody who can help me with this. There's just got to be!"

But, who?

Unbidden a name sprang into Eric's mind—a person so obvious that he couldn't believe he hadn't thought of it before. Betty! Betty would know what he should do. Who better to know what Kirsten was feeling than the woman she lived with?

Eric leaped up from the swing just as a gigantic clap of thunder burst across the sky and rain began pelting the earth. "That's it!" he shouted, racing down the steps into the sudden downpour. "By God, I'll go see Betty tomorrow. With any luck Kirsten will be home by the weekend!"

With a joyous whoop Eric flung his arms wide and threw his head back, spinning crazily in a circle as he reveled in the sensation of the cold raindrops running off his upturned face.

"By the weekend!" he shouted to the heavens. "She'll be back by the weekend! In my house, in my bed, in my arms!"

Eric sat at Betty Zimmer's big kitchen table, staring at her back as she poured him a cup of coffee. He had been so anxious to see her this morning that he had run his favorite gelding almost into the ground in his haste to get to town. But now that he was here, he didn't know what to say, and the shyness he had fought all his life was rendering him all but speechless.

Thankfully Betty saw his consternation as she set his cup in front of him and started the conversation herself.

"I assume you're here to talk about Kirsten."

"Yes," Eric nodded, taking a gulp of coffee and setting the cup back on the saucer with a clatter.

Betty sat back in her chair and looked at him expectantly until it became clear he wasn't going to say any more.

Finally after several excruciatingly silent moments, she said, "So what do you want to know?"

Eric swallowed hard and said quietly, "Has she . . .

271

told you what happened between us?"

"Yes."

Another long silence.

"Do you . . . do you believe her?"

"Let's say, I think there are problems between you that need to be talked out, but I don't believe for a minute that you'd want Elsie Swenson when you had Kirsten."

Eric could feel himself flush, but he looked up from his cup and met Betty's gaze squarely. "I don't want Elsie. I never did. I just don't know why Kirsten won't believe that."

Betty shrugged. "Elsie can be a very compelling liar."

"I know," Eric nodded. "But I don't understand why Kirsten would believe her over me."

"I don't know either, Eric," Betty commiserated. "Kirsten has never confided to me exactly what Elsie said, but I know that Elsie told her that you and she had been alone several times and made it sound like those times had been spent . . . intimately."

"That's crazy!" Eric flared. "I've never been alone with that little witch for more than ten minutes, and, believe me, even when I was, being intimate with her was the last thing on my mind!"

This heated confession was met by an almost imperceptible smile from Betty.

"Do you love Kirsten?" she asked flatly.

Eric's eyes softened. "Yes," he answered.

"Then why don't you do something to set things right between you?"

"I've tried!" he said defensively, his voice rising as anger replaced his innate shyness. "I went to her shop yesterday and told her I wanted her to come home. She practically threw me out!"

"Exactly!" Betty snorted. "You *told* her to come home."

Eric nodded dumbly.

"Don't you think it might have been a better idea to *ask* her? She probably thinks you just need some help slaughtering another hog!"

Eric closed his eyes for a moment, tamping down his temper. "That incident was a long time ago," he growled. "A lot of things have changed since then."

Betty looked at him speculatively for a moment. "Maybe Kirsten doesn't know that things have changed. You say you love her, but have you ever told her?"

"What do you mean?"

"Just what I say! Have you ever told Kirsten you love her?"

"She knows. She must."

"Why?"

Eric's eyes narrowed for a moment as if he were warring with himself over how much to confide. "Before she left, she and I were . . . intimate," he muttered. "That wouldn't have happened if I didn't love her."

Despite herself Betty started to laugh. "Oh, Eric, making love to a woman is hardly proof of a man's devotion. Men do it all the time with women they don't care a hoot about!"

Eric's eyes turned flinty. "Well, this man doesn't!"

Betty sobered, realizing the truth in his words. "I know that," she said softly, "but I'm afraid Kirsten doesn't. You should have told her you love her."

To Betty's surprise Eric started to laugh, a sound so filled with relief and joy that Betty found herself smiling in response.

Rising from his chair, he planted his hands on the table and leaned close to Betty's face, still grinning. "You mean, all I have to do is tell the girl I love her? Well, by God, I'll go do it right now!"

"Wait a minute!" Betty cried in alarm, standing up and pushing the exuberant man back into his chair. "I said you should have told her already. I didn't say that telling her now would solve anything."

Eric's smile faded. "Why not?"

"Because," Betty said dejectedly, sinking back into

her chair, "it's too late. After the harsh words you two had yesterday, I don't think she'd believe you."

Eric winced, embarrassed that Betty obviously knew what had passed between him and Kirsten the previous afternoon.

"And, besides," Betty continued, "Kirsten is leaving for New York on Saturday."

"Leaving Saturday?" Eric gasped, forgetting his embarrassment. "How can she be leaving so soon?"

Betty shrugged. "She opened her bakery to make enough money to leave. She's done it."

"She couldn't have made that much so soon!" Eric protested.

"No?" Betty chuckled mirthlessly. "With every eligible man in this town buying pies and cookies from her every day . . . just to have a chance to spend a little time with her? Why, that bakery of hers has made more in three weeks than most would in three months."

Eric's face darkened. "Who's hanging around her?"

Betty smiled inwardly, pleased with his reaction. "Never mind," she said with a dismissive wave of her hand. "Kirsten doesn't care about any of them. The point is that she's leaving in four days, and if you don't want to lose her you're going to have to think of a way to prevent it. And barging into her shop shouting that you love her isn't going to do it."

"You don't know that for sure," Eric argued.

"No, I don't," Betty admitted. "But after what happened between you yesterday I think she needs a lot more than a simple declaration of love from you. At this late date, it would probably just make her think that you want something from her."

Eric shook his head. "I don't understand any of this. What could Kirsten possibly think I want except for her to come back?"

"Oh, I think she'd believe you want her to come back. But I think she'd also wonder why. What you need to do is show her that you want her to come back for the right reasons—because you love her and want

274

her to be your wife, not because you need your clothes washed or your floors scrubbed."

Eric's lips tightened with offense at Betty's implication, but before he could voice his indignation she continued. "What you need to do is launch a campaign."

"A campaign? What kind of campaign?"

"A campaign to win Kirsten back!" Betty barked, annoyed with his lack of imagination.

Eric sat back in his chair, his expression pensive. "A campaign," he murmured.

"Yes, a campaign! You need to woo her, seduce her, make her see that you love her."

Eric smiled at the thought of seducing his wife. "I'll be happy to do that," he chuckled, "but I don't see how it's possible in four days."

"It's not," Betty sighed. "You need time to court her, and in order to do that you're going to have to figure out a way to keep her from leaving on Saturday."

"Well, short of stealing her train ticket, I don't know what I can do."

Suddenly Betty's eyes widened and a huge grin lit up her face. "She hasn't bought her train ticket yet," she said, her voice conspiratorial, "but, I know for a fact that all her money is in a little box under her mattress in her room."

"Under the mattress!" Eric exploded. "Is she crazy? Why didn't she put it in a bank! Why, anybody could steal it from her at any time!"

"Exactly," Betty said meaningfully.

Eric gaped at the older woman, unable to believe what she seemed to be suggesting. "You can't be serious!" he gasped. "You think I should steal her money from her so she can't leave?"

"I didn't say that," Betty answered primly. "All I said was that her money is under her mattress, and, as you said, anybody could steal it. Kirsten never goes to her room till well after ten o'clock at night. That would give a robber ample time after dark to climb that big tree outside her window, sneak into her room, take the money, and disappear without anyone being the wiser."

Eric stared at Betty in astonishment, then suddenly threw her a smile so brilliant that her elderly heart skipped a beat and she blushed like a schoolgirl.

Rising, he clapped his hat on his head and took two steps around the table, pulling Betty out of her chair and enveloping her in a big hug. "Thank you," he whispered, kissing her weathered cheek. "You're a true friend."

"Oh, get on with you," Betty giggled, pushing him away and patting her tight bun back into place. "Just remember, all I'm doing is helping you buy a little time. The rest is up to you."

"I know," he nodded earnestly, "and I promise I won't let you down."

"Don't worry about letting *me* down," Betty said, shaking a warning finger at him, "just don't let that little girl down."

"I won't," Eric vowed, turning toward the back door. "I love her beyond my own life, Betty. I just have to make her believe that."

Opening the door, he flashed her another grin and disappeared down the steps.

Betty closed the door behind him and touched her hand to her cheek where he had kissed her. With a small, girlish giggle, she sighed and whispered, "Oh, Kirsten, you lucky girl!"

Chapter 24

"I must be absolutely nuts!" Eric, perched on a tree limb fifteen feet above the ground, looked down at the sodden earth beneath him and shook his head. "God, if my younger brothers could see me! I'd never hear the end of it!"

Pulling himself to his feet, he reached for a large limb above him, testing it to see if it would bear his weight. Confident that it would, he hefted himself up to the branch and squatted atop it, one arm wrapped securely around the oak's stout trunk. Thank God he and his brothers had spent their youth climbing trees. At least he wasn't afraid of heights, and even though the branch he was on was wet and slippery he was secure in his footing.

He straightened to a standing position and found himself level with Kirsten's window. He sighed with relief when he saw that despite the rain she had left the window open a crack, making his entry much easier than if he'd had to try to pry it open from his precarious perch.

Leaning forward, Eric braced one hand against the side of the house and used the heel of his hand to raise the window until it was fully open. Then, grabbing the sill with both hands, he hoisted himself up and wiggled through the small opening, landing on the bedroom floor with a loud thump.

For a long moment he lay motionless on the floor, praying that his arrival had not been heard below. When he was finally confident that no one had raised an alarm, he got carefully to his feet, squinting in an attempt to get his bearings in the dark room. Reaching out with both hands, he felt around in front of him, taking one careful step at a time so he would not bump into the furniture.

However, his groping hands missed the rocking chair, and a soft grunt of pain escaped him as he stubbed his toe against the hard mahogany rocker. Again, he stopped, holding his breath until he was sure that he hadn't been heard below.

Slowly, his eyes became accustomed to the darkness, and he was able to make out the shadow of a small, canopied bed directly in front of him. He crept toward it, squatting down when his knees hit the side rail. Pushing both arms under the mattress, he searched for the box Betty had told him was hidden there.

His knuckles ran into something hard and metallic, and with a sigh of profound relief, he gave the object a tug, pulling it toward him until he held the small box safely in his hands.

He was relieved to see that it didn't have a lock on it, enabling him to simply remove the money from within, rather than having to steal the entire box.

Flipping the lid open, his eyebrows rose in surprise at the large stack of bills lying inside. "There must be a hundred bucks here," he breathed, inexplicably proud that his resourceful little wife had turned such a tidy profit in such a short time.

Scooping up the money, he quickly shoved the wad of bills into the pocket of his denims, then shut the lid and pushed the box back under the mattress where he had found it.

With a smile of satisfaction he started back toward the window, careful to avoid the chair he'd tripped over before.

He almost made it.

He was just throwing one leg over the windowsill when the door opened and in walked Kirsten, carrying a candle. Eric froze, paralyzed with indecision as he watched her walk toward the bed. Should he jump? My God, the drop was at least twenty feet and he would break his leg if he landed the wrong way. With the cold September rain pelting down outside, he'd probably freeze to death before morning. For a moment he had a terrible vision of being found in the morning, lying cold and dead in the yard below the window with Kirsten's money clenched in his lifeless fist.

But what was his alternative? Kirsten had not turned toward the window yet, but it was only a matter of time before she noticed the chill in the room and came over to inspect. He couldn't just sit there straddling the sill, He had to do something!

In or out, Wellesley! You either brazen it out and face her or you jump and risk breaking your fool neck!

The decision was made for him. Some infinitesimal movement must have caught Kirsten's eye, and with a gasp she turned toward the window. "Who's there?" she demanded, her voice shrill and frightened. Grabbing the candle up from the nightstand where she'd placed it, she held it out in front of her, tryng to identify her late night intruder.

"Who is it?" she repeated. "Make yourself known or I'll scream!"

"Damn it!" Eric cursed to himself, wishing he'd jumped.

With a sigh of resignation, he threw his leg over the sill and dropped back into the room. "It's me, Kirsten," he said quietly.

"Eric?" Her voice was stunned. "What are you doing here? How did you get in here?"

"Through the window," he admitted lamely.

Kirsten walked slowly toward him, holding the candle out in front of her as if she still wasn't convinced it was him. When she got close enough for the flame to reflect the dark planes of his face, she gasped, "It *is* you!

279

What in the world are you doing here?" Taking another step toward him, she continued, "Did you really climb in through the *window?*"

"Yes," he answered.

"Why?" she demanded, her voice a mixture of disbelief, anger, and amusement.

Eric took a deep breath, praying that the tactic he was choosing was the right one. "I wanted to see you."

Eric heard Kirsten's sharply indrawn breath, then saw her hurry over to the bureau, dipping the candle to light the wick of a small kerosene lamp. The light flared and illuminated the room enough that they could now clearly see each other.

For a long time neither of them spoke. Kirsten's hair was down and her prim calico dress was unbuttoned almost to the waist, testimony to the fact that she had obviously begun undressing as soon as she had entered her dark room.

Despite his ludicrous predicament Eric's warming gaze swept over her and he felt his manhood suddenly swell in heated appreciation of the provocative picture she presented.

Kirsten noticed the path Eric's eyes had taken, and with a small gasp she clutched at her gaping bodice, her cheeks flaming with embarrassment. "Eric!" she snapped, her voice sharp. "I want you to tell me right now what you're doing here and why you came in through the window. If you wanted to see me you could have come to the front door or, better yet, come to see me tomorrow at the shop."

Kirsten's heightened color and lame attempt to cover herself was doing much to inflame Eric's already rising lust, and he suddenly found that his throat was dry and his hands were shaking. "I wanted to see you alone," he rasped. "There's been too much talk about us already and I felt we needed some privacy."

"Well," Kirsten responded, her nervousness apparent as she tried to rebutton her dress, "this is hardly the time or the place."

"I think it's the perfect time and place," Eric murmured. As his eyes followed her fingers' fumbling movements, his erection strengthened and grew.

Kirsten saw the lusty fire leaping in his eyes, and suddenly his intent seemed clear. "No! You have to leave . . . now! We've said everything there is to say to each other and it's better if we just leave things the way they are."

"You don't mean that," Eric countered. He took a slow, meaningful step toward her, his gaze settling on her lips.

Kirsten's eyes widened, and despite herself she glanced downward. Eric's rampaging desire was fully evident, pressing insistently against his jeans. The flaming passion evident in his eyes made a chill run through her, and for a moment she had a crazy impulse to tear off her dress and press her naked body against him.

Again her eyes flicked down to the huge bulge in his pants, and unconsciously she licked her lips, causing Eric to groan in reaction. Kirsten heard his needy call, and from deep inside her came a warm, liquid answer. She closed her eyes and took a deep, shuddering breath, trying hard to harness her quickly escalating desire.

"Eric, you must go," she ordered, but her resolve was quickly waning and her entreaty held little conviction.

"Don't make me leave, sweetheart," Eric pleaded. He took another step toward her. "Please . . ."

"No!" Kirsten said, trying to sound firm even as her traitorous nipples hardened to pointed little peaks with his approach. Ignoring her body's primitive call, she continued, "You shouldn't be here. It's over between us. You know that. I'm leaving for New York on Saturday and I intend to get a divorce as soon as I get there. Now, please, don't make this any harder than it already is. Just go!"

"Kirsty," Eric said, his voice low and reasonable, "you don't want a divorce any more than I do. Let me stay with you tonight and we'll work this out. There's no reason why I shouldn't be here, sweetheart. I'm your husband."

The low timbre of his voice was so seductive that Kirsten swayed toward him. But suddenly a vision of Elsie smirking in satisfaction as she told Kirsten what she knew about Eric's body, rose before her. The mental picture was so painful that Kirsten winced and took a hasty step backward. "Don't say you're my husband!" she cried. "You quit being my husband the first time you made love to Elsie Swenson!"

Kirsten's stubborn accusation did much to cool Eric's overheated body, and a surge of anger coursed through him, replacing the throb of passion he had so recently been experiencing. Clenching his hands at his sides, he took an angry step toward her. "How many times do I have to tell you that I never made love with Elsie Swenson?" he raged.

"You can tell me as many times as you want," Kirsten hissed, her face so close to his that he could see the pain deep in her eyes, "but that doesn't change the truth!"

"The truth," Eric shouted, "the truth! Lady, you wouldn't know the truth if it jumped up and bit you! You want the truth? Well, here it is!"

And burying his fingers deep in her flaming hair, he pulled her head back and covered her lips in a bruising, desperate kiss. He expected her to fight him, to pull away, slap him, kick his shins, something. But Kirsten rarely reacted as he thought she would, and he was astonished and delighted when instead of pushing away from him she wrapped her arms around his neck and parted her lips beneath his.

Feeling her unexpected surrender, Eric's lips softened, his kiss becoming gentle and seductive as his tongue subtly invaded her mouth.

He disentangled one hand from her thick hair, running it down her cheek and neck until it settled on her breast where her bodice still gaped open. His

282

thumb provocatively stroked her nipple, causing it to harden and peak. With a groan he moved his hand inside her chemise, running his sensitive palm over the excited little nub until Kirsten squirmed and moaned in reaction.

Still kissing her, Eric dropped his other hand to her bottom, pulling her hard against him and rubbing his erection against her abdomen. "Love me, Kirsty," he choked, lifting his mouth from hers and gazing into her passion-glazed eyes. "Please, just once more . . ."

Drunk with desire, Kirsten nodded weakly, her hands fumbling at the buttons of his shirt. But a white-hot need had descended on Eric and he couldn't wait any longer. Yanking his shirt out of the waistband of his jeans, he ripped it upward, causing the abused buttons to spray in all directions. Kirsten blinked in surprise, then giggled, and in a like move ripped open her bodice.

In clumsy, frenzied abandon, they tore at their clothes, peeling them off their hot bodies and throwing the pieces willy-nilly around the room. In a matter of seconds Eric stood before his wife wearing nothing but his light linen underwear while Kirsten was reduced to only her chemise and stockings.

She was just bending over to roll down her stockings when Eric's voice stopped her. "Don't," he murmured, his voice shaking with desire, "let me."

With a small nod Kirsten backed up a step and sat down on the edge of the bed. Eric dropped to his knees in front of her, leaning forward and grasping the hem of her chemise to pull it slowly over her head. Kirsten raised her arms to help him, lifting her full breasts and throwing her head back to invite his kiss as the discarded chemise drifted to the floor.

Eric did not disappoint her. Running his fingers down the insides of her upraised arms, he drew his hands forward to caress her silken bosom. As Kirsten slowly dropped her arms, he cupped her lush breasts and bent forward, pressing his face against her soft skin. His warm breath raised goose bumps all over her body, and she shivered deliciously.

Eric raised his head, gazing up at her with hot, dark eyes, then leaned back on his haunches and slowly began unrolling her stockings.

Seductively he worked the silk over her knees and down her calves. Kirsten leaned back on her elbows, closing her eyes and drinking in the sensation of his strong fingers stroking the taut, sensitive flesh of her calves.

When both stockings were removed, Eric lifted her foot, running his thumb along her arch until she squirmed and twisted in reaction to the erotic massage. Then, lowering his head, he began kissing her toes, one by one, before slowly working his way up the inside of her foot to her ankle and past her calf, pausing only to lick the soft skin behind her knee. Subtly he inched his body forward, causing Kirsten to unconsciously spread her thighs. Then with a small smile of anticipation he abandoned her knee, kissing his way up the inside of her thigh until he was a mere breath away from her moist, throbbing womanhood.

He hesitated, waiting to see if she would stop him.

Kirsten guessed his intent and her eyes widened with incredulity at his boldness, but she was of no mind to stop him. As his lips descended and she felt his warm, wet tongue stroke the very core of her being, she dropped back on the bed, a moan of ecstasy escaping her. The sensation of Eric's intimate caress was indescribable—a budding, building tension that made her want to pull away and, at the same time, press closer. Her entire being seemed to be centered on the hot eroticism of his questing tongue, and inexorably she moved ever closer to her climax, feeling like her whole body might fly apart at any moment.

The moment came, and with a cry of surrender Kirsten gave in to the pounding waves of ecstasy which crashed over her—the erotic, pulsing contractions seeming to go on forever.

When the passionate convulsions finally ebbed and stilled, she closed her eyes; sated, spent, and more relaxed than she'd ever been in her life. At that moment all she wanted to do was rest . . . and relive the stunning moment. But despite her satiation she experienced a feeling of incompleteness, and as Eric stripped off his undergarment and rose from his knees to stand beside the bed and gaze down at her, she knew what he wanted.

The heat in his eyes again warmed her, and she realized that she wanted it, too. Dropping her eyes from Eric's face, she paused a moment to admire his heaving chest and the tightly ribbed muscles of his abdomen before allowing her gaze to feast on the great aroused beast of his masculinity.

Reaching toward him, she ran her fingertips along the underside of his manhood, causing him to throw his head back and bite down hard on his lower lip. "Can I do to you what you just did to me?" she asked throatily.

A shudder coursed through the entire length of Eric's body, and it was a moment before he could speak. Even then his voice was so hoarse that Kirsten had to strain to hear him. "Yes, but not now," he rasped. "I couldn't stand it now."

Kirsten smiled, instinctively understanding what he meant. Sitting up, she wrapped her cool fingers around his hot, throbbing arousal and purred, "So, Mr. Wellesley, just what *do* you want now?"

Eric squeezed his eyes shut, knowing that if he watched her caress him any longer, it would send him over the edge. "Kiss me, Kirsty," he whispered.

Intentionally misunderstanding him, Kirsten smiled and leaned forward, placing her mouth around the swollen head of his manhood and kissing him while she swirled her tongue around and around the fiery tip.

It was more than Eric could stand, and with a choked apology for his haste he fell on her, slipping easily into her warm, aroused body.

She was ready, no, more than ready, and by his third

deep thrust, she matched his frenzied rhythm. Wrapping her slender, silken legs around his flexing loins, she whispered words of encouragement until he came with a hoarse shout of release, plunging again and again as he filled her with his hot, potent seed.

Finally, with a groan, he collapsed on top of her. They lay absolutely motionless for a long moment, Kirsten taking in deep draughts of air as she breathed in the scent of him. He smelled sweaty, musky, and as he moved to kiss her, she recognized her own essence clinging to his lips.

Tiredly she raised a limp hand to stroke his ebony hair. He was heavy as he relaxed against her, and she shifted under him, trying to alter her position so his massive chest would not squeeze the very breath from her.

Sensing her discomfort, Eric rolled to his back, taking her with him until she was lying on top.

He sighed a long, satisfied sound that made her smile. She tucked her head into his neck, her breath warm against his throat, and, still intimately joined, they drifted into a deep, dreamless sleep.

Chapter 25

Eric woke early and for a moment he didn't know where he was. His sleepy gaze drifted about the unfamiliar room, finally coming to rest on Kirsten sleeping next to him. He smiled and allowed himself a moment to study her serene face. She looked almost ethereal with the early morning sun casting its soft rays across the delicate curve of her cheek.

Eric lay very still, sublimely content just to gaze at his beautiful wife. Finally, *finally,* things were right between them.

Then he remembered the money. His eyes widened in horror as it suddenly dawned on him what a precarious predicament he was in. He had to somehow get out of bed, get the stolen money out of his pants pocket, and return it to the box under the mattress—all without waking Kirsten.

It wasn't going to be easy. They lay closely entwined, wrapped in a lovers' embrace with limbs entangled and lips nearly touching. Slowly, Eric withdrew his right leg from where it lay intimately nestled between Kirsten's thighs. Luckily his careful movement did not wake her, but the loss of his warmth made her move closer, snuggling her head against his broad chest. Her warm breath wafted across his nipple and Eric winced as he felt his manhood stir to lusty life.

He frowned, cursing his body's traitorous response

to his wife's unconscious sensuality. Closing his eyes for a moment, he willed himself to think of something other than the sensation of Kirsten's soft breasts pressing provocatively against his side.

Stop it! he silently berated himself. *You've got to get out of this bed and get the money back in that box before she finds out you took it!*

Promising himself that if he was successful in his quest to return the money they could spend the rest of the morning making love, he slipped out of bed and crept over to where his pants lay on the floor. He pulled the wad of bills out of the pocket then turned back toward the bed, grimacing as he realized that the box was under the mattress on the side where Kirsten was sleeping.

Can't be helped, he shrugged, padding silently over to the side of the bed and sinking to his knees. Kirsten suddenly turned over so she was facing him, her face mere inches from where he was kneeling. Eric held his breath, praying that she wouldn't open her eyes. She didn't.

Slowly, very slowly, he pushed his arms under the mattress at the spot where he remembered the box being. It was much more difficult to wedge his arms between the mattress and the bedsprings with Kirsten's weight pressing against them, but finally he felt his fingertips touch the box. Closing his eyes, he began slowly pulling it toward him.

"What are you doing?"

Eric's eyes snapped open at the sound of Kirsten's sleepy voice. "Nothing!" he blurted, jerking his arms out from under the mattress.

Kirsten looked at him, her expression puzzled. "Why are you kneeling there?"

"I, ah, I was just looking at you."

"From the floor?"

"Well," Eric stalled, his mind working frantically as he tried to come up with a plausible explanation for his ridiculous position, "well, you were lying this way and I couldn't see your face from the other side of the bed, so I came over here to get a better look."

A small, pleased smile tipped the corners of Kirsten's mouth. "That's sweet," she yawned, stretching like a drowsy cat.

"Kind of dumb, I know," Eric laughed, rising quickly to his feet and tossing the wad of bills on the floor near his jeans. With a quick, surreptitious side step, he kicked the bills under his pants, then turned back to Kirsten, hoping he didn't look as guilty as he felt.

But Kirsten wasn't looking at Eric's face. As he circled the perimeter of the bed, her eyes were glued on his midsection. "Not dumb at all," she purred, blatantly admiring his partially aroused manhood, "if that's the effect watching me sleep has on you."

Profoundly relieved that her attention had been distracted by his unwanted erection, Eric grinned. "Yeah," he chuckled, glancing down, "just think what a kiss might do."

Kirsten moaned in anticipation as he climbed back into bed, pulling her over on top of him so the entire length of their bodies touched.

"Guess I don't even need a kiss," he smiled, directing her hand downward until it closed around his rapidly swelling length.

Kirsten shivered as she felt him swell in her hand, his surging arousal exciting her unbelievably.

Suddenly she rose to her knees, throwing back the covers. "I want to look at you," she murmured, her eyes raking his magnificent body before settling on his hot, pulsing shaft. She drew in her breath, awed by the size and power of him. Glancing up at his dark passion-hardened face, she whispered, "You must be the most beautiful man in the world."

"Hardly," he chuckled, reaching down and cupping Kirsten's breast in his hand. "Maybe the best-endowed, but certainly not the most beautiful. My brothers Seth and Adam win that award."

"You're wrong," Kirsten countered, leaning forward to allow him better access to her rosy nipple, "no one could be more beautiful than you are."

"I'm glad you think so," Eric breathed, mesmerized by the provocative sway of Kirsten's lush breasts as she crawled up the bed toward him. Crouching over him, she placed her hands on either side of his head and lowered her breasts until they brushed against his lips.

Eric's eyes fluttered closed, and with a low groan he drew a hard little nipple into his mouth, caressing Kirsten's breast with one hand, while running his other hand down her body until he reached the soft hair at the juncture of her thighs. Opening his eyes, he gazed up at her where she still knelt above him. As if in answer to his unspoken question, her mouth parted slightly and she thrust her hips forward, rubbing her wet warmth against his hand. As she rocked back and forth, Eric stroked her intimately, then extended a finger into her soft, welcoming depths.

With a gasp Kirsten straightened, arching her back and reveling in the feeling of Eric's finger deep inside her.

Eric's breath was coming in short, harsh gasps as he watched his wife take her pleasure. "You like that?" he whispered.

"Yes," she moaned, throwing her head back in an agony of sensation.

"Then I'll show you something else you'll like." He removed his hand from her, smiling at her small cry of distress. "Don't worry, sweetheart," he promised, "this will be even better."

Quietly directing her to straddle him, he grasped her by her hips and slowly, carefully, set her down on his straining manhood.

"Ohhh . . . ," Kirsten groaned as she felt him filling her, "oh, Eric!"

Eric glanced down, watching Kirsten slowly lower herself on to his shaft. For a moment he felt a twinge of apprehension that she wouldn't be able to handle all of him, but he underestimated the depth of her desire. Despite the fact that she felt like she might split in two, Kirsten was determined to take all of him into her and wiggled her hips back and forth until he was buried deep inside her.

For a long moment Eric lay perfectly still, drowning in the sheer eroticism of Kirsten's tight little body enveloping him so completely. But Kirsten had other ideas, and with a quick wiggling movement she reclaimed her husband's attention.

Eric smiled provocatively as he looked up into his wife's luminous, passion-intoxicated eyes.

"Aren't we supposed to do something now?" she asked, her voice shaky and breathless.

"S'pose we could," he teased, rotating his hips slowly until she gasped with delight. "We could do that. Or, how about something like this?" Very slowly he lifted her up nearly the full length of him, then brought her back down.

Kirsten's shriek of pleasure made him laugh with exultant male satisfaction and lift her again. This time when he lowered her she gasped, "Can you do that faster?"

"God, you're a demanding little wench," he growled with mock ferocity, "but, yes, I suppose I can."

Firmly gripping her hips, he set a rhythm which Kirsten quickly matched, tightening her thighs against his sides and increasing their pace until they hurtled over passion's precipice together. Their simultaneous shout of joy and fulfillment resounded off the walls of the small room, echoing and reverberating as she collapsed against his chest.

As they drifted back to earth Eric pushed Kirsten's tousled hair back from her face and kissed her tenderly. "You're something, you know that, Mrs. Wellesley?"

With a tired little smile, Kirsten kissed him back and murmured, "Do you still want me to be Mrs. Wellesley?"

"What do you think?"

Rolling off him, Kirsten propped her head up on her hands, her expression suddenly serious. "I hope you do."

A look of sheer contentment settled on Eric's handsome face. "Kiss me, Kirsty," he whispered.

Surprisingly, Kirsten shook her head, determined to exorcise the demon which still stood between them. "I need to ask you something first."

"What's that?" he smiled, idly brushing his thumb across her nipple.

"Did you . . . did you ever do this with Elsie?"

Eric's thumb stilled. For a moment he just stared at her with a look so incredulous that it startled her. Then an anger, dark and forbidding, suffused his face. In a fury he pushed her away and leaped out of bed. "How can you ask me that? *How?*"

"Please, Eric," she entreated, sitting up and pulling the sheet up to cover herself, "just tell me you didn't. That's all I want."

"I've told you and told you and *told you,*" Eric raged, pacing furiously back and forth the length of the bed. "After what we've shared in the last twelve hours, how can you doubt me?"

"Just tell me now that you never made love to Elsie and I'll never mention it again!"

Eric came to an abrupt halt at the side of the bed, his eyes black with pain, his posture rigid. Clenching his hands at his sides, he loomed over her and in a low, choked voice, said, "No, Kirsten. I'm not going to tell you again. If we're going to have a marriage, then there has to be trust between us. I find it impossible to believe after the night we've just spent that you could question my feelings for you, I refuse to spend any more time trying to talk you out of it."

"I don't think I'm asking so much," Kirsten insisted, her voice trembling and tears glazing her eyes. "You've told me many times that there was nothing between you and Elsie. But now, when I need to hear it from you just once more, you refuse. Why, Eric? Was Elsie telling the truth, after all?"

A pain so intense that it almost sent him to his knees shot through Eric. *How* could she still doubt him? *How?* After what they'd just shared . . .

If possible, his face became even angrier. "You know, Kirsten, sometimes I think you *want* to believe I've been having an affair with Elsie. So why don't I just tell you I have and make you happy? Yeah, sure, I've made love to Elsie. Lots of times. In my bed, in hers, at the hotel, in the barn, in the haystack—anywhere! Anywhere and anytime we could find a place and a moment, we've done it. And she's good, Kirsten. Damn good. Maybe even better than you, although I'd have to think about that one awhile. So, now you know. Are you happy?"

"You're lying!" Kirsten screamed. "You're lying!"

Eric shrugged. "Maybe I am and maybe I'm not. At this point, that's for you to decide."

"Get out!" Kirsten shrieked, tears streaming down her face. "Get out of here! I never want to see you again. I hate you!"

"Now, there's something *I* can believe," Eric shouted back, yanking on his jeans and shrugging his buttonless shirt over his wide shoulders. Leaning over to pick up his boots, he spotted the roll of bills on the floor, and with a smile of perverse pleasure he scooped it up and stuffed it back into his pocket.

Striding over to the door, he paused a moment, turning back toward his sobbing wife. In a voice so low it was almost inaudible, he said, "You know, Kirsten Wellesley, you're a fool."

Then he was gone.

Chapter 26

Dear Stu,

I know it's been a long time since I wrote you and I'm sorry for not answering your last letter sooner.

I'm writing now because I need some advice with a personal problem and you're the best person I know to help me.

Paula is the only member of the family I've corresponded with in the last few months and I don't know if she's told you, but I got married in June.

Unfortunately, my wife, Kirsten, and I have had some problems and we're not currently living together. Most of what has happened has been my fault, but no matter what I try to do to straighten things out between us, nothing seems to work.

Since I know you and Claire had some trouble when you were first married, I'm hoping you could tell me what you did to make up with her when things got rough.

I love Kirsten, Stu, but I'm afraid I'm going to lose her. Please write back as soon as you can with any advice you might have. Thanks.

Eric

P.S. Give my love to Claire and the kids. By the way, how many do you have now?

With a sigh Eric reread the letter to his brother and placed it in an envelope. Stuart was his last hope. If he couldn't help him then Eric knew he was lost.

He shoved the letter in his pocket and rose from the kitchen table, slamming his hat on his head and hurrying out to the barn. If he mailed the letter right away, hopefully Stuart would respond before Kirsten could again save enough money to buy her train ticket back to New York. Eric knew he had successfully postponed her departure by stealing her money, but he was also sure that as angry as she was with him now, she'd probably work doubly hard to earn it back as soon as possible.

As he rode into town he again mulled over the events of the last day. How could things have gone so wrong? If only he hadn't gotten caught in Kirsten's room, if only he hadn't seduced her, if only he'd just told her what she wanted to hear ... If only, if only, if only! How could one man make so many stupid mistakes in such a short time?

Eric had always thought himself to be a reasonably intelligent, civilized human being ... until he met Kirsten. But ever since the day she'd stepped off the train in Rose Meadow, it seemed like everything he said or did was boorish or insensitive. What had the girl done to him to turn him into such an ass?

Please, Stu, he thought desperately as he raced his horse down the road, please tell me what I should do to get her back. And, *please,* tell me fast!

Pulling up in front of Bjorklund's General Store, Eric quickly dismounted. Although he dreaded having to pass by the four old geezers clustered around the potbellied stove, there was no help for it. Lars Bjorklund was postmaster of Rose Meadow and handled all the town's mail out of his store.

Sailing through the front door with the letter clutched in his hand, Eric vowed not to let himself be goaded by anything the old men might say. Not pausing to even say hello, he rushed by them so quickly that none of them had time to do more than look up in amazement.

"In a hurry, Eric?" Ezra wheezed.

"Must be a mighty important letter!" Hershel Locke added.

Eric ignored them. Reaching the back counter, he set the letter down in front of Lars and said quietly, "How long will it take to get this to Boston?"

"Did you hear that, boys?" Ezra cracked. "Eric's sending a letter all the way to Boston!" Leaning back in his chair, he called, "Who in tarnation do you know all the way out in Boston, son?"

With a resigned sigh Eric turned toward the old men. "My brother. It's . . . it's his birthday."

"Well, that's right thoughtful of you to remember him," Hershel noted. "Why, Harold here ain't never sent me a birthday card!"

Harold Locke's wizened old face screwed up in an annoyed grimace. "Now why the heck would I send you a birthday card? I see you every day, you old fool!"

"Well, it still would be nice to be remembered on your birthday," Hershel grumbled.

An immediate argument erupted between the ancient siblings, and Eric turned back to the counter, relieved that he was no longer the object of their interest. "How long, Lars?" he repeated.

"'Bout a week, I'd guess," Lars answered, picking up the letter and weighing it. "And it'll cost you three cents."

Digging in his pocket, Eric tossed three pennies down on the counter. A week! That meant it would be two weeks before he would get an answer, even if Stuart wrote back the day he received his letter.

"Did you hear about what happened to Kirsten?" Lars asked, interrupting Eric's thoughts.

Eric's heart slammed against his ribs. "No," he said, hoping his voice wouldn't betray him.

"She was robbed last night," Lars said, keeping his voice low enough so that the old men couldn't hear.

"Robbed?" Eric gasped, his eyebrows lifting convincingly.

"Yeah. Someone broke into her room and stole all the money she's earned at her bakery."

"Is she okay?"

"Yeah, I guess she wasn't there."

"Well, thank God for that."

"Anyway, she lost everything she's saved." Lars's voice trailed off meaningfully, but Eric remained silent.

"Guess that means that she can't leave on Saturday," Lars added.

"Yeah, guess it does," Eric agreed. "Gotta go, Lars. Make sure that letter gets posted today, okay?"

"Sure, Eric," Lars answered, obviously annoyed with Eric's seeming lack of interest in Kirsten's misfortune, "I'll make sure your brother gets his birthday card."

"Thanks." With a quick nod, Eric hastened out of the store.

He didn't have to wait two weeks for an answer to his letter. The following Saturday when he walked into the general store to buy supplies, he was met by Lars eagerly waving a yellow envelope at him. "You got a telegram this morning!" he called excitedly. Western Union had recently opened a small office in Rose Meadow and telegrams were still a rarity, causing much speculation amongst the townspeople when one did arrive.

"Yeah?" Eric said, his heart racing.

"Don't know who it's from," Lars announced, thrusting the envelope toward him, "but it must be something mighty important. Hope it's not bad news."

With a nod of agreement Eric ripped open the envelope and unfolded the short missive.

Will be in Minneapolis on business 9–18. Stop.
Meet me at Winslow House Hotel. Stop.

Will talk about problem then. Stop.
Stuart. Stop.
P.S. Four kids—another one due in January.
Stop.

"What's the date today?" Eric asked, looking up
from his wire into Lars's expectant face.

"The fourteenth, I think," Lars responded, his
curiosity rampant. "Was your telegram good news, I
hope?"

"Great news," Eric grinned. "Absolutely great."

Lars grinned back and nodded hopefully. "Yeah?"

"Yeah! See ya."

Pivoting on his heel, Eric strode out of the store,
leaving a very disappointed Lars Bjorklund staring
after him.

Eric walked through the massive double doors of
the Winslow House and looked around with interest.
The hotel, built in 1857, had been the first luxury hotel erected in the fledgling city of Minneapolis.
For twenty years it had reigned as the Queen of St.
Anthony, and even though other more modern hotels
had been built in the years since, Winslow House was
still an impressive structure with its high ceilings and
thick, forest green carpets.

Quickly Eric's eyes scanned the lobby, lighting upon
a tall, ebony-haired man lounging in a large velvet
chair. With a broad smile Eric hurried across the lobby
to where the gentleman sat. "Stu! How are you?"

At thirty-seven, Stuart Wellesley was still considered
by most of Boston's elite social set to be the most
handsome and charming man in Massachusetts. Tall,
with jet black hair, gray eyes, and a wide, sensuous
mouth that had made many a debutante swoon with
longing, he was an imposing figure as he rose to greet
his younger brother with the signature Wellesley smile.
"Eric," he beamed, standing up and clasping his broth-

er's hand in a warm, fraternal handshake, "God, it's good to see you!"

The two men, so similar in appearance yet so different in personality, stood for several minutes exchanging pleasantries and catching up on the last two years. More than one lady passing through the lobby cast a covert, appreciative glance in their direction, but the men seemed oblivious to the interest their striking presence generated.

"What are you doing way out here on the frontier?" Eric asked.

"Business," Stuart answered. "I'm meeting with father's old friend J.J. Hathaway. He's developing a number of resort hotels on the far west side of Minneapolis and I'm interested in investing."

Eric shook his head in wonder. "Did you smell the potential profit all the way out in Boston, Stu?"

Stuart laughed. "Hey, I've got a family to support. And it's growing all the time!"

"Yeah, you said in your wire that you're going to be a father again. How is Claire?"

Stuart's eyes grew soft at the mention of his adored wife. "Absolutely incredible for a thirty-one-year-old woman having her fifth child. She won't slow down for a minute even though I keep telling her to take it easy. But, you know Claire—there's no stopping her. She loves a baby around the house and she's just thrilled we're having another one. Frankly, so am I."

"I'm happy for you, Stu," Eric smiled. "You seem to have gotten everything you ever wanted."

"I'm a lucky man," Stuart agreed. "But, from your letter, I take it that luck has been passing you by lately."

With a dejected shake of his head, Eric muttered, "It's my own damn fault. I knew I shouldn't get married. But I did it anyway, and now I've fallen in love with the girl."

"That doesn't sound like a problem to me," Stuart noted, chuckling.

"Wouldn't be, except that now that I've finally

realized I love her, she wants a divorce."

Stuart frowned. "Do you think she cared about you when you got married?"

"Yeah, I think so."

"But she doesn't now?"

"Doesn't seem to."

"Sounds like a simple timing problem to me," Stuart shrugged. "Let's go up to my room, order some food, and talk about this. If you really love your wife, Eric, then there's got to be a way to set things to rights."

"I hope so, Stu. God, I hope so."

Long after the food was eaten, the wine drunk, and Stuart's fine cigars smoked, the brothers still sat talking. Eric told Stuart everything, from his dismay over Kirsten's fragile delicacy the first time he had seen her, to their last night together, spent in what he hoped would be passionate reconciliation, but which had ended in the bitter argument that had caused their current estrangement.

Stuart said little except to ask a question now and then, chuckle at the story of the boiled laundry, and shake his head in sympathy as Eric finished his tale.

When at last Eric was silent, Stuart leaned back in his chair, mulling over all his brother had told him. "What I don't understand," he said, his voice pensive, "is why you just didn't tell her you've been faithful. It seems like this whole mess could have been avoided if you would have just told her what she wanted to hear. Especially when it's the truth!"

"I know" Eric nodded miserably, "but, I was so Goddamned hurt that after the night we'd spent together she'd still doubt my fidelity, I just couldn't give her the satisfaction of telling her again. I know it was wrong of me, and, believe me, I regret it."

"Well," Stuart said, leaning forward and pouring himself another snifter of brandy, "you've got to tell her. That's all there is to it. If you want her back, you've got to tell her."

"I don't know how," Eric admitted. "At this point I don't think she'd even see me, and even if she would I just can't walk into her bake shop and say, 'I've always been faithful. There's no one else but you.'"

"No," Stuart chuckled, "I don't think the bake shop is the right place, either. But telling her that she's the only one is exactly what you have to say. You just have to figure out a way to say it that she'll believe."

"But how? How have you told Claire you're sorry when simple words won't do it?"

Stuart smiled—a faraway look that bespoke of many a memory. How many times, especially in the turbulent early days of his marriage, had he agonized over exactly that question? How to say you're sorry . . .

Pulling himself back to the present, he looked at Eric with a wry smile and said, "Well, there was one instance when we almost split up, and I seem to remember that an emerald-and-diamond ring said a lot of things I couldn't."

Eric shook his head. "That won't work for me. I can't buy Kirsten's love."

"And you think I could buy Claire's?" Stuart asked, laughing. "Come now, Eric. You know her better than that! No, Brother, it wasn't the ring that did it, it was the note attached to it."

"Note?"

"Yeah," Stuart smiled, his mind traveling back over the years, "a short, simple little note tied to that ring said everything I'd been trying to say and didn't know how to."

"And it really made a difference?"

"Guess so. She's still mine after twelve years."

"A ring, huh?" Eric ruminated. "You really think that would work?"

"Oh, it doesn't have to be a ring. It could be a necklace, a bracelet, a brooch, anything. But I think a ring is more personal. To me, it's the most intimate piece of jewelry a man can give a woman."

"Yeah." Eric nodded. "I like the idea of a ring."

"Then I suggest you give it a try. Just make sure the note says what you want her to know."

Eric nodded his understanding and sat back in his chair, swirling the dregs of his brandy around the bottom of his glass. A long comfortable silence descended as the men finished their drinks. With a yawn Eric pulled out his pocket watch and snapped it open. "Jesus, Stu! It's two in the morning!"

"I know," Stuart nodded. "I'm beat. I haven't been awake this late since . . ." His voice trailed off.

"Since when?" Eric asked curiously.

"Since the night before I left on this trip," he laughed, throwing Eric a lecherous wink.

The men rose from their chairs, making plans to meet the next morning and visit a small exclusive jeweler Stuart knew.

Eric opened the door into the hall, then turned back to his brother, throwing his arm around Stuart's shoulder. "How can I thank you, Stu?"

"Not necessary," Stuart grinned. "Just patch things up with your wife and then bring her out for a visit. From what you've told me, I know I'd like her—as long as she doesn't try to do my laundry."

Eric laughed heartily. "It's a deal, big brother, and I promise, I won't let her anywhere near your underwear!"

The train ride home seemed interminable. Eric had spent most of the previous night staring at the ceiling of his hotel room trying to decide what to write on the note he would attach to the diamond ring he'd purchased.

He'd been sorry to say good-bye to Stuart at the train station. It had been so good to see him—so good to have someone close to talk to. Somehow Stuart, as he always had, made all of Eric's problems seem solvable. For the first time in years Eric regretted living so far away from the rest of his family.

Idly he looked out the train window, but soon grew bored with the stark fall countryside. Shifting to a new position on the train seat, he felt the hard bulge of the tiny velvet box in his pocket. With a small smile he pulled it out. Snapping the lid open, he gazed down at the exquisite ring nestled within, thinking how beautiful it would look on Kirsten's long, tapered finger.

The stone was magnificent—a flawless, two-carat blue diamond, stunning in its simplicity and the perfect complement to the narrow gold wedding band he'd given her when they'd been married.

How was he going to present it to her? He couldn't just walk up and hand it to her. It had to be done subtly, so that she would have time to consider his note before they saw each other again.

But how?

Many miles passed as Eric pondered this question. Then suddenly, just as the train was pulling into the tiny Rose Meadow station, his face lit up with a dazzling smile.

He had it—and it was perfect!

Chapter 27

Eric peered through the window of Kirsten's bake shop, straining his eyes in the late night darkness.

A steady rain fell, the heavy clouds obscuring any light the meager sliver of moon might have provided. Eric was freezing, his wet hair plastered to his head as icy runnels of water ran down his face and the back of his neck. His boots had long since given up the battle of protecting his feet from the wet ground, and now, after lurking outside the bake shop for more than an hour, even his socks were soaked, encasing his numb feet like icy cocoons.

Satisfied that the door he had heard closing earlier really had been Kirsten leaving, he reached into his jacket pocket and withdrew a small knife. It was no great challenge to jimmy the flimsy door lock except that twice he had to stop to blow on his fingers. Although he was wearing gloves, the relentless rain had long since penetrated the soft leather, chilling his fingers until they were stiff and clumsy.

Despite the horrendous weather Eric was determined that tonight he would put the plan he had formulated on the train into action. Ignoring his chattering teeth, frozen ears, and numb feet, he doggedly twisted his knife between the door and its frame until he heard the lock snap.

With a gusty sigh of relief he opened the door and

stepped into the warm shop, oblivious to the puddle he was creating as water streamed off his clothes and boots.

His eyes were already well accustomed to the inky darkness, and he quickly spotted the object he sought. His boots squished noisily as he hurried toward a huge ceramic bowl sitting on a small table near the back of the store and covered with a soft, linen towel.

He clamped his teeth down on one finger of his right glove, freeing his wet hand from the clammy leather and reaching into his breast pocket to extract the diamond ring he had purchased. A tiny strip of paper which he had wound around the ring's shank after carefully penning "You're the only one. E." now hung wet and limp from the gleaming gold band. He painstakingly rewound the soggy message around the ring, cursing the dark night which prevented him from seeing if the ink had smeared.

Lifting the linen, he smiled in satisfaction. A large dome of bread dough sat in the bowl where Kirsten had set it to rise overnight. Eric had seen her set bread dough out many times while they had lived together and had counted on her doing so tonight.

With a smile he poked his finger into the dough, creating a small, round tunnel into which he stuffed the ring. He closed his eyes for a moment, mentally picturing, as he had hundreds of times in the past few days, Kirsten's surprise and delight when she kneaded her dough in the morning and found his fabulous gift and his note telling her what she so wanted to hear.

He had planned his strategy carefully, waiting until Friday night to bury the ring so she would find it Saturday morning and come out to the farm to thank him. And what a reconciliation he had planned! He had already bought a large steak and dug two huge potatoes out of the kitchen garden for a romantic dinner. And, afterward, he would light a fire in the great stone fireplace in the parlor and make love to her in the plush softness of the Aubusson rug. Then

Sunday they would attend church together so everyone in Rose Meadow would know they had reconciled.

Eric's loins tightened just thinking about the following night, and with a hopeful sigh he pulled the towel back over the bread dough and left the shop.

Saturday came and went—with no Kirsten.

The day passed with agonizing slowness for Eric, who spent most of his time pacing up and down the front porch, looking out over his fallow fields and waiting for the sight of Kirsten's horse coming down the road.

By the time the sun set, he was frantic—and angrier than he'd ever been in his life. Why hadn't she come? The only possible explanation he could think of was that she just didn't care. That his gift—and his message—had meant nothing to her. As his fury and despair increased, his mind conjured up terrible images of Kirsten finding the ring, reading the note, and tossing it aside, her lip curling in disdain at his pathetic efforts to reconcile with her.

How dare she treat him like this, he thought furiously, lighting his umpteenth cigarette of the day. He had done everything, *everything* he could to make amends for his stubbornness the morning they had argued, and still she rejected him. Well, let her! He didn't need her—had never needed her. He would go to church tomorrow morning, give her money back to her, and tell her that he would personally drive her to the damn train station!

By now Eric had worked himself into a full-blown rage, and with a snort of contempt for his own foolishness he flicked his cigarette butt into the muddy driveway and slammed into the house, determined that he would fix himself the best steak dinner of his life.

He was late for church and it was Kirsten's falt. If it

307

weren't for her he wouldn't have drunk himself into a stupor and passed out on the sofa in the parlor.

Then this morning, when he had finally opened his dry, burning eyes, he was suffering the agonies of a hellish hangover—his head pounded, his stomach rolled, and his body felt like he'd been pummeled by a prizefighter.

With a groan he had pulled himself up to a sitting position, clutching the back of the sofa as he squinted, bleary-eyed at the mantle clock. Seven-thirty! My God, church was at nine and he still had to do his morning chores!

Damn her! he thought irritably, lurching to his feet and reeling unsteadily toward the kitchen, she'd never been anything but trouble! Just wait till he saw her this morning! By God, when he got done telling her exactly what he thought of her she'd wish to hell she'd never answered his first letter!

By the time he finally arrived at church and slipped quietly through the big double doors, everyone was seated and the service was well underway.

Sliding into a back pew, Eric sat down carefully, trying hard not to jar his aching head. Sweet Jesus, he thought, closing his eyes against the brightness of the sun streaming through the window, even his teeth hurt!

Opening his eyes a slit, he looked around, trying to spot his wife. He found her seated toward the front with Sarah and Ole Lindquist, looking like she didn't have a care in the world—like she wasn't responsible in any way for his current agony.

The service dragged on endlessly, and when Pastor Anders mounted the pulpit steps, a thick sheath of papers clutched in one hand, Eric groaned. It was obvious the good man intended to regale his congregation with one of his long-winded, rambling sermons.

Closing his eyes again, Eric gave in to his tiredness, his chin dropping to his chest as the minister's flat voice droned on and on, lulling him into a state of near unconsciousness.

Finally, the pastor's voice faded away, and with great effort Eric raised his head, relieved that the sermon had finally reached its conclusion. Just a few more prayers, one hymn, and it'll be over, he silently comforted himself.

But Pastor Anders wasn't quite finished and in an important voice boomed, "Before we conclude our service today, I have an announcement to make."

Eric forced himself to open his eyes and direct his attention to where the clergyman still stood high in his pulpit.

"Gunnar Larson asked me to help him find the rightful owner of this."

With disbelieving eyes Eric watched Pastor Anders hold Kirsten's diamond ring aloft.

"Seems Gunnar found this diamond ring in a chicken sandwich yesterday," the pastor announced.

Startled gasps and choked bursts of laughter erupted from the congregation as everyone started excitedly speculating about how a diamond ring could find its way into a sandwich.

Barely able to control his own mirth, Pastor Anders continued, "Yes, I know it sounds crazy, but Gunnar swears it was in his sandwich and he has the broken tooth to prove it!"

At this point the entire congregation, with the exception of the hapless Gunnar and the gaping Eric, exploded in great gusts of laughter.

"Quiet, please," the pastor commanded, holding up his hands in an effort to control his chortling flock. When the congregation had finally settled down, he continued, "Now, Gunnar has no idea where the ring came from. He thought it was perhaps from his bread, but the loaf came from Kirsten Wellesley's bake shop and she says she's never seen this ring before. Also, Gunnar says that there was a fragment of paper stuck to the ring when he pulled it out of his, er, mouth, which is also very strange."

A noisy buzz again rose from the parishioners as

they tittered over this latest twist to the mystery.

"At any rate," Pastor Anders said loudly, again halting the flow of conversation, "if any of you recognize the ring and can show proof that you own it, please see me after the service. If no one claims it by next Sunday, then the ring will be returned to Gunnar to do with as he pleases."

Eric slumped down in his pew, totally devastated. What the hell had happened? Was it possible that Kirsten hadn't noticed the ring when she'd kneaded the dough? Eric's mouth turned down angrily at the corner. More likely, she'd found the ring, read the note, and purposely left it in the dough. Perhaps she even hoped to embarrass him by making him publicly reclaim it so everyone in town would know what a fool he'd made of himself.

Well, he wouldn't give her the satisfaction. Let Gunnar keep the ring. He could take it to St. Paul and sell it for all Eric cared.

With a dark look Eric glanced over at Kirsten, surprised to find that she was turned around in her pew, looking back at him, a bemused, questioning expression on her face. The instant their eyes met, she turned away again, but for a long moment Eric continued to stare at her back, trying to decipher what her look had meant.

Was it possible she hadn't found the ring? Hadn't seen his note? Eric sighed miserably, realizing there was no way to find out without coming right out and asking her. And somehow he knew he couldn't bring himself to do that. He just couldn't face the possibility that she might tell him she had found it but had purposely left it in the bread as an eloquent way of letting him know that she didn't want it—or him.

Lost in his brooding, Eric wasn't even aware when the long service finally ended, realizing it only when the people seated next to him rose to leave.

With a mumbled apology that he was blocking their exit, he hurried out of the church, walking over to where his horse was tethered and turning to look back at the church doors.

He saw Kirsten come out of the building and took a halting step forward, torn between his desire to talk to her and his pride. He saw her look around the churchyard, and with his heart in his throat, he waited for her eyes to light on him.

Just as he saw her gaze settle on him, he felt a tug on his sleeve. Glancing over to see who was trying to get his attention, he sucked in his breath in annoyance. It was Elsie, standing too close and smiling at him with a look calculated to make Kirsten's blood boil.

Eric immediately looked back at Kirsten, not even responding to Elsie's greeting. But Kirsten had already turned away and was hastening down the church steps, her head high and her back rigid.

His heart sinking, Eric turned angrily toward Elsie, jerking his arm out of her clinging grasp. "What are you doing?" he demanded.

Elsie's eyes widened with well-practiced innocence. "What do you mean, Eric?" she asked, pursing her lips in feigned offense. "I just wanted to say hello. It's been so long since I've seen you, I was even considering riding over to check on you this afternoon. I know you're, ah, alone now and I thought I'd stop over to see if there's anything I could do for you."

Eric looked down at the woman who was responsible for so many of his problems, his eyes darkening. "So you'd like to come over and see me, would you?"

"Oh yes," she beamed.

"Well, I'm going to tell you something, Elsie, and I want you to listen very closely so you understand every word I say. Okay?"

Elsie nodded, her expression expectant.

"I don't want to see you. Not here, not at my place, not anywhere. In fact, if I'd been marooned on a desert island for the last twenty years and hadn't seen a woman in all that time, I *still* wouldn't want to see you. Am I making myself clear? Just nod your head if I am."

Elsie's face reddened with anger, but she slowly nodded.

"Now, here's something else I want you to understand," Eric continued, his voice deadly quiet. "You stay away from my wife. If I ever hear that you've said anything, *anything,* to ever upset Kirsten again, I'll make you wish you'd never gotten on that train in New York. Do you understand?"

Again Elsie nodded.

"Good. Don't forget it."

And turning on his heel, Eric walked over to his horse, mounted, and rode away.

For a long time Elsie stared at Eric's rigid back as he rode off down the road. He didn't want her. *He really didn't want her!* My God, she thought hysterically, clapping a shaking hand over her mouth, if Eric didn't want her, she was going to have to spend the rest of her life with Olaf! Dear God! How could her plans have gone so wrong?

Late that evening Eric lay in his big bed thinking about the look Kirsten had given him in church. For hours he had played and replayed her expression in his mind, trying again and again to decipher from that one brief glance if she knew about the ring. The more he thought about it, the more sure he was that she had never found it. Somehow she had just folded it into her bread dough, shaped it into a loaf, and baked it—innocently selling the bread to Gunnar Larson without ever suspecting what it contained.

So where did that leave him?

"Where it leaves you, buddy," he muttered to himself, "is nowhere. How do you get her back now that you've blown Stu's suggestion?"

Another gift was out. Anything he would do now in that regard would be anticlimatic. What he needed now was another idea—another suggestion. But what—and from whom?

With a sigh Eric turned over on his side, wearily punching this pillow. He'd figure out something tomorrow. Tomorrow he'd come up with the perfect plan to get Kirsten back.

When Jim Landers arrived at his telegraph office the next morning, Eric was outside the door, pacing back and forth in agitation.

"Morning, Eric," Jim smiled, pulling a key out of his pocket. "Need to send a wire?"

"Yeah, right away," Eric nodded.

Unlocking the door, Jim walked into the office, pausing to pull up the window shades before he stepped behind the counter. "Here you go," he said, shoving a small piece of paper and a stubby pencil toward Eric. "Soon as you get it written, I'll send it off."

"Thanks," Eric nodded, picking up the pencil, then setting it down again as he looked at Jim speculatively. He didn't know the telegrapher well since Jim had just moved to Rose Meadow when the Western Union office had opened a few months before, but what Eric did know of him, he liked. Silently praying that his instincts about the man were right, he said, "Jim, the wire I'm sending is personal and it could cause me a lot of embarrassment if anyone found out what it said."

Jim wasted no time putting Eric's mind at ease. "I understand," he nodded, "and, believe me, you don't need to worry about a thing. I wouldn't be in business long if I didn't keep people's confidential wires confidential. Whatever message you're sending, it's your business and no one will hear it from me."

Eric breathed a sigh of relief. "Thanks," he nodded. "I appreciate it."

Bending over the scrap of paper, Eric penned his message, then shoved it back toward Jim. "Send it as soon as you can, please, and mark it urgent."

"Will do," Jim promised as Eric hurried out the front door. Despite the fact that he had sent thousands of wires in the five years he'd been a telegrapher, he leaned over this one and read it curiously. His face split in a wide grin as he read the short message, and for a brief moment he wished he could share the contents with the entire citizenry of Rose Meadow. He'd love to be the one to answer the question uppermost in everyone's minds. With a sigh of regret that his professionalism would force him to keep this titillating bit of information to himself, Jim walked back to his transmitting machine and tapped out Eric's wire.

Stuart Wellesley
Marblehead, Massachusetts

Ring was a disaster. Stop.
Any more suggestions? Stop.
Please advise immediately. Stop.

Eric

Chapter 28

Stuart's response was swift, brief and informative. He had four suggestions for his brother.

1. Take her on a vactaion.
2. Admit you love her; tell her you've never cheated.
3. Give her a baby—fast!
4. If none of these work, find a different wife.

Eric chuckled as he read the wire. He would be happy to adopt three of Stuart's four suggestions. As for the fourth, well, that wasn't even an option.

After picking up his telegram, he strolled over to the Rose Café for a cup of coffee. He missed Kirsten's coffee. She might not have known how to make a drinkable cup when they'd first married, but she'd quickly learned to make the best coffee he'd ever tasted. He hadn't even realized how he'd come to look forward to that first cup she always had waiting for him when he came in from milking—until it, and she, were no longer there.

Pulling Stuart's missive out of his pocket, he laid it on the café table, studying his various alternatives. Stuart's first suggestion appealed the most. A vacation. It was exactly what he and Kirsten needed. Time alone spent at their leisure, getting to know each other again without any interference from other people or mundane daily tasks. Eric smiled to himself as he thought about how that leisure time might be spent: talking over their problems, putting to rest the misunderstandings between them; then, relaxing, taking walks, sharing meals, making love. God, it sounded *so* good.

But even if he could find the time and an appropriately romantic place, how would he ever talk Kirsten into going? They were hardly on terms where he could simply ask her if she'd like to go away with him for a few days. Eric's eyes rolled, just thinking about what her response to that invitation might be.

Leaning back in his chair, he took a long drink of coffee and stared vacantly out the café's front window. What would it take to make her agree? Probably nothing short of subterfuge. Somehow he had to think of a reason for her to go with him. But what? It had to be something important, something vital enough to his future that she would be willing to put aside her hostile feelings and accompany him.

More than an hour passed as Eric lounged at the small table, drinking cup after cup of coffee and pondering his dilemma.

With a distracted air, his gaze drifted around the small, deserted café. It really was a dreary little place, he thought, frowning at the bare walls. The food was good, the coffee was great, but the atmosphere was depressingly Spartan. It was no wonder that even though it was nearing noon, he was the restaurant's only patron.

They'd make a lot more money in here if they'd fix this place up a little. A few pictures on the wall would do wonders.

Idly, he thought that he should probably donate a few of his many paintings. God knew they weren't doing anybody any good stashed away in the loft of his barn, and they would make a big difference in here.

Narrowing his eyes, his artist's mind envisioned a beautiful woman's portrait hanging on the barren wall

316

over the lovely old oak bar.

His mind drifted as he recalled the first time he had seen such a painting. It had been in the main salon of the famed Stanford Hotel outside of Minneapolis.

As always the thought of the Stanford Hotel brought a fond smile to his lips. It was the stunning grandeur of that portrait that had convinced him to fulfill his long repressed desire to paint.

Lost in his memories, Eric leaned back in his chair, tipping it onto its back legs. His expression grew distant as he thought about the first time he had visited the Stanford.

It was six years ago. His father, on a trip from Colorado to Minnesota to meet with his old friend and business partner, J.J. Hathaway, had stopped briefly in Rose Meadow, inviting Eric to accompany him on his journey to Minneapolis.

Eric had eagerly accepted, delighted to have a chance to spend a few days with his beloved father while James Wellesley and J.J. Hathaway held their meetings in the chic privacy of the Stanford. Mr. Hathaway owned the huge eight-hundred room hotel which he had built high on the banks of Lake Minnetonka, a large, multi-armed lake full of bays, channels, and islands which gouged a meandering twelve-mile path through the lush green forestland west of Minneapolis.

The elegant hotel had lived up to every story Eric had heard about it. But what had struck him most was the "Portrait of a Lady" which graced the south wall of the hotel's main salon. He had spent hours standing in front of the painting, studying the artist's technique, especially the nuances of color, light, and shadow, which seemed to cause the beautiful woman's smile to change as the sunlight streaming through the huge windows waxed and waned with the hours of the day.

It was after that weekend that Eric had tried his own hand at painting. For the next six years he had spent the long cold days of winter painting landscapes, trees, flowers, and portraits of his family. It was his ultimate goal to paint a picture similar to the one at the Stanford, but he had never found a suitable woman to pose for it.

But that was before Kirsten. She was perfect—everything he'd dreamed of for his masterpiece. His eyes drooped as he envisioned the portrait he could create if only Kirsten would agree to pose.

"That's it!" The front legs of Eric's chair hit the café's floor with a sharp crack. "I'll take her to the Stanford and paint her in the main salon!"

Realizing that he was talking out loud, Eric glanced around self-consciously, sighing in relief when he found that he was still the café's only customer.

A smile tipped the corners of his mouth as he thought of spending time alone with Kirsten at the exclusive resort. October was nearly upon them, and the oak, elm, and maple leaves would be turning, festooning the lake's shoreline with magnificent hues of red and gold.

It was the perfect setting for romance, and by painting Kirsten's portrait they would be forced to spend long secluded hours together, offering him the perfect opportunity to seduce his reluctant wife back into his arms—and his life.

The only hitch in his otherwise brilliant plan was that Kirsten would probably refuse to go with him. By now he was sure she must have figured out who stole her money, and she was undoubtedly so angry with him that she wouldn't even see him, much less do him the favor of posing for him.

Eric frowned. That damn money! He should never have taken it.

Then suddenly his eyes widened as the seed of an idea sprouted in his mind. Money! He'd tell Kirsten he needed money and that he'd been offered a lucrative commission to paint a portrait for the hotel. Somehow he'd make her believe that he was broke, so broke that he was in jeopardy of losing his farm and all he owned. Surely she must still care enough about him that she wouldn't want to see him lose the farm! Why, he could even tell her that he'd stolen *her* money in a moment of mad desperation.

But would she believe him? In all the time they'd been married, they had never discussed finances, and Eric doubted that Kirsten had any idea of the full extent of his worth. Still, his house and its furnishings bespoke wealth, and she must have been aware that there was never any shortage of money when she wished to purchase something.

He'd just have to think of some way to make her believe he'd lost his fortune. Maybe he could tell her that he'd made several bad investments and had mortgaged the farm in a vain attempt to salvage them. He cringed at that idea, hating the thought of making himself look so inept in front of his wife. But if the ploy would convince her to accompany him to Minneapolis, his embarrassment would be worth it.

Rising from his chair, Eric hastened toward the café's front door, eager to put his plan into action. His first step would be to send a wire to J.J. Hathaway, asking him for his complicity in the planned deception. If Mr. Hathaway agreed to corroborate his story that he had been commissioned to do the painting, then surely Kirsten could not suspect him of having any ulterior motives.

Eric's mind was working feverishly as he trotted down the road toward home. This mad scheme just might work—if only Kirsten would agree to pose.

Certainly, he told himself with assurance, if she knew her refusal would cause him to lose everything, she couldn't say no!

"No."

Kirsten shook her head in adamant negativity. "Absolutely not."

"But, Kirsten, please, I need your help!"

"No, Eric. I won't go with you. I'm sorry, but that's my final answer."

319

Eric stood in front of the display table in Kirsten's little shop, desperately trying to think of some way to make her change her mind. With an effort he strove to keep his voice low so that the other customers, who he could tell were dying to hear the latest domestic dispute between the Wellesleys, couldn't eavesdrop.

"Can't we talk about this?" he muttered.

"I don't see any point," Kirsten retorted loudly, slamming two pies down on the table, "my answer isn't going to change."

Eric glanced around warily, frowning at the amount of attention Kirsten's statement had attracted. Leaning across the table toward her, he whispered, "Won't you at least hear me out? You owe me that."

Kirsten sighed in exasperation, her eyes boring into his. "I don't owe you anything, mister!" she hissed. "But I suppose if I don't hear you out you'll never go away, will you?"

"Probably not," Eric grinned, elated that he'd at least elicited that much cooperation from her.

"All right! When do you want to talk?"

"As soon as we possibly can," he answered, his smile blinding. "How about tonight? I could come up to your room."

"NO!"

Eric cringed as every head in the store turned toward them.

"Okay, okay. It was just an idea. How about if I take you to supper at the hotel?"

Again Kirsten shook her head. "That won't work either. It's too public, and, besides, this discussion isn't going to take long enough to last through supper."

Eric frowned in disappointment. "Okay, you name the time and the place."

Kirsten thought a moment, then with a curt nod, said, "I'll ask Betty if we can use her parlor. Eight o'clock tonight."

"Eight it is," Eric nodded. "I'll be there." And tipping

his hat jauntily to the women standing near the front door, he exited the shop.

"I still see no reason why I need to be involved in this. You can hire a model to pose for your painting."

Eric blew out a long, frustrated breath. He and Kirsten had been sitting in Betty's parlor for half an hour, but, despite all his arguments, he was getting nowhere. "I told you before, I can't afford a model!"

"Then find a picture of a woman you admire and paint from that!"

"Kirsten, it wouldn't be the same! I wish you'd try to understand. This is my one chance to have my work really seen—by all the right people—and the portrait has to be perfect!"

Kirsten eyes narrowed. "I never knew that you had the slightest interest in having your work 'seen.' I thought you just painted for your own enjoyment."

Eric shrugged. "For a long time I did, but now I need money if I'm going to save the farm, and accepting this commission is the only way I can think to earn it. But," he continued, his voice beseeching, "if the painting isn't my best work, Mr. Hathaway may not even buy it! That's why I need your help so desperately, Kirsten."

"How did this Mr. Hathaway even find out about you?"

Eric thought fast. "He's an old friend of my father's. I guess Pa told him I paint."

Kirsten nodded, accepting his explanation. Rising from the settee where she was sitting, she walked over to the window, gazing out at the still autumn night. When she finally spoke again, her voice was strained. "Why don't you ask Elsie to pose, Eric?"

Eric closed his eyes. He'd been waiting for this, but, still, Kirsten's quiet words hit him like a punch in the stomach. Getting up from his chair, he walked over to where she stood. "Because I want you."

Kirsten continued to stare out the window, her eyes

321

haunted. "Why? Did Elsie turn you down?"

Eric's lips thinned as he struggled to keep his temper in check. "I didn't ask her," he said, the sincerity in his voice convincing her that he was telling the truth. "I want you."

Kirsten lowered her gaze, looking blindly at the floor. She couldn't give in to this! She couldn't! But as much as she wanted to deny it, the quiet entreaty in Eric's voice was having the same effect on her it always had. It took every bit of willpower she possessed not to turn around and step into his embrace. He was standing so close behind her that she could scarcely breathe—his potent male allure so compelling that she felt like she was being drawn by a powerful magnet. She stared at her knuckles, watching them whiten as she gripped the windowsill and fought against the desire racing through her.

"Kirsty," Eric whispered, his breath soft against her ear, "did you know I'm the one who stole your money?"

His unexpected confession made her turn toward him in astonishment, her swinging hair brushing against his face. "I thought so," she breathed. "But, why?"

"Because . . . because . . ." Eric's voice was strangled as he tried to force the lie through his lips, but the words just wouldn't come. Instead he whispered, "I'm sorry, sweetheart. I'll give it back to you."

His unconscious endearment nearly brought Kirsten to her knees, and, not trusting herself to speak, she simply nodded.

An endless moment passed as the couple looked at each other, their faces so close that their breath mingled. A wisp of Kirsten's hair had tangled itself into Eric's and with a self-conscious little smile she reached up and pulled it free.

Eric held his breath, praying for a sign that she wanted him to kiss her. It didn't come. Instead she sidled out from where she stood trapped between his body and the window, stepping hurriedly away from him.

Her quick movement was devastating in its implication, and with a small sigh of defeat, Eric shook his head and walked out of the room.

He went straight to the front door, but when he reached it, he paused, his voice quiet. "Thanks for hearing me out, Kirsten. I appreciate it."

He was halfway down Betty's walk when he heard her soft call. Turning back toward the house, he saw her silhouetted in the doorway. He stood and waited, his expression searching, but Kirsten remained silent. Finally, figuring that she must not have called him after all, he turned back toward the street.

"Eric?" Her voice was small, tentative.

Again he paused, but this time he didn't turn around. "Yes?"

"I'll go."

Chapter 29

"I want one thing understood," Kirsten said, turning to Eric who stood next to her on the platform of the Rose Meadow train station, "this trip is strictly a professional arrangement. We're not going as husband and wife. We're going as artist and model. Period."

"I understand," Eric nodded, looking down the tracks at the approaching train.

"And I want you to know, too, that I'm using the money you're paying me to pose for you to buy my train ticket back to New York. I'll be leaving as soon as we return."

"I understand," Eric repeated, still refusing to look at her.

"Most of all, I want your promise that while we're on this trip, you won't put any pressure on me to change my mind."

Eric finally turned toward her, his face dark with repressed anger. "Why would I?" he asked coldly.

Kirsten blinked. "Oh. Well, good. Then we're agreed that this is a business relationship and that's all."

"Absolutely," Eric growled, taking her arm and leading her down the platform to where the train had pulled to a blowing, steaming stop. "Come on, let's board."

Momentarily taken aback by Eric's sudden animosity, Kirsten allowed herself to be pulled along the platform, but her slim velvet traveling suit did not allow her much freedom of movement, and she was no match for Eric's long, angry strides. Finally, breathless and exasperated, she wrenched her arm out of his grasp and said, "Slow down, for heaven's sake! The train is not going to leave without us. We're the only ones boarding!"

Instantly slowing his steps, Eric took a deep, calming breath. "I'm sorry," he said. "I didn't mean to rush you."

With a curt nod, Kirsten again accepted the arm he held out to her.

Sam Harkins, the train depot's ticket agent, was greatly enjoying this latest interchange between the battling Wellesleys. He had been astonished when the couple had arrived together that morning, carting enough luggage to indicate a lengthy absence. "Second honeymoon?" he asked innocently, throwing Eric a knowing grin.

Eric pretended he didn't notice the man's leering look and wiggling eyebrows. "Two round trips to Wayzata, please."

"Wayzata, eh?" Sam repeated. "The rich folks' stop. You two vacationing at one of them fancy hotels up there on that big lake?"

"It's a business trip," Eric answered curtly.

"Well, we don't see many folks headin' for Wayzata, I'll tell you, not for business *or* pleasure! Thought nobody but them snobby Easterners stayed at that place."

"How much for the tickets?" Eric demanded, fighting hard to keep his annoyance in check.

Sam named the price, then added, "When you comin' back, Eric?"

"Two weeks."

"Two weeks? Woowee! That must be some business you got goin' on. Who's takin' care of your farm all that time?"

"I've hired someone," Eric answered shortly.

"And how about Mrs. Wellesley? What's she gonna do up there? She got business, too? Oh, and by the way, who's gonna run the bakery while she's gone? I'd hate to think I'm not gonna be able to buy any of them cakes of hers for two whole weeks."

Eric sighed, wishing desperately that the nosy old codger would just give him his tickets so he could make his escape. "Betty Zimmer's going to keep the bakery open. May I have my tickets please, Sam?"

"What? Oh, sure, Eric. Here." Pushing the tickets through the grilled window, Sam added, "Well, you two have a good time now and be sure to stop by when you get back. I want to hear all about your trip!"

Eric nodded, scooping up the tickets and fleeing the window as fast as he could.

"Hee, hee, hee!" Sam chortled, watching Eric hurry down the platform to where Kirsten was standing. "Business trip, indeed. Sure as shootin', the only business that boy's got on his mind is the business of gettin' his wife back in his bed! Just wait till the boys down at Bjorklund's hear about this!"

Boarding the train, Eric and Kirsten settled themselves into seats facing each other just as the snorting, puffing monster jerked into motion.

"What time do we get there?" Kirsten asked.

"About two."

"Have you arranged for transportation to the hotel?"

"Didn't have to. The steamboat will be at the station waiting for us."

"Steamboat? What steamboat?"

Eric smiled, relishing the fact that for the first time he was going to be able to treat his wife to the kind of luxury she had known in New York. "The *Minnetonka Princess,*" he supplied. "J.J. Hathaway, my father's friend who owns the Stanford Hotel, had a twenty-five-hundred passenger steamboat built to ferry the hotel's guests around the lake on sightseeing excursions. It also travels every day to the train station to pick up and drop off the hotel's guests."

Kirsten's mouth dropped open. "That's incredible! Imagine, a steamboat cab!"

"You're going to love this place, Kirsty," Eric enthused, warming to his subject. "Hathaway touts that the Stanford is the most elegant hotel west of New York City. It draws summer visitors from all over the country—especially from down South. They come up the Mississippi on the big riverboats and spend July and August at the Stanford to escape the heat."

Kirsten looked dubious. "It was hardly cool here in July and August. I can't imagine people coming to this area to get away from heat!"

"Oh, but the Lake Minnetonka resorts are a lot different from Rose Meadow," Eric chuckled. "The shoreline is thick with forests which provide a lot of shade and the hotel has huge covered verandas that catch the lake breezes and stay cool virtually all day long."

"It sounds wonderful, Eric," Kirsten smiled, finding herself caught up in her husband's enthusiasm. "A lot like Saratoga."

"I've heard people compare it to Saratoga. In fact there are some New Yorkers who say it's better."

Kirsten thought back to the happy summers of her childhood spent, in large part, at the famous Eastern resort. "It couldn't be better than Saratoga," she murmured. "Nothing could."

Eric noticed her wistful look and frowned to himself. Damn! The last thing he wanted to do by bringing Kirsten to Wayzata was to make her homesick for New York! His goal was to make her forget New York, not long for it! Quickly he changed the subject. "Are you hungry? There's a dining car on the train. I thought we could have lunch."

Kirsten shook her head. "No, I'm fine. Besides, you know how expensive train food is. I don't want you to spend any money needlessly. We'll just wait and eat at the hotel. Didn't you say that they're supplying our meals and rooms as part of your compensation?"

Eric hesitated a moment. "Ah, yes, they are. But there won't be a meal available there until tonight. We have to eat something before then, and even though I may be having some financial problems, I think I can still afford lunch."

He nearly choked on his words. God, he hated this subterfuge! He was starving and he wanted lunch! But he realized he better get used to his self-imposed austerity program. Unless he wanted to admit to Kirsten that he was lying to her and that, in actuality, his financial situation was such that he could afford to buy the whole damned train if he wanted to, he'd have to continue with this sham.

"I'm really not hungry," Kirsten insisted, reaching into her reticule and pulling out a large red apple. "But I figured you might be since you usually are, so I brought this along to tide you over."

Eric stared at the apple in wry amusement. Leave it to Miss Practical to think of everything! Reaching out, he took the apple from her outstretched hand. "Thanks," he said softly, "I appreciate the thought. This should hold me just fine."

Their trip continued pleasantly. For the first time since she'd agreed to accompany Eric, Kirsten relaxed, relieved that he had agreed to the stipulations she'd demanded on the station platform. As usual Eric didn't say much, but he seemed content, leaning back against his plush seat and watching the scenery turn from the barren, flat farmland of southern Minnesota to green, fertile valleys and hills as they neared the juncture of the Mississippi and Minnesota Rivers near Minneapolis.

At the St. Paul station they changed trains, boarding a small, short-haul commuter which chugged its way westward across the Mississippi and out into the verdant countryside.

"Look at all the lakes!" Kirsten marveled, gazing out the train's expansive windows. "Why, you can see a lake in every direction!"

"Pretty, isn't it?" Eric smiled. "The glacier really did

its work here. Seemed to gouge a lake out every couple of miles."

"It's so beautiful!" Kirsten breathed, her nose pressed to the window in her excitement.

Eric nodded, but his mind was not on the beauty of the terrain. Rather, it was on the dazzling countenance of his enraptured wife.

He spent the remainder of their journey covertly watching Kirsten, while secretly planning how he would woo her during the next two weeks.

They disembarked at the small, bustling Wayzata station and headed directly down an embankment to a set of large wooden docks where several steamboats sat, roaring and belching great plumes of smoke into the cloudless autumnal sky. The air was cool and crisp, with a slight breeze coming from the lake, blowing soft tendrils of Kirsten's flaming hair around her face.

Boarding the huge, lavish *Minnetonka Princess,* they stood by the rail, looking out over Wayzata Bay.

"This lake must be huge!" Kirsten exclaimed.

"It is. We're at the very eastern end of it now, but it goes on for miles and miles. Don't worry, we'll have a chance to see it all while we're here."

"Oh, I doubt that," she countered, turning to him with an indulgent smile. "After all, you're here to work, not vacation! I would imagine that Mr. Hathaway will expect you to spend your days painting, not sightseeing."

"Well, of course he expects me to paint," Eric said quickly, silently chastising himself for his slip, "but, he knows that artists can only work when the light is just right. There will be some times during the day that I won't be able to paint, so I'm sure we'll have time to look around a bit."

"That would be nice, of course," Kirsten nodded, "but, the most important thing is to get the painting done as quickly as possible. I wouldn't want Mr. Hathaway to think we were taking advantage of his hospitality."

"No, of course not," Eric sighed. "I'm fully aware of the reason we're here, Kirsten, but I might as well warn you. After you've spent a couple of hours standing perfectly still in one position, you'll be glad to call it quits and move around a little."

At that moment, the *Minnetonka Princess* backed away from the Wayzata dock, ending all conversation as the mammoth steamboat's deafening whistle sounded and black smoke spewed high into the air. The gigantic paddle wheel dug into the water, throwing a fine spray over the passengers clustered at the rail, and with a bone jarring shudder the boat headed into the bay.

They arrived at the hotel's dock just as the bright autumn sun began its spectacular descent toward the western horizon. Eric smiled as he looked up at the luxurious edifice before him. It was just as he remembered. The huge, sprawling hotel spread across the lake's high bank, looking much like a Spanish palace. Large, double-tiered verandas extended the length of the long building, affording each of the guest rooms with a magnificent view of both the lower and upper arms of the lake. The first-floor veranda was completely screened in, protecting its guests from the nasty, stinging mosquitos which rose out of the nearby marshlands every night at dusk to prey upon their hapless human victims.

Atop the hotel's steeply pitched roof were multiple cupolas, each with a flag waving from its summit like so many ladies' handkerchiefs fluttering a welcome in the soft, cool breeze.

As Eric reached out a hand to help Kirsten into a waiting carriage to begin the ascent up the steep hill leading from the dock to the hotel's front entrance, she paused a moment, looking around in awed astonishment. "This is the most magnificent resort I've ever seen!" she confided to him quietly. "No one in New York would ever believe a place like this exists out here on the frontier."

"Oh yes they would," Eric laughed. "Half the guests

331

who visit here are from New York! The word has gotten out, I can assure you."

The carriage completed its short trip up the long, sweeping drive, stopping in front of the hotel's massive double doors. Eric quickly climbed down, then turned to assist Kirsten.

Without releasing her hand, he walked back to where the driver was unloading their baggage, digging into his pocket and pulling out a coin to tip him.

"You shouldn't have to do that!" Kirsten whispered as they proceeded up the front steps. "Surely if you told the man that you're just working here, he wouldn't expect a tip!"

"Forget it," Eric muttered. "A quarter isn't going to break me."

Kirsten frowned at her husband, obviously annoyed with his spendthrift ways, but said no more.

They swept through the huge doors and entered the hotel's massive lobby. As Kirsten got her first look at the magnificent foyer, she stopped dead in her tracks, sucking in her breath in disbelief.

"Red, isn't it?" Eric chuckled.

Dumbstruck, Kirsten merely nodded. The entire lobby was decorated in shades of red and gold. Red wallpaper, red-and-gold draperies, even the thick, soft carpet beneath their feet was red. Looking down at the carpet, Kirsten leaned toward Eric and whispered, "Is the carpet velvet?"

"Yeah," he whispered back, smiling. "Not bad for the 'frontier,' right?"

Kirsten nodded, her eyes wide.

They proceeded across the room to the registration desk where an impeccably groomed older gentleman stood waiting for them.

"Ah, Mr. Wellesley, hello! So good to see you again, sir. It's been a long time."

Eric cringed as Kirsten's eyebrows rose in surprise.

"Nice to see you again, too," Eric mumbled, picking up the pen the desk clerk held out to him and leaning over the register. "Is Mr. Hathaway here?"

"Yes, indeed, sir. He's been waiting for you. Told me to inform him the minute you arrived."

With the briefest of nods, Eric shoved the register back across the counter.

The desk clerk turned away briefly, plucking a large gold key from out of a bank of pigeonholes. "Suite 364, sir," he said, tapping a small bell with the palm of his hand. A porter immediately appeared, nodding at Eric and Kirsten with a decidedly servile attitude.

"Why don't you go on upstairs and get settled?" the clerk suggested. "Your baggage is already on its way up to the suite. I'll notify Mr. Hathaway that you've arrived. He told me he'd like to see you this afternoon, if possible. Would five o'clock be convenient?"

Kirsten gaped at the desk clerk in stunned disbelief while Eric simply nodded and said, "Any time that's convenient for Mr. Hathaway is fine with me. I'm at his disposal."

"Fine," smiled the clerk. "Five o'clock it is, then. I'll send a boy up to show you to Mr. Hathaway's office when the time comes."

"Thank you," Eric muttered, grabbing Kirsten's elbow and hastening her away from the fawning man. He'd have to talk to Hathaway right away and instruct him to tell the staff to quit acting like he was an honored guest instead of a commissioned workman. Otherwise his carefully planned ruse was going to be exposed before his plans even got underway.

As they sped across the lobby, Kirsten whispered, "Why is everyone treating you like you're the President of the United States? Don't they know you're an employee?"

"I don't know," Eric shrugged. "Maybe they don't."

"But the desk clerk must! He said Mr. Hathaway had been waiting for you. He must know why you're here."

"I don't know!" Eric repeated. "Maybe good manners are just so ingrained in the staff here that they treat everyone the same, regardless of who they are."

Kirsten's expression was doubtful. "That doesn't make any sense. And what's this about a suite? I thought we'd probably be assigned a couple of little rooms under the stairs somewhere."

Eric sighed, his frustration mounting. "Kirsten, I don't know any more about this than you do. But if they want to treat us like royalty, why fight it?"

"Because," she said patiently, "if room and board is part of your payment for the portrait, it would make sense to spend as little as possible on lodging and get as much as possible in cash."

Eric closed his eyes, finding it impossible to argue with such sterling logic. "We'll talk about it later," he hedged. "The middle of the lobby is really not the place. Besides, that porter waiting to take us up in the elevator is beginning to look annoyed, so let's go!"

"Elevator!" Kirsten gasped. "They have an elevator?"

Eric chuckled. "The first one ever installed west of the Mississippi."

"I don't like elevators," she shuddered, "they scare me."

Eric looked at her in astonishment. Never, in all the time they'd known each other had he ever heard Kirsten admit that anything scared her. Feeling a sudden surge of protectiveness, he slipped his arm around her shoulder. "Don't worry, sweetheart," he whispered, his mouth close to her ear, "I won't let anything happen to you."

With eyes full of yearning, Kirsten looked over at the sweeping staircase. "Couldn't we just take the stairs?"

Eric smiled benevolently. "If you want to."

"I do."

Signaling to the porter that they would take the stairs, Eric gently cupped Kirsten's elbow and headed in that direction. Their room was on the third floor and as they slowly ascended the staircase, Eric wondered how he was going to explain that they would be sharing it. He knew Kirsten was going to balk, probably insisting that he get her separate accommodations, and somehow he had to talk her out of it.

They strolled down the third-floor hallway, following the porter who had met them at the elevator doors. Eric had specifically instructed Mr. Hathaway to assign them a small room, but obviously the man had not listened. The porter proceeded down the entire length of the wide hallway, stopping in front of a set of carved double doors at the very end of the corridor. He placed the key in the lock and with a sweeping gesture flung open the massive portals, ushering the frowning Eric and the gaping Kirsten into the spectacular suite.

"I hope you'll find everything satisfactory, sir," he said, turning to Eric.

"I'm sure it will be fine," Eric answered, reaching in his pocket for another coin while studiously avoiding Kirsten's eyes.

With a quick, subservient nod, the porter handed Eric the door key and backed out of the suite, closing the door behind him.

Eric cast wary eyes on Kirsten, but she was paying no attention to him. Without a word, she lay her reticule on a small table and looked around the room. They were in the parlor portion of the suite and Eric could tell by the path Kirsten's eyes were traveling that she was gauging how many bedrooms were attached. Since there was only one interior door in the room, the answer was pretty obvious.

Walking over to that door, Kirsten flung it open and stepped inside.

Eric waited.

When she reappeared, he braced himself for the explosion he was sure was imminent, but to his surprise it didn't come.

Instead Kirsten simply looked at him, her eyes cool and expressionless. With a leisurely tread that belied her seething anger, she walked across the suite, pausing to pick up her reticule. Then, in a soft, velvety voice, she lowered the boom.

"Eric, would you do something for me?"

Astounded that she didn't seem to be upset in the least by the sleeping arrangements, Eric beamed and answered, "Sure, sweetheart. What do you need?"

"I'd like you to go downstairs and ask that porter to come back up and get my bags. I'm going home now."

Chapter 30

"What?" Eric gasped, a surge of panic racing through him. "You can't go home!"

"Watch me!" Kirsten snapped.

Moving quickly toward the door to block her exit, Eric forced his voice into a conciliatory tone. "Kirsty, what's wrong?"

"What's wrong," she hissed, "is that you lied to me."

Eric gulped, silently cursing the damn desk clerk. "What makes you say that?" he asked, hoping his voice didn't betray his roiling emotions.

"This makes me say that!" Kirsten blurted, throwing her arm wide in a gesture that encompassed the whole suite. "You told me we'd have separate rooms. You promised that this trip was strictly business and that you wouldn't put any pressure on me to . . ."

"And have I put any pressure on you?" Eric interrupted.

"Well, no," she admitted, "but, there's only one bedroom here."

"So?"

"So, there's also only one bed!"

"There's a sofa," Eric said reasonably, pointing to a small settee centered in the parlor.

"Oh, sure!" Kirsten laughed sarcastically, glancing with disdain at the delicate four-foot long piece of furniture. "And I just bet you're going to curl that huge body of yours up on that every night for the next two weeks."

"I will if you want me to," Eric said quietly.

Kirsten paused, not knowing what to say in the face of his immediate agreement. "You can't sleep on that, Eric. You'd be crippled by morning."

"Then I'll ask Mr. Hathaway to give us another room."

"You will?" she asked, her voice small.

"Absolutely. I'll ask him when I meet with him this afternoon."

Kirsten didn't know whether to be relieved or disappointed by Eric's ready capitulation to her demands. "Will you have to pay for another room?"

"Probably," Eric shrugged, delighted that Kirsten was reacting exactly as he'd hoped. He knew that offering her her own room was a gamble, but in the face of her distrust and obstinacy, it was the only way he could think to prevent her from leaving altogether.

"Can you afford that?" she asked.

"Can I afford not to?" he countered. "They'll take the money out of my pay, but if you leave there won't be any pay. What choice do I have?"

Kirsten bit her lip. Maybe she *was* wrong about his motives in bringing her here. Laying her purse back on the table, she said softly, "I can sleep on the settee."

It was all Eric could do not to jump for joy. With an effort he strove to keep the triumphant glee out of his voice. "Are you sure?"

"Yes," she responded, nodding. "It's kind of short, but I usually sleep curled up anyway."

"I know," Eric said, his voice slightly husky as he remembered those two heavenly nights when he'd awakened to find her curled up against him.

As if she could read the thread of his thoughts, Kirsten blushed and turned away. "It's almost five," she said breezily, "you better get ready for your meeting."

Nodding, Eric headed toward the bedroom, entering

338

the sumptuous room and looking longingly at the huge, canopied bed. It took very little imagination to picture Kirsten nestled against him in its soft depths. With a Herculean effort, he dragged his eyes away and marched over to an ornate commode which stood in the corner.

At least she's not leaving, he thought. *She may not be in your bed yet, but, at least she's in your room.*

Trying to convince himself that the first step of his carefully planned seduction was a success, he turned his thoughts toward his upcoming meeting with Hathaway. He sincerely hoped that he could escape the jovial man's company quickly. He wanted dinner. Never, when he'd concocted this cock-and-bull story of financial woes for Kirsten, had he considered that he'd have to starve to death to convince her of his plight!

"Are you sure we should be eating in here?" Kirsten whispered as they walked into the Stanford Hotel's main dining room.

"Absolutely," Eric whispered back. "We get three meals a day. *Every* day. Now, quit worrying and let's eat!"

They were barely seated when a formally clad waiter approached them. With a smiling nod, he handed them two leather bound menus and said, "Good evening, Mr. Wellesley, Mrs. Wellesley."

Kirsten gaze flicked up to the waiter in astonishment. How did he know their names? "Good evening," she replied, her expression puzzled as she looked over at Eric.

"Evening," Eric muttered, furious that Hathaway had obviously still not alerted the staff as to his supposed purpose for being here. "What's ready?"

The waiter's eyebrows lifted in startled offense at the curt tone in Eric's voice. "The roast beef is ready, sir. So is the chicken."

"Good," Eric said, snapping his menu closed and

holding it out to the man. "I'll take the roast beef—a double cut, and lots of potatoes."

"What kind of potatoes, sir?"

"It doesn't matter. Just bring a lot of them."

"Very good, sir," the waiter nodded, appalled by Eric's rudeness. He was well aware that Eric was one of *the* Colorado Wellesleys, but as far as he was concerned this particular man was just a prime example that a huge fortune didn't necessarily denote good manners.

"And you, madam?" he said, turning his attention to Kirsten, who was sitting with her menu still closed in her hand, gaping at her husband.

"Oh!" she said, pulling her eyes away from Eric. "I'll have, let me see, fish, I think. Do you have fish?"

The waiter smiled at her with patronizing patience. "Yes, indeed. The finest in Minnesota, madam—caught right out here in our lake this very morning."

"That sounds wonderful," Kirsten nodded, "I'll have it."

When the waiter finally completed taking their order, including recommending a wine which Eric instantly agreed to, and headed back toward the kitchen, Kirsten turned on Eric in a fury.

"Why were you so rude to that man?" she demanded. "And why did you order wine? I'm positive that isn't included in your daily ration."

Eric nearly choked on the water he was drinking. *Daily ration!* Good Lord, Kirsten made it sound like she expected them to eat bread and water!

"I wasn't trying to be rude," Eric assured her. "I'm just starving to death and I want to eat now!" As if to prove his point, he reached across the table and plucked several crackers out of a small basket. "And, as far as the wine is concerned, I don't care if it's part of my 'ration,' or not. I want a glass."

Kirsten looked at him, intrigued. "I've never seen you drink wine in your life," she laughed. "You and I never had it at home."

Eric's heart leaped at her unconscious mention of his farm as "home." But, not wanting her to see how pleased he was by her slip, he merely shrugged nonchalantly and said, "Well, I enjoy a glass of wine when I'm out. You and I just never went out much."

"No," Kirsten answered dryly, "we didn't. Too much work to do for that."

Before Eric could respond to her subtle dig, the waiter reappeared with their meals. Conversation came to a dead halt as Eric tore into his food.

"You really are hungry, aren't you?" Kirsten chuckled.

"Yeah," Eric nodded, barely pausing as he scooped up another forkful of mashed potatoes and thick, brown gravy. "I haven't eaten since yesterday, except for that apple you gave me."

"Yesterday!" Kirsten exclaimed. "You mean you didn't have any breakfast this morning?"

"No," Eric shook his head. "I didn't have time. I had to get the chores done and then fill Joe Wheeler in on how to take care of things while I'm gone, and I didn't have time to make anything for myself before I had to meet you."

Kirsten lowered her head, feeling an unexpected surge of guilt that Eric had no one to cook for him now that she was gone. "I wish I'd known," she murmured. "I would have brought you some pastries."

"Thanks," he smiled, pleased by her concern, "but I made it okay. The apple helped."

Looking up at him, Kirsten felt a moment of unaccountable sadness. The whole time they'd lived together, she'd cursed the never-ending chores she'd faced every day. But now she realized that she actually missed some of those wifely duties. She knew she could happily live her entire life without ever cleaning out another privy, but when she thought back on how Eric's face would light up when he walked in to find a fresh plate of cookies or a fruit pie, she felt an inexplicable sense of loss.

When their plates had been cleared and the last drop of wine consumed, Eric rose from the table and pulled back her chair. "Let's go in and look at the salon," he suggested. "I want to get an idea of where we should pose you before I set up tomorrow."

They strolled across the massive lobby, arm in arm, oblivious to the admiring looks cast their way by other guests and the hotel staff. Eric's dark handsomeness contrasted with Kirsten's tawny beauty drew many eyes in their direction, and as they disappeared into the private salon, ladies' fans snapped open to cool flushed cheeks and men glanced at each other knowingly, sharing looks of appreciation.

Eric walked into the salon, his eyes darting immediately to the wall above the grand piano where the "Portrait of a Lady" had hung. He breathed a sigh of relief when he saw that the wall was bare. At least J.J. Hathaway hadn't forgotten to take down the painting! He didn't know how he would have explained to Kirsten the hotel's pressing "need" for his work if the magnificent portrait had still been present.

He looked fondly around the familiar room, his expression wistful as he remembered the last time he'd been in it—standing in front of the portrait with his father by his side as he confessed to him his secret desire to paint. And his father, ever supportive of his many sons' dreams and aspirations, had encouraged him, instilling in the shy, conservative Eric the confidence to make his closely held dream a reality.

For a moment a feeling of profound sadness washed over him as he thought about how much he missed his father. James Wellesley's death had been so unexpected, so shattering, that Eric, the most sensitive and introspective of the seven boys, had never completely recovered from his loss.

"Where do you want me to pose, Eric?" Kirsten's voice shook him from his melancholy reverie, and with a slightly embarrassed smile he pointed toward the piano and said, "There. Against the piano."

Eagerly, Kirsten walked over to the piano, standing slightly at an angle and artfully resting an elbow on the instrument's gleaming surface. "Like this?" she asked.

"Something like that," he agreed, nodding. "The elbow's good. I'm going to have you holding a lace handkerchief in your other hand."

Kirsten walked back to where he stood near the door. "I brought several things with me that I thought would be appropriate for me to wear."

Eric's mind was miles away, his artist's eye already gauging light and distance and depth. "You don't need to worry about that," he muttered distractedly, shifting his focus to another window as he compared different angles, "Your dress came today."

"My dress?" Kirsten asked curiously. "What dress?"

Jerking himself back to reality, Eric's eyes widened in horror as he became aware of what he'd just said. He couldn't tell Kirsten that he'd contacted a fashionable dressmaker in St. Paul, paying her a small fortune to design and sew a dress to his exact specifications. He'd even gone so far as to ask Betty Zimmer to measure one of Kirsten's dresses so that he could send the dressmaker her exact measurements.

"Oh, didn't I tell you?" he asked in feigned surprise, keeping his voice light and guileless. "The hotel is supplying a dress for you to wear."

"Why would they do that?" Kirsten asked, frowning. "And, how could they have a dress made without my measurements?"

"Well," Eric hedged, thinking fast, "they wanted to design the dress themselves so that the colors would match this room. And, as far as your measurements are concerned, they asked me."

"How did *you* know?"

"Oh, I just guessed, but I think I was close enough that it should fit pretty well. If it doesn't, you can always pin it or something."

Kirsten looked doubtful. "Well, all right, if you're sure the dress will do credit to your painting."

Thinking of the exquisite, ice blue satin gown which was, even now, hanging in a closet in J.J. Hathaway's office, Eric chuckled and said, "Don't worry, my lady. I won't allow you to wear anything less than the very finest Mr. Hathaway's money can buy." And bending over her hand, he kissed it gallantly.

With a small giggle, Kirsten pulled her hand out of his grasp and said, "Come on. If you have to get up at dawn to set up your supplies, we better get to bed."

Eric swallowed hard, thinking just how much he'd love to "get to bed" with Kirsten. "You're right," he said tightly. "I was just thinking about that myself."

Chapter 31

Kirsten lay awake long into the night, tossing restlessly in the hotel suite's huge, sumptuous bed. It was well past midnight and although she knew that Eric wanted to get started with the portrait early in the morning, sleep eluded her. When they had returned to the suite after dinner, Eric had insisted that she take the bedroom after all, arguing that she was the one who needed to look fresh and rested in the morning.

Despite the late hour, she could hear him through the bedroom door, moving about just as restlessly as she was as he fought to get comfortable on the hard, too-short settee.

"Serves him right for not making it clear to the hotel that we needed two rooms," she muttered irritably, but, still, a small twinge of guilt niggled at her as she thought about how truly uncomfortable he must be.

Kirsten's mind drifted back to the lovely dinner they had shared and how right it had seemed to again sit at the same table, chatting and eating together. What was it about eating that was so intimate?

No, she thought wryly, it wasn't just eating, it was eating with Eric. She had shared thousands of meals in her life with other people and never did she feel the same sense of intimacy that she did when she sat across a table from her husband.

Your soon to be *ex*-husband, she reminded herself

firmly. She had to stop thinking of Eric as her husband. It was obvious he had. Despite the day they had spent together, Eric had maintained a distance, treating her with unfailing charm and good manners, but, also, with a polite aloofness that made her feel more like an old and dear friend than a wife.

"And that's exactly what you want, isn't it?" she demanded to the empty room. Of course it was. As soon as these two weeks were over, they would return to Rose Meadow, she would take the money he was paying her, plus the pilfered hundred dollars he'd promised to return, board the train for New York, and leave his life forever. Eric's disinterest was exactly what she wanted. Their ill-fated marriage was over and her romantic feelings for him dead.

Kirsten flopped over on her back and stared miserably at the ceiling, a tear tracing its way down her cheek. If all that was true, then why did her knees still turn to jelly every time Eric looked at her?

Eric was already in the salon ready for Kirsten when she joined him the next morning. His easel was set up, his paints set out, his colors already mixed on his palette. What he wasn't ready for was the way Kirsten looked when she entered the room, wearing the blue satin dress he'd had designed for her.

She was a vision. The sheen of the midnight blue cloth against the alabaster whiteness of her skin and the fiery hue of her hair was so breathtaking that he was dumbstruck. He'd known that the color and fabric he'd chosen would set her skin and hair off to their best advantage, but he'd never dreamed that any woman could look as beautiful as she did with the sun glinting off her hair and reflecting off the magnificent diamond teardrop necklace which lay nestled in the high curves of her lush breasts.

He had told her that he had borrowed the necklace from a jeweler friend, but, in actuality, he had purchased it for her at the same time he had purchased the cloth for her dress. As he gazed at the necklace gently rising and falling with her breath, he wondered if he would ever have the opportunity to tell her it was hers. Probably not, he thought with a small sigh, considering that the inexpensive garnet earrings he had purchased at Lars's store when they'd first been married, still lay under a pile of underwear in his bureau drawer.

"Where do you want me?" Kirsten asked, gliding across the room toward him.

In my bed!

"Right here, in the curve of the piano," he answered, his voice thick with repressed desire.

"Are you getting a cold?" she asked in alarm, concerned by the huskiness of his voice.

Not trusting himself to speak again, Eric simply shook his head. Taking Kirsten by the elbow, he steered her toward the piano, turning her until she stood at the angle he wanted. "Now, put your arm along the top like you did last night," he directed.

Kirsten obediently placed her arm along the piano's polished surface. "Here?"

"Yes."

"What should I do with my other arm?"

Eric picked up a large white lace handkerchief which was lying on a small table. "Hold this," he said, handing it to her. "Let it trail down the skirt of your dress."

"Like this?"

Again he nodded, utterly charmed by her natural grace as she stood before him. She was a born model.

Walking back to his easel, he stood next to it for a moment, cocking his head slightly and staring at the overall effect she presented. "Something's wrong," he said.

"Wrong?"

"Yeah, I think it's the set of your shoulders."

Looking surprised and slightly offended, Kirsten

looked down at her shoulders. "What's wrong with them?"

"Nothing's *wrong* with them," Eric chuckled. "It's the way you're holding them. Relax and drop them a little."

Kirsten did as he bade, but he still wasn't satisfied. "Actually I think it's the way your dress is positioned. Lower the sleeves a little."

Setting down the handkerchief, Kirsten tugged at the sleeves of the dress, pulling them down until they fell slightly off her shoulders. "Is this better?"

Eric swallowed hard as even more of her breasts were exposed. "It's better, but it's still not right. The bodice is wrong now."

Glancing down at the low-cut bodice, Kirsten shrugged. "What do you want me to do with it?"

"Here, I'll fix it," he said, setting down the brush he was holding and walking over to where she was standing. Dipping his thumbs into the bodice, he gave it a gentle tug downward, causing Kirsten to jump.

Eric looked at her with alarm. "Did I hurt you?"

"No," she answered quickly, not wanting him to know that her startled movement had been caused by the sensation of his hands touching her breasts. She was embarrassed by her reaction to him, especially since he was obviously not feeling the same at all.

Kirsten realized that she was seeing a whole new side of Eric. Eric Wellesley, the artist, was an entirely different man from Eric Wellesley, the farmer, or Eric Wellesley, the husband. His touch was impersonal, distracted, an artist posing his model and nothing more.

She couldn't have been more wrong. The feeling of Kirsten's warm, creamy breasts pressed against his hands had shot tremors of desire through Eric which were almost overwhelming. It was only by sheer dint of will that he was able to impassively adjust the bodice of her gown without grabbing her and ripping the damn thing off.

Reluctantly he removed his thumbs and stepped back. "There, that's better," he muttered, quickly retreating behind his easel before his traitorous body betrayed him to his disinterested wife. "Now, lift your chin a little and think about something delicious. I want a little, faraway smile—the kind of look you'd have if you were thinking about something you really want, but you're not sure you'll ever get."

You, Kirsten thought, assuming exactly the kind of longing, wistful smile Eric was looking for.

"There! That's it! Now, hold it. Don't move a muscle." And, dabbing his brush into the paint spread across his palette Eric started his masterpiece.

It was the hardest work he'd ever done. Years of painting had taught him the importance of keeping a detached eye, of viewing his model as an object to be observed, then transferred through his brush to the canvas. But painting Kirsten was different. Never had he been so acutely aware of how much he loved her as during those first moments when he began painting the contours of her exquisite face and the lines of her delicately curved body.

It was a gut-wrenching experience; draining, exhausting, and exhilarating. His brush moved as if by magic as he used his medium to tell the world of his love for this woman. He knew, even in the very first moments as paint covered canvas, that this would be his greatest work. For the first, and undoubtedly the last time in his life, he was working out of love, and all the passion and longing he felt for Kirsten was visible on the canvas in front of him.

Two hours passed in total silence as the couple worked together. Eric was completely unaware of the time until he suddenly noticed that the sun had shifted, causing the shaft of sunlight coming through the window to wane and finally disappear altogether. He sighed and reluctantly laid down his brush, loath to have to quit.

"Okay, Kirsty," he said quietly, "we're done for

today. You can relax now."

With a sigh of relief, Kirsten sagged tiredly against the piano, lifting her aching shoulders and flexing her stiff knees. Her movement was almost painful as blood rushed into limbs which had been held absolutely rigid for two hours. A little groan escaped her, causing Eric to turn and look at her in surprise.

"Are you okay?" he asked, concern etched on his handsome features.

"Yes," she smiled. "I'm just stiff. I never dreamed this would be such hard work!"

"Why didn't you tell me you were tired?" he asked, taking her by the arm and guiding her toward a plush chair. "I would have stopped a long time ago."

"I didn't want you to stop," Kirsten answered, sinking gratefully into the chair. "You seemed to be making such good progress that I wanted you to keep going."

Eric looked at her searchingly for a moment, surprised at her consideration.

His gaze was so warm, so soft, that Kirsten felt a moment of panic. "After all," she said quickly, "the longer you paint every day, the sooner we'll be done here and can go back to Rose Meadow."

Eric felt like he'd been punched in the stomach. So, that was it. Kirsten wasn't being considerate, she merely wanted to get this obligation over with and get on with her life . . . a life without him. The spell which had been lingering over them was suddenly broken, and in a harsh, businesslike voice he retorted, "Well, from now on, tell me when you've had enough. I don't want you fainting on me."

Hurt by his callousness, Kirsten nodded and rose from the chair. "I'm going up to change," she announced and turned toward the door.

"Fine," he called after her, cursing himself for letting the moment between them get away, "I'll clean up here and then meet you in the dining room for lunch."

Without turning, Kirsten nodded and disappeared

350

out the door.

"Damn!" Eric cursed aloud. "You stupid, damn fool!" With a feeling of frustration and defeat, he turned tiredly back toward his dirty brushes.

The next two weeks flew by. Kirsten and Eric's days took on a pattern: rising early, eating a hurried breakfast, then spending the morning working together. More than once Kirsten thought she might collapse from the strain of the endless hours of standing rigidly still next to the piano as Eric's work took shape. But the intensity and satisfaction which she saw written on his face as the painting progressed was a heady incentive for her to stand, uncomplaining and motionless, for the long, tedious hours.

In the afternoons Kirsten would read or nap or play cards with the other guests at the opulent resort while Eric continued to paint, filling in backgrounds and shading in completed portions of Kirsten's dress and handkerchief.

Their evenings were spent together, enjoying quiet dinners and taking long walks in the cool fall evenings. They would return to the hotel late, often stopping in the opulent bar for a nightcap before retiring to their room.

In all this time neither of them ever mentioned their marriage or its impending demise. After the first morning of posing when Eric had adjusted Kirsten's dress, he never again touched her, except in the most proper and accepted manner, taking her arm as they descended the hotel's sweeping staircase or placing a hand lightly on the small of her back to usher her through a door or guide her between tables in the crowded dining room.

Retiring for the evening was a never-ending agony, which, unbeknownst to either of them, was shared by both. Every night as they parted for their respective rooms after a brief, chaste kiss, Eric hoped that Kirsten might ask him to share her bed, and at the same time Kirsten prayed that he wouldn't draw away after the brief touch of his lips to her cheek, but, rather, draw her into his arms and kiss her till she swooned.

But it didn't happen, and as the days passed and the portrait neared completion, both of them became more and more moody and introspective.

Inevitably, the final day of their stay arrived. As usual, Kirsten walked into the drawing room shortly after eight. But instead of finding Eric in his usual place behind the easel, she found him dressed in a pair of wool worsted pants and a sweater, sitting on a sofa directly opposite the piano.

"What's going on?" she asked, her brows knitted in confusion. "You're not wearing your work clothes."

"No," he smiled, a look of satisfaction on his face, "I don't have to. The work's done."

Kirsten whirled toward the easel, her eyes sparkling with excitement. "Oh, Eric, is it really? When did you finish?"

"Last night," he answered happily, rising from the sofa and coming to stand next to her in front of the covered easel.

"But you didn't tell me yesterday that you were that close."

"I didn't think I was, but after you left for your walk yesterday afternoon, I finished it."

"And you didn't say anything at dinner?"

"I didn't want to tell you until I could show you. And I didn't want you to see it until this morning when the light was good."

Kirsten pressed her hands to her cheeks, gazing at him with shining eyes. "May I see it now?"

Closing his eyes for a brief moment and casting a heartfelt prayer heavenward that she would approve, Eric nodded and slowly lifted the light cover.

Kirsten was awestruck. Never had she seen a more

glorious work of art. It was her, but, then again, it wasn't, for she knew that she had never looked so beautiful.

"Eric," she whispered, "it's . . . it's magnificent."

Eric released a breath he hadn't even realized he was holding. "Do you honestly think so, Kirsty?"

"Oh, yes," she breathed. "Do I really look like that?"

"To me you do," he answered, his voice so low she hardly heard him.

"I don't know what to say," she sighed, turning toward him and looking at him as if for the first time. "I never realized what it would feel like to be . . . immortalized."

Eric chuckled, a soft rich sound which rumbled up from his chest and made Kirsten's heart pound erratically. "Do you really like it, sweetheart?"

"I think it's the most beautiful painting I've ever seen," she answered truthfully, and reaching up, she placed her hands on his cheeks and kissed him softly on the mouth. "Congratulations, Eric."

For a moment Eric was so dumbfounded by Kirsten's soft caress that he didn't react at all, and by the time he had the presence of mind to lean toward her and lift his arms to draw her closer, she was already pulling away.

She didn't look at him, didn't see the look of yearning and loss in his eyes. Embarrassed by her own impulsiveness, she turned quickly back to the portrait, stepping closer to look at it in greater detail. "You know," she said brightly, still not meeting his eyes, "I think this calls for a celebration. Since we aren't leaving until tomorrow and the painting is done, I think we should spend the day enjoying the resort."

When Eric still said nothing, she turned toward him, trying to gauge his reaction to her suggestion. "What do you think?" she smiled. "Wouldn't you like to see some of the sights? You've hardly been out at all during the day, and the leaves are just gorgeous now that they've all turned. Wouldn't you like to spend the day on the lake?"

"Yes," he answered softly, "I would."

"Good," she answered, a happy smile on her lips. "I'll go up and change and maybe you can see about booking us on the *Belle* for an excursion this afternoon."

"Sure."

Nonplussed by Eric's odd behavior, Kirsten threw him a last, slightly puzzled smile and hurried out of the room.

All the way up the stairs, she thought about how Eric's lips had felt when she'd touched them with her own, and a little thrill of anticipation skittered down her spine. *A whole day. A whole day with him! Please God, make him ask me just once more if I'll stay. Just once more!*

Chapter 32

Eric did a whole lot better than just booking them on the *Minnetonka Belle* for an excursion around the lake. He arranged with the hotel kitchen to pack them a picnic, then hired a small sloop to sail over to a heavily wooded island where he knew they would be alone.

It was a wonderful plan, he thought happily, as he sat in the lobby waiting for Kirsten to come back downstairs. Inspired even! Stuart himself couldn't have done any better.

It seemed like an eternity before Kirsten descended the staircase, dressed in a light gold-and-orange day dress which set off her coloring and made her cheeks glow with good health.

"Did you book us on the *Belle?*" she asked as she approached.

"No, I thought we'd sail over to the island."

"Sail! Do you know how to sail?"

"Yes," he chuckled, "as a matter of fact, I do."

Stooping down to pick up the heavily laden picnic basket, Eric took Kirsten's arm and escorted her out the front door of the hotel and down toward the docks.

"Where did you learn how to sail?" she asked as they walked across the lawn, dodging an energetic group playing croquet.

"When I was a kid I spent a summer with my brother in England. He taught me."

"You have a brother in England?" Kirsten asked, astounded by this incredible bit of information.

"Yes. Miles. He's the oldest."

Kirsten shook her head, once again reminded of how very little she actually knew about the man she had married. "You've never mentioned him."

"You've never asked."

Having no answer for that, Kirsten smiled. "You're right."

They reached the dock and Eric helped her into their small rented sloop. Kirsten looked about the tiny craft with trepidation. "Are you absolutely positive you know how to do this?" she asked.

"Why?" he grinned, detaching the anchoring line and throwing it up on the dock as he stepped down into the boat. "Don't you know how to swim?"

"Swim?" she gasped. "Well, yes I do, but, you know how to do this well enough that we won't capsize, don't you?"

"Don't worry, Kirsty," he laughed, loving the feeling of being responsible for her well-being. "I promise you won't get your hair wet. Just sit back and enjoy the day. I know what I'm doing."

And he did. His control of their little boat was masterful and they reached the island without mishap. Eric furled the sail and jumped into the shallow water, hauling the boat up on shore. Holding his hand out to Kirsten, he helped her out of the boat, then reached back into the small craft and pulled out the picnic basket and blanket which he had stowed earlier.

"Come on," he smiled, taking her hand. "I know a place that's perfect for picnicking."

A thrill shot through Kirsten as she felt her small hand being enclosed in Eric's large, calloused one. At that moment she felt like she would follow him to the ends of the earth if that's where his picnic spot was.

Fortunately, however, it wasn't quite that far. They walked about a quarter of a mile toward the interior of the island until they reached a large clearing. The spreading oaks overhead had lost much of their dense summer foliage, creating a soft bed of leaves over which Eric spread the blanket.

Sitting down, they unpacked the picnic basket and eagerly dug into the fried chicken, corn bread, and fresh crisp vegetables the hotel had packed for them.

"This is a beautiful spot," Kirsten smiled, looking around their secluded bower in appreciation. "How did you know about it?"

"I was here a few years ago with my father," Eric told her, his mouth full of chicken. "He had business meetings with Hathaway and I spent a morning exploring over here. Not many people come over to the island now, but I'm sure that's going to change. I've heard J.J. has plans to develop it into a picnic grounds and dance pavilion."

"Oh, I hope he doesn't do that," Kirsten said. "It would ruin the island's beauty if it were crawling with people all the time."

"You have a point," Eric conceded, "but you have to admit it would be a great place to have a dance."

Kirsten's eyebrows rose. "I didn't know you like to dance, Eric."

"There are a lot of things I like to do that you don't know about."

Kirsten dropped her eyes, surprised by his provocative comment. Looking around for something to busy herself with, she pulled two large pieces of chocolate cake out of the picnic basket and handed one to Eric.

"I love chocolate," Eric announced, lying back in the leaves and taking a huge bite of the cake. "When I was a kid, my mother used to send all the way to New York for cocoa so our cook could make us cakes and candy."

Again Kirsten's eyes widened in surprise. "Your family had servants?"

Eric hesitated, angry with himself that he was unwittingly divulging too much about his family's wealth. "Well, ah, yeah. With eight kids, my mother couldn't handle everything herself so she hired a couple

357

of women to help. They come real cheap out West."

"Eight children," Kirsten mused. "It never ceases to amaze me when you talk so calmly about a family that size."

"It doesn't seem strange to have a family that size when you're part of it," Eric said, brushing cake crumbs from his hands and rolling over onto his stomach. "I can't imagine being an only child."

"Well, it's not much fun. It's very lonely."

"I'm sure it is," he nodded. "I'd never want just one child. All my married brothers have big families and I've always figured I would, too,"

His unthinking comment about having a family cast an immediate pall over their conversation, and desperately Kirsten tried to think of a change of subject that would break the heavy silence.

"So," she said quickly, seizing upon the first topic she could think of, "when are you going to show Mr. Hathaway the painting?"

"Show Hathaway?" Eric asked, his mind still on her reaction to his leading comment about a family.

"Well, yes!" she laughed. "Don't you think your client will want to see the work he's paying you for?"

"Oh, sure. Sure! I'll show him when we get back."

"It's a truly beautiful painting, Eric," Kirsten said.

Eric smiled. "Thank you, madam," he said quietly, sitting up and leaning close to her. "I think the quality of the work is a direct reflection on the quality of the model."

Kirsten blushed, charmed by his compliment and excruciatingly aware of how close he was sitting to her. "That's very nice of you," she whispered. "Thank you."

"No," he smiled, leaning even closer until his lips were just a breath away from hers, "thank *you*." And before she could react to this latest onslaught to her senses, he lowered his mouth to hers, kissing her softly.

She began to pull away, terrified by the feelings he was evoking in her, but he wouldn't let her. As she began to draw back, he followed her, placing his hand on the back of her head and rising to his knees as he continued to kiss her.

Despite her trepidation at where the kiss might lead, her mouth softened beneath his and she lifted her hands, burrowing them into his hair.

He reacted with a sharp intake of breath, wrapping his arms around her back and pulling her up to her knees till she was pressed against him.

She could feel his rapidly rising arousal pressing insistently against her, and drawing on her last vestige of sanity, she tore her mouth away, sitting back on her heels and looking at him in horror.

"We can't do this!" she gasped.

It took Eric several deep breaths before he could get his raging desire under control enough to speak. When he did, his voice was hoarse and choked with need. "Why not?" he rasped, reaching for her again. "It's so good between us, Kirsten!"

"We can't!" she insisted. "It's not right."

"What do you mean, it's not right?" he retorted, his voice angry and frustrated. "You're my wife!"

It was a mistake to remind Kirsten of their relationship, and immediately she bristled. "Not for long!"

Blowing out a long, furious breath, Eric raked his hands through his hair and shook his head. "I don't understand you!"

"I know," she whispered brokenly, "you never have."

With a groan of despair Eric tried once more. "Kirsten, why do you keep fighting me when it's so good between us. Why?"

"Because," she said, rising to her feet, "as you told me yourself, it was even better between you and Elsie."

Eric stared at her in disbelief, trying to tell himself that he'd heard her wrong—that after all they'd shared in the last two weeks, she couldn't still believe he cared for someone else.

Why had he lost his temper that morning and said those things to her? And how could he ever make her believe that it had only been anger and frustration that he made him lie to her?

Looking into Kirsten's tear-glazed eyes, he shrugged in defeat and said, "You're right. We are no good for each other. Every time I get close to you, you end up crying."

Kirsten wiped furiously at the tears which had spilled over and were now running down her cheeks. "I know," she gulped, "strange, isn't it?"

Eric shook his head. "No, sweetheart, not strange. Just sad."

Without another word, the couple gathered up their picnic supplies and headed back to where their small sailboat sat happily bobbing in the late afternoon sun. They silently boarded and made the return trip across the lake, docking at the hotel and proceeding in mute agony up to their suite.

Kirsten immediately walked into the bedroom, closing the door softly behind her and sagging down on the edge of the bed. She didn't hear Eric leave a few minutes later. She didn't hear anything—except a sound deep within her that she knew was her heart breaking.

Kirsten had insisted that on this last night of their stay, Eric should take the bedroom. He had argued that it didn't matter, that he had become accustomed to his uncomfortable little settee, but she was adamant, stating that he deserved at least one night of comfort.

For the first time since arriving at the Stanford, they didn't have dinner together. Kirsten emerged from the bedroom at seven that evening, looking composed, if a bit pale and drawn, but Eric was nowhere to be seen. Thinking that he must be downstairs, picking up a newspaper or perhaps validating their train tickets for the following morning, she sat down in a large comfortable chair to wait.

The grandfather clock's silver pendulum swung back

and forth with incredible slowness, the minutes creeping by until, finally, they stretched into hours. But still Eric didn't return.

Finally, at nine, Kirsten hefted herself out of the chair and returned to the bedroom, changing out of the lovely evening gown she was wearing and pulling on her nightgown. Her stomach growled loudly, reminding her that it had been many hours since she had last eaten, but she was too tired and depressed to consider going downstairs and dining alone. Besides, after today's disastrous picnic, she didn't feel hungry, despite her stomach's protestations to the contrary.

She gazed longingly at the large, soft bed, wishing she could climb under the downy quilt and sleep for about a hundred years, but she had promised the bed to Eric, so with a weary sigh she picked up a blanket and pillow and headed back into the parlor.

The settee was appallingly uncomfortable and Kirsten felt a terrible rush of guilt when she thought about how miserable Eric must have been sleeping on it for the last two weeks. But despite her discomfort, she fell asleep quickly, exhausted from the trials of the heart-wrenching day.

Eric sat at a small table at the back of the Stanford Hotel's luxurious men's lounge. The dark, smoky room was a blessed respite from the sparkling bright chandeliers and tinkling women's laughter so prevalent in the rest of the hotel.

"Just what I need," he muttered to himself, refilling his brandy snifter from a large cut-glass decanter. "Somewhere where no women are allowed!"

He gazed about the nearly empty room, wondering why there weren't more men taking advantage of the restricted bar. "Maybe everybody else is just too stupid to realize how good it is to be a single man," he growled.

"Did you say something, sir?" A soft feminine voice

from close behind him made Eric wheel around in surprise.

"Nothing that has anything to do with you, miss," he answered, rising slightly from his chair. "Are you aware that this is the men's lounge? No women are allowed."

"Oh, a few of us are," she smiled, her voice low and slightly husky. "You're Mr. Wellesley, aren't you?"

"Yes," Eric answered, squinting to try to bring his uninvited guest into focus. "But who are you?"

"I'm Jocelyne," she murmured, slipping into the chair opposite his at the table, "but my friends call me Josie."

"Well, Josie, you shouldn't be in here. If the manager sees you, he'll throw you out."

"Don't worry about that," she assured him. "Why don't you buy me a drink?"

Her bold request finally registered in Eric's alcohol-fogged brain, and he realized where he had seen her before. As in most fine hostelries with a clientele of wealthy businessmen, the Stanford employed several charming and discreet young women who were, for a weighty price, available to male guests as "personal companions."

Several times during his stay at the Stanford, Eric had seen these pricey ladies of the evening lunching quietly together in the dining room or sitting outside in the sunshine during the warm fall afternoons. He had even once pointed them out to Kirsten, asking her if she had any idea who they were, then laughing heartily when she answered that she thought they might be a group of wealthy sorority girls enjoying one last weekend at the lake before returning to college.

As he took a closer look at the woman sitting across from him, he realized that she was the same girl he had noticed staring at him one day as he and Kirsten had strolled arm in arm along the lakeshore. Gazing now at her pretty, expectant face, he said quickly, "I'm not looking for company, miss."

"Oh," she sighed, pursing her mouth in a disappointed little moue, "what a pity." And, picking up her small beaded reticule, she rose to leave.

"Wait a minute," Eric blurted. "If you really want that drink . . ."

Smiling, she sat back down, looking over meaningfully at the bartender. "Where's Mrs. Wellesley this evening?" she asked casually.

"*Mrs.* Wellesley," Eric drawled sarcastically, "is upstairs, nursing a very large case of offended sensibilities."

"Oh?" Josie questioned, taking a delicate sip of the champagne cocktail the bartender had silently set in front of her. "Now who would offend such a lovely lady?"

"I did," Eric admitted.

"No! How did you do that?"

"Tried to take liberties with her."

Josie giggled. "But, Mr. Wellesley, how does one 'take liberties' with one's own wife?"

"Well, Josie," Eric said, his words slightly slurred as he leaned back and took another large swallow of brandy, "if one is married to my wife, one is accused of taking liberties simply by trying to kiss her."

Josie's eyebrows rose imperceptively in well-concealed surprise. For the past two weeks, she had watched the handsome Mr. Wellesley dote on his beautiful young wife, his affection so blatant that Josie had felt a surge of envy every time she saw them together. What wouldn't she give to have Eric Wellesley look at her the way he looked at Kirsten? She had thought the couple to be deeply in love and was now finding it nearly impossible to believe Eric's words. Could Kirsten Wellesley really be foolish enough to reject her charming and virile husband's attentions?

"Perhaps," she suggested, "you just approached her at a bad time."

Eric shook his head. "No, that's not it. She doesn't

want me anytime. She's leaving me."

The look on his face was so sad, so woebegone, that Josie's heart went out to him. "Leaving you? Surely, you're mistaken!"

"No," Eric shook his head sadly, "no mistake. She's going back to New York. Tomorrow—after we get home. I thought I could save our marriage if I brought her here. I thought a vacation might change the way she feels about me, but it didn't. She just doesn't love me, and there's nothing I can do to make her."

For a long moment Josie stared at Eric, knowing that she was in a perfect situation to make her little fantasy about him come true. The man was totally vulnerable—and hers for the taking. Josie had known many, many men and she knew an easy mark when she saw one. But despite her secret desire to see Eric Wellesley naked and kneeling above her in the darkness of her small room, something stopped her. In a flash of crystal clarity she realized she didn't want him for a lover for one night. She wanted him for a friend for the rest of her life. So instead of seducing him, she decided to help him.

"You know what I think, Mr. Wellesley?"

"No," he said, forcing his flagging attention back to her.

"I think that you're making a mistake about your wife. I think she's very much in love with you."

"You're wrong. She's never loved me."

Josie shook her head, thinking back on the times that she had seen Kirsten Wellesley throwing covert looks at her husband that were so hungry that Josie had been surprised the couple didn't tumble to the ground right there on the beach in front of her.

"I also think," she continued, her voice soft and persuasive, "that if you go upstairs right now, scoop her up in your arms and take her to bed, you'll find that she won't say no."

Eric smiled wistfully as Josie again rose and picked up her small purse. "I'm afraid you're wrong, Josie," he

364

said sadly. "She always says no."

Josie smiled and leaned over to give Eric a soft kiss on the cheek. "She won't say no tonight," she whispered. "Trust me. I'm rarely wrong."

Before Eric could argue any further, Josie swept away in a swirl of satin skirts, heading for another small table and another lonely man.

Kirsten didn't know how long she had slept, but she was suddenly startled awake by a pair of strong, muscular arms lifting her off the settee. Her eyes snapped open in alarm, and for a moment she fought desperately against the stranger in whose viselike grip she was being held. Her fears were quickly allayed, though, as from out of the inky blackness, she heard Eric's voice, soft and caressing.

"Shh, sweetheart. It's just me."

"What are you doing?" she asked, her voice still trembling with the fear she had felt.

"Taking you to bed," he whispered, burying his lips in her hair as he carried her toward the bedroom.

"But I told you I'd sleep out here tonight," she protested weakly, leaning against the rock-hard sturdiness of his massive chest.

"I want you to sleep in here."

"Really, Eric, I'm perfectly all right on the settee. In fact, I was sound asleep."

"I want you to sleep in here," he repeated.

"But it's your turn to have the bed."

"I know."

Suddenly his intentions became clear and Kirsten's eyes flared wide. "Eric! Put me down!"

"Okay," he whispered, lowering her gently to the softness of the big bed.

A candle sat burning on the nightstand, allowing Kirsten to see his face as he sat down on the edge of the bed and leaned over her. His eyes were fathomless as she stared up into their dark depths, and for a moment she felt like she could drown in them.

"What are you doing?" she whispered hoarsely, knowing she should leap right out of the bed and flee the mesmerizing man looming over her.

"Taking my wife to bed," he answered calmly.

Kirsten gasped. "Are you drunk?" she demanded.

"A little."

"And you're planning to . . . force me?"

"No," he smiled, leaning over and kissing her gently near her temple. "I'm planning to make love to you."

His lips trailed down her cheek to her neck, then back up toward her ear, making goose bumps spring up all over her body.

"Eric," she pleaded, squirming with delight as his tongue touched her ear, "we can't do this."

"Yes we can," he whispered back, his warm breath tickling her ear and making her shiver. "This is the last night we'll ever have and I want to have something to remember for the rest of my life. Please, Kirsty, just give me tonight."

Kirsten knew she should protest, knew she should tell him she didn't want his kisses, his caresses, his passion. But she did. Oh God how she did! And he was right. This was their last night together and she wanted something to remember, too.

With a little moan of surrender, she wrapped her arms around his neck and turned her head so that her lips met his.

His response was immediate. With a groan he stretched out beside her, and for the first time since he'd picked her up off the settee she realized he was naked. Naked and aroused past anything she'd ever known before.

The feeling of his hot, hard erection throbbing against her thigh was a powerful aphrodisiac, and blindly she clutched at him, seeking his mouth in a frenzy of feminine need. A coil of desire unfurled somewhere deep within her, and for the first time in her life Kirsten surrendered completely to the primal, sexual call of her woman's body. This aroused, questing male clasping her so intimately against his body was her mate, and, for this night at least, she would deny him nothing.

Wiggling out from under him, she shifted on the bed, trying to sit up. But Eric, blinded with lust, groped for her, frantic to pull her back into his arms.

"Don't leave!" he panted.

"I'm not," she assured him through shaking lips, and reaching down she pulled her nightgown over her head, freeing herself from its gauzy confines. Throwing the unwanted garment on the floor, she turned back to her husband, whispering, "I want to feel your skin on mine."

"Oh God, Kirsty," Eric moaned, kneeling before her as he reached out a trembling hand and touched her breast, "you're so beautiful. The most beautiful thing I've ever known."

Kirsten smiled, her eyes closing as his soft words swirled around her brain and his fingers feathered over her nipples. She felt like she was drunk, intoxicated by the sound of his voice and the sensation of his hands on her body. She drew a deep breath, throwing her head back in ecstasy as she breathed in his male essence. He smelled warm, musky, and excited, and her nostrils flared wide as she drank him in.

They were both kneeling now, facing each other as their fingertips explored each other's bodies and they kissed with a passion neither of them had ever dreamed possible.

Eric threaded his hands into the fiery splendor of Kirsten's hair, pulling the flaming cascade over her shoulders and burying his face in its softness. "Your hair is like silk on fire," he murmured throatily.

"And yours is like ebony satin," she returned, stroking a disheveled lock back from his forehead. Leaning forward, she again captured his lips, rubbing her thumbs over his hard little nipples as he dropped his hands to the curve of her waist and kneaded the soft skin.

367

Kirsten held her breath as she felt his fingers fan down her abdomen, tangling themselves in the fiery down at the juncture of her thighs, then reaching lower until his middle finger slipped deep inside her. Her muscles contracted, and instinctively she moved herself up and down, creating a semblance of the friction she longed for.

With a low, animal-like growl Eric tumbled backward into the pillows, straightening his legs between Kirsten's thighs and grasping her hips to lift her onto his huge, pulsating staff.

But with a quick shake of her head Kirsten stopped him. "Not yet," she whispered, pulling out of his grasp and staring at his huge manhood in excited fascination. "There's something I want to do first."

Before Eric could protest this delay, she dipped her head, cupped his length in one hand and softly kissed the swollen tip of his hard shaft.

Eric groaned in erotic torment, writhing beneath her and daring her to new boldness. "Ever since you did this to me that morning," she confided, her voice throaty, "I've wondered if you'd like it as much as I did." And, taking him into her mouth, she gently sucked on him, running her warm, wet tongue up and down his length and swirling it around the hot, wet head.

"Kirsten," Eric groaned, tossing his head back and forth on the pillow in an agony of sensation, "Kirsten, I don't think I can take this . . . torture."

Lifting her head, Kirsten looked up into her husband's dark, passion-hardened face. Never had she imagined she could bring him the pleasure she was now witnessing, and with a triumphant laugh she said, "Then, by all means, I'll end it." And, throwing one leg over his hips, she lowered herself slowly onto him. A moan of pure, animal ecstasy erupted from Eric as she slid slowly down his throbbing organ, and for the first time Kirsten realized the extent of the power she held over him. Determined to give her husband the most unforgettable climax of his life, she set herself to her task, arching her back until her hair swished against his thighs and propelling herself up and down on his pulsing manhood until they came together with a shout. Their mutual climax went on endlessly as Eric pumped his seed into Kirsten's receptive body, filling her until she felt she would burst, and planting their future deep within her.

When the spasms finally subsided, Kirsten collapsed on top of him, her face buried in his neck, her breasts pressed against his sweaty chest. She lay there for a long time until finally, very gently, Eric lifted her off his manhood and lowered her limp body to the bed. Without a word, he slipped his arm around her shoulders and pulled her up next to him. Then, with a sigh of utter contentment, he kissed her and slept.

For a long time afterward, Kirsten lay quietly next to her sleeping husband, her body sated by his lovemaking, but her mind tortured by sorrow.

She'd spent the happiest moments of her life with this man, and yet even he had admitted that tonight would be their last together.

Slowly Kirsten turned her head to gaze at Eric as he slept. He was beautiful. So beautiful that she wished he'd wake, wished he'd pull her over on top of him and make love to her again.

At that moment Kirsten knew that she'd sell her soul for just one more hour spent beneath Eric's virile body as he gifted her with the rapturous splendor of his love.

Chapter 33

"How can I ever face him?" Kirsten fretted, pacing the length of the suite's parlor. "How could I have acted like that? What must he think of me?"

Beside herself with embarrassment, Kirsten bit down on a perfectly manicured nail, heedless of the time and attention she'd spent on her hands and nails since they'd been at the hotel.

It was shortly after seven in the morning, and although Eric had not even stirred in the big bed they had shared, Kirsten had been awake for hours. She didn't know what had awakened her, but with the cold light of dawn came feelings of shame that she doubted she'd ever get over.

Her midnight wish that Eric would make love to her again had certainly come true. The night they had spent had been unbelievable; scandalous, carnal, lusty, and indecent—a feast for the senses that surely no good Christian woman would ever participate in, much less initiate! They had made love three more times after their first wild encounter, doing little more than dozing for an hour or so before they woke and started all over again.

Kirsten's face reddened just thinking of the things they'd done. What would Eric think when he finally awoke? That she had the soul of a prostitute, probably! One thing was for sure—she'd never be able to look him in the eye again.

She'd always heard that regular sex between a husband and wife was a normal and expected part of marriage, but certainly, not all women approached the marriage bed like she had last night—like some starving beggar at a banquet. In fact, most of the matrons she'd known talked about the marital act as some sort of necessary evil whose only reward was the possibility of begetting a child.

Certainly the last thing on her mind last night as she and Eric had rolled around in a frenzy of passion and desire had been children!

"What in the world came over me?" she asked herself miserably, sinking down on the little settee and burying her head in her hands. "I acted like a common trollop!"

No wonder Eric didn't love her! A man would never say "I love you" to a woman who acted as she had. As if in validation of her fears, Kirsten realized that despite all that had gone on between them last night, those three words had never passed Eric's lips. Oh, he'd whispered words of passion to her, words of encouragement, words of satisfaction and ecstasy, but never had he uttered the three words she wanted to hear so badly.

All that remained now was to get through the next few hours. As soon as they arrived at Rose Meadow, they would part, and tomorrow or the next day she could board the train for New York, leaving Eric Wellesley and this whole agonizing chapter of her life behind her.

But little did Kirsten know as she sat wallowing in misery, that, even at that moment, she was carrying a little part of Eric Wellesley within her that would never allow her to leave him completely behind.

Eric awoke and looked around for a moment in confusion. Then, remembering where he was and, more importantly, who he was with, he smiled and turned his head toward Kirsten's pillow. Surprised to find it empty, he raised himself on an elbow and looked around the bedroom for her. She was gone.

An unaccountable finger of fear traced up his spine and, throwing back the covers, he bolted out of bed, tearing across the room and opening the door into the parlor.

He spotted Kirsten sitting on the settee, her head propped on her hands and a look of such utter misery on her face that he gasped in alarm.

Kirsten had not heard the door open, and for a long moment Eric just stared at her, trying desperately to negate what he was seeing. But the look on her face was undeniable. She regretted last night.

His heart sank as he realized that nothing had changed. He'd been a fool to believe that one night of bliss would make her love him.

All he had to do was look at her now to know that the hours they'd spent locked in each other's embrace had meant nothing to her. Perhaps she'd felt she owed it to him, but obviously this morning she regretted her sacrifice.

Feeling utterly devastated, Eric quietly closed the door and sank down on the edge of the bed.

Realizing how deeply he'd mistaken Kirsten's feelings the previous night, he vowed to salvage some modicum of dignity by making today's inevitable separation as painless as possible.

Rising, he trudged wearily over to the closet, pulling open the double doors. He was surprised to find it stripped of Kirsten's clothes. Glancing around, he noticed two large suitcases already packed and sitting by the bedroom door, another sign of how anxious she was to get away from him.

Hurriedly dressing, he packed the remainder of his clothes, pondering how best to approach this horribly awkward situation. Deciding the best way to alleviate Kirsten's embarrassment would be to act as if nothing unusual had happened between them, he opened the bedroom door and stepped into the parlor, an impersonal smile fixed upon his face.

"Good morning," he said cheerily, wincing when he saw her jump.

"Good morning," she croaked, turning startled, embarrassed eyes on him.

"Are you all packed and ready to go?"

"Yes," she responded, rising from the settee and clasping her hands in front of her.

Reaching into his vest pocket, he extracted their train tickets, making a great pretense of checking them. "Our train is at eleven, so we have plenty of time. Do you want some breakfast?"

"No, thank you," she said quietly.

Knowing full well that she had eaten no supper the night before, Eric frowned. "You really should eat something, Kirsten," he advised.

"I don't want anything, *thank you,*" she said shortly, turning away and hurrying off to the bedroom.

A pain twisted through Eric as he watched her disappear through the door. This was even worse than he'd first suspected. She wouldn't even look at him!

Determined to put an end to this ludicrous situation, he marched into the bedroom. Kirsten was standing with her back to him, looking out the window.

"Kirsty," he said softly, walking up behind her, but careful not to get too close. "About last night . . ."

Whirling, Kirsten looked at him with eyes like those of a trapped rabbit. "Don't say anything, Eric. Please! *Just don't say anything!*"

"Kirsten," he began again, taking another step toward her.

"No!" she blurted, her voice rising. "I don't want to talk about it. It was a mistake. An unforgivable mistake and I *don't* want to talk about it! Just go have your breakfast and leave me alone. Please!"

Knowing all was lost, Eric nodded once and stalked out of the room.

The train ride home was the worst two hours either of them had ever spent. They again had seats across from each other, but, unlike their first journey during which they had chatted and laughed, the entire trip was made in stony silence. For much of the time Kirsten kept her eyes closed, feigning sleep in an effort not to have to meet Eric's eyes. They both knew that she wasn't sleeping, but, to her great relief, Eric played along with her sham and didn't disturb her. Every time she opened her eyes, however, she found him staring at her, his dark eyes cool and expressionless. Somehow his emotionless gaze cut more deeply than if he'd come right out and told her that he found her wanton behavior reprehensible.

They arrived at Rose Meadow shortly after noon, silently disembarking from the train and standing stiff and miserable on the station's platform as they waited for their luggage.

"How was the trip?" Sam Harkins, the ticket agent called, hurrying down the platform toward them.

"Unforgettable," Eric muttered, trying to force a smile that never made it to his eyes.

"Unforgettable, huh?" Sam chortled, looking meaningfully at Kirsten. "You feel that way, too, Mrs. Wellesley?"

"It was very nice," Kirsten said quietly, turning away to watch the porter descend the train stairs with their bags.

"I figured you two'd be back today," Sam continued, hefting the bags onto a cart, "so I told old Russ to be here with his wagon to pick you up."

"Thanks, Sam," Eric nodded, reaching into his pocket and handing the man a quarter. "I appreciate the thought."

"Sure thing, Eric. You two heading straight out to your farm, or are you stopping in town first?"

"I'll be going to the bakery," Kirsten answered quickly.

Sam shifted his eyes toward Eric to see his reaction to this comment, but Eric merely nodded and headed off down the platform to where Russell Nelson's wagon was parked next to the station.

Russell loved to talk, a trait which Eric usually found incredibly annoying but which today seemed like a godsend. The trip to Betty Zimmer's was made in record time and neither he nor Kirsten ever had to say a word.

They pulled up in front of Betty's house, and before the wagon had even come to complete stop Eric jumped down and headed around the back, lifting Kirsten's bags out of the wagon bed and heading for the front door.

Russell climbed down and extended a hand to Kirsten, who smiled her thanks, then hurried after Eric.

She opened the front door and Eric stepped through, not even pausing to answer Betty's friendly greeting. Proceeding directly up the stairs, he waited in front of Kirsten's bedroom door for her to unlock it, then stepped inside and set her bags down with a thump. Turning toward his silent wife, he said tonelessly, "When are you leaving?"

Kirsten swallowed hard, not knowing if she would be able to find her voice to answer his question. "Maybe tomorrow," she murmured, "but, more likely, the next day. I'll . . . I'll need to stop by the house to pick up the rest of my things. Is there some specific time you'd like me to do that tomorrow?"

Eric shook his head. "I'm going to be real busy tomorrow . . . you know, catching up on chores and things. You can come anytime. It doesn't matter."

Kirsten nodded, then lowered her head as she realized that she didn't know what else to say.

The silence between them extended endlessly until, finally, Eric cleared his throat and said, "Okay, I'll see you tomorrow then."

Without looking up, Kirsten nodded again.

Blowing out a long breath, Eric took a step toward

the door. "Good-bye, Kirsty."

Kirsten hesitated a moment before lifting her head, not wanting him to see the ocean of tears lurking just behind her eyes.

But, she needn't have worried. He was gone.

"Please, Betty, it's just two or three dresses and a pair of shoes. They're right together in the closet. It would only take a minute to run in and get them." Kirsten looked at the frowning older woman with hopeful eyes.

"No." Betty Zimmer shook her head adamantly. "I'm not going to be a part of this, Kirsten. You want to leave your husband, that's up to you. But I'm not going to help you. Period." And with a huff of disapproval the portly older woman turned on her heel and marched out of Kirsten's room.

"Well, thanks a lot," Kirsten grumbled. Then, with a sigh of resignation, she tied on her bonnet, grabbed her shawl, and headed out the door, determined that if she was going to be forced to face Eric again, she might as well get it over with.

Kirsten knocked for the third time, but still no one answered. Finally admitting that Eric wasn't in the house, she turned around and shielded her eyes with her hand, scanning the fallow fields for the sight of him. She didn't see him. Frowning, she walked out to the barn, pulling back the heavy door and poking her head inside the dark, musty interior.

"Eric?" she called.

No answer.

"Eric, are you in here?"

No answer.

Suddenly something warm and solid hit the back of her legs and she nearly jumped out of her skin in fright. Whirling around, she looked down to find Durango, his tongue lolling and his tail wagging furiously.

"Hello, boy," she smiled, squatting down and rubbing the big dog behind the ears. "Where's your master?"

Cocking his head as if pondering her inquiry, Durango let out a loud bark and then loped off toward the house. Puzzled, Kirsten followed him. Mounting the front porch again, she knocked more loudly, wondering if Eric was somewhere in the house where he couldn't hear her pounding. But despite her repeated efforts, he still didn't respond.

Frustrated and annoyed that he had obviously left when he told her he'd be home all day, Kirsten tried the front door. It was unlocked. Pushing it open a crack, she leaned her head in and called, "Eric, are you home?"

Silence.

For a moment she hesitated, debating whether she dared just go upstairs and get her clothes when Eric wasn't home. She finally decided that she might as well. She had booked passage on tomorrow morning's eastbound train, and God knew she didn't have time to drive all the way out here again.

She stepped into the house, closing the door softly behind her as she gazed around the familiar foyer. She hadn't expected to feel anything, but somehow seeing the furniture she'd dusted so many times and standing on the shining wood floor she'd polished with such care caused a lump to form in her throat.

Although she knew she shouldn't, she walked into the parlor, pausing in the doorway as her eyes scanned the walls, admiring the beauty of Eric's artwork. Unbidden, tears rose in her eyes and she bit her lip hard in an effort to quell her wayward emotions. "Stop this!" she told herself. "You're acting like a fool!"

Turning, she walked quickly down the hall and climbed the stairs, determined that she wouldn't give in to the wave of nostalgia and loss that was quickly overwhelming her.

She hurried down the upstairs hall, looking neither

left nor right as she headed for the small bedroom she'd slept in for so many months. Keeping her eyes trained directly in front of her, she walked into the little room, marched over to the wardrobe and pulled open the doors. It was empty.

With a gasp of surprise she stared into the vacant closet. Where were her clothes? Surely Eric wouldn't have gotten rid of them. He knew she was coming back for them. She'd told him she was!

Maybe he'd set them out for her, she thought suddenly, turning in a circle as she look around the room for any trace of her belongings. But there was nothing.

Becoming more annoyed by the minute, Kirsten left the small bedroom and walked down the hall toward the master chamber. Maybe there might be some clue as to Eric's whereabouts in his room. Hopefully he hadn't misunderstood her yesterday and thought she wanted him to bring her clothes to her in town. But, no, that didn't make sense. She would have passed him on the road.

With an irritated shake of her head, she rounded the corner into his bedroom. The sight that met her stopped her dead in her tracks.

There, on the wall over Eric's huge bed, hung the portrait he had painted of her. For a full minute Kirsten just stood and stared, unable to come up with any rational reason why it was hanging in Eric's bedroom.

"Looks nice there, doesn't it?"

With a sharp scream of terror, Kirsten whirled around, clapping her hand over her chest as she found Eric standing less than a foot behind her. "You scared me to death!" she accused, furious that he had sneaked up on her. "Don't ever do that again, Eric!"

Eric held his hands up in front of him and tried hard to conceal the smile that threatened. "Sorry, sweetheart," he said, not sounding sorry at all.

"Why is this picture here?" Kirsten demanded,

pointing an accusing finger at the portrait.

"Why do you think?" he countered.

Suddenly Kirsten thought of the most logical reason. "Oh, Eric," she said, her voice low and sorrowful, "didn't Mr. Hathaway accept it?"

"He never had the chance. I decided to keep it for myself."

Kirsten looked at him like he had lost his mind. "What do you mean, you decided to keep it? I thought you needed the money Mr. Hathaway was paying you to paint it."

"No." Eric shook his head. "I don't."

"You don't?" Kirsten asked dumbly.

"Nope."

There was a silence as Kirsten tried to make sense of what he was telling her. "Did you get the money you needed somewhere else?"

"No. I never really needed any money."

"What?"

"I'm rich, Kirsty. Richer than Minnesota dirt."

Another silence fell and Kirsten wondered if she was losing *her* mind.

"If you didn't really need the money," she said slowly, "then why did you tell me you did and take me all the way up to Minneapolis to pose for you?"

Eric smiled wryly. "Why do you think?"

"Quit answering every question with another question!" Kirsten ordered, suddenly suspecting she'd been duped.

"Okay." Eric nodded agreeably. "I lied to you, and I took you to Minneapolis for two reasons. First, I really did want to paint a portrait of you, and, second, it was the only way I could think of to get you alone for a while."

Kirsten's voice was barely audible as she asked the next question. "Why did you want to get me alone?"

Eric's answer was equally quiet. "I hoped if we spent some time alone together, away from the farm and away from Rose Meadow, you might come to love me."

Kirsten clapped shaking hands over her mouth. "Oh God, Eric!" she moaned.

In a second he had closed the gap between them and drawn her into his arms. Tilting her head back, he rained kisses all over her face while in a choked voice he entreated, "Don't leave me, Kirsty. Please don't go back to New York. Stay here and be my wife."

"I can't!" she sobbed, trying to extricate herself from his embrace.

"Why *not?*"

"Because you don't love me!"

Eric immediately dropped his arms and moved back a step, gaping at her in stunned disbelief. "What? You think I don't love you? Are you crazy?"

Kirsten shook her head, too distraught to speak.

"God, Kirsten," Eric groaned, raking his hands through his hair in utter frustration, "I wish you could have known me before you knew me."

Despite herself, a smile quirked the corners of Kirsten's mouth. "You wish I'd known you before I knew you?"

"Yes!" he reiterated, still not realizing how funny his words were. "You can't imagine what I was like before . . . before you!"

"What were you like, Eric?"

"I was quiet, reserved. Of all my brothers, I was the calm, sensible, dignified one."

"But you're still quiet and dignified," Kirsten insisted.

"You think I'm quiet and dignified? My God, girl, do you have any idea the things I've done since I've know you? Any idea what I've done because I loved you and wanted you so badly? Kirsten, I've climbed through windows, I've stolen money, I've broken into bakeries in the middle of the night so I could bury diamonds in bread dough."

Kirsten gasped. "That was you who did that?"

"Of course it was me!" Eric barked, annoyed that Kirsten had interrupted his tirade. "And that's not all either! I've also pretended to be a starving artist. I've coerced my father's best friend into treating me like a tradesman when he knows I'm as rich as Midas. I've settled for apples on a train when I wanted steak and potatoes. And you think I don't love you?"

For a long moment Kirsten just looked at him. "You do love me, don't you?" she breathed, hardly daring to say the words out loud.

"Yes, sweetheart," Eric answered, picking up her hand and kissing it. "And something else, too."

"What's that?" she whispered.

"I've always been faithful to you. There was never, *ever* anything between Elsie and me. You've always been the only one, Kirsty. I swear it!"

With a cry of joy Kirsten launched herself into Eric's arms. "I love you so much," she cried, burying her face against his chest and soaking his shirtfront with tears of relief and joy. "I want to be your wife so badly. I want to stay here with you and bake tarts and slaughter hogs and give you sons!"

Eric chuckled, a warm, rich sound from deep inside him. "I'll take care of the hogs myself," he laughed, "But you can help me with the sons anytime."

Kirsten raised wary but hopeful eyes to him. "And, you're sure you don't care that I'm a . . . a wanton?"

Astounded by her outrageous question, Eric pushed her back far enough so that he could see her face. "A wanton?"

"Yes," Kirsten nodded, lowering her head in embarrassment. "After the way I acted the other night, I figured you wouldn't want to be married to a woman who was so . . . so unladylike."

"Oh, Kirsty," Eric laughed, pulling her to him again, "the only thing that might make me not want to be married to you is if you ever *stop* being 'unladylike.'"

"Do you really mean that?" Kirsten asked, her eyes shining with love.

Scooping her up in his arms, Eric walked over to his big, soft bed and lowered her to it. "Since you don't have to catch a train today after all, maybe you'd like me to show you just how much I mean that."

"Oh yes," Kirsten breathed, shivering in anticipation as she saw her husband's eyes darken with passion, "I'd like that very much."

And, so, he did.

Author's Note

I hope all of you enjoyed Kirsten and Eric's story. The bride's handbook which Kirsten refers to while trying to learn to be a housewife actually exists.

It is titled *Buckeye Bride* and was given to my great grandmother at the time of her marriage in the early 1870's. About half of the book is devoted to recipes and there really is a section entitled, "Pickles—Every Man's Favorite Snack"!

The other half of the book is filled with household hints for the young wife including such gems as "the greatest cause for the loss of a man's affection is poor cooking," and "carpets can be kept clean in the winter by throwing bucketsful of snow on them and then expediently sweeping it out the door, thus freeing the rugs of dirt and dust." Pity the poor young wife who became distracted during this chore and allowed her "bucketsful of snow" to melt!

Buckeye Bride has been handed down from mother to daughter in my family for four generations. Although, in 1992, we find most of the "helpful hints" amusing, it gives me a wonderful sense of continuity to try recipes that I know my great grandmother made while her Eric was out plowing the fields on their huge, Minnesota farm.

Jane Kidder
Scottsdale, Arizona
May, 1992